FIONA McINTOSH

BETRAYAL

TRINITY: BOOK ONE

www.orbitbooks.co.uk

ORBIT

First published in Australia in 2001 by Voyager,
HarperCollins*Publishers* Pty Limited
First published in Great Britain in 2006 by Orbit

A CIP catalogue record for this book
is available from the British Library.

ISBN-13: 9–781–84149–457–9
ISBN-10: 1–84149–457–7

Typeset in Garamond 3 by Palimpsest Book Production Limited,
Grangemouth, Stirlingshire

Printed and bound in Great Britain by
Mackays of Chatham plc, Chatham, Kent

Orbit
An imprint of
Little, Brown Book Group
Brettenham House
Lancaster Place
London WC2E 7EN

A member of the Hachette Livre Group of Companies

www.littlebrown.co.uk

For my special Trinity —
Ian, Will and Jack McIntosh

Acknowledgments

My sincere appreciation to family and friends. A few deserve special mention. Thanks to: Pip Klimentou who, fearful that my mornings and nights would blur, has given our house an 0600 wake-up call each day for the past eighteen months. Anne Maddox, my draft reader, whose enthusiasm is so intoxicating I wish I could bottle it! Paul Meehan, my laugh wizard and sounding board for all things magical. My parents, Monnica and Fred Richards, for their endless support. Bryce Courtenay for his advice and encouragement. My editor, Nicola O'Shea, for her help and friendship, and Stephanie Smith for seeing *Betrayal*'s potential when it was just another nervous manuscript.

And . . . especially, to Ian.

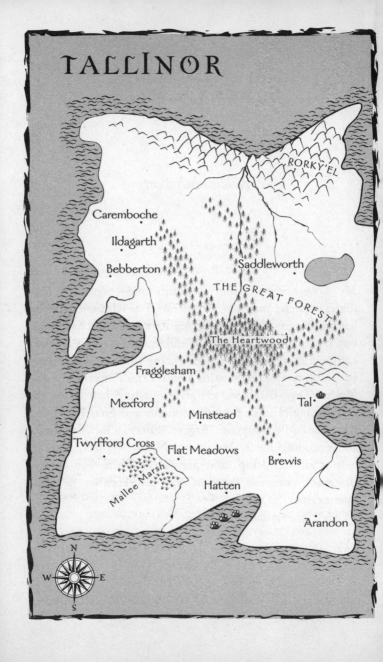

TALLINOR

RORKY'EL

Caremboche

Ildagarth

Bebberton

Saddleworth

THE GREAT FOREST

The Heartwood

Fragglesham

Mexford

Minstead

Tal

Twyfford Cross

Flat Meadows

Brewis

Mallee Marsh

Hatten

Arandon

N
W E
S

PROLOGUE

Mild, cloudless and still. It was a perfect day for an execution. Sallementro cast an experienced gaze around the gathering crowd and wondered at its subdued mood. It was nearing noon. The prisoner would be led out shortly, or so a nearby watcher announced to no one in particular. People nodded, spoke in hushed tones and shuffled their feet. The gathered hardly seemed to notice the contrived tomfoolery up front as a hired buffoon tried to warm up the crowd's anticipation of justice. If anything they turned away; ignored the boisterous behaviour and kept their own quiet thoughts.

It was all very curious, Sallementro thought.

He had arrived in Tal only that morning. Another wandering minstrel, hoping to catch the ear of a wealthy noble who might avail himself of a troubadour's services to woo his mistress or impress his friends. Perhaps, Sallementro mused, he might even be invited to perform at the royal court. That would be a coup.

He pulled himself back to the present. Whilst the execution was all the talk of the city's inns and markets, the musician had not, as yet, had the chance to learn more about its victim. That the young man was important was obvious. Why else would King Lorys himself proclaim his death sentence and by such an antiquated method?

Crucifixion and stoning. Sallementro shivered. It was barbaric but it was going to make for a fine ballad. He began to hear the first few notes in his head as he edged his way through the people.

Raised in the fertile counties of the far south, he had gone against his father's wishes. Generations of his family had farmed the rich soils around Arandon and had amassed an enviable name and wealth. He was expected to support his eldest brother's needs; ensure the family holdings were consolidated. Sallementro argued he was the third son and expendable but this had never yielded any success with his irate parents. His mother shrieked during their many arguments that she would prefer him to choose the Cloth than this. A wandering singer! Arrogant and stubborn all of them, they could not imagine a greater blight on the family's good name. Sallementro had never wanted to be anything else though.

And then there were the strange dreams with the mysterious woman who demanded he follow his chosen path, urging him to wander far and wide to practise his art. The dreamspeaker whispered across his sleeping thoughts of a young woman in need – not just of his friendship but his protection.

Odd. He was a songster not a soldier. Who could he protect? He cringed at his mother's angry voice. He was no hero.

The woman was relentless though, invading his dreams for ten summers. He had been travelling the Kingdom now for another ten summers and felt as though he had known her all of his life. Yet in truth he knew only her voice and her wishes. Lys . . . was that her name? Stupidly, he could never quite recall.

Sallementro had never told anyone about her but he silently acknowledged that the mysterious woman had a strange hold over him. It was she who had given him the courage to stand up to his family; she who had empowered him through her whisperings to leave them and pursue his singing. Who was she?

His musings came to an end as a fat hand shoved him. He was in the midst of a stream of apologies for treading on the rotund lady's toes when heads began to turn in unison. His victim lost all interest in him. Sallementro followed her several wobbling chins to gaze at the north tower, towards which people were pointing and staring.

'There she is!' someone brayed.

The minstrel found himself holding his breath as he watched a young woman step out onto the balcony. She was flanked by two burly guards. The woman shook off their steadying hands and defiantly lifted her chin. As she did so, the midday sun glinted off a pale gem-like oval attached to her forehead. The crowd murmured as one.

Looking at her Sallementro felt his heart skip and the chorus of his song came crashing into his mind. Here she was. The girl whom he had heard about for two decades. The dreamspeaker spoke true. Sallementro felt an instant, aching bond with the beautiful, sad-faced woman who was staring solemnly back at the crowd. At last he had found her. And now he must protect her.

Tension, which had been building all morning, suddenly flared. Some people called out words of encouragement to the girl whilst others shook their heads or wept.

'Who is she?' Sallementro thought he had whispered to himself.

'She's the lover,' his ageing neighbour replied. 'Worth dying for I'll say.'

'I beg you, tell me her name, sir.'

'Why, she is Alyssandra Qyn.'

Further conversation was drowned by a fanfare of trumpets heralding the sovereign's arrival. King Lorys and his Queen, Nyria, were the most successful royals ever to rule Tallinor and their close and happy union was legend throughout the surrounding kingdoms.

Right now though, Sallementro noticed, there was no trace of joy in the pair. Stiff and with an unfocused gaze, they barely acknowledged the lukewarm cheers from their people, nor did they glance towards the beautiful girl. A good thing too, Sallementro thought. She wore a gaze of pure hatred and it was firmly fixed on the King.

'If looks could kill, Lorys would be in his death throes right now,' murmured a man standing in front of Sallementro.

'Her looks *could* kill, you fool,' breathed another neighbour. 'She's an Untouchable, remember. Brimful of magic. See the jewel on her forehead?'

Sallementro had heard of the Untouchables. He recognised the disc of archalyt which branded her one of the clan of sentient women who lived in the remote northern region of the Kingdom. Protected from all persecution by the Inquisitors, they were warded from using their powers by the enchanted gemstone. When a woman joined the clan, a sliver of the stone, polished to a glass-like oval, was pressed onto her forehead. If she was genuinely sentient, the disc adhered instantly. There it remained for ever, to prevent magic being used by her or against her.

'What does the stone mean to others?' Sallementro asked the man nearby, who seemed to know about it.

'You must be a southerner, minstrel, not to know about archalyt!' the man replied.

'Enlighten me then and I shall create a song for it,' Sallementro suggested artfully.

His informant was in rare good humour. 'The archalyt means she has the King's protection. No man may touch her, ever. That goes for the pig Inquisitors too.'

Sallementro nodded and looked back at the young woman on the balcony. He could see the glittering stone more clearly and, without realising it, began to rhyme words for the opening verse of what he already knew would be one of the best songs he would ever create.

A cry went up. 'Ware, the dead man comes!'

Some of the younger women were already crying. Sallementro was astonished. People began to call to the condemned prisoner even though they could not see him yet. He glanced up at the balcony again. Alyssandra Qyn had finally dragged her death stare from the King. Her eyes now followed the steps of her lover.

One young woman was crying so hard she swooned. Sallementro helped her friends to pull the girl to her feet. More people were becoming agitated as the prisoner came closer. He decided the prisoner must be an extraordinary fellow to provoke such an outpouring of grief.

He was right.

The condemned man, Torkyn Gynt, squinted at the noon sun. It pained his eyes after seven days in the black dungeon. A ringing in his ears blocked out most of the sounds in the castle bailey. He entered it between a column of soldiers, all of whom he knew well; all of whom reluctantly guided him to the execution plinth. Tor was a favourite son of Tallinor. These soldiers of the elite Shield had tutored him in every skill, from downing ales to swordplay. Little did any of them know, he thought, that he needed no weapon to defend himself. The gods had given him enchantments so potent and powerful he needed nothing more than his own magic but he had promised he would not use that power today. Instead, for the sake of Alyssa Qyn's safety, he would face his death. He would die courageously. He would meet his destiny.

He passed by women who echoed his own fear in their tears as they wept openly. The men's faces were blank but inside they thanked their gods they were not in his place.

Tor's heart was pounding so hard he felt sure it would burst and kill him long before any stone hit its mark. The manner in which the King he loved had decreed he must die terrified him. In fact he was surprised he could actually put one foot in front of another right now.

Put on a brave show for them, my boy. Don't allow the scum Inquisitor Goth the pleasure of watching you show your suffering.

He heard Merkhud's words over and again but it was so much easier said than done. Earlier, when he had been allowed a final visit from his mentor, the old man had acted strangely.

Gripping Tor's hand Merkhud asked, 'Do you trust me?'

'I always have,' Tor lied. He knew too much now about Merkhud's past to believe every word he uttered was not driven by secret manipulations.

'Then trust me now,' the old man said.

Merkhud's normally gentle voice was thick with pain. He was choking back his own fear at what lay ahead for the boy he regarded as a son. And at what was still ahead for both of them.

Could he pull off this wild plan? Could such a magic truly be wielded?

This was the last time he would embrace this fine young man; the man he had deliberately betrayed.

A hard, brief kiss to the side of Tor's head and the old man struggled to his feet and rapped on the cell's heavy timber door with his walking stick. All too soon it swung back and Tor noticed that Merkhud was wiping away tears before the gaoler stepped in. Merkhud turned, looking a century older in that moment of grief. His words were cryptic, whispered only for Tor's superior hearing.

'No matter what happens today you must trust me and listen. Shut out the noise and your fear and listen for me. I will come.'

Tor nodded gravely but did not understand what the old man was saying. He let it pass. There was nothing to be achieved now.

'Promise me you'll be brave for her and for me. And find forgiveness for your King. He knows not what he does.'

And then Merkhud was gone.

Tor suddenly felt very alone. He could not reach Alyssa via the mindlink; she must be wearing the archalyt again. They thought it was part of her for ever. They had not counted on his strange, indetectable magic which removed it at a touch. Now she would wear it for good. He hated them for marking her.

Alyssa had been spared an identical barbaric death though; that much at least he had achieved, convincing his King to pardon her involvement in what he had claimed was a seduction not an affair. Lorys, he noted, had agreed without much pressure. Tor had seen it and so had Queen Nyria: fascination . . . desire . . . lust.

Tor understood. Alyssa was an exceptional beauty and if that could save her from death, why not?

The gaoler cleared his throat from the cell doorway, a little lost for what to do. He liked the boy. Always had. Didn't everyone? He began to close the door as quietly as possible, then offered something which he hoped might help. 'Not long now, lad. An hour or two maybe.'

His words were no comfort. Tor's resolve broke. Tears fell for himself: for the pitiful way in which he was to die and the stupidity of his actions which had brought him to this monstrous conclusion. He cried too for Alyssa, who had never asked for anything but his love, yet he had betrayed her twice. He wept for his parents. Would they have made the journey to Tal to witness their famous son's untimely end? His greatest despair, however, was reserved for two newborn infants he would never know. Not even their mother, his beloved Alyssa, knew they were alive. That was his third betrayal of her and now he would die and she would never know the truth.

'Tor . . .' Someone called his name gently. It was Herek, wondering if he needed help.

Had he stumbled? The sharp sunlight, the cries of the crowd and his own heartbeat. It was too much. Now they were asking him to sit on a special chair: it was the Chair of the Damned, he realised. He would sit here now and hear why he was to be stoned. It was purely protocol — everyone gathered knew why Torkyn Gynt was to be slaughtered — but the Chair of the Damned was a final chilling reminder that death was imminent, stretching the ordeal just a little longer. It gave the victim a few last moments to repent his sins, beg forgivness, beg for mercy — whatever he felt moved to say or do. It gave the audience, traditionally hungry for blood of the accused, the opportunity to watch him suffer the terror of these final moments.

Tor sat, suddenly bewildered and stared at the dust on the ground. He could not look at anyone. One of the most senior of the courtiers who had presided at the trial in the Great Hall unrolled a parchment and read aloud its length of accusations. The actual sentence would be read shortly but only after the executioner himself had been introduced.

Tor could not bear to listen to their words any more. Instead he called himself within; shut out all of the people and allowed his thoughts to drift back. Back to where it had all begun, on that balmy afternoon in Twyfford Cross seven summers previous . . .

I

A Bridling at Twyfford Cross

Torkyn Gynt was young, adventurous and bored. He hated being an apprentice scribe but it was expected by all that he would continue Jhon Gynt's excellent work. He watched his father squinting at the letter he was working on with the Widow Ely. The older man's eyes were failing and the day when his son would have to take over was fast approaching.

Today, however, they would spend the warm, sunny afternoon working at Twyfford Cross. A more sleepy, uneventful village Tor could not imagine. He felt like yelling his frustrations aloud as he heard the Widow Ely whingeing, yet again, about her sore hip. His mood was broken by the miller's old dog Boj, who ambled over to the walnut tree beneath whose cool canopy they were working. Boj nudged Tor's hand. His days of being a champion mouser were over but everyone in the village loved the old rogue.

Guilt stabbed at Tor as he watched his father struggling to read back the letter to the cranky widow. He offered to take over and sighed to himself as he dipped the nib into the ink. Life did not get much less exciting than this, he decided.

As he scribed her boring words, his thoughts embraced more alluring sights than the widow's beefy hips. The curve of Alyssa Qyn's breasts brought a smile to his face. His client's hacking cough unfortunately brought him back to the tiresome present. That and an urgent prod from his father, who knew better than most what a daydreamer his son was.

Rubbing his ribs and glaring at Jhon Gynt, Tor heard it. His strangely acute hearing picked up the ominous sound. His mother always said his ears were sharp enough to hear the birds breathing in the trees; a gift from the heavens she called it. Tor eventually realised this was her way of acknowledging – without actually admitting – that he possessed extraordinary powers. These were not times to be gifted with sentient ability; in fact it was a curse to possess any magic. So nothing was ever said openly. His strange and powerful talents had been kept hidden now for fifteen summers.

Widow Ely's voice droned on. She hardly noticed Tor unfold his long legs from beneath the table and stand but Boj did. Disturbed from his doze, the dog waddled off.

Tor listened. Riders! Many of them and travelling fast. He did not need to see them to know they represented danger. Jhon Gynt was shocked to see ink, parchment and nibs suddenly scattered and hear his son yelling.

Too late. They were upon them in moments. Boj was trampled on his way across the street as a dozen riders came at full gallop into the village square. The face of the man in charge was unmistakable. Tor had not seen him before but vivid descriptions by others assured him this man was Chief Inquisitor Goth.

Goth's face was a tortured mound of flesh. Savagely pocked, one side lay slack whilst the other twitched incessantly, giving his right eye a permanent tic. His sneer turned into a nasty smile as he drank in the village's silent shock. Boj, almost dead, still managed to snap at the heels of Goth's mount. A sword was driven into the dog's belly to finish the cur off but inwardly Tor cheered his courage. Some of the folk flinched at Boj's cruel death but held their tongues from a familiar fear.

Tor blinked his distinctive, cornflower blue eyes. He could feel his power gathering.

His father must have sensed it because he squeezed his son's shoulder. 'Don't do anything foolish, Torkyn,' Jhon murmured.

Goth stared at the villagers. They were still, watching the reviled Inquisitor carefully, waiting for his inevitable command. He allowed the silence to hang just a moment longer, relishing the fear he created wherever he rode.

When he spoke his voice was vaguely effeminate, its high pitch always a surprise for new listeners.

'Good people, it's been a while since we last visited. I see you have rebuilt the alehouse.' He nodded towards the White Hart.

The inn had suffered the firebrands of the hated Inquisitors three winters previous. The sweating innkeeper groaned. Goth's small, sharp eyes picked him out instantly.

'Ah, Innkeeper Pawl,' he cooed, 'fret not. This time I'm sure the village will give me what I want.'

His fellow riders, dressed in their black cloaks and purple silks, sniggered.

Tor sensed a movement to the back of them and noticed a lone horseman turn into the street. He was old. Wispy grey hair struggled from beneath the brim of his hat and flapped around a silvery speckled beard. The rider paused, taking in the scene ahead before urging his fine black stallion forward.

Rhus, Goth's second, had also noticed him and signalled his chief. Goth turned, lifted his eyes in irritation and cursed.

The stranger spoke. 'What evil do you do here, Goth? Tell me, has some poor child seen animal shapes in the clouds and frightened you in your sleep? Or perhaps that poor creature I see at your feet had some profound ability to . . . what? Sniff out bones from the air, maybe?'

Somebody choked on a laugh but most of the village folk remained silent. No one who challenged Goth lived long enough to tell the tale. Tor shifted to get a better look and was glad to see Goth's complexion now almost matched his expensive purple silks.

'Like you, I carry out the King's work, Physic Merkhud.' Goth was struggling to remain calm, hating the royal healer for his untimely appearance.

The old man sneered. 'Never compare my work to your ignoble doings, Goth.'

'Oh, I'll be sure to pass on your sentiments to his majesty,' Goth replied sweetly, regaining some composure.

The older man shook his head. 'Don't trouble yourself. I shall tell him myself when I share a meal with their majesties next.'

Merkhud knew that would sting. The Inquisitor may ride under the King's banner but Merkhud was the King's oldest, dearest friend. He promised himself he would take up the matter of Goth more vigorously with King Lorys.

The Inquisitor was obviously at Twyfford Cross for a bridling, Merkhud thought sourly. Lorys's loyalty to this barbaric law to punish all sentients was primitive. Surely the centuries of persecution of these empowered innocents must soon end. Innocents may well be the very people to save Tallinor's precious throne in years to come, he concluded to himself.

A stable boy appeared and took his horse's reins but Merkhud did not move. He had eyes only for the Chief Inquisitor. Goth's ire was at boiling point; Merkhud had ruined his fun. All pretence at civility fled. He waved Merkhud aside and addressed the villagers, his shrill voice carrying loudly.

'We come for the woman known as Marya.'

A woman cried out and more wails joined with hers. He loved to hear them scream. He lifted his voice above the din.

'She is sentient and has no place in our society. In the name of King Lorys, I pronounce she be embridled. Bring her forward immediately . . . or this whole village will be torched.'

Heads turned towards a group of four women. The eldest began to yell a stream of helpless abuse, beating her chest as she sank to the dust. This amused the riders; more so when her daughters began crying. Only the youngest refused to break down, a plain woman with languid dark eyes that hardened as she stared at Goth.

Tor could sense it coming though her power was weak.

He felt her about to hurl it uselessly towards the Inquisitor when a calm voice spoke via a suddenly opened mindlink.

It's no good, Marya. They are shielded well with archalyt. Go quietly and your sisters and mother will live. If you fight, he has the excuse he wants to kill you now along with your family. The voice was firm but tender.

Tor was rocked. He looked wildly around. Who had spoken with this power? Before he could check himself he began following its magical scent, reaching out with his own senses, scrambling after a barely remaining trace . . . back to the old man. Tor locked on for just a moment and then, petrified at what he had done, snapped away. He was too late. Tor saw the shock of discovery register on the stranger's face. He looked away, back to Marya who was being forced to her knees in front of Goth's horse. The retreat was not fast enough; the stranger was equally gifted at chasing a scent.

Physic Merkhud's gaze burned into the side of the young scribe's head . . . the intruder. Tor needed to escape. This was exquisitely dangerous. How could he have been so stupid after years of control? Although the exchange had occurred without note from the Inquisitors, Tor realised he was now indelibly marked by someone infinitely more subtle in the use of the Power Arts. Someone who could conceal the use of magic like he could.

'Father, we must leave,' he said and hurriedly bent to pick up his paperwork, nodding apologetically towards the Widow Ely. She only had eyes for the grisly scene unfolding in front of her.

Jhon Gynt grabbed his son's arm. 'Torkyn . . . he expects an audience for the bridling. I like it not either but we must remain for fear of stirring his anger.'

Tor looked over at Merkhud and this time their eyes locked. The surprise had still not left the old man's face.

Goth had taken the opportunity to outline to the gathered how he had tracked the girl down, homing in on her magic and marvelled at her stupidity in using it so carelessly.

Finally he gave the command. 'Bridle her!'

Marya became hysterical, struggling and scratching at the men who held her. She was sending strikes of power at all her captors but, as Merkhud had warned, they and their horses were shielded by the mysterious archalyt, which reflected her power back at her.

Tor could not bear to watch her agony. Without further thought he cast a spike of his own power at her which stunned her temporarily. He could sense the old man's horror at his audacity but refused to meet his eyes.

As the girl slumped to the ground, her mother cried out loudly to the heavens, begging the gods to unleash their wrath on the scum who would take her daughter.

Fortunately, Goth was too immersed in watching the dull leather bridle, studded with the same archalyt, being lifted from its sack to hear the mother's scorn. Several of his men busied themselves with unnecessarily pinning down Marya's limp body whilst another lifted her head. Rhus pulled the headpiece onto her face, slipping the metal bar between her teeth. Marya regained consciousness and began whimpering, her tongue pinned down painfully by the bar. They snapped the lock at the back and hammered the two pins firmly into place. Rough hands pulled her to her feet and ripped her clothes from her body. She stood unsteadily; naked, bridled and trembling, silenced by fear.

Many of the men from the village who knew her looked away, ashamed for the girl's bared flesh and of themselves for not being able to protect their own.

Torkyn could feel himself losing control when the soothing voice entered his head again. *This is not your time boy. Do not reveal yourself now*, it warned.

Once more Tor sensed the stranger's eyes boring into him from across the street. He was so taken aback by the intrusion on his thoughts that the well of power within him temporarily subsided. As he watched, the village blacksmith was escorted to the humiliating scene. He carried a brand bearing the mark of a sentient: the hated star sign.

'Now brand her as you've been instructed, blacksmith . . . or die.'

The smith knew Marya well. His only son, a serious lad, was very fond of the girl and had begun to talk of marriage. He could not move.

'Do it!' shrieked Goth, his high voice almost snapping with the tension.

He leapt down from his horse in a fury when the command was ignored for the second time, and pulled the smoking brand from the blacksmith's limp grip.

'Kill him,' he said.

Rhus did not hesitate. He hacked off the smith's head with such force it rolled down the street, coming to rest next to the mangled Boj. People began to scream. Goth barely paid any notice to the twitching, headless body from which the lifeblood gushed. Making sure two of his men were holding Marya firmly by the arms, Goth savagely pressed the smoking brand against each of her small breasts. As the smell of fresh blood mingled with that of smoking flesh, he finished his handiwork, pressing the brand between her legs.

Goth addressed his pale, shocked audience. 'Another evil one, safely delivered. Now she'll tempt men no more to spawn evil sentient bastards.'

Satisfied, he threw the brand aside and suggested to innkeeper Pawl that he and his men had acquired quite a thirst from this afternoon's dusty ride. The trembling man gestured towards the door of his inn.

Marya's wreck of a body was thrown into a waiting wagon by two of the riders. One by one the villagers ignored the risk and covered her with their own clothes, touching her tenderly and whispering promises to take care of her family. She heard none of them.

One of the village men picked up the smith's head and reverently placed it on the chest of the pitiful, blood-drenched corpse, which was carried away quietly by his fellow folk.

No one bothered with Boj.

Tor knew he must get as far away from this harrowing scene as quickly as he could. Striding towards his father's small wagon, he threw his belongings into the back and grabbed the reins. He dared not look at the old man. As soon as his father had climbed into the seat next to him, he guided Lady out of the village towards the safety of Flat Meadows several miles to the east.

Tor and Jhon Gynt shared not a word on the journey home.

2

The Floral Dance

The Midsummer Floral Dance was Tor's favourite local event. In spite of his distracted, melancholy mood since the bridling, his spirits lifted greatly as he guided the wagon to Minstead Green that morning.

One of his earliest memories was holding his mother's hand, watching while the village girls weaved their intricate patterns of steps. He still loved the colour and pageantry of the festival.

This was the first year he would attend Minstead on his own and the sense of freedom was seductive. It was made particularly intoxicating by the fact that Alyssandra Qyn would dance for the first time this year. She had reached womanhood and was permitted to take a husband if she chose.

He longingly watched her gossiping with the other girls on the Green. She smoothed her honey-coloured hair; its golden glints sparkled in the sun. There had never been anything vain about Alyssa, though her radiance was plain to all. With her mother long dead and Lam Qyn in his cups most of the time, she rarely had the benefit of the invaluable parental guidance Tor enjoyed. Alyssa had virtually raised herself, caring for her drunken father as best she could, and now earned the family's pitiful income from her salves and simple herbals.

Tor had been captivated by her from the moment they first spoke. Dangerously, some years back, she had opened a link, cast out randomly and locked onto him. When it happened, the shock caused Tor to spill a pot of ink across a new tablet of paper which resulted in a fiery scolding from his normally good-natured father. Tor had no defence. How could he blame a cheeky nine year old who lived on the other side of the river? Through him she listened to the rebuke and when it was over whispered, *Sorry, whoever you are.*

From that time they had linked daily, wondering with each conversation if the Inquisitors would sniff them out. As children, it had seemed vaguely dangerous fun. Now, older and wiser to the horror of discovery, they quietly marvelled at their invisibility. Both had agreed to restrict the link to each other, as it was obviously something about one or both that kept them safe.

Tor sighed. There was not a prettier girl in the surrounding villages, though it was Alyssa's strength and companionship he most adored. He revelled in the whispers of the ladies nearby agreeing that she was a great beauty but bristled at the suggestion that a wealthy merchant would sweep her off her feet one day soon.

This was precisely why he intended to speak to her in earnest today. They so rarely saw one another and though they linked often he worried that she may not welcome his offer of marriage. Nevertheless, he had promised himself he would pledge his love and ask for her hand just as soon as he caught that damn posy of flowers.

Tor imagined the culmination of the Floral Dance when the girls would close their eyes, then loft their flowers high over their shoulders. The eligible men would try to catch the posy belonging to the lady of their choice. The tradition of the dance held that any man who proposed marriage, without the flowers having left his clutch, would have his wish accepted. The girls believed that if they became betrothed on the day of the Floral Dance the marriage would be happy, their first child a son and their husband would remain faithful.

This summer some forty women had gathered on Minstead Green with their bright meadow flowers held together by woven straw. Plain or beautiful, the spinsters of Minstead all looked lovely dressed in their finest cottons. Alyssa had chosen a soft green linen. Fashioned simply, it showed off her slim neck and tiny waist to perfection. It also cunningly matched her eyes. Tor knew she must have gone without many meals to afford the fabric.

Tor was not the only fellow smitten by her charms and he realised this. A quick glance was all it took to confirm that too many of the young bachelors had eyes only for Alyssandra Qyn.

She stopped fussing with her dress and hair, looked over and smiled. His heart raced.

I'll kill you Tor, if Rufys Akre catches my flowers! she said across the link.

Mmm, imagine those gravestones for teeth waiting to nibble you each night.

He laughed as he cast this thought to her and Rufus

Akre, standing next to him, looked at him strangely, wondering what was so funny.

Just catch my posy because if desperate Rufus doesn't, Eli Knox has already told me he will.

Tor looked around for Eli and saw the handsome storekeeper talking with friends, his head nodding towards Alyssa as he spoke.

Tor scowled. *Don't worry about me. You just worry about throwing it straight!*

There was never any doubt in his or Alyssa's thoughts who would catch her posy. It would not have mattered whether there were twelve dozen men of a mind to win her attention that day; the posy belonged to Tor. He had magic on his side and he wielded it with exquisite subtlety that afternoon, guiding her clutch of daisies, bells and cornflowers through the air to his lifted hand at the completion of the Floral Dance. He clung to her posy tightly even though seven men blundered into him, knocking him backwards to the ground; a few even daring to wrestle for it, Eli Knox being one of them.

Alyssa bounded over. 'Claim your prize, my Lord,' she said, effecting a terrible curtsy.

This was the final insult for Eli Knox. 'Your father's pickled mind is rubbing off on you, Alyssa, if you believe a poor scribe like Gynt can give you a decent life.'

Tor could not help himself. He spiked Knox who suddenly found himself unable to complete a sentence without a profound stutter.

Tor mimicked him. 'Oh, Kn-Kn-Knox, Anabel Joyse said you could have her f-f-f-flowers.'

Anabel Joyse was an excessively large, ruddy-cheeked spinster of middle years with a thatch of flaming orange hair and just four teeth. She had given up the Floral Dance years previous but her terrifying legend lived on with the young men.

'F-f-f-you, Gynt;' Knox stuttered.

'Oh and f-f-farewell to you too, Knox. Come on, Alyssa.'

He grabbed her hand and they ran away from the Green, eventually finding themselves near the Minstead stables. It was the first time in many days that Tor had been able to laugh: the Twyfford Cross bridling had seriously unsettled him. Though he had daydreamed of it many times, cursing his shyness, he had every intention today of asking Alyssa if she would be his wife. He had the Floral Dance on his side. He could not fail now.

She leaned back against the stable. 'You nearly lost my posy, you oaf!'

'But would I have lost you?' he asked, wanting to kiss her.

Alyssa decided he was never going to pluck up the courage so she did it for him. Pulling him to her, she gave him no choice but to close his lips against hers. The kiss was so much more delicious than in his dreams. The reality was slow, deep and so passionate he lost all ability to hear. Silence reigned in his world. Only Alyssa's sweet, soft mouth mattered.

Alyssa finally pushed him back from her. They were both breathing deeply.

She looked serious. *Ask me*, she said via the link.

Tor was about to speak when he heard a horse shift in its stall. Glancing over her shoulder, his ardour died the second he caught sight of the fine black stallion bearing the royal Tallinese oriflamme. He stepped back from Alyssa, staring with disbelief into the murkiness of the stable, where lazy flies buzzed around the horses.

Tor? Alyssa shook his arm. He did not respond but the alarm on his face was plain. She felt him snap their link shut.

'Whatever's wrong?' she asked aloud, trying to see what he was looking at so intently in the shadows of the stable.

Tor's mind was spinning with fright. The grisly scene from Twyfford Cross came racing back. He unwrapped her arm from his and turned to face her slowly.

'We have to go.' He said it quietly but deliberately.

'Go? Go where?'

'Away from here,' was all he said, taking her hand and pulling her back towards the Green.

She switched back to the link, her irritation clear. *Tor what's going on? I thought we were—*

He cut her off. 'No link,' he said aloud, fiercely.

He pulled her across the street and past the Green towards his father's wagon where Lady was chewing contentedly on a bag of oats.

'Stop it, Tor! You're frightening me.' Alyssa refused to budge.

'We must get away from here, then I will explain everything.'

Tor kept walking but Alyssa had not moved. 'Tell me now,' she said, confused, her voice filled with disappointment.

As Tor swung angrily around he saw him. The old man who had been at the bridling. The King's man. The man of magic.

Physic Merkhud had indeed been looking for the young scribe ever since he had witnessed that arrogant trickle of magic against the hapless Marya at Twyfford Cross. It had surely saved her life but could so easily have sounded the death knell for the scribe. And yet Goth and his dark band of Inquisitors had not so much as twitched an eyelash in acknowledgement of such power being wielded before their eyes. The discovery of the boy and his potent, indetectable magic had stunned Physic Merkhud, and he grasped hungrily at the thought that this was the One. In three centuries of searching, none but his own unique magic had gone undetected by the Inquisitors.

The tall handsome lad was running from him once again. He would not lose him this time.

Alyssa followed Tor's startled gaze. His thick dark hair had come loose from its thong and his strange, brilliantly blue eyes were wide and blazing at an old man standing at the edge of the Green. She made her fateful error then, angrily re-opening the link and speaking deliberately across it.

Who is that man? Why are we running?

Merkhud, startled for the second time in almost as many days, shifted his gaze from the young man he was following to the beautiful young woman standing on the other side of the street. There they rested with wonder, as Torkyn Gynt knew they would.

It was as if everyone in Minstead had stopped in their tracks at the precise second Merkhud heard Alyssa's voice on the link. Children playing, women talking in groups, couples laughing – all still, held silent in their acts of normality, while Tor's life flipped into anything but. And all he could hear was the pounding of his heart.

He forced himself to breathe deeply before speaking across the link, not caring now that the mysterious man could hear, anxious only for Alyssa's escape.

Alyssa, if you do nothing else for me ever again, go now. Take the wagon and leave. No, don't even mention where to. I'll get word to you soon. Now go.

He turned and began to walk away from her.

Tor, wait! she cried.

Go! he screamed. And she did, running towards Lady, stung by his coldness and aggression.

Tor did not wait to watch what the man did. He knew he would already be hurrying back to the stable. Instead he veiled his mind from Alyssa, broke into a sprint and headed across country, taking care to stay as far away from the roads as possible.

3

Stones of Ordolt

It had been two days since the second sighting but Tor remained badly shaken. He had spun a tale of being roughed up by drunken revellers as they left Minstead, saying that Alyssa had escaped unhurt but with the wagon and Lady. One look at his dishevelled appearance and distressed expression and his parents could believe it. Fortunately the story gave him the excuse he needed to lay low at home.

Tor felt terrible about lying to his parents and the extra burden it created for his father. They had always lived frugally, in a small stone dwelling in Flat Meadows. It was a village of no fascination other than its excellent inn and its proximity to the main road, which led to the capital of Tal. His father worked hard to provide a good home for his family and to give his son a trade. His mother earned a small wage cooking for the local inn.

She had recently bustled back into the house; it was never quiet when Ailsa Gynt was home and Tor listened absently as she chatted about the marvellous fruit pies she had baked today.

She pulled one of them out of her big basket and set it down on the scrubbed table in the kitchen where Tor sat. The scrumptious aroma alone would normally send his stomach into spasms but not today.

'I smuggled one out for you, son. You need fattening up . . . you've been looking so pale these last days.'

Tor said nothing. He was desperate to link with Alyssa but he had been unable to reach her. Curious. He could imagine what she was thinking, what strange ideas she would conjure from his silence after his harsh behaviour at Minstead. If only he could talk to her and set her mind at ease. She was veiling, he decided, and yet there was no veil of hers he could not navigate his way around. This, if he was being honest, did not feel right.

His mother continued chattering, oblivious to her son's anguish, moving about her kitchen with practised ease and a surprisingly light step for such a heavy woman. Tor often wondered how he had managed to turn out so tall and slender with such short, round people for parents.

He had missed the question.

'I said, are you still feeling poorly, Tor?' his mother repeated.

He shook his thoughts clear. 'Er . . . no, much better today. I'll be able to work tomorrow,' he replied.

'Well, about time, Torkyn!' said Jhon Gynt, but not unkindly, as he entered through the back door. 'There's a mighty storm brewing, mother. Look at the sky.'

Tor joined his father at the door. Bruised clouds were gathering in dark clumps and the day's early breeze had stopped making the trees show their respect. The late afternoon had become ominously still. The air felt brittle, expectant.

'Are you worried about Lady?' Tor asked guiltily.

'No. Alyssa will have the sense to have her in that barn of theirs and this storm may not even hit Mallee Marsh. Lady's better off where she is. I'll need her by Fourthday though, son, so I hope you're well enough to get over there and bring her back by then.'

Tor nodded and felt his father's hand on his shoulder.

'All right, let's see what treat Mother Gynt has in store for us,' his father said kindly.

The storm banged angrily against their front door two hours later.

Ailsa Gynt shivered. 'I hate thunder and lightning — sends a chill up my spine,' she commented from her rocking chair, fingers travelling swiftly with a needle and yarn.

'Why?' Tor said, yawning and closing his book.

'Oh, it's silly, but my grandmother always used to say it was a bad omen . . . you know, that perhaps the gods are angry.'

'Oh Ailsa, my love, stop that nonsense,' Jhon grumbled gently. 'Son, I can hear that back gate swinging against the wall. It's going to come off its hinges if we don't secure it.'

Tor pulled on a large hat and blanket from the hook by the back door and loped off. As he left, a hand of lightning lit up the sky, swiftly followed by a deafening crack of thunder.

'That was close,' Ailsa muttered, sewing frantically. 'The gods must be furious!'

Jhon Gynt clicked his tongue in feigned irritation and returned to his accounts. It was then they heard a different sort of banging on their front door.

*　　*　　*

Tor marvelled at the theatrics of nature above him, but did not tarry for the rain was hard and furious, turning the yard into slimy mud. He cast to Alyssa for the umpteenth time in two days and again found only strange bleakness on their link. Tor felt so glum he allowed the rain to pummel him for a few moments. Then, gingerly edging his way around the deepening puddles, he heard his mother calling to him from the back step. He squinted through the rain and could see her beckoning for him to hurry.

What now? he thought irritably.

He stepped back into the house, uselessly trying to stamp off the water from the drenching as he hung the sodden blanket and hat back on the hook. When he turned he felt his stomach flip. Between his parents, and smiling benignly, was the old, silver-haired stranger. Instinctively Torkyn shielded himself and his parents in an instant.

Impressive, said the old man directly into Tor's head. *But fear me not, I am no enemy of yours.*

Jhon Gynt was speaking. Tor wanted to shake his mind clear of the old man's touch. His father sounded overwhelmed by the importance of their evening visitor.

'Torkyn, this is Physic Merkhud. He tends their majesties, King Lorys and Queen Nyria.' His father's emphatic look suggested he show due respect.

Why do you stalk me, old man? Tor slammed back across the open link whilst effecting a neat bow to their guest.

Merkhud nodded courteously in return. *Patience, boy. I will explain all*, and then the link was cut. He spoke aloud. 'Forgive me, please, for this late and dramatic arrival. I'm due in Tal by Firstday but had to talk with your son before I left the district. We met at Minstead a few days ago.'

'Oh, you didn't mention that, Tor,' his mother chided as she bustled the old man into a comfortable chair near the fire. 'Now, have you eaten?'

Food was ever the first thing that came to his mother's mind, Tor thought sourly.

Merkhud, by contrast, looked delighted. 'Well, to tell you the truth I've been riding all day and haven't had the chance to nibble on so much as a crust.'

Music to her ears, Tor thought, trying to force a polite expression onto his face. Was this the bad omen his great-grandmother's superstition had warned about, he wondered? Another crack of thunder answered him.

'You must be chilled, Physic Merkhud. Let me get you a warming nip of something,' Jhon Gynt offered.

It was rare his parents had guests, let alone one with the ear of the King, and they were obviously going to enjoy it, Tor decided. He did not allow the shield to slip but returned to his seat, curious and frightened, wondering where this was leading. The men made polite small talk whilst Ailsa moved noiselessly and efficiently about her kitchen. As the conversation wore on, Tor could not help but become fascinated with the physic's talk about life in the capital, Tal.

The old man had a smooth, musical quality to his voice and close up appeared anything but threatening. His beard, though long, was trimmed neatly and the wispy hair was now tied back so his deep grey eyes were visible amongst friendly wrinkles.

'What's King Lorys like?' Tor asked as their guest leaned back into his chair for Ailsa to place a tray on his lap.

'Thank you,' Merkhud said softly, smiling directly into

Ailsa's eyes. He turned to Tor. 'Um, Lorys . . . let me see now. He's an exceptional King. Far better than his father and grandfather before him who both ruled with fear. Lorys has an empathy for his people; he and Queen Nyria—'

'Then why does he allow his people to be maimed, tortured and killed? What is he afraid of?' Tor hurled back.

He enjoyed watching Merkhud's lips purse in reaction to his aggression. Their guest covered his irritation by eating some bread.

'He's a good man, Tor, but if he has a flaw it's his traditional intolerance of sentients. He blindly follows his ancestors and their archaic laws which, at the time, were passed from fear. It makes me sad too.'

Ailsa returned with a bowl of steaming stew. 'Here now, this should warm your old bones.'

Her rabbit stew, with its blend of spices and fragrant herbs, was famous in the district. She set down a plate with some extra hunks of bread thickly smeared with butter.

Merkhud needed no further encouragement and set about consuming the delicious, simple fare. 'This really is an extraordinary stew,' he uttered between mouthfuls and Ailsa beamed.

She wanted to return to her sewing but thought it impolite, so she smoothed her skirts instead, cleared her throat and stared at her husband, willing him to make some sophisticated conversation. Her son, she could see, wore a sullen countenance. His normally radiantly blue eyes were blanked dull; they looked like those of the rabbit she had killed earlier that day. She did not understand his bad humour but this visitor was far too important to ignore.

Jhon Gynt took the hint. 'So, Physic Merkhud, having you share a humble meal in our house is a pleasure, but you said you needed to see Torkyn?'

Direct as usual, his wife thought, abandoning all hope of a long evening in fine company. She picked up her sewing.

Merkhud had just finished cleaning up the rich, sticky gravy with a hunk of the bread. He sincerely wanted to lick the remains of that juice from his fingers. Instead he dipped them into the water bowl on his tray, picked up the accompanying napkin and set about cleaning his hands and whiskers. All of this gave him precious time to think.

'You'll forgive my frankness,' he said finally.

Jhon Gynt nodded. 'I'd appreciate it.'

Merkhud looked directly at Tor when he spoke.

'I am aware that your son is sentient . . . Please, let me finish,' he said as the boy's parents gasped and he felt the shield around them tighten.

Get out of here, physic! Torkyn snarled across the link.

His mother was jabbering and his father was on his feet.

'Let me finish, please. I'm not here on the King's business and I am certainly no member of the butchers who go by the name of Inquisitor,' Merkhud implored.

Then more emphatically and directly at the boy. 'Tor, you do not intimidate me so stop your threats. You do, however, amaze and reassure me. In you I see hope for us all.'

'He speaks in riddles.' Tor waved his hand as if to dismiss the ravings of an old man, but once again strengthened the shield around himself and his parents, terrified of what the sentient physic was capable of.

Jhon Gynt's normally gentle voice sounded suddenly commanding.

'Physic Merkhud, forgive my son's indiscretion . . . whatever he's done. We don't discuss Torkyn's power for obvious reasons. That you bring it into the open so casually is very frightening for all of us after his lifetime of hiding it. Please say what you've come here to say. I fear this is no visit of chance.' An icy look was sent towards his son to ensure he gave no further interruption.

Merkhud nodded his head. 'You are correct, Jhon Gynt. This is no social visit. I am sentient too.' He allowed that to hang between the four of them for a moment. 'And, like Tor here, the Power Arts I wield go strangely unnoticed by Goth and his merry band. I know not why.'

He lied. He had to.

'Until I witnessed your son use his powers to help that poor girl at Twyfford Cross, I had never met anyone else in my life whose magic was undetectable.' Again he lied.

The silence was heavy. He knew the boy's parents had no clue if or when their son wielded his magic and felt sure they had forbidden him all of his life to use those skills. He took a deep breath, knowing this was the critical moment he had quested towards for so long and time was so short. He could not fail now.

'With Tor's consent — and yours, of course — I would like him to come to Tal and be my apprentice.'

'At the Palace! Why?' Ailsa shrieked, unable to contain herself.

'By the light, man! Are you mad? It would be like giving him to Goth. We might as well paint a sign on his forehead that reads "bridle me",' Jhon Gynt bellowed in a rare show of rage.

'No, Gynt, you're not thinking. I've just told you that both your son and I can wield our power without detection. He will be safest at the Palace under my absolute protection. No one would dare touch him there, and no one will. I will teach him the healing craft. He will be my successor at the Palace: wealthy, respected and safe from the barbarians who roam this land. Who knows, perhaps it is Tor who will bring about change with me . . .'

Merkhud stopped himself. He was excited, clutching at his one sparkling chance. Surely this boy was the One. He must not lose him.

Come with me, boy, he whispered across the link. It was only then he saw the light shining in Tor's strange blue eyes and knew he had won.

'You want us to give you permission to take away our son – our only child?' Ailsa Gynt's tears were already flowing.

'I am asking you to give him into my care and, at risk of being dramatic, to give him to the people of Tallinor.'

'Physic, have you ever had a child? Do you know what it is to give up a son?' Jhon Gynt's voice was gritty with emotion.

For a moment it felt as though the world had stilled. The sound of the storm outside seemed to fade to silence. Merkhud's reply was barely more than a murmur.

'I do. I had two sons, once. The first beautiful child died almost as soon as he was born. The second boy was a gift to soothe our hearts and I loved him more than I have loved anyone . . . but he too left us, tragically. It was a long time ago and I've been lonely and embittered ever since. Turning my back on the many young men who have begged to be given a chance to learn, to train and perhaps take my place one day.'

No one said anything.

'What's in this wine, Jhon Gynt? My old gums have not flapped that precious piece of information ever.'

'Physic Merkhud, in truth this must be Torkyn's decision. I will not force or even ask him to leave us – heaven knows, I am in need of his eyes and hands here. But it's a grand opportunity for him – much grander than a father dare dream for one of his own.'

They all looked at Tor who was sitting quietly. He swallowed hard, casting a sideways glance at all the things familiar to him in the room.

'I'd like to go.'

Merkhud felt a flare of triumph but kept his expression sombre as he turned to the boy's crestfallen parents.

'May I have a word with your son alone?'

On the pretext of clearing up his tray Ailsa busied herself in the kitchen. Jhon excused himself.

Merkhud turned back to the young man whose magic was potentially more powerful than anyone now in the land. A young man who might hold the secret to the Trinity.

'Are you sure you want this?'

Tor's brow wrinkled. 'Yes, Physic Merkhud, I think so.'

'Please, Tor, be very sure about this. It is not a decision to take lightly nor is it one you can easily turn back on once made. If you only *think* you are sure, then perhaps you are not yet ready.'

Merkhud's gaze was hard and unblinking. He had no intention of giving up the boy of course, but he also needed this young man to be committed. It would be no easy adjustment to life at the Palace.

Straightening up, Tor held out his palm and concentrated on it. Merkhud looked puzzled but took his lead and watched. Soon there was a shimmering above it and a hazy vision materialised of three small spheres in dazzling colours. Merkhud held his breath. He was not mistaken: Torkyn was showing him the Stones of Ordolt.

'Tor.' His voice was raspy. 'Where have you found these, boy?'

Tor sounded as though he was speaking from faraway. 'I dreamed about them last night, I think.'

He moved his fingers and the orbs weaved gently around them, their fiery colours glinting and sparkling as they caught some of the candlelight. Then he snapped his hand closed. 'Do you know what they are?' His voice was normal again. He was focused.

Merkhud knew now he had been right about Tor. He lied once more. 'No, no, I don't, but they are certainly beautiful. Have you no idea?' he asked hopefully.

'I don't. I just know that this dream, your arrival and the way I feel right now all point me to going with you.'

Tor had already decided he would be taking Alyssa with him too, but he chose to keep this to himself for now.

The old man sighed deeply. The Host had told the truth. Someone was here to save the land. His search, the first part of his quest which had spanned fruitless centuries, was over.

Now for the difficult part, Tor told himself. He found his parents sitting quietly in their small room. He noticed – perhaps for the first time – how very sparse it was. There was nothing fancy about this room. It was where hard-working, honest people found their rest and their humble pleasure. Only the bed was soft – his mother loved a soft mattress – other than that the furniture was hard and ever practical.

The only item of whimsy was a small series of drawings Tor had done as an infant, which his mother had bound into a leather file. They leafed through the primitive pictures from time to time, laughing together. It amused his parents that Tor had always drawn the family as four. As a young child he had insisted he had an older brother, drawing him as a large and menacing figure, sometimes even talking to the imaginary person. There was no brother. The Gynts put it down to Tor's longing to have one, but that was impossible. The local physic had made that painfully clear to them.

Tor did not know what to say, so he shrugged apologetically.

'It's all right, Torkyn, this is the right decision.' Jhon Gynt was comforting himself as much as his son.

Ailsa started weeping again and Tor crossed the room in two strides. He could not bear this from the woman who was always in control of the situation. He rocked her gently. Soon he felt his father's strong arms wrap themselves around them both and hold them tight, all but keening with his own despair.

Tor lost sense of time. He could not tell how long they remained like that or when the tears finally subsided. Afterwards they talked of nothing of consequence for a few minutes; awkward conversation he would not be able to recall later. Finally, as silence once again hung heavy between them, his father took Tor's hand in his own as his mother did the same on his other side.

'Mother and I must share something special with you.' Gynt cleared his throat. 'This is difficult, Tor. It's a secret we have kept for fifteen years. I had hoped we would never have to share it with anyone, least of all you, but now that you are leaving, it's our duty to tell you.'

Tor felt the hairs on the back of his neck stand up in anticipation of what was coming. For some reason, he just knew it was going to be bad.

'Tell me nothing. I don't want to hear this . . . please. I – whatever it is, it doesn't matter to me.' He searched his father's face but found only resignation and a weighty sadness.

'You must know this, Torkyn.' Jhon pulled his son close. 'Although you bear our name, child, I did not sire you and your mother did not birth you.'

Tor felt his world spin momentarily into a dizzying darkness, and out of its inky depths three brilliantly coloured orbs hastened towards him. The sensation was menacing and he must have yelled out for the sound helped him return to his parents. His father was shaking him by the shoulders.

Tor shook his head in disbelief. He could see his father talking, yet he could hear nothing save the faint thump of his blood pounding in his ears. He shook his head again to clear it.

'Tor, are you listening to us?' His mother's red, weepy eyes implored him as much as her words.

'Look at me, son, and hear my words,' Gynt said as he held Tor's face and stared directly into his eyes. 'A woman came to our town fifteen winters ago. With her she had a magnificent baby boy, all swaddled up and crying he was.' His father smiled ruefully in memory. He let go of Tor's face and dropped his hands to his lap.

'And this beautiful boy had no parents. Both had been killed; a fire we were told, which had claimed everything they had bar the child who had been spared. There was no other family. The woman had happened along whilst the village folk were fighting the fire. Someone had put the babe in her arms and she nursed it through the night. The next day no one stepped forward to claim the child. It was a poor village, you see, and one more mouth to feed, another body to clothe, was just too much.

'The woman found herself with a few-months-old babe and she herself simply passing through on her way to Tal.'

Tor wanted to stop the words but his father continued.

'She took the boy, travelling many miles with him before arriving in Flat Meadows where she paid for a room overnight at the inn. Well, you know Mother Gynt – she took pity on the woman and her heart almost burst to see the child, homeless, without the love of his mother and endlessly whimpering. She had an instant bond with him which soothed his wails. As is your mother's way, she fell hopelessly in love with the boy and begged the woman to let her keep him.'

Ailsa took over. 'You were irresistible, Torkyn. I loved you from the moment I set eyes on you, and with each passing year I loved you more, child. Your father and I could not get with child, you see. We had tried for so many years.'

She threw a knowing glance at her husband, who returned it as he remembered the nights of love in this same bedroom.

Tor looked at his mother. 'And she gave me to you?'

'Yes. You were helpless, homeless and unwanted. We were not wealthy but we were comfortable. We had no children but so dearly wanted a child of our own. We wanted you. It wasn't a hard decision, Tor, you were so easy to love.'

'Nobody asked any questions?' Tor asked incredulously.

'Why, yes, of course. Lots of questions were asked by the Flat Meadows folk,' his father replied. 'We told the truth and before long the questions stopped and you were accepted as Torkyn Gynt, our son.'

'And the woman?'

'She moved on to Tal, I imagine. She seemed very happy to find a good home for you and she left immediately. We've never heard from her again.' Ailsa looked at him uncomfortably. 'Why, would you prefer we had let you go on with her and live what sort of life, I wonder?'

'No, but this is such a shock. I . . . well . . . have you ever thought of finding out more about my real parents? Who they were? How the fire happened?'

It was his father's turn to look uncomfortable. 'No, Tor, we haven't. You were a blessing – a gift from the gods.'

Tor shuddered involuntarily at his father's words.

'They were dead. We had no reason or business to go in search of ghosts. You were ours. We just wanted to give you a home of love and laughter,' Ailsa said gently.

'And that you did.' He squeezed her hand tightly. 'Is there any more to this tale?'

Jhon Gynt stretched. 'No, son. That's the only secret we have ever kept from you. But your mother and I knew this day of reckoning would probably come. From the early days we knew you were special, but we ignored it.

You were sensitive enough to realise you are blessed with a dangerous gift. I have to say, after talking at length with Physic Merkhud, I trust him. He will protect you as you tread your own path now.'

'When do you leave us, child?' Ailsa wondered aloud, not really wanting an answer.

'Merkhud has given me a purse. He wants me to buy a horse and some stout boots and come when I'm ready. He leaves tomorrow but I thought I'd wait a few days and help you with the letters over at Beckynsayle . . . er, perhaps leaving Sixthday . . .' Tor's voice trailed off.

Ailsa poked her husband in the ribs. 'What about the stones?'

'Oh ay, the stones. Almost forgot.' Jhon Gynt tuttutted to himself and reached over to a small cupboard. He rummaged through the drawers and pulled out an old sock from which he took a small pouch of very soft animal skin, the contents of which clinked together. Tor looked puzzled.

'Yes, well, I'm as curious as you to know what these are all about. The beautiful woman with the golden hair told us these were tied around your neck when they rescued you.'

Gynt tipped the contents gently into his palm: three small, dull spheres clunked into his hand.

'She was very clear, though, with her instructions. You were to have these when you were . . . of an age, she said.'

Ailsa stared at the orbs. 'We asked what she meant by of an age, but she only said we'd know the right time to give them to you.' She looked up. 'I imagine this must be the right time, my child.' Her voice was soft.

'Here, Tor, keep them safe,' Jhon said. 'I'm stumped

as to why she insisted you have them. All I can think is that they belonged to your birth family and for that reason alone I've always considered them precious. At least it's something you have from them.'

Jhon dropped them into Tor's hand where the orbs blazed into spectacular colours.

'Light strike me!' Ailsa reached out her hand to Tor.

'It's all right. They feel safe . . . um . . . comforting even.'

He shrugged to give an appearance of casual acceptance which he certainly was not feeling. Here they were: the very stones he had dreamed of the night before and later conjured in a vision for Merkhud. He was definitely making the right decision in going with the old man.

His father looked uncomfortable at the sight of the magical stones blazing their colours, and held out the small skin pouch. 'Put them away, Tor, and keep them hidden. It wouldn't be a good idea for you to show those to anyone, not even Merkhud.'

Tor tipped the stones back into the pouch and nodded. 'No, you're right, though how do you think I find out what they are for?'

It was his father's turn to shrug. 'My advice is to leave them. If they have a purpose, I'm sure it will make itself known to you. Promise me you'll keep it as our secret; show no one. The golden-haired woman . . .' Jhon Gynt stopped awkwardly then cleared his throat. 'She said they were magical and were never to be shown to anyone but you. We were to impress upon you that they were to be kept secret.'

He covered Tor's hand which held the pouch of stones with his own. 'I don't understand any of it, son. Not your strange skills nor these, but I fear it is perhaps leading to something none of us can know or understand.'

He smiled at Ailsa. 'Well, come on, mother, no more sadness. Our boy's off to the Palace. We should be proud not miserable. Let's all away to bed, and tomorrow no work – we'll go to Rymond for the day and sort out Torkyn's horse, get him those boots and perhaps a new shirt for his journey. Who knows, we may find that yellow silk you've been lusting for, woman.'

Ailsa did at least smile. Tor's spirits lifted as well. He knew they were going to be fine, and he could not help but feel excited for his future. However, there was one more hurdle to leap and that was to convince Alyssa Qyn to come with him.

As he could not reach her on the link, he would go to her village the day after tomorrow and tell her everything.

4

Alyssa Qyn Disappears

Alyssa walked into the cottage and called to her father to see if he was home. Not that he would have noticed or cared anyway. These days he spent increasingly more time in a drunken stupor talking to his ghosts. She could forgive him the women. He had loved her mother, of that she had no doubt. Rather than fall prey to the number of well-meaning ladies who had called upon him in the early days, he had found his solace with the women who required no love from him, only his money.

The tears came easily now. What could possibly have upset Tor so badly that he had yelled at her and forgotten all about catching the posy? She had been sure he was going to find the courage and ask her the question she longed to hear.

Everything had been perfect until the old wretch with the wild grey hair had ruined it. Who was he? Worst of all, now she could not open a link to Tor, though she had tried many times. Her efforts to cast hit a mysterious blankness. Why was he punishing her?

Alyssa washed her face in an effort to pull herself

together, knowing her gruff father could stagger in at any moment.

When Lam Qyn did return he was, as usual, very drunk. His daughter, ever wary of his moods, fell into a well-practised routine of cheery talk as she pulled off his boots and helped him to the table. A steaming bowl of soup was quietly placed in front of him. Then, as he sat staring into his dish, she kept up her quiet flow of meaningless conversation, hoping it would lull him into eating and finally sleep.

She might have been successful if she had not begun humming to herself when she was clearing his plate away. His temper stoked lightning fast and his movements were surprisingly swift for a drunk man. Alyssa did not even see it coming. His large hand hit the side of her face with such force that the dish she held shattered itself on the opposite wall. Her knees banged painfully to the flagstones. She could not feel her cheek; it was instantly numb.

'That would be your mother's tune and I won't hear it sung again in this house!' he raged at her.

Through her tears, she watched her father stagger back out of the cottage and disappear into the night. He would not be returning soon.

She hated her life. The only shiny part of it was Torkyn Gynt. Being able to talk to him while they grew up in different villages on either side of the river had been her only solace in a lonely, loveless existence.

If only her mother had survived birthing the daughter she had barely lived long enough to hold close. Was that it? Did her father blame her for the loss of the woman he adored? Oh, how she needed her friend Tor now. She wept. Hours passed.

Alyssa finally roused herself and made her way to the tiny room where she slept. She poured some water into the bowl from the jug on the rickety table. Although it was icy cold, she forced herself to put her face directly into it in an attempt to clear her mind.

Using the flannel she cleaned herself thoroughly, rubbing pointedly around her neck where Tor had stolen a brief kiss and scrubbing her lips of his passion. Towelling herself dry, her grief hardened. She was very angry now. Something more than fear for the old man — more like respect — had burned in Tor's eyes. Those large, mesmerising blue eyes. Alyssa shook her mind clear of his face.

She pulled on some fresh clothes and went down the narrow stone stairs, hating her house and terrified her father might return. She poured a draught of water to steady herself, but it was no surprise that the pitcher slipped from her trembling grip and smashed on the flagstones when a figure appeared in the doorway. Alyssa tasted blood. She must have bitten her lip.

'Dear me,' a voice said kindly as its owner made a tentative entrance, pulling off a bonnet and shawl.

'I'm sorry . . . I thought you were . . .' Alyssa didn't finish. 'Who are you?'

'Oh, I was just passing, wondered if the family here might let an old lady rest in their barn for a short while.'

Alyssa hardly listened. She sank to the floor, her skirts soaking up the spilt water, the tears of relief and frustration rolling freely.

'Oh, my girl. Here, you must not cry. 'Tis only water and that old earthenware jug can be replaced easily enough.'

The woman, old but surprisingly strong, firmly helped Alyssa up and, after seating her on a chair, set to cleaning up the mess. Alyssa watched distractedly. The old girl was no threat; if anything, the company was soothing.

'You're welcome to rest awhile here. There's no one home but me.'

The old girl nodded her thanks and began to hum quietly to herself. It was a lullaby and her voice was like a balm for Alyssa's pain. She did not remember the herbal tea being made but soon enough firm fingers wrapped her own around a mug, its contents sweetened with honey. Now where had that come from? The thought passed as quickly out of Alyssa's mind as it had arrived. She sipped contentedly in her silence, concentrating on nothing other than the pretty tune.

At some stage candles were lit, shutters closed on the moonlight and she felt herself being guided back up the stairs again. She was gently undressed, her hair tied back loosely with a ribbon, and then she was laid oh so softly in her own bed. The covers were drawn up and she was tucked in in the same way her father used to do when she was little and he loved her. She thought she smiled at that distant memory but she couldn't be sure.

The lullaby continued softly on the fringes of her mind. Her lids were heavy and sleep beckoned seductively. She slept dreamlessly and all the while the old girl sat quietly beside her bed, wrapped in a faded and well-used shawl, murmuring the same gentle lullaby tirelessly.

Alyssa woke refreshed. The anxiety had not deserted her but a tantalising smell of hot cakes got her up and out of her bed swiftly. How had she got into this nightshirt,

she wondered, as she pulled it over her head and felt the
gooseflesh surface on her skin at the chill.

She pulled back the shutters. A very light drizzle hung
almost mist-like, with the sun nothing more than a bright
smudge behind a blanket of grey cloud. She shivered and
pulled on some warm clothes. They were worn, like all
her few garments, but her new good humour prompted
her to brush her hair vigorously and tie it up with the
one silk ribbon she possessed.

She remembered the strange but generous old woman
who had appeared last evening, and presumed she must
have stayed the night for her father had never learned how
to cook. She wondered briefly where he could be and
whether she should go looking for him.

Alyssa would normally find him on the street or in a
corner somewhere, recovering badly from the previous
night's carousing. She would clean him up, put him to
bed to sleep it off, feed him later when he awoke, listen
to his angry sorrows over his meal and then hopefully
have him sober and clear-minded enough to tackle his
various chores. She sighed. It was a pitiful life they both
led.

Tor edged into her mind but she pushed him away
with a forced smile. She would not think of him now. She
would try to open the link later. She knew he had to
collect Lady soon or his father could not go about his
business. Alyssa hurried downstairs, only to feel her good
humour evaporate as she saw the woman tying on her
bonnet and readying to leave.

'Ah, there you are. You look well, my girl. I'm so very
relieved.' The old woman beamed and pulled on her shawl.
'I'll be on my way then, lass. I hope you didn't mind my

staying the night? I just couldn't leave you in such a state, and so scrawny too. Here, look, I've made you some hot cakes and there's a pot of tea brewing, so get some of it into you and I'll rest easy.'

She waddled over and hugged the stunned girl, then turned to pick up her cloth bag. Alyssa ran to the door and slammed it shut. The wild look in her eyes made the old woman exclaim, her hand clutching her throat.

'You . . . you can't leave. You can't leave yet, I mean. I want to talk to you.' Alyssa fought the tears. 'Please, I don't even know the name of the person who has been so kind to me.'

The old girl studied her and then, to Alyssa's relief, put down her bag and removed her bonnet.

'My name is Sorrel.'

She sat down and folded her hands neatly in her lap.

Determined to hold her longer than the pleasantries would allow, Alyssa quickly poured two mugs of the tea.

'And your name is. . . . ?' Sorrel sipped the tea.

'Oh, I thought I must have told you last night. I'm Alyssandra.' She offered the old lady one of the hot cakes. 'But people around here call me Alyssa,' she added.

'That's a very lovely name you have.' Sorrel nibbled her hot cake.

'Thank you. My father made it up. My mother's name is . . . er, was Alyssa. She was very beautiful, I'm told.'

The old woman responded gently. 'I lost my mother early too. It's hard on a girl. How old are you now?'

Alyssa took a sip of her herbal tea and winced. The heat burned where she had bitten her lip the night before.

'Fifteen summers.'

'Ah . . . this is an age when a girl misses her mother

most,' Sorrel said before switching easily into relating tales of her life as a travelling herbwoman.

Alyssa found her stories fascinating, particularly as she too had a good understanding of herbcraft. The old woman then brought her story into the present, casually describing her most recent journey into Flat Meadows, where the village was apparently abuzz with gossip that one of its own was off to the Palace at Tal.

'Everyone seemed so proud and excited. I happened to meet the lad — very handsome he is with those strange blue eyes. My, my, those Tal women will steal his innocence within hours of his entering the city gates.'

She laughed conspiratorially but there was no laughter in her eyes. Instead, they watched the girl carefully.

Alyssa felt confused. 'I know quite a few people at Flat Meadows. Er, did you get the person's name?'

'No . . . I'm not sure I did. I was just passing through and stopped nearby the inn for a supper. Big lad, he is. Very shiny dark hair, brilliant cornflower blue eyes . . . like I've never seen.'

'Torkyn Gynt,' Alyssa said flatly, an almost deranged look creeping into her own eyes.

'Never got his name, my girl. Ah now, wait, that's right. Gynt does ring a bell. Father's the local scribe around these parts?'

Alyssa nodded miserably.

'Well, they were all buying him ales and congratulating him. The celebrations spilled outside, that's how I got to learn about it. The innkeeper mentioned he was going to be an apprentice to the famous Physic Merkhud.' She coughed, banging her chest. 'Whoever he might.be.'

Alyssa's complexion had turned pasty. 'I know Gynt

but I had no idea he was planning to leave. Did anyone say when he was going?'

Sorrel shrugged. It was deliberately casual. 'This morning, I gather from all the excitement. The whole village was planning to turn out to farewell him.'

Alyssa stood abruptly and began to clear the table. Her heart broke in that moment, though she remained composed. 'Oh? I'm sorry I missed those festivities.'

It took all her willpower to prevent herself showing her true feelings, which were ranging from anger to terror to grief as she cleared away the crockery. Sorrel had not added anything more to the conversation on Tor. It was not her fault; she could not know they were sweethearts with a betrothal understood.

Alyssa forced herself to change the subject even though she desperately wanted to know more. She adopted a bright voice and began describing her own life.

'I can't tell if he blames me for my mother's death somehow,' she concluded sadly of her father.

Sorrel stood and stretched. 'Do you look like her?'

'Yes, I'm told by the few who knew her that I'm her image.' She shrugged, suddenly embarrassed, realising that she had told Sorrel earlier how beautiful her mother was.

'Well, my dear, I would suggest that he loved your mother so much that every time he looks at you it hurts him all the more. He probably doesn't get on with this life because he is constantly reminded of his old one.'

'Do you think so?' Alyssa felt as though a door had been opened.

'Perhaps you should stop doing all that you do for him. Maybe it's time for you to leave and make your own way,' the old girl said, brushing at crumbs on her clothes.

'But how would he feed himself, stay sober? Who would look after him?'

Sorrel snorted. 'He would!'

Alyssa was shocked but she also felt a twitch of excitement at such a suggestion.

'And where would I go? I'm fifteen with no money, no prospects, and you're telling me to leave my village.'

Sorrel smiled and started to adjust her shawl around her shoulders. Alyssa felt rising panic.

'Are you leaving now?'

'Yes, my girl. It's time Sorrel moved on. I have a long journey ahead of me and that silly old donkey braying out there is telling me the sun is getting high and we must cover eight miles to Twyfford Cross before the eve.'

Once more the old cloth bag was picked up.

'Perhaps, Alyssandra, you'd walk with me a while?' She moved with purpose to the door, opening it to a damp afternoon. The drizzle had stopped but the sky still looked mournful.

And then Alyssa genuinely shocked herself. She ran after Sorrel, startling the donkey.

'Sorrel! Take me with you.'

The old woman stopped and turned around. She looked grave but not surprised. 'You don't even know where I'm going after Twyfford Cross.'

'I don't care. Just let me come with you. I'll be no bother and I can cook and take care of myself. I can run errands. I know how to saddle. I can write. I can earn money for us. I understand the herbals . . .'

She was anxious, staring at the old girl.

Sorrel looked to the sky momentarily and then back at

Alyssa with some resignation. 'I know you want to escape a miserable life, but what else are you running away from, lass? There's more to this my big nose tells me.'

Sorrel's nose was huge, particularly when she twitched it for effect. Alyssa's laugh was brittle with her grief over Tor, but she took the old girl's hand in her own and squeezed it.

'You're right, there is more but I'm not ready to talk about that yet. If I go away perhaps there's a chance my father will pick up the pieces of his life and build a new one without my mother's memory haunting his every waking moment through me.'

Sorrel put her arms around her. 'What will you tell him, lass?'

'I'll write him a no – You mean I can come with you?' She held her breath.

'Well, I don't seem to be able to get rid of you, do I?'

The girl's scream of thanks startled Kythay the donkey. The animal reared and pulled hard on his tied reins, hurting himself. Alyssa was startled herself. She approached the wide-eyed animal murmuring a nonsensical stream of sounds. Reaching out, she gently stroked his forehead and down to his velvety nose. The wild look faded from his eyes and he stopped pacing and stamping the ground. In the time it took to pick up an apple Kythay had returned to his ponderous munching as though nothing had happened.

Sorrel's eyebrows were arched. 'That was impressive. You have a way with simple beings, then?'

'Always have . . . that's why I was good with Tor.' She whispered the last to herself before turning on her heel.

'Pardon me?' Sorrel's hearing was still razor sharp.

'Oh nothing. So, will you wait whilst I pack? There's hardly anything anyway.'

'Only bring what you are prepared to carry,' the old girl called.

She stared after Alyssa for a moment or two, then deliberately faced away from the cottage, focused and cast her simple message.

The girl is mine.

She felt his sigh of satisfaction before the measured reply came back.

This has been a fortunate day, Merkhud replied.

5

The Rescue of Cloot

Tor had been chewing on dust for hours when he finally eased his sore buttocks off Bess, the mare his parents had suggested he buy with some of the money from Merkhud's rich purse. He was almost limping as they drew level with the ornately carved stone pillars which stood sentry to Hatten. Tor spat more dust before leading the mare into the bustling streets. Finding an inn was the main task.

Merkhud had insisted that he bed down in reputable establishments, as had his parents who had given him a list of suitable lodgings. This promise he meant to keep, but when he arrived at The Pig and Whistle a fire had wrecked its chances of a busy season this year and, as a result, the second and third inns on his list were brimming with guests when he finally found them.

Although he was exhausted Tor knew his priority was to care for the horse. After such a long ride she needed fresh hay, sweet water and a well-earned bag of oats. In fact he was convinced Bess was giving him an accusatory look as they passed a welcoming stable.

'How about a rub down at Hatten's premium inn for

horses?' he asked the willing mare as he stroked the white blaze on her forehead.

Tor paid the stableboy and then tossed him another coin. He found himself in a gregarious mood, relishing the thought of a bath to ease his aches, a hearty meal for his grumbling stomach and an ale or two to help forget Alyssa's lovely face.

'Here's an extra half regal for you — make sure she's really comfortable tonight, eh?' he said to the stableboy.

Introducing himself as Bart, the lad assured Tor the horse was in the best possible hands.

Tor was already walking away when he heard a scuffle and raised voices. He turned back to see a burly man clutching the thin arm of a young woman, who was struggling and cursing at him. Passers-by were laughing. It took only a moment before the bristly faced man was pushing his bulk and his charge in front of Tor.

'Stop!' The voice Tor realised, with some surprise, was his own.

'Mind your own business, you stupid youth. She's mine.' The big man's breath was enough to force Tor backwards a step. He barely ducked the well-aimed cuff.

'Yours! You brute, Goron — I wouldn't be yours for all the gold in Largoth. Now let me go, you devil's turd.'

The young woman emphasised her demand by kicking the hapless Goron between his legs. This raised another chorus of laughter from the gathering crowd. Poor Goron found himself on his knees in agony.

Even Tor had to smile. 'I think this young lady would prefer it if you allowed her to take her leave,' he whispered to the man.

He could not resist adding some clarity to this

suggestion by releasing a spike of balled air squarely into the man's stomach. Onlookers saw only that Goron winced, buckled again and let go of the scrawny girl's arm. She bounded off, swift as a hare, turning just once to grin at Tor before disappearing into the mayhem of the busy streets.

The crowd dispersed as quickly as it had gathered. Friends helped Goron to his feet and assisted him to limp to an alehouse, where Tor guessed he could soothe his wounded pride as much as his wounded groin.

Tor picked up his saddlebag and wandered back towards the town square. He was being led by his nose to a popular stall where a woman was selling skewers of roasted meat. He joined the queue.

There was obviously some event taking place in the main square for he could hear loud bursts of hooting and laughter. Tor imagined there must be a play of some sort being performed. Finally it was his turn. The woman looked up at him, a sour expression on her face. 'How many?'

'Two, please.' He dug into his pocket for a couple of royals. It would not do to rummage through his pouch of coins; that would be asking for trouble.

The woman dipped the skewers with their still sizzling chunks of meat into a sticky, dark sauce, and he exchanged his coins for the dripping, succulent food.

Turning, he pulled the first chunk off with his teeth. As he walked towards the square, he was too busy rolling the hot meat around his mouth to notice what the noise was about. The simple food was delicious enough to bring a smile to his face as he wiped the juices from his chin.

It was the first heartfelt smile to crease his face in days.

Since finding Alyssa's home deserted, then her father drunk in the village square, yelling obscenities and shaking a crushed note in his fist, Tor had felt lost. Alyssa had gone. Disappeared with some herbal woman to who knows where . . . or why. Her message had been brief, loving towards her father but made no mention of Tor. Surely she could not still be angry? He had told her he would contact her. He had made the detour to her village to ask the question he had wanted to ask at Minstead Green. He had hoped to persuade her to come with him. She would have said yes, he knew it. Why would she just leave?

He shook his head clear of Alyssa for the umpteenth time but he could not shake the pain of loss.

Tor arrived at the rear of the crowd in the square. The shouting he had heard he now realised was jeering. This was a mob and they were taunting something. He skirted the throng, two dozen people thick in some places, to get a better look. The second skewer of meat was forgotten for the time being.

Pushing through the people proved difficult so he walked back to one of the square's permanent shops. A man's voice announced something but it was lost in the moment whilst people shooshed one another. Tor levered himself up onto a small ledge. What he saw shocked him.

Kneeling in the middle of the square was a dazed man who appeared to be mumbling to himself. He was severely deformed, with a face that would scare children, and cause polite people to look away and the less polite to stare. He was crippled too, Tor assumed, from the twisted appearance of one leg. Adding to the poor wretch's woes, his dealers in punishment had nailed his right ear to a post

and his hands and feet were tightly bound. Tor could see
that the angry red welts around his wrists were bleeding
in places.

The jeering mob was taking delight in pelting him
with rotten fruit and one canny vendor had even taken to
selling fish heads for a drack apiece. Men, presumably his
captors, kicked him. The victim could do nothing to help
himself yet he made no sound. Wittingly or unwittingly,
the cripple gave his audience no satisfaction and this infuriated his torturers.

Tor wondered what crime this man could possibly be
accountable for. He finally found his voice and asked the
shopkeeper.

'Caught peeping in the ladies' bath-house.'

'That's all?' Tor's exclamation caused the man to step
back.

'We don't like his sort around here. Scares the little
ones and the fine ladies. Just his appearance at the market
yesterday saw business take a turn for the worse. I tell
you, it's unsettling for folk. He's no good to anyone and
should have been done away with at the hour of his birth.'

Tor snarled at the smug shopkeeper. His lighthearted
mood of just moments ago had evaporated. The roasted
meat juices which lingered in his mouth now tasted acidic.
He tossed the second untouched skewer at the shop front
where it was fought over by several very lean dogs.

Suddenly the noise of the jeering, the smell of the
people gathered and the memory of the humbled,
deformed cripple overwhelmed him. Tor was tired too.
He needed that bath, some ale and a place to rest and
forget what he had witnessed. He strode away with
purpose, pushing past yet more people streaming into the

square to get a look at the prisoner. As he shouldered his
way past a buxom woman, her flesh all but wobbling in
anticipation of the ghoulish entertainment, he heard the
gentle voice in his head. *Help me . . . please*, it said.

Tor whipped around. 'Who said that?'

A couple looked at him as though he was hearing voices,
which he found grimly amusing.

The voice spoke again in its deep yet gentle pitch. *I
am innocent of the charge. Won't you help me, please, Torkyn
Gynt?*

He ran back towards the shop front and returned to
his ledge, ignoring the protestations from the keeper. Once
again the scene of humiliation assaulted him. He wanted
the man to look at him; wanted proof that it was the prisoner speaking to him and not his imagination.

He cast across the link. *Who is this?*

*Cloot. I am the prisoner. I am wrongly charged and seek your
help Torkyn Gy—.* The man's voice broke as a nasty blow
from one of the guards smashed into his nose.

Tor could see more blood, this time spilling from the
man's face. He felt incensed. This persecution was a
pursuit of entertainment rather than justice; he was sure
of it.

Cloot . . . the link is open, draw on my strength if you can.

He pushed strongly through the crowd this time, with
no idea why he had suggested the prisoner should attempt
to use him as support. He had never tried such a thing,
did not know whether it could be done. It was simply all
he could think of, and as for reassuring the poor wretch
that he was coming . . . it was ridiculous. What was he
supposed to do and why was he doing it?

Still, Tor neither excused himself nor wavered in his

direction as he pushed through the gawking, jeering audience. Finally his height allowed him to keep Cloot in his sights. He was astonished by a new sensation: the cripple had turned the link into a physical connection, skimming off Tor's reserves of energy to hang onto consciousness.

Now he was at the front of the crowd and several disgruntled people wondered at the youth's arrogance in pushing past. He noted the same brute of a guard aiming another kick. He had to stop it. With no time for sophistication he used a trick which Alyssa had taught him, sending a brief but blinding pain into the eyes of Cloot's tormentor. The guard halted with a look of shock, before screaming and falling to the ground.

Tor drew level with the prisoner.

Thank you for staying, Torkyn.

The voice in his head was full of pain and there was no time for pleasantries. The confused guard was climbing to his feet and Tor knew he could not risk a second spike of magic so close on the last. Inquisitors were always around and may suspect something even if they could not detect it.

Then a new voice spoke.

'Good people, please, hush yourselves. Corlin, would you be so kind as to ask your brave guards here to desist from injuring their prisoner further. I'm sure he has no plans to leave just at the moment.'

The last comment drew titters from the immediate onlookers. Tor studied the man who was now arguing with the head guard. He seemed at ease in front of all the people; almost amused, in fact, by his own participation in the show.

Corlin did not share his good humour.

'This is not your business, Cyrus, nor your jurisdiction, I might add. I'm acting on behalf of the good people of Hatten.'

'That's Prime Cyrus to you and your fearless guards, Corlin, and by the looks of the prisoner I'm certain his punishment is complete. Do tell me again what it is he is accused of?' The Prime's voice dripped dangerously with sarcasm.

Corlin was angry at the breach in protocol but the man before him outranked him. He took a breath and faced the people, speaking theatrically, hoping to resurrect some of the previous enthusiasm.

'He stands accused of peeping during the ladies' session at the baths this morning.'

It suddenly sounded ridiculous. The crime considered heinous several hours ago, when several of the wives of the town's most prominent and wealthy citizens had levelled the accusation, now seemed petty.

The Prime was a tall, broad-shouldered man with thick, dark hair and a closely cropped beard. He wore no badge of office and was dressed in simple dark breeches and white shirt. His voice was clear and deep and his grey eyes had a sparkling quality, as though in perpetual merriment, which he demonstrated fully now by lifting his head and laughing. In fact he roared, and many in the crowd joined in. Even Tor, relieved at finding himself forgotten in the scene, found himself grinning.

'Ha! The rich and pampered ladies who frequent the baths should be secretly delighted that anyone should want to peep at their ample backsides and thunderous thighs.'

By now it seemed that everyone but Corlin and his

sidekicks had dissolved into laughter. Tor noted, however, that the Prime's eyes were no longer smiling when they returned to rest on the cripple's tormentors. And his voice was as cold as a winter's stream.

'Release this wretch, Corlin, and go and find some bigger game to amuse your apes with. This man's punishment – just or unjust – is complete.'

'Says who?' snapped Corlin, who thought he had been in charge of proceedings.

'Says I!' The Prime's eyes were glittering dangerously dark now. 'Release him immediately on my order. Call off the thugs who masquerade here as men of the military and don't even think of reaching for your sword. Your head will be rolling in this very gutter before it is out of its sheath.'

Corlin hissed a threat. 'I will live to see you regret this, Prime. Another stage, another day, and don't be too sure it won't be your own head the dogs fight over.'

He turned swiftly, drew a large knife and cut the bonds on Cloot's hands and feet. His final act was to scowl meaningfully at the hushed crowd before pushing past, his helpers falling in step behind him.

The people who, minutes earlier, had been crying for blood now saw the cripple for what he was. They began to drift away, embarrassed.

'I'd be obliged if you told me who you are and what you were planning to do a few moments ago,' enquired Cyrus, now standing above Tor who was still crouched next to Cloot.

An unspoken message passed between Tor and his crippled friend. Tor stood, finding himself eye to eye with the Prime, which was a new experience for both of them.

Each was used to being the tallest of men. Tor noted with relief that the man's eyes had resumed a certain mellowness and he opted for his usual explanation when he found himself in an inexplicable situation: a characteristic shrug.

'I asked you for your name, boy,' Cyrus reminded quietly.

'Tor, sir. Torkyn Gynt.'

'And you hail from. . . . ?'

'I've just arrived from Flat Meadows, Prime. I . . . um . . . I stabled my mare and was strolling around the town hoping to find a room for the night and stumbled across this . . . er, him.' Tor nodded towards the prisoner who remained silent.

'Do you know him?'

'No, sir, er Prime, I don't. Well, he spoke . . . No sir. No, I don't . . . not exactly.'

This made Cyrus glare at him again. He enunciated his words very carefully in case Tor had not understood the original question.

'Have you or have you not met this person before? Don't be clever with me, boy.'

'I have not,' Tor replied, relieved he could answer with honesty.

The Prime squinted as he tried to read Tor. It was a look his two lieutenants knew intimately. He possessed an uncanny ability to judge the integrity of someone. Everyone in the royal corps knew to fear that look if they were not being entirely truthful. Tor held the gaze steadily and, though tempted to look down and kick a stone or shuffle his feet with the embarrassment he felt, resisted the urge.

Cloot, his head still attached to the post by the nail

in his ear, grunted in pain. Cyrus cast a glance at the prisoner and then back at Tor. Finally he extended a large and surprisingly well-manicured hand at the boy.

'Well, Torkyn Gynt, if you don't know this man then you're a fool.' He smiled broadly which took Tor by surprise. 'But a courageous one. I'm glad someone had the bollocks to think about standing up to that sadistic swine . . . though the gods only know what you had in mind.'

His smile, ferocious and brilliant in intensity, disappeared as soon as he looked back at the man on the floor. 'Help me, boy. Let's get the halfwit free.'

'He's not a halfwit, sir; his name's Cloot . . . er, Prime Cyrus.' Tor's leap to defend was sprung too fast.

Cyrus peered at him with raised eyebrows and a grim yet bemused expression. He said nothing, the look was enough.

'I mean . . .' Tor was about to start gabbling. He knew he had made an error. 'With respect, Prime, from what I can tell, he may be mute as well as a cripple, perhaps not an idiot though.'

Tor grinned. He hoped it would help, and he felt sweet relief when the Prime's brow puzzled.

'You're a physic as well as a warrior, then?' Cyrus's sarcasm was gentle this time.

'No, sir. Well, yes, sir. I'm training to be one, that is, sir. I just think he would have cried out . . . er, from the pain if he could talk. Don't you think so?'

Cyrus growled quietly to himself. He locked his knife behind the carelessly banged-in nail. 'Now for the nasty bit,' he said, before releasing Cloot who fell helplessly against Tor. 'You poor sod,' Cyrus muttered, noticing just how badly hurt the man was. 'Wait whilst I get help, Gynt.' He stalked away.

Cloot, still in Tor's arms, turned his large head to face the boy. His misshapen features, pulped by the beating, somehow rearranged themselves into a smile. *Thank you*, was whispered into Tor's mind.

Tor was moved by the man's dignity. 'Rest, Cloot.'

Cyrus returned with two of his men in tow, dragging a cart.

'Get him loaded on there, Riss,' he ordered. 'Gently, man, he's half dead already.'

Tor stood up. 'What happens now, sir?'

'My men will see him to the alms hostel. If old man Jonas is not in his cups yet he'll patch him up as best he can and perhaps find him a pallet for the night. It's the best we can do.'

Cloot was slumped on the cart. Riss, with the help of his mate, was beginning to wheel him away. Tor knew it would happen: Cloot's voice was back – urgent and laced with pain but also anxiety. *Tor! We must remain together*. Cloot was still drawing on Tor's energy to remain conscious.

Tor had to try. 'Prime Cyrus!'

The Prime had already swung himself up into his saddle. 'Good luck, Gynt.' He turned his horse.

Tor leapt after him, as well as shouting to the men laboriously wheeling Cloot away. 'Ho, you men, wait!'

'What now, boy?' growled Cyrus. 'I've wasted enough of the King's time on this affair already. Speak!'

'I'll take care of him,' Tor blurted.

'You'll what? What the hell are you talking about, Gynt?' Cyrus turned his horse back.

Tor really did not have any idea what this was about. What did Cloot mean by saying the two of them had to remain together, and how did he know his name? It was too strange, and yet the last few days had been so full of strange happenings that nothing should really surprise him.

He followed his instincts.

'Prime Cyrus. Please, let me look after him. I can't imagine what kind of care he'll receive at the alms house with him being a cripple and the man the town has just beaten half to death . . . Well, why would anyone bother to help him? He'll die. We both know this, so what can it hurt if I help?' Tor didn't know what else to say.

Once again the Prime studied him. 'Why do I get the distinct feeling that you are not telling me everything, boy? What possible good can you do him? Granted old Jonas is a bit of a butcher but I can't think of anything better.' He looked almost kindly down at Tor. 'There's nothing you can do for him, Gynt. Go on home with you. Back to your village and forget about this ugly event.'

Tor stepped towards the cart. 'It matters to me. This man will die if I don't help him. I have a little money. Perhaps I could afford a better physician for him.' Tor knew he was grasping. He would have to come up with something better than that.

'You have money? Money to burn on a half-dead, retarded cripple you apparently don't know?' The Prime sounded understandably incredulous.

Think, Tor, think!

'It was honestly earned, sir, and I might as well spend it on doing something to guarantee myself a place in heaven than pissing it into the gutter tonight.'

Tor waved his hand nonchalantly, hoping the show of bravado would sway Cyrus. It did.

'Have him, Torkyn Gynt. He's paid his dues. He's a free man. Good luck to you both.'

With that the Prime turned to his men, barked an order and rode off without looking back.

Riss cleared his throat a little too loudly. 'Where d'you want him, boy?'

'Er . . . what?' Tor raked his hand through his hair.

'Prime's orders. We're to take him to wherever you are staying.'

Tor could see from the dust on the man's clothes that it had been a long day of marching and he had probably been looking forward to a few ales rather than wheeling a cripple around.

'I have no place to stay,' Tor said.

Riss looked as though he was going to step forward and club him. Instead he growled, 'Halfwits stick together it seems.'

'Look, I've tried to find an inn but it's so busy tonight and I've had no luck. How about helping me find somewhere? I'll pay you,' Tor blurted desperately as both men cursed him.

'You're very free with your money today, lad,' Riss said in a tone which suggested he didn't think Tor had any.

'How much?' Golag's voice, silent up to now, grated as though it wasn't used often enough.

'Find me a room, a physic and a hot stew and I'll pay you both a duke apiece.'

Tor had already guessed that these infantrymen were paid less than that each week. It was an exorbitant sum but it was worth it if they would help. He could not fault

Merkhud's generosity of purse but would need to be frugal after this.

Both men whistled through their teeth. The offer was irresistible, Tor hoped; to his relief Riss nodded. They each took a handle of the cart and the wheels squealed as Tor pushed from behind. He had no idea where they were all headed but he was grateful to the two soldiers who mumbled quietly to themselves as they navigated a path down the crowded main street.

Tor squeezed Cloot's arm. *Not long now* he eased gently into the pained mind of his friend.

There was no reply, save another pull on his strength.

The scenery began to change: they were on the fringe of the town in a more rundown district. Turning into a cobbled alley they bumped their way through the narrow pass overhung with densely built houses. At the end of the alley they entered a small square which was a mass of activity and riotous colour. Bright bunting was being hung and stalls were being set up. The smell of onions cooking and various meats beginning to sizzle took hold of Tor's stomach and squeezed tightly. He was ravenous.

He caught up with Riss. 'What's going on?'

'They're crowning the King of the Sea tonight.'

'King of the Sea?' Tor looked confused.

'I thought you were from around these parts, Gynt. How come you don't know about the Harvest Festival?' Riss spat expertly.

'I've led a quiet life, Riss. I remember my parents talking about this once, but I've never been out of the district until now. What happens?'

The cart rumbled slowly around the large square as

Riss explained to Tor that although Hatten was generally a wealthy town now, the people had not forgotten its humble beginning when the area began to build its wealth on fishing and wine. Its grape juices were not as fine as the smaller vineyards of the sun-drenched valleys south of the capital, but this region supplied most of the Kingdom's commonly drunk wine. Each year at the end of summer, when the huge schools of prized lokki fish arrived to fill the fishing trawlers and the vines were laden with bunches of fat fruit, the farmers and fishermen gave thanks.

A festival had grown up around the annual harvest, based on choosing a King of the Sea and a Queen of the Vines. It was believed that when the royal pair lay together they would propagate the following year's harvest. The ritual had been observed for almost two centuries and these days it was a huge event for Hatten.

All the fishing boats would be in port tonight and the inns filled with landowners, captains, sailors and vineyard workers as well as visiting merchants and ordinary people passing through to observe the festivities and join the fun.

No wonder there's nowhere to stay, Tor thought.

'And as this year's Queen was crowned last night, tonight it's the turn of the King, and then the merry-making for them and the town begins,' Riss continued.

Golag's grimy face and yellowed teeth leered into view. 'Perhaps I'll be chosen. Wouldn't mind giving that Eryn one.' His voice sounded like boulders rubbing together, and he grabbed his crotch to emphasise his point.

The men stopped the cart.

'Who's Eryn?' Tor asked as they lowered the front end.

'Aw, she's just one of the whores chosen as Queen by

the town's menfolk. But I don't think Golag stands a chance, eh, Golag?' Riss poked his grubby friend in the ribs and laughed.

Tor frowned. 'So now the women choose the King. Is that how it works?'

'No, boy. The Queen chooses her own. Light strike me! That Eryn won't be spreading her legs for anyone ugly tonight. Fucking the likes of us is strictly on a pay as you go basis.'

'Pay as you come,' Golag corrected, pleased with his jest.

Both soldiers found this most amusing; their mirth became even louder when they saw Tor blushing.

'Er, right. I think I understand now. Thank you, Riss.'

Tor's attempt at a polite end to the conversation provoked more laughter. He decided to change the subject swiftly and looked around. They were standing in front of an inn called The Empty Goblet and he could hear loud singing and men's voices.

'Are we here?'

Riss had composed himself but Golag was still banging his chest to stop the hacking cough which followed his guffaws.

'Yes, boy. I reckon we can find you a small room here tonight, with some luck and some change to grease old Doddy's palm.'

'How much?' Tor didn't want to pull out his pouch of coins so he dug around in his pockets. He found some barons and small copper. Golag grabbed the lot.

'Hey!' Tor pulled at Golag's filthy sleeve.

'And don't forget my duke,' the soldier growled into Tor's face.

Tor had put two dukes into his shirt pocket as they had made their way here and was now very glad for such foresight. He gave Riss both coins.

'What happens now?'

Riss cleared his throat and spat again. The gob gleamed on the dust by Tor's toes.

'Get the halfwit onto your shoulders, lad, and follow me.'

There was no point in trying to talk to Cloot now. Tor found he was becoming used to the sensation of Cloot pulling on his energy. He pushed another parcel of energy into his half-dead friend, feeling the loss keenly, and hefted Cloot awkwardly onto his right shoulder. Stooping, Tor staggered as he followed Riss inside. The noise was deafening. It was a soldiers' inn all right and they all looked and smelled like Riss and Golag. He followed, waiting impatiently under the dead weight of Cloot as Riss said something to the fat man behind the counter. The innkeeper pointed a pudgy finger upstairs.

Riss turned to Tor. 'Top floor. I'll find the doctor and then that's my part of this deal done.' He smiled and briefly shook hands, which Tor found reassuring.

He nodded at Riss gratefully and began the challenging ascent. Stopping several times, twice to let giggling girls and soldiers stumble past him; he finally reached the second-storey landing which had only three rooms. Tor opened the first door and closed it hurriedly when he saw a young prostitute, hard at her work.

'Damn!' he muttered, feeling the colour rise in him instantly.

There were two choices left. He lumbered towards the door at the end of the airless corridor. This room was

empty. It was also tiny. He tried to lay Cloot gently onto
the mattress of the cot but he was so weary his load slipped
and Cloot dropped with a crunch. Tor flopped down on
the floor beside the bed, worried and exhausted. A short
while later there was a knock and a young girl, about ten
summers old, entered balancing a jug of water and bowl.

'The physic is behind me,' she gabbled.

A man spoke. 'Are you Gynt? The one with the retard?'

Tor sighed and stood tiredly. 'Yes, I suppose that sums
things up.' He nodded towards the bed.

The doctor, whose name was Freyberg, laid his walking
cane against the cot and immediately began tut-tutting
to himself. Together they removed Cloot's rags and both
drew a sharp breath at the palette of colour across his
body. Angry purple bruises from the earliest wounds
blended with the dull pink of the most recent, with
promise of a much deeper colour to come. These were
interspersed with distressing bright red splotches showing
bleeding close to the skin's surface, due most likely,
Freyberg commented absently, to broken bones.

Doctor Freyberg kept up a quiet, continuous muttering
to himself as he examined his patient. Finally the old man
rolled up his sleeves and opened the satchel he had brought
with him. He pulled the cork from a bottle of a dark,
viscous substance which smelled strongly of cloves and
handed it to Tor.

'Pour some into his throat. It will help take the edge
off the pain.'

Tor obeyed, holding Cloot's head gently as he tipped
the blackish liquid into his swollen mouth.

'His teeth, sir? I mean, could he be swallowing any broken
teeth with this?' he asked as he handed back the bottle.

The doctor snorted, then eyed the boy from beneath bushy brows, one of which expertly held a monocle in place.

'Well, I should imagine swallowing broken teeth is the least of this man's problems, but if it reassures you, my boy, I have already checked and it appears his teeth remain whole . . . though that seems to be the only part of him which is.' He looked at Cloot and then back at Tor, adding gently, 'However, I'm impressed that you thought to mention it, Gynt.'

This pleased Tor. Long before Merkhud had put the thought into his mind about training as a practitioner of healing, Tor had felt a similar calling.

'I'm heading for Tal, Doctor Freyberg,' he blurted. 'Physic Merkhud has taken me on as his apprentice. I'm to learn the healing arts.' He was unable to help the pride which swelled in his chest at finally saying this out loud.

The man returned Tor's smile. 'Why, that's just marvellous. I haven't met the great Merkhud but he is very well known to the Tallinese. His reputation, however, is known to everyone. I can't imagine you'd have a more talented teacher and at the Palace too.' At this he blew out his cheeks. 'What an opportunity for a boy . . . But now wait, I seem to remember some talk of Merkhud having never taken any scholars under his wing—'

'You're right at that,' Tor cut in excitedly. 'I'm his first apprentice.'

'Then I shall have the honour of giving you your first lesson, young Gynt.'

The doctor returned to surveying his patient.

'But I must tell you, your sad friend here is very

damaged from the cursed beatings of his captors. I'm not sure of the extent of his problems – not yet anyway – so if you are going to be of any help, you must promise to be brave. He is hurt terribly,' he added.

Tor nodded gravely. He could hear the sounds of the early merrymaking in the square cranking up a notch in intensity. Through the tiny window the soft late afternoon light gave the attic room a warm glow.

'His name is Cloot, sir. I'm called Tor.'

The doctor acknowledged this with a barely perceptible nod before continuing briskly.

'From what I can tell immediately, Tor, Mr Cloot has several broken ribs, a broken arm on his left side, a disjointed shoulder on his right side and a broken wrist on the right side too. He is severely concussed, probably from a particularly nasty blow just here,' he said, pointing to Cloot's temple. 'And if his jaw is not broken then it is cracked badly around this point.'

Tor remained silent.

'His cheek may also be fractured and his nose is quite obviously broken. He will have a couple of shiners by tomorrow – if he lives that long – and this ear has a nasty tear . . . Did they nail him to that damn post?'

Freyberg did not wait for a reply. 'There's some bad bleeding here and here – if he has ruptured inside then there's very little we can do but I'm hoping against hope that it is due to the broken ribs. The man's a marvel, though. How he is still alive is a wonder.' He began to rummage through his bag again.

Tor didn't have to wonder. The increasingly intense headache and weakness he felt told him enough about how Cloot was still alive. He desperately needed to rest.

Cloot was draining him. The doctor was still talking but Tor did not hear.

'I'll need your help . . . What's wrong, Tor? You look as white as fresh milk. Are you squeamish, is that it? Sit down, sit down.'

The old man fussed until Tor did sit down on the small stool near the window. He dragged in some air, willing the nausea and faintness to dissipate. Taking the black phial which the doctor held outstretched, he looked up confused.

'Just sniff it – it should help.'

Tor sniffed and regretted it the same instant, gagging and then coughing and spluttering. His eyes watered and his nose ran. He must have glared through his noisy discomfort because Doctor Freyberg snorted loudly, this time with humour, then handed him a second, even smaller phial after breaking the glass seal.

'No, doctor, I won't, thank you – I like not your herbals,' Tor croaked.

'Trust me, Tor. This really will make you feel better. The other – simple but powerful smelling salts. I apologise.'

Tor didn't think he looked in any way chastised but took the phial and swallowed the contents. It had a pleasant taste. Not sweet but not bitter either, with a soft flavour of something he had never tasted before. He liked it and did, indeed, feel brighter almost immediately.

'Good, isn't it? It's called arraq,' Freyberg said, looking his way.

'What is it?' Tor licked his lips.

Freyberg began to clean Cloot's face gently as he spoke. 'It's a berry. Violet-skinned with bright red fruit. The berries are tiny and rare. They bloom only during Thaw and for a very short season. As soon as the ice and frost show the first signs of melting, I'm out hunting my arraq berries. But 'ware the raw berries – exquisitely poisonous, young Tor.'

'I've never heard of them before.' Tor smelled the empty container and committed the bouquet to his excellent memory. 'How do you prepare them?'

'Perhaps I'll be able to show you one day. It's a messy but simple process of boiling them furiously down to a syrup. But if you want to poison someone, the juice of a few berries will kill them efficiently; a few drops will paralyse. Not many people know this.'

The doctor was now gently sponging Cloot, removing the grime which added to the mess of his body. He began humming softly as he did so. Tor stayed quiet, inwardly marvelling at the renewed strength he felt and even took the risk of sending another silent bolt of it into Cloot.

'I need your help, Tor, to set Cloot's broken bones – are you feeling up to it?'

'Yes, I want to help.'

They worked for the next hour or so, gently easing joints and limbs back to their positions and sweating, despite the early evening's mildness, over straightening his bones as best they could. After this the doctor instructed Tor where to apply the special salves and ointments he pulled out of mysterious pockets in his bag and showed him how to bind the broken bones. Finally, as twilight claimed the dusk and the noise in the street and from the inn below began to overwhelm their voices, the doctor straightened his back and sighed.

'That's it, Gynt. He's in the hands of his gods now; I

can do no more for him.' He looked searchingly at Tor. 'I lie. There is one more thing I can do.'

He dragged a small bottle from his bag. Inside was a pink liquid.

'I use it on fatally injured patients. If the worst happens and you see more of these red splotches appearing, or if your friend starts to cough blood, you give him this. Tip it down his throat and say a prayer for his soul.'

Tor was shocked. Pure arraq juice, he guessed.

'We won't need it, Doctor Freyberg.' His voice was raspy and he was embarrassed to realise his eyes were misting up.

'I know, my boy. I hate to lose any patient, but if and when he regains consciousness he may be in tremendous pain and could die in agony. This will speed him on his way, that's all.' He pressed the bottle into the boy's hand. 'It's a gentle death, Tor,' he added softly.

Tor could hardly bear it. He was exhausted physically and emotionally.

'How much do I owe you, doctor?'

The doctor almost winced at his tone and busied himself clearing things back into his satchel.

'I am offended greatly by this person's suffering. I will not accept your money, Tor.' His kind smile overwhelmed Tor who slumped on the stool. 'And as for you, son, I recommend you use the money to get a hot bath, a hearty meal and a few ales. Mr Cloot is going nowhere for a while so rest and get your strength back too. You look strapping enough and yet you seem weakened – are you sickening for something?'

'No, sir – I've just been travelling for several weeks and skipped too many meals.' He lied expertly and hated himself for it, particularly to this generous soul.

'Until tomorrow then, Tor.'

Tor listened to the doctor climbing down the stairs, the sound soon lost in the noise of men's voices soaring from the inn's front room. He studied the strange, sleeping man's face, trying to look behind the puffiness and horrible bruising. This was not a handsome fellow. His large nose swooped down almost to touch his protruding bottom lip, whilst his forehead appeared unnaturally deep. Oversized ears and a mad thatch of dark hair would have made him seem freakish if not for the intelligence Tor had seen mirrored in those pained eyes earlier. The man was mute but he was certainly not cretinous as most instantly assumed.

Tor gave his umpteenth sigh as he contemplated, once again, the thought which had niggled since Doctor Freyberg had said there was nothing else he could do. His attention was momentarily distracted by frenzied movement at the foot of the bed and he watched with horrified fascination as a small army of ants dealt with a struggling, dying cockroach. They began expertly to dismember the wretched creature while its rapidly decreasing number of legs thrashed furiously in the air. One particularly enthusiastic foot soldier was doing his damnedest to haul one enormous leg off on his own. Tor admired the tiny ant, up against a seemingly impossible task but unwavering in his dedication. Perhaps the ant inspired him.

Tor took a long, deep breath, pushed up the sleeves of his rough shirt and gently laid his hands on Cloot's chest. He closed his eyes, summoned the Colours and felt his fingers begin a familiar tingling as the room turned silent and grey.

6

King of the Sea

In spite of his fatigue, Tor felt refreshed after washing and changing his dusty clothes. He joined the boisterous crowd of soldiers downstairs, feeling lost and a bit lonely amongst men who all knew each other.

His spirits were boosted when the roasted meat and a cup of strong ale were set down in front of him. The girl melted away again, lost between the shoulders of beefy men. The colour of her hair reminded him of Alyssa and he was swamped by a fresh wave of despair about where she had gone and why she had left without word. Almost unconsciously he cast, seeking her out, begging inwardly for her response. Nothing. Just the blackness. He poked at it. There was no hint of Alyssa's familiar scent.

Too occupied with eating a sorely needed meal and thinking on Alyssa, he did not notice company had arrived until the soldier had undone his scabbard and set the blade on the table. Tor picked up his own mug and, raising it slightly towards the newcomer, took a long draught.

'To your good health, Gynt,' Prime Cyrus said quietly. 'How goes it with the freak?'

'His name is Cloot, Prime Cyrus. The doctor holds little hope that he will survive this night.' He held the soldier's keen gaze.

The Prime leaned back and rubbed his battle-grey eyes. 'Tell me about yourself, Gynt, you intrigue me.' His voice was friendly, open.

Tor could not help but like Cyrus. He sensed a sophisticated man not afraid to resort to violence. His senses also told him this was a loyal man, one who would put his men before himself and his sovereign before anyone.

'So little to tell, Prime Cyrus. Not long ago I left my village where I've lived all of my life and now I'm on my way to Tal.'

Cyrus nodded towards Tor's cooling meal. 'Please.'

Tor returned to his food. The Prime gestured to a passing serving girl for a refill of his ale. 'How old are you?'

'Old enough,' Tor said awkwardly, his mouth full.

'And you're heading for Tal . . . Why?'

'Why not? The capital seems the most logical place to seek my fortune.' Tor was beginning to feel like cornered prey.

'Is your father a farmer, Torkyn?'

So he remembers my name. Tor was impressed again.

'No, sir, he is the scribe for our district. We live at Flat Meadows. Perhaps you know it?'

'Indeed. Well, I know its inn. I have stayed there but not in a long time. And the father is prepared to let the intelligent son go and not follow the profession. This seems strange.'

Tor pretended to drink what was left in his mug, though he had emptied its contents already, using the time to think. The Prime was honest, of that he had no doubt, but the man was also being too inquisitive.

'My father's a great believer that all men should broaden their minds before settling down to a profession or . . . family.' He held the Prime's gaze innocently.

'So you plan to return to Flat Meadows?' Cyrus asked slowly.

'I have no plans, Prime Cyrus. Why all these questions, if you don't mind me asking one?'

'Because whatever happens in Tallinor is my business,' Cyrus replied. 'The security of our realm is my responsibility and I like to know when folk with strange friends and even stranger ways are making a beeline for our capital.'

The Prime sat back, his half-drunk mug of ale cradled loosely in his lap. Tor was not fooled by the casual manner; the soldier was clearly enjoying himself.

'I'm just suspicious by nature, but somehow I know our paths will cross again, Gynt, and then I'll have your story.' He stood. 'Here's to your fortune then, in Tal.'

Cyrus rebuckled his scabbard and, without much more than a nod, disappeared towards the inn's door. Soldiers parted shoulders swiftly to let their revered leader pass through.

The interrogation over, Tor decided he needed fresh air. He cast to Cloot upstairs and established that he was still unconscious and would probably remain that way for a while.

Outside the revelry had escalated. The main square, now a riot of colour, dance and music, was lit by hundreds of scented candles burning inside brightly decorated, waxed paper lanterns that hung in long strands. Their gentle, spicy fragrances were blown by a soft sea breeze around the streets.

Tor found himself watching a young couple dancing close, laughing and kissing. Too much seriousness in my life, he berated himself. It is time just to relax. Alyssa would contact him when she was ready. Cloot was safe upstairs. The Prime and he had reached a quiet truce and his first carnival was awaiting impatiently. He straightened his shirt, checked the pouch of money and the orbs – which, he noted, now emitted a constant, just perceptible hum – and joined the revellers.

Dizzy from dancing with three of the local lovelies, Tor was in the middle of a challenge to lift the incredibly fat lady in her chair when his fruitless exertion was brought to a sudden end by the loud tolling of a bell.

People immediately began spilling out of inns and various side streets, hurrying to get the best vantage point in front of a makeshift stage in the centre of the square. A robed man stepped up onto the stage and began to quiet the happy mob.

'Good folk, be welcome. Our sincere thanks to the generous people of Hatten, who have once again given us a memorable day – and night – of festivities. But now the moment we've all been celebrating towards has arrived: our new Queen of the Vines must pick her King of the Sea.'

The crowd roared its approval.

'I would now ask all the bachelors who consider themselves worthy of Kingship to come forward. No more than twelve men will be presented so make haste!'

The bell tolled again and Tor laughed with the crowd as a mad scramble of men, young and old, started trying to climb the stage. The ladder had been taken away so they were having to haul themselves up the hard way. Some tripped in their dash to the platform. A few fell in their desperate attempt to hoist themselves up or others pushed them away much to the merriment of the onlookers. As always a few hardy souls made it and were preening themselves proudly above the crowd.

One minute Tor was enjoying the hilarious antics, the next he was in the air. With a rush and a wild cheer, his captors dumped him unceremoniously onto the podium. Tor spun around just in time to catch sight of six burly soldiers in fast retreat. Scowling, he scanned the back of the crowd and, right enough, there was Prime Cyrus wearing a sardonic smile, his mug raised in a toast.

Tor was furious. He found himself being hastily arranged into the two lines of suitors for the Queen's hand but consoled himself that she would never choose him, so let them have their fun.

Loud horns heralded the arrival of the Queen. Ceremonial music piped up and everyone began to bow in mock homage to their sovereign. From afar she was stunning. Raven hair was polished to a gleam and hung to just below her narrow shoulders. She was dressed in an almost transparent gown of palest green gauze which clung seductively to her narrow hips and small, full breasts. A dazzling golden cloak sparkled and fluttered around her. The woman was closer now, smiling at her subjects. Tor straightened himself up and, without real-ising it, began to selfconsciously smooth down his white shirt. The girl's cheeks were pink with excitement. Her large eyes were shining with the enjoyment of all this attention. All in the crowd could see her naked body clearly defined beneath the wispy thin shift.

Tor recognised her as being the girl he had saved from the beating today. That cheeky young sprite of a thing who had not even offered thanks. This was the Eryn they spoke of, the whore Golag had joked about.

She winked! Was that at me or someone else, he wondered indignantly.

The soft breeze teased her nipples and he could see them swelling through the veil of her gown. She really was ravishing.

The master of ceremonies calmed the frenzied cheering and announced the procedure – which everyone but Tor already seemed to know by heart. Each suitor must first negotiate the impossible: a fifteen-stride walkway of slippery, flopping, dangerous lokki fish in their death throes. Delicious cooked but able to inflict nasty injuries to stray fingers, toes – in fact, any human flesh they could latch onto with their razor-sharp teeth. And if the teeth did not catch the foolhardy suitor, then the saw-toothed fins would, lacerating shins and calves. Each bare-legged suitor had to 'tread the fish' to reach his Queen and be crowned King of the Sea. Triumphant suitors in previous years had made the dash but not without enduring an ordeal of pain and lasting wounds. No one had ever made it across without injury.

One after another the suitors fell into the slimy, frenzied mass. Two hardly advanced beyond their point of entry, leaping back and yelling as thrashing fins whipped across their legs leaving savage slashes. Others tried to pursue their quest, screaming their pain as they tripped, stumbled, and ultimately succumbed. Within minutes the walkway was stained bright red as blood mingled freely with sea water and dying fish. The crowd loved every minute of it.

Finally it was Tor's turn. He was the last to tread the lokki.

Perhaps it was the arraq working its own particular magic, and no doubt fatigue and one too many mugs of ale were clouding his judgement. Not long ago he had been drooping over Alyssa. Right now he was eyeing a pretend Queen he seriously wanted to claim as his own. He convinced himself to get into the spirit of the festival rather than fight it.

He could hear the soldiers heckling him. Tor really did not want to end up slashed and bleeding but he glanced once again at Eryn, who seductively stretched the front of her gown so little of her firm body was left to his imagination. As he stepped onto the landing of the walkway, Tor fleetingly recalled Merkhud's warning, but lust had him in its grip now and the Colours were roaring up inside of him.

He pushed out with his power, casting a spell over the dangerous mass of sea monsters. Planting his feet firmly on two of the giant lokki, he let go with the power. Momentarily calmed, the two thrashing, slippery fish seemed to glide over their dying brethren.

It was over in moments, so quickly the crowd barely had the chance to consider how such a thing could be achieved. Tor alighted at the other end of the walkway and pandemonium erupted in the crowd. A new King was to be crowned. The worthiest of all suitors in the history of this savage contest would rightly claim throne and Queen.

In the noise and warmth of this still, late summer night, desire pounded in Tor as he bowed before his Queen. Amidst the revelry Eryn turned to him and took his hand.

'I never did thank you for saving me today. I hate Goron! Hope his balls are the size of melons after I kicked him!'

And then she was sweetly waving to her subjects while Tor's feet were quickly washed by two handmaidens. Their two thrones were picked up and walked through the square.

Tor momentarily found sense within his clouded mind and suddenly thought that he had to get back to Cloot.

'Where do we go now?' Tor called to Eryn over the heads of the people.

'You'll see soon enough,' she said suggestively.

She is adorable, Tor thought helplessly, falling back against his throne. As they left the square he caught sight of a very bemused Prime Cyrus lifting his ale once again and giving a single Tallinese salute.

The happy mob carrying the thrones snaked their way up towards the Summerhouse where the 'royals' would be left for the night to consummate their 'marriage'. It was believed that the joining of this King of the Sea and Queen of the Vines would ensure prosperity for the following year's harvest of lokki and grapes.

Feeling extraordinarily tired, Tor sensed the link slice open weakly. It would not hold. He grabbed at it, locking onto the fragile call from Cloot. Tor did not need to hear him; he could tell immediately that the man desperately needed more life-giving strength. His own energy reserve was so depleted he used it all in a last desperate bolt of healing power which he cast to Cloot. He let go, feeling the world spin as he slumped back, his head lolling to one side.

Eryn noticed and put her hand on his arm and nodded towards the front of the line. They had arrived.

'Just do what I do and it will all be over quickly,' she murmured.

Tor watched as women began to throw vine leaves on the path. At its end he could see a small structure dwarfed by a huge single tree at the top of another very gentle incline.

'The Summerhouse,' she said, taking his hand. 'Let's go.'

They walked slowly up the path, alone this time, whilst the crowd sang a final song to the King and Queen who would now be expected to consummate their mock-marriage. It was a lusty song of fertility.

The threshold of the Summerhouse was gently illuminated by headily perfumed candles and strewn with fragrant herbs. A large bed was draped with soft muslin. It was the only furniture, other than a small table set with supper and wine.

'Kiss me,' Eryn said and then saw his confusion. 'You have to kiss me and then they'll go.'

Tor's thoughts fled to Alyssa and back. He made a silent plea to the gods not to allow Alyssa to eavesdrop on this particular night of his life. As Eryn's mouth closed on his he heard the applause of appreciation. The kiss continued long, soft and slow. Tor somehow found the strength to scoop Eryn into his arms and enter the Summerhouse. He laid her on the bed and their lips finally parted.

Frantic desire coursed through him, but even as he lowered himself he felt the final heroic reserves of his energy flee. His last conscious act of that day was to murmur an apology to the young woman who lay beneath him, hideously offended.

Parrots were making a commotion outside the Summerhouse. Startled awake by their happy racket, Tor looked vacantly around the room until he remembered the previous night. He could almost see the shape of Eryn pressed on the sheets and could smell her lingering perfume.

Recalling his sad performance, Tor cursed loud and colourfully. Then he remembered Cloot.

Still fully dressed from the previous night he hurriedly swung long legs to the ground and moved swiftly from the bed. He found his boots placed neatly by the entrance and pulled them on without noticing the tiny note stuck inside.

As he sped off down the hill towards the city, Tor threw his mind to Cloot, anxious of what he might find.

You're awake!

I am now, thank you.

I've disturbed you? My apologies.

Not really, there's a physic here. I gather his name is Freyberg.

Tor stopped. *Is he wondering over the miracle of your recovery?* he asked sheepishly.

No, not at all. We were actually discussing where the fish might be running today.

Tor heard Cloot chuckle deeply in his head and bristled with embarrassment. How was he going to explain this away to Freyberg?

I'll be there shortly.
And I'll be waiting, Cloot said.

In the smallest room at The Empty Goblet, Doctor
Freyberg was furious. He banged his monocle into his left
eye.

'And what are you smiling about, Mr Cloot?' Freyberg
demanded, knowing it was a pointless exercise. He probed,
with no small wonder, at the healed limbs and once pulpy
bruises which had paled almost to nothing.

The patient shook his ugly head and wiped the grin
swiftly.

'Ah, so you can hear?'

Cloot nodded.

'Well, you have no need of my services any longer. It
seems angels paid a visit here last night and did my work
for me.'

They could hear someone taking the steps two at a
time and moments later Tor clattered into the room,
breathing deeply from his efforts. Freyberg snapped his
case shut and swung around theatrically.

'Welcome, Gynt. I have the most extraordinary tale to
relate.'

He pushed his hands into his pockets so the boy
wouldn't see them shaking. Freyberg was not sure whether
he felt unsteady from the miracle of the work he had
witnessed or from the terror it evoked.

He had been a physic for thirty-three years and, like
his father before him, had served Hatten for all of his
professional years. Freyberg knew he was good. No, he
knew that he was an exceptional doctor and yet, with all
his experience and skills, he also knew that nothing was

going to save Cloot's life last night. Now, very much alive and healed, the mute sat before him, and damn him if a dopey grin was not spreading across his ugly face again.

Tor acknowledged the physic with a stiff bow. He looked over at Cloot, saw him sitting up on the bed and could not help but return the huge grin.

'Doctor Freyberg, I'll explain everything, I just need to talk to Cloot,' he muttered as he closed the door. He was at Cloot's side in two strides and gripped the man's huge hand tightly.

'Talk! How do you talk to a mute?' Freyberg plonked himself into the only chair in the room. He stared angrily out the small window at the marketplace below, listening to the boy's excited onesided conversation.

'I thought you were dead at one point, Cloot. I was so scared.' Tor felt his eyes filling with hot tears. He'd done it. He had saved the man's life.

Hush, boy. Don't dig a deeper hole for yourself, Cloot murmured in Tor's head and nodded slightly towards the doctor. He raised his other hand and tapped Tor's head lightly. *There is much for me to share with you, but right now I must rest, and you must think of something very impressive to tell the doctor*. He sagged back onto the bed.

Tor let go of the man's hand first and then his mind. He faced Freyberg, who was snatching nervously at his beard. This was a good man sitting in front of him. He did not want to lie but admitting he was sentient was as good as signing his own death warrant. Merkhud had gone to some pains to point this out before he left.

Do not use your powers on this journey at all. Don't be tempted to show off. Don't interfere with anyone or anything. Just mind your own business and get yourself quickly to Tal.

That's all Merkhud had asked and had Tor done that? No. Goron, Corlin and his thugs, Eryn, Cyrus, Cloot, Doctor Freyberg: six or more lives he had already touched with his magic having barely spent sunrise to sunrise in this city.

Freyberg's voice cut into his thoughts. 'There's absolutely no use trying to dream up a plausible excuse. Just tell me how in the name of Light this man is alive today.'

Tor stood. Cloot's tired eyes followed him.

'It was me . . . I did this.' Tor's voice was flat. He was genuinely scared now, for his very life depended on how the doctor felt about the use of the power.

'You're sentient.'

It was not a question but Tor answered anyway.

'Yes. I couldn't just let him die.'

'What am I going to do with you now, boy? You realise I'm under royal oath to turn you over to the Inquisitors?'

Freyberg turned angrily towards him. Tor remained silent.

'Barbarians that they are!' the doctor spat. 'And is Physic Merkhud aware of your power, young man?'

Tor hesitated as he stepped onto perilous ground. 'He is.' He held his breath.

Cloot pretended to doze. Freyberg twisted his beard in a frenzy of troubled thoughts. The airless room was silent for a long time.

'Right! If it's good enough for the famous Merkhud, then who am I to interfere? I really have never appreciated what all the fuss is about the power and if you can do this for a broken man, just think of the good empowered people could do for the Kingdom!'

Dr Freyberg stood and stared hard at Tor. He felt almost sorry for the tall, handsome youth.

'You mean you won't be telling anyone about this?'

'I will not.'

Tor took a step towards the doctor and awkwardly hugged the man his thanks.

Freyberg was solemn. 'This is a wonderful but dangerous gift you have, son. You'll have to be far more careful how you use it in future. The next person may not be as impressed as I.'

Tor nodded.

'I must go, my boy. I have a long day of appointments but I'm worried about how you'll explain away Mr Cloot's miraculous recovery.'

'I really hadn't thought past trying to save his life but I'll think of something,' Tor said, raking his hair with his fingers.

'Well, think quick, boy. The innkeeper here is a notorious gossip. It will be around this city like wildfire. My best advice is for you to get out of here immediately. Use the cover of night and get as far away from this town as you can.'

Freyberg left soon after and, as Cloot was asleep again, Tor headed downstairs and consumed an enormous breakfast. Whilst the woman laid out his food, she answered his query for directions to the famous Hatten public baths.

Feeling so much better for the food, and chewing on an apple, Tor meandered through the narrow lanes, enjoying the brightly painted colours of the tall walls and the bright washing hung on short poles from shuttered windows. He even kicked an inflated pig's bladder around with some of the children and, just for a while, forgot he was anything more than a wide-eyed visitor to a big town.

Resuming his walk he continued until he came into a small square which he recognised from the ornate fountain the serving lass had described. He joined a short queue of men dropping coins into the hand of an old and bored-looking attendant, who duly handed them a piece of folded linen.

'How much?' Tor asked as he drew level with the attendant.

'Well, handsome, for a peek at what hangs between your legs, I'll let you in for free,' cackled the crone. Tor noticed, with no little revulsion, she had not a tooth in her head. The hoots of laughter around them goaded her on.

'Or come out the back wi' me now, I'll pay you instead!' The hag found this especially amusing and Tor was again treated to a full view of her aged gums.

A young man pushed past him. 'It's two bits.' He flashed a smile.

Tor dropped the coins into her grimy palm. He snatched the towel and followed the man, relieved to escape the woman's horrible laugh.

He caught up. 'Thanks.'

'Don't mention it. She's revolting but she does that to everyone she can, so don't be flattered.'

'I'm not. My name's Tor Gynt, a traveller.'

'Pleased to meet you, Tor. I'm Petyr, town slut.'

He took some delight in watching Tor's shock.

'Well, come on, Tor, don't be such a prude. I need a bath; so do you by the look and smell of things.' With a wrinkle of his nose he walked ahead.

The sounds of men's voices increased in volume as Tor

rounded a stone pillar behind the undressed Petyr. The bath was huge, surrounded by massive murals of naked people cavorting through forests which reached up high into the vaulted ceiling. He was staring. Petyr was saying something to him which he missed.

'I said are you coming in, handsome, or do you plan to stare at naked men instead?' Petyr called as he floated on his back.

'Don't call me handsome.' Tor was irritated.

'Why ever not, you fool? When did you last look in the mirror? You are handsome and such a strong build! Ah, but I see you are not comfortable with it yet. Well, you will be, my friend, you will be.' Petyr waded off, amused.

Tor took time to scrub himself properly using one of the gritty cubes of soap left in pots around the baths. He realised it had been days since he had last bathed. Tor relaxed into the warmth. When Petyr returned Tor mentioned the impressive architecture and concept of the public baths.

'Do you want help washing your hair?' Petyr's green eyes, framed by long, dark lashes, had a roguish glint.

Mortified at Petyr's suggestion, Tor threw several handfuls of water over his own head before striding to the steps and getting out. He grabbed his linen and wrapped it quickly around himself.

Petyr stepped out. 'You seem very edgy, Gynt. I won't bite.'

'Look, thanks for your company. Perhaps we'll see each other around.' He sounded so polite he wanted to bite his tongue out.

'I doubt we move in the same circles, Gynt, but I'm

told you didn't finish the job you were picked for last night with Eryn. How disappointing.'

Petyr had finished drying himself and was stepping neatly into his clothes. Tor had stopped dancing on one foot to clamber into his breeches.

'You know Eryn?'

'Like a sister.'

'Then you'd know where I can find her?'

'I might.'

'Petyr, please will you tell her I'm sorry. It was nothing to do with her.' He finished dressing.

'Farewell, Tor. Perhaps I'll mention it, but then again, perhaps I won't. Nice talking with you.' He tossed his towel into a nearby basket and walked away.

'Wait!'

Petyr turned back. Tor flipped his own towel into the basket.

'I'm at The Empty Goblet.'

Petyr laughed. 'That fits.' Then he was lost in the crowd of men headed towards the main doors.

Tor sat down on the narrow stone ledge which ran the perimeter of the walls. Feeling gloomy he began to pull on his boots and it was only then that he saw the note which had fallen inside. His spirits lifted when he realised it was from Eryn. Her writing was atrocious but he managed to work out that she seriously wished she had stuck with the ardent, carrot-haired farmer last night.

He intended to make good with her if he could. But right now it was time to return to Cloot and find out more about his strange friend.

7

Dreamspeaker

The Empty Goblet was a hive of activity as Cyrus and his company made preparations to depart Hatten. The men were eager to leave: they had been on routine patrols through the middle towns of the Kingdom for many weeks.

Cyrus was as popular with his soldiers as he was with the Tallinese who made him welcome wherever he travelled. Curiously though, despite women flocking to him, it was whispered that he never involved himself in liaisons. His wife, a beautiful, fragile creature, had died giving birth to his son a decade previous. When the infant had also died he had been so lost in grief that friends had feared for him. King Lorys had always liked the dashing young captain and when the old Prime died, Lorys did not hesitate to promote Cyrus over three more senior contenders. It was an honour for someone so young, though Lorys had never regretted his choice for Prime of the Shield, and was glad that the security of Tallinor was in the hands of Kyt Cyrus.

'You've settled the account with that rogue Doddy?' Cyrus asked his captain.

Herek nodded. 'I gave him only the agreed price we set last spring.'

'Good, though I don't doubt the slime watered the men's ale.'

'Do you want me to go back and—'

'No,' Cyrus cut in distractedly. 'No, it just occurred to me he'd fleece us somehow. Innkeepers seem to think that because we wear the King's crest we have access to his purse.'

The captain remained silent.

'Herek, we leave at daybreak. Inform the men.'

'Yes, sir.'

'How many days?'

'Two, sir – if we get a good trot around the Great Forest.'

'We must move swiftly then. I'll be with Mayor Reyme most of today if you need me. Otherwise, just get the men readied. You know what to do.'

The Prime nodded at Herek before looking towards the door. He was pleased to see Torkyn Gynt walk in, looking decidedly more chirpy after a bath and visit to the barber it seemed. Cyrus acknowledged Herek's snap to attention yet was more interested in how the youngster had got on the previous night.

'Ho, Gynt.'

'Prime Cyrus. Still here?' Tor was on his way to the stairs but walked back to where Cyrus was seated.

'As you see.' Cyrus nodded towards one of the stools at his table.

'When do you make tracks?' Tor asked, seating himself and briefly casting to Cloot. He discovered Cloot was awake and was about to speak with him but stopped himself.

'What happened?' Cyrus was grinning good-naturedly at him.

Tor came back to the conversation and was puzzled. 'What happened when?' Two ales had found their way to the table.

'Just then. You asked me when we were making tracks; I replied but you seemed to be focused on something else. Surely I'm not that tiresome?'

'Apologies.' He had to do that better from now on. 'It's been a strange couple of days and my head is anywhere but where it should be.'

'I don't doubt it, Gynt, after last night. How did you perform anyway?'

'All right, I think . . . didn't hear any complaints.'

'Ha!' Cyrus liked this boy. Draining his mug he banged it down on the table. 'I shall look forward to seeing how you get on in Tal, young Gynt. Until then, travel safely.'

Tor stood and took the Prime's outstretched hand firmly in the Tallinor manner.

'Oh, by the way, Gynt, good luck with Merkhud. If you ever have need, you can reach me through the Palace Guard,' Cyrus said, eyes shining with amusement.

Tor was shocked. 'How do you know?' he stammered, sure he had told no one but Doctor Freyberg.

'It's my job to know.' Cyrus tapped his nose.

'The Light guide your way home, Prime Cyrus.'

'It always does, Gynt.' A slight nod of his head and the master of swift departures left the inn.

A powerful friend to have at the Palace, Tor thought as he ascended the two flights of stairs and walked into his small room.

You look well, Cloot, he remarked and settled himself in his spot by the window.

Cloot, seated and relaxed on Tor's bed, had obviously gone to some trouble to clean himself up. From somewhere in his small sack of belongings he had produced a clean shirt.

I am well. His voice had a rich timbre in Tor's head.

Tor took a deep breath as he turned slightly to gaze out at the buildings across the marketplace.

How do you know my name? he asked quietly, not turning from the window.

I have known it all of my life.

Tor was alarmed but he forced himself to continue. *Who told you about me?*

Lys.

A woman?

Yes.

And who is she?

I have no idea, Cloot replied flatly.

Well, how does she know me?

You would have to ask her, Tor. Cloot shrugged apologetically.

And, what is your purpose?

Cloot shook his head slightly. *Of my ultimate purpose, I am not advised but I—*

Tor turned sharply to eye Cloot whose large, ugly face was softened by compassionate understanding. He put his hand up to stop the boy's frustration.

Tor, let me tell you what I do know rather than what I do not, and perhaps we can put together some of the pieces of this curious puzzle.

He continued after Tor nodded with resignation. *I come*

*from an almost unknown region in the far northeast of the
Kingdom which my people call Rork'yel but I've heard it referred
to as Rock Isle by some of the oldest northerners, which is odd
because it's certainly not an island.*

He noticed Tor blink with irritation and cleared his
throat.

*Ever since I was old enough to be aware of dreams, I have
been visited by a woman who calls herself Lys. She never shows
herself but she is always there. For all of my life she has told
me of a person — Torkyn Gynt his name — to whom I am
bonded.*

Tor interrupted. *What do you mean, bonded?*

I'll explain but first, have you ever heard of the Paladin?

Tor shook his head.

*Well, what I'm about to tell you will mystify you as much
as it did me for many, many years, until Lys wore me down
into acceptance of my life's charter. I have never discussed this
with anyone — not even my own family, who may never forgive
me for leaving them several weeks ago.*

Cloot sounded strained when he mentioned his family.

Go on, Cloot.

The man sighed. *There are ten members of the Paladin.
One is chosen from each of the Kingdom's ancient peoples. Mine,
the Brocken, have lived in our region for hundreds of years. Since
I was old enough to understand her words, Lys has told me that
I am one of the ten.*

He fell into a heavy silence.

But what does this have to do with me?

The Paladin are guardians, Tor. Cloot spoke now with
gravity. *There are two of us who will protect you with our magic
and our lives.*

But why? Tor could suddenly hear his own heart

beating. His tongue was dry, his hands wet with perspiration. He really did not want this answer.

Because you are He. You were given to save our world and I was bonded to you as one of your protectors as soon as I was born, probably long before you were born.

Tor's barely controlled anger slammed into Cloot's mind. *It doesn't make sense Cloot — just listen to me. I'm a simple scribe's son. I've led an ordinary life in a small ordinary village where nothing more exciting happens than the Twyfford fair!*

Cloot remained calm and spoke gently. *And yet here you are, that simple scribe's son, on his way to the royal Palace, apprenticed to the most famous physician our land has known and who just happens to be a powerful sentient.*

But that's got nothing to do with it! Tor snapped, secretly shocked that Cloot knew of Merkhud's powers.

The Light it hasn't! What about the powerful magic you wield? Do you think that doesn't interest him? Look at what it has done for me and you've barely tapped it, Tor. Think about it. What did it feel like to heal me? Once you understood what was required, it was like eating one of Goody Batt's pastries — simple and irresistible!

Fine. I've saved you, Tor spat. *Next the world, but what am I saving us from?*

Cloot shook his head. *That I don't know, boy. Perhaps Lys will tell us.*

Tor poured himself a mug of water from a pitcher. He drank, calmed himself, refilled the mug and handed it to Cloot.

All right. Tell me what else you know, he said, resuming his seat.

His friend smiled. *Lys told me to wait. Each visit she*

would insist on my patience. I spent fifty summers waiting.

You what? You're fifty summers old? Tor spluttered. *But . . . but . . .*

Yes. I am old in your terms but we Brocken are a strange race, Tor. We live long and I am still very young in the minds of my elders.

Your parents are alive?

Why, of course, and my older brothers and sisters and even my grandparents, and they are all livid that I've left Rork'yel. A brilliant smile lit his ugly face.

Tor couldn't help but laugh out loud. *Cloot, have you any idea how strange this all is for me? A few days ago I was spilling ink and being scolded by my father. Now I'm under the protection of a strange, very ancient . . . Brocken, is it? And being told it's up to me to save our land from who knows what.*

Believe it, Tor. You must accept as I have. Consider how strange it is to hear about some child yet to be born and then, fifty summers on, you're told to leave your home and your family to find and protect him.

They sat in silence for a while, thinking about how their lives had been thrown together.

Has Lys told you what she wants from me? Tor wondered.

No, but she has suggested we just follow our instincts and events will unfold. Cloot shrugged.

Unfold? Light! What am I getting myself into? Is there anything else I should know? Er, wait a moment, you said you were sent to find me. How did you know where to look?

Cloot swallowed the contents of the mug and stretched. *Lys came to me in a dream last full moon and said it was time. She said I was to leave before dawn and when I asked her where I should go, she told me I would know when I woke. She was right. When I woke just before dawn I could sense you. It was as though I was gathering in a length of luminous colours as I travelled across Tallinor. That's how I recognised you: your colours are blindingly strong.*

You see me in colours?

No, I followed the colours I sensed and they were connected to you, and if I hadn't been accused by that loutish corporal of – what was it . . . peeping? Cloot snorted, *I would have reached you outside of Hatten rather than under such dangerous circumstances.*

What were you planning to say to me? Here I am, the great – and very old – Cloot, your protector?

Well, no, I had in mind to wrestle you from your horse and challenge you to a power struggle, so infused was I with this new magic. Why should a scrawny lad like you get to save the world? Why should not a noble and, dare I say, handsome Brocken have the honour?

Cloot was being theatrical, waving his arms in the air and Tor's nervous mirth bubbled over. It was reassuring for both of them to hear him laugh.

To tell you the truth, Tor, I had no idea what I would say – or was supposed to do – once I found you. I was simply following my nose, as Lys instructed. As it turned out, you found me.

This magic you say you now have . . . why didn't you use it?

Well, that would have been intelligent, would it not, to ensure attracting attention to myself? I hear they bridle anyone who shows the slightest trace of the power. No, Lys warned me to not draw any undue notice to myself. She said my looks alone do enough . . . not that I know what she meant by that! So I took her advice and made sure I got my ear nailed to a post and every soul for miles around clustered to look at me and jeer at me and throw nasty things at me. Yes, I went to great pains to go unnoticed.

Tor enjoyed Cloot's humour; he felt genuine warmth for his new friend. *What magic do you possess?*

Cloot shrugged in his habitual way. *I honestly don't know because I haven't tried to do anything. I surprised myself when I reached out to you yesterday and spoke without anyone else realising I was doing it. If I hadn't been in such a difficult position, I would have done a jig of glee on the spot!*

There was a light knock at the door. Tor crossed the room in two easy strides to answer. It was the young serving girl, bringing up fresh candles and water. Tor allowed her to enter and noticed her petrified glances towards Cloot, who was sensibly pretending to sleep. If the girl's tongue got wagging that he was up and healed, then new dangers would present themselves. Initially impressed at his friend's presence of mind, Tor did not appreciate Cloot suddenly dropping his jaw open and snoring menacingly. The girl let out a terrified squeak and hurried out of the room.

Busybody!

Tor sighed. *So, what now, O my protector?*

I go where you go, Torkyn. We're bonded, remember? Not that I want to do this, mind. I can think of any number of things I'd rather be doing in my homeland. Right now I'd like to be strolling down to Goody Batt's to see what's cooking in her kitchen. Cloot's voice trailed off dreamily in Tor's head.

Right then – if you don't have one, here's my plan. Tomorrow night we leave for Tal . . . and in secret. I'll need to get a horse for you and beyond that we'll just have to see what happens. And who in the name of Light is Goody Batt?!

8

Miss Vylet's

It was several hours later and fortunate that they had the
link to argue across.

No, I will not!

Cloot, you have to trust me, Tor implored.

*What? That you'll catch me on a cushion of magic should
I fall, or that you'll cast a spell to patch me up again?* Cloot
just stopped short of sneering. He hated heights and what
Tor was suggesting was outrageous.

Tor reached across and squeezed his friend's hand. *No,
trust me that I won't let you fall in the first place.*

Where you go, I go, Cloot grumbled with weary resignation.

*Now look, I've worked it out and I've done a run-through.
All we have to do is cross the rooftops for a couple of buildings
and then I've found a way we can get ourselves to street level
relatively easily. Oh, and one more thing. You'll be wearing a
skirt and shawl — they're in there.* Tor pointed to a sack in
the corner.

He left the room quickly, snapping closed the mindlink
before Cloot roared.

There was one final task to complete prior to their pre-dawn escape. If his directions were right he needed to make his way down towards the port and a brothel called Miss Vylet's. He found it, attached to The Lookout, an inn popular with those who arrived in Hatten by ship and the ships' skippers. Tor expected it to be a roughhouse part of the town but the buildings were well kept.

Walking into Miss Vylet's he reeled from the noise of a hundred or more loud conversations above the din of drunken singing. Tobacco smoke caused a bluish haze to settle around the drinkers and merrymakers. Scanning the room for Eryn he could not see her and felt a knife of disappointment slash through him. He pushed his way to the inn's counter and ordered an ale. He paid his coppers, turned his back against the counter and leaned on his elbows, watching the activities.

There were various women, dressed provocatively in low-cut silks, serving drinks and meals. Some were sitting on laps and lighting pipes for the patrons. Miss Vylet was a clever woman: the ale was good and the smell from the kitchen told Tor's experienced nose that she ran an honest inn, which ensured its patrons returned over and again. She not only took their money for food, drink and accommodation but next door could take their money for the satisfaction of other needs.

To encourage her guests' desires, she had her pretty troupe of girls showcasing themselves most efficiently. He watched one fresh-faced young woman in a scarlet gown that hugged her perfectly proportioned body superbly, deliberately lean low over a table to gather up the mess of three wealthy men who had finished eating. The man closest to her got himself such an eyeful of smooth, pert breasts that he was ready to negotiate the price on the spot. The girl knew of it, of course. She caught someone's eye up on the landing and was strolling off arm in arm with the man before he could think it over.

Tor followed her glance upstairs and saw a straight-backed, slim woman of some sixty-five years seated there. Her dark, roving eyes took in everything. She caught his look and acknowledged his smile with an amused arch of her eyebrow.

She had to be Miss Vylet.

When Tor turned back he noticed another pretty woman had already taken the scarlet girl's place and was busily clearing the same table. Yes, Miss Vylet was a very clever woman, he concluded. And rich, no doubt, for the money changing hands over the counter was brisk and plentiful.

He drained his mug. As he shouldered his way towards the door he knocked someone's arm, causing his ale to spill. Tor apologised and the man good-naturedly waved the mishap away and bent to wipe the froth from his pants. As he did so Tor caught sight of a familiar cascade of raven hair. His breath caught to see her in animated conversation with a man upon whose knee she was perched. The man he had tipped ale onto stood upright again and Eryn was once more lost in the crowd.

Tor moved closer to the door and into a better position to see her. She looked ravishing and her companion was laughing at some story she was telling while tracing a hairy hand along her spine which was only vaguely covered by a crimson gown. She was laughing as she teased him. Tor seethed. He had no right to but he felt a fury grip him dangerously.

A woman squeezed by, carrying a small tray of drinks. Tor touched her elbow to get her attention.

'You couldn't afford me, sonny,' she said, not unkindly. 'But believe me, I'd love to.'

Her amusement and innuendo diffused his fury immediately. 'I'm sorry, I didn't mean that,' he said.

'Oh . . . well, pity.' She smiled.

'I'm wondering if could you tell me whose lap Eryn is sitting on . . . er, that is if it doesn't break any rules here.' He needed his grin to work its charms this time.

'Well, we're not supposed to but . . .' The hesitation told Tor his charms were in good shape. 'Where is she anyway?' she said, looking around.

'Over there, in the corner.' Tor nodded his head in the direction but deliberately kept his back to Eryn.

'Oh, yes. Um, that's Captain Margolin. Adores Eryn. Always visits whenever he's in Hatten, spends up big in here and refuses any other girl.'

Tor felt grim but he made sure his expression did not betray him. He grinned. 'I see. Am I pushing my luck to ask you the name of his ship?' Tor was thinking fast now, his smile gleaming at the girl.

'Let me think now. Well, you would have to double-check with someone who knows it for a fact but I think she's called the *Majestic*. Why, is something wrong with her?'

And that gave Tor his plan.

'No, I . . . er . . . simply have a message for Eryn, that's all.' Tor tried to sound offhand.

'I'm her friend, Elynor. I'll pass it on but you'll have to be quick.' She nodded towards the balustrade on the floor above. Miss Vylet was watching them.

Tor shook his head casually as if considering her offer.
'Look, thanks but don't worry, I'll see her a bit later.' Tor
feigned a smile and made to leave.

He heard Elynor snort. 'You'll be waiting a long time,
handsome. Margolin buys her for the whole night.'

Tor felt sick. He hurried into the cool night air, dragging in a lungful of it to clear his head and nostrils of
the noise and smoke. This was stupid. He should just
forget her and go back to his inn. He looked up the street
and as he did so a young lad trotted past him. Tor whistled him back.

'Want to earn a duke?'

'I don't whore.' The boy could barely be eight years
old and his reply shocked Tor.

'I don't remember asking you to . . . er . . .'

'Well, that's what most people are about in there,' the
boy said, nodding his head towards Miss Vylet's. 'If it's
not fucking the girls, then they're after fucking some lad
and I just likes to be up front wi' them. I live around
here and gets asked all the time whether I'd like to earn
a penny or two.'

He stared at Tor who was lost for words at that moment.

'So, tall man, how do I earn the duke?' The boy clicked
his fingers towards Tor's face as if to bring him to his
senses.

'Well, shorty,' Tor replied, regaining his wits, 'I'll give
you a duke to go into this inn and pretend that you've
run all the way from the dock. You must find a captain
called Margolin, who is sitting in the alcove two windows
down from where we stand, and tell him there's a fire
aboard his ship. It's called the *Majestic*. Tell him he's
needed immediately. Run out as fast as you can and I'll

meet you on the next corner and double your money.'

The lad blinked once. 'You're on. Where's my money?'

'Oh no, you don't. Let's run through it again.' Tor couldn't imagine he had the plan down pat.

'Look, mister, do you want this job done or not? I'm late and much as I'd like a few extra pennies it doesn't make a ha'peth of difference when my mam's skinning my backside. Yes or no, I don't care.'

The cheek of him. Tor pulled out the money, dropped it into the boy's small palm and told him to hurry. He was inside before Tor could say more, a look of contrived panic suddenly fleeting across his small face. Tor watched with amazement through a window as the boy gave a brilliant performance, pushing dramatically through the legs of drinkers, even stumbling once and daring to wink through the glass. Tor had to move to the next window to catch the finale. At first the captain looked bemused, then his expression changed to alarm as the boy's tale unfolded, his arms waving and eyes wide and bright. Margolin pushed Eryn off his lap, dug into his pocket and tossed her some coins, then remembered something and turned and kissed her hand before pointing towards the door in explanation. The boy took off between the legs of people and tables and the captain was unable to keep up.

Tor quickly ran up the street and hid around the corner and within seconds his small accomplice scampered around as well, grinning gleefully.

'You owe me another one,' he said, not even out of breath.

'And I'll pay it gladly. You seem adept at this sort of thing.' Tor liked the kid with his mad thatch of black hair and green eyes. He gave him a third coin.

'Cor! Three!'

'You earned it. What's your name?'

'Locklyn . . . Locky.' His eyes gleamed at the money in his hand.

They could hear Margolin running in the other direction towards the dock. The conspirators laughed.

'I'm Tor and you were great.'

'Hope she's worth it, Tor.' Locky's grin spread across his face and then he winked and was skipping off.

'Hey! Hope your mam doesn't spank you too hard,' Tor called after him.

Locky looked back over his shoulder. 'I lied, I don't have a mam. My sister looks after me!' And he was gone.

Tor strolled back into the inn and looked for Eryn. Elynor was standing next to her at the bar, both waiting for their orders to be placed on their trays. Eryn looked irritated and Elynor was explaining something to her.

Tor glanced up at Miss Vylet whose all-seeing gaze had been resting on him since the second he had set foot back in her establishment.

You'd better have enough coin to pay for her, young man. Her voice was calm and deliberate in his head.

Tor could not hide his shock. He stopped and hoped to the Light that his mouth had not gone slack.

I do, he cast tentatively across the mindlink.

Then welcome to the house of Miss Vylet.

Her lined face creased into the sunniest of smiles and Tor saw in that moment the great beauty Miss Vylet had obviously been in her youth. He found his own grin and flashed it but the smile was wiped when a mug of ale was tipped over his head. He should have felt her coming.

'You bastard!' Eryn hurled at him, along with the mug which caught him painfully on the cheekbone.

Heads were turning and those around him were laughing. Eryn had been careful not to splash other patrons with her liquid fury.

'How dare you!' She was very angry.

Her hair shone gloriously, Tor noted despite his discomfort, and in another moment of strange clarity he remembered Merkhud's warning to remain as inconspicuous as possible on his journey. He had taken being conspicuous to dizzying new heights. First the marketplace, then the marriage ceremony, now this. He was tired of it all and his patience snapped. He grabbed Eryn's elbow and brooked no argument as he angrily led her outside.

He cast to Miss Vylet, *Back in a moment*, and heard her chuckle softly. It was she who closed off.

Outside the air chilled the cold ale on his body further but the more Eryn struggled, the tighter his grip bit into her arm. She stopped, went limp, even pouted.

'If you didn't expect to see me again, why this note?' He waggled a crumpled piece of paper in front of her.

'I wanted to know if you had the courage to face me again,' she spat and bent her small finger up and down, suggesting his manhood had never been up to the task.

'I'm here, am I not?' Tor could not think of anything less ludicrous to say.

'Yes, and I wish you were not. Captain Margolin is worth a lot of money to me and you've just ruined it. I've been waiting since the beginning of summer to see him. You're hurting me.'

She began to fight back tears, which swiftly killed Tor's

wrath and replaced it with weariness of this strange life
he was leading. He let go of her arm.

'I'm sorry about the captain, Eryn, really I am. I came
tonight to tell you that I regret what happened the other
evening, which had nothing to do with you, and wish I
could explain it better than that.'

He sighed, remembering the eventful day. 'It's a day I
want to forget, except I haven't been able to forget how
beautiful and funny you are and how much you deserved
my apology . . . And well, now you have it.'

He raked his dark hair off his handsome face and Eryn
quietly marvelled at his total ignorance of how heart-stopping he was.

'Now, I have one gold piece left and it's yours, which
I hope makes up for what you lost from not being with
Margolin tonight.'

He dug out his last coin, a heavy gold sovereign, and
put it in her hand, closing her fingers around it. He bent
his head, kissed the hand which held the money and
walked away.

'Tor, wait!' She tried to catch up with him but he
increased his long strides.

Eryn picked up her gown and broke into a run. She
finally grabbed him by his damp jacket and spun him
around. Light! He really was the most handsome man she
had ever laid eyes on.

'Tor, please wait . . .' She caught her breath. 'You'll
die of cold before you reach wherever you're going.'

He looked pained, she thought, and suddenly sad. It
began to drizzle and people started ducking for shelter.
A breeze picked up across the water and blew straight at
them.

He fixed incredibly blue but tired eyes on her. 'Hurry back, Eryn, or you'll be the one with a cold and that would be shocking for business, I imagine.' He winced at his own nastiness and at watching her flinch from it too.

Eryn's smell and her warm nearness reminded him too much of Alyssa. A great sadness descended on him. He had to go. Her eyes were searching his and he did not know what for. He bent, kissed the top of her head and pulled her hand from his shirt. 'Goodbye, Eryn, good luck.'

'No, damn you, Torkyn Gynt, you don't just toss me a coin and walk away. At the very least you might as well have what you've paid for.'

He wanted to go. 'Go find Margolin then. Tell him to fuck you and tell him it's on me as I've already paid the fee.'

She was visibly shocked. Her hand flew to her throat and Tor hated himself. She slapped his face hard and, without another word, turned and stalked down the street. He let her go, watching her wrap her arms around herself as protection from the chilling drizzle which was rapidly turning to rain. He was glad. The business was unfinished but the matter was clearly settled.

His face stung. Tor dug his hands deep into his pockets and trudged away from The Lookout. He thought about Alyssa, cast along the path he knew so well and hit the dense void he had expected. He would give anything to hold her close just once more. He checked on Cloot and found him sleeping. He was pleased to feel all of Cloot's strength was back. As he rounded the corner which would lead him away from the port, Miss Vylet's soft voice suddenly breezed into his head.

She doesn't deserve that.

He surprised himself with a smooth, immediate response. *Stay out of this, Miss Vylet.* He kept walking.

So cowardly, Torkyn. I hope Merkhud chooses more wisely next time.

She shut the link viciously.

Merkhud! She knew about Merkhud. Tor's head swam with possibilities.

Who are you all? he screamed into the link and then began running. Running back towards The Lookout. The inn was still busy though the crowd had thinned out and there was no sign of either Miss Vylet or Eryn.

'You again?' It was Elynor, tray in hand, other hand on hip.

'Is Miss Vylet here?'

'She's next door and that's all you get, handsome, whoever you are.' She left him.

Still shivering slightly, Tor pushed past the heavy drapes shrouding the small archway which connected the brothel to the inn. The noise drifted away as he stepped through a second, even more heavily curtained opening into a lamplit foyer. A beautiful creature, dazzling in a deep gold gown, arose from behind a small screen and gave him a wide smile.

'Welcome, sir,' she said then faltered as soon as she assessed his age. 'Er . . . can I help you?'

He didn't hesitate, surprising himself. 'Yes, you can . . . um?' Tor gave an enquiring look and the girl immediately offered her name.

'Thank you, Mya. I'm looking for Eryn. I believe she arrived a short time ago.'

Mya was just about to give an answer when he felt,

rather than heard, someone behind him. He turned.

'Good evening.'

'Sir, this is Miss Vylet,' offered Mya in a rush.

Tor stepped towards the older woman, bent and kissed her hand.

'It's a pleasure to meet you again, madam,' he said aloud for Mya's benefit, adding through the link, *I imagine we have plenty to talk about.*

Indeed, she replied and cut the link.

'Mya, Mr Gynt and I share a mutual friend. Please fetch Eryn to my study when I ring for her. In the meantime, I would like to take wine with this handsome fellow. Perhaps you'd be kind enough to send some through.'

With that she dismissed the astonished girl, offered her arm to Tor and led him down a small passageway to her private rooms. Miss Vylet's salon was the most elegant room Tor had ever seen, though he readily admitted to her he had not seen many elegant rooms. She smiled warmly at his comment and asked him to make himself comfortable in one of the large armchairs near a small open fire.

He sank down and warmed himself. Next to this morning's bath, had anything ever felt this good? Yes, Alyssa's kiss, Eryn's warm body next to him in the bed. He shook his head to clear it. His host was holding a small tray and closing the door with thanks to someone. She set down the tray with its decanter of plum-coloured wine and accompanying small glasses.

'I like to take a glass of Bethany each evening,' she said, pouring a measure of the syrupy specialty of Tallinor's northern region. She handed it to him, poured another and then seated herself opposite. They gently raised glasses

to each other. Miss Vylet sat in a comfortable silence and
Tor felt tired enough to enjoy the peace. He was getting
used to being studied. He closed his mind as a precaution. It felt strange but secure.

She probed and was impressed.

'I see you've acquired a veil.'

'I think it's necessary, don't you?' He meant no insult.

'Oh, indeed, and no doubt long overdue. A word of
advice. Train yourself always to keep your mind that closed
to anyone but those you want to have a link with, such
as . . . er. . . . ?'

Miss Vylet waited for Tor to offer a name.

He shook his head and wasn't sure why. Instinct
perhaps.

'There's no one at present who can talk to me in this
way, other than you of course, Miss Vylet.' He drained
the delicious Bethany and laid his glass carefully back on
the tray.

'Oh, come now, Torkyn. How about Physic Merkhud
to name one?'

'Perhaps he can but he has not done so,' Tor answered
carefully.

'And no one else has ever spoken to you via the link?'
She could not hide her curiosity.

'Actually yes, there was someone once but that link
has been damaged and we've not talked in a long time.'

It was the truth. In deliberately being obtuse, Tor left
his host in the situation of either having to delve deeper
and therefore appear more than just curious, or to let
alone. She acknowledged silently that he would do well
in the diplomatic circles of the royal Court.

'Well, just heed my advice, Tor. It will serve you loyally.'

'Miss Vylet, may I ask you a question?'

'Of course.'

'How much would it cost me to purchase the services of Eryn for the whole of tonight?' He kept a straight face despite her astonished expression. This clearly was not the question she had anticipated.

'Light, child! Would you know what to do with her?' The glass was stopped halfway to her mouth.

'I suppose that's my problem.'

She had recovered herself. 'Well, why don't you ask Eryn yourself?' She leaned over to pull on a cord. 'She'll be here shortly. Now, what else do you want to ask?'

'About Merkhud obviously. How you know him, how you know me, how we are all connected perhaps?'

'I've known Merkhud for most of my life. I think I've secretly loved him for all that time too.' A little laugh escaped her. 'We are loyal friends and speak often.'

'By mindlink?'

'Of course. He certainly doesn't come calling at the brothel, if that's what you mean. As to how I know of you, he mentioned you would show up in Hatten and simply asked me to see you through safely.'

'May I ask how you were to do that?'

'Eryn, Petyr, Locky. They're all in my pay in some form or another.' It was the turn of her eyes to twinkle. Her guest had not seen that coming.

'You mean you planned all of the meetings?'

'I did.'

'And Cloot?'

'Is this the freak whom you helped the other day in the marketplace?'

Tor nodded.

'No, I have no knowledge of that strange fellow. What happened to him anyway?' She held out her hands to warm by the fire.

'Oh, I paid for a room at the inn for a night and a local doctor saw to him. He disappeared during today, I know not where. The physic said he would probably die and I'm just glad he had the good grace not to do it on my bill.'

Tor lied smoothly and again wondered to himself whether this was instinctive. Something was forcing him to keep Cloot as secret as possible. Miss Vylet was nodding. He was glad to hear a soft knocking at the door.

'Come, Eryn,' Miss Vylet said.

Eryn entered; she had changed into a diaphanous pale blue shift. Tor took a deep breath and stood. Eryn refused to look at him.

'You called for me, Miss Vylet?'

'I did, yes. Eryn, you know Mr Torkyn Gynt here?'

Eryn nodded, her eyes firmly on her satin slippers.

'Well, he has just asked me an extraordinary question. He wishes to spend tonight – the whole of what's left of tonight, that is – with you. He has asked me how much this might cost and I thought it would be best if you sorted this out directly with him. I fear too much may have already passed between you two to make this a comfortable trade. It is your choice, my dear.'

Eryn finally looked up at Tor, her eyes defiant. 'He's already paid – a gold sovereign, madam.' She dropped the heavy coin into the older woman's palm. 'More than enough to buy me for the night.'

She hadn't taken her eyes from Tor's. They burned angrily.

'In that case, my dear, you'd better show him to one of our special rooms.'

And with that Miss Vylet turned and bid Tor a warm goodnight. 'Enjoy your stay, Mr Gynt, and please call in any time you find yourself travelling through Hatten again. My best to our mutual friend and good luck in Tal.'

She disappeared through another door in her study. Only a heavy silence remained.

'Follow me, please.' Eryn's voice was brittle.

'Eryn, wait a moment.' Tor felt horribly uncomfortable. Suddenly this was no longer an idea which appealed.

She ignored him. 'It's this way.'

Eryn walked out of the door. He paused but had no choice but to follow. She was already at the top of the stairs and disappearing down a darkish corridor lit by flickering candle lamps. He took the stairs two at a time and at the top glimpsed her walking into a room at the very end of the corridor.

Tor walked slowly, his tread heavy. This did not feel right. Light though, she was lovely; more so when she was angry and her eyes blazed as they had. He arrived at the door. Everywhere around him was so quiet that he knocked gently. She opened it. His mouth went dry in an instant for she was naked.

'Close it, please, I won't be long.'

He watched her shapely bottom move with tantalising, rolling grace to the four-posted bed. She pulled the drapes across. 'Whenever you are ready, sir.' Her sarcasm was barely concealed.

Enough. Tor strode across the room and ripped back the drapes with such force that she almost shrieked. Instead she gathered up the sheets around her thin shoulders and stared angrily at him.

'Enough, Eryn. None of this is to my liking or of my doing. You chose me for the wedding ceremony, remember, and now I hear from Miss Vylet that you were her spy. You were told to find me, which you did so expertly almost as soon as I arrived in Hatten. Then Petyr at the baths and Locky . . . you're all "friends", I gather?'

He shook his head at how gullible he had been but gave her no chance to retaliate, holding up his hand to silence her.

'Thank you for being part of the elaborate scheme. The sovereign's yours. You've certainly earned it.'

He threw the curtains closed, stepped up to a small table where wine was set out, drank a draught and, with no further word, headed for the door.

'They're my brothers, not my friends.' Her voice was urgent yet sullen.

'What?'

'I said they're my brothers – Petyr and Locky.' She poked her head out from the drapes. 'Don't go,' she said quietly and disappeared, re-emerging a moment later with a satin wrap around her. 'I mean it. Really . . . don't go, Tor.'

She walked to him, took his reluctant hand and made him sit by the fire with her. 'It's cold out there tonight.'

Tor barked a tired laugh. 'Especially when you've been rained on.' She had not let go of his hand and began massaging it.

'All right. No apologies. A truce instead. Agreed?'

'Agreed,' Tor replied with relief. 'Now what?'

'Finish what we started last night, except this time there's no guile. I'm here because I choose to be, not because I have to be or because you've paid.'

'Your writing is atrocious. Do you know that?' he said suddenly, remembering her note.

She laughed. 'Be grateful I can write at all. Most of the girls can't.'

'Who taught you?'

'Margolin and a few others who liked me enough to spend a little of their precious paid time on teaching me rather than just—' Tor cut her words off with a hand across her mouth.

'Don't say it, Eryn. You're better than that.'

'Am I?' she said wistfully. 'Not really. I rather like this life, Tor, so don't go trying to change me.' She meant it.

He pulled her close. 'May I finish that kiss, at least? If you only knew how furious I was to wake up and realise I'd missed my chance.'

All trace of seriousness drifted away as she turned to face him. They kissed gently and then deeply. When Eryn finally pulled back she studied his face.

'Was that kiss just for me or are there more of us in this room?'

'Oh, there might have been a few others in there somewhere,' he teased.

She swiped at him playfully and tried to get up from the floor. He grabbed her wrap to prevent her and in doing so it came off. Eryn rushed for the bed with Tor leaping behind her. They hit the mattress hard, only to hear a sinister crack as the bed's main beam gave way. This made them laugh and the more they tried to shoosh each other, the worse it got.

'Light! What is Miss Vylet going to say?' she said, finally composing herself.

'Don't worry about it.' He kissed her shoulders and then her neck.

'Get those disgusting clothes off,' Eryn said in a dreamy voice as Tor traced a finger over her body. 'And I know this is your first time too, so don't be bashful. You've got yourself the best teacher this side of the capital!'

Curiously, it was Prime Cyrus who flashed into Tor's mind as he pulled off his damp shirt and breeches. He felt the Prime's presence, just for a moment, on the edge of his mind. Strange – Cyrus was calling to him for help. The vision passed as he lowered his body down next to Eryn.

9

Shapechanger

The Company of King's Men clattered along the road to Tal at an easy pace. No need to push the horses nor the men. Each could almost smell the capital now, at worst two days ride away. Summer was putting on a last hurrah of warmth before autumn made its arrival: the trees had already begun to don their multi-coloured finery to ensure a grand welcome. Children, farmers and even a small band of tinkers raised their hands in greeting as the Company passed by.

The Prime was none too happy about the noises of appreciation which many of his men made as they passed a small vineyard of women bent to their work, but his mood was too light to reprimand them harshly. The grapes the women picked would make the delectable sticky wines which the nobles liked to take with their sweet courses at feasts, and by all accounts it would be a splendid year. Although Cyrus was a lover of fine wines and could appreciate the sunny silkiness of a golden Syric, it was always the voluptuous beauty of the powerful reds which his palate craved. He thought about the dwindling supply of superb Moriett he kept in his rooms at the Palace. He imagined himself relaxing in his favourite chair; perhaps even by the fire, for the nights were certainly becoming chill enough. Yes, he could almost taste the liquid velvet.

Herek ruined his musings. 'I thought we'd push on to Brewis, sir. The weather's fine enough and that means we could probably make the city's outlying villages by nightfall tomorrow. Perhaps even to Sherwin. Then it would be an hour's ride in the morning.' Herek's voice was questioning. It would be the Prime's decision alone.

The Moriett called him. 'Agreed. Let the men know and then pick up the pace. If we're going to make Brewis, let's do so before dusk.'

Herek understood. Brewis, a small village, pretty as a picture, sat on the edge of one of the long fingers of the Great Forest. No Tallinese was comfortable roaming the forest at night, and the horses became particularly skittish if not settled well before dark closed in around the mysterious wood.

The hamlet of Brewis was visible from the crest of the rise in the road where Cyrus and his two lieutenants had stopped. Surrounding Brewis were the fields of impossibly pretty lavenders for which it was famous; it supplied all of the Kingdom's nobles with these fresh herbs for their floors. Pointing directly at the village was the finger of the southwestern fringe of the Great Forest. Brewis was still two miles away but Cyrus was keen to make camp.

'Over there, sir,' Herek said, pointing to a smallish depression in the land.

Cyrus cast a keen eye across the landscape. 'That's the best we're going to do. Let's get them moving before our

light goes.' He cantered ahead whilst Royce, the other
lieutenant, waved on the men.

By the time the sky had spread its mantle of sunset
colours across Brewis and the night's chill was just biting,
the men had set up camp and their fires were dancing.
The Prime had ordered ale be given out, which pleased
the men no end and they drank to his health which he
accepted graciously. He held his men's loyalty very
preciously and went to enormous lengths to ensure that
all who served him were well cared for. There was not a
man under his command who did not give the Prime his
loyalty willingly.

One of the supplies men ambled up and offered him
a mug of ale.

Cyrus smiled. 'I won't tonight, but my thanks.'

He wanted a clear head for tomorrow, and besides with
the Morriet so close he could not think of downing an
ale in its stead. He would wait.

The man shrugged and limped off to a nearby fire,
muttering about there being more for the others. Cyrus
smiled again, his eyes falling on his other lieutenant.

'C'mon, Royce, a song is in order, I think.' He motioned
for the lieutenant to sit in the centre of the ring of small
fires.

While the men were all cheering and clapping for
Royce, who was swallowing down the contents of his mug
with his lute in his free hand, Herek saluted.

'Yes, Herek?' Cyrus looked up from where he was
sitting.

'All's secure, sir. Four men on watch, all sides, sir, and
we'll be rotating every hour.'

'Good job, Herek. Now relax and have an ale, man.

All that snapping to attention makes me twitchy.'

'Er . . . yes, sir, thank you, sir.' Herek snapped another salute for good measure and went in search of ale.

Cyrus leaned back on his bedroll. He was in no hurry to sleep, though he felt full and relaxed and warm. Royce possessed an excellent voice. He was in good spirits tonight, not just from the ale – being newly married he was looking forward to seeing his young wife. He sang lusty songs and drank the rest of the evening away, as did the men until they all drifted off.

Cyrus was surprised more ale was not drunk. The men were clearly tired for they seemed to hit their bedrolls far earlier than he would have thought. Oh well, this was fortunate. It would mean a prompt start at first light.

Lieutenant Royce, still in high spirits from his songs and unable to settle, swapped with one of the men on watch who couldn't stop yawning. 'Go ahead, Cork, I'll take this one.'

He was rewarded with a grateful grin and another huge yawn. Royce caught Herek's attention and pointed that he was taking the northern watch. Herek nodded. He too felt damnably weary yet was surprised that the men had turned in so early.

The clouds had closed in so the moon was hidden. Before midnight all the men were snoring happily in a lightly drunken sleep.

Only Cyrus slept clear-headed and shallowly, as was his custom.

The intruders waited another hour to make sure the confection in the ale had worked. They melted out of the blackness and if Cyrus heard the low owl hoot it did not disturb him unduly. As he rolled over in his slumbers to warm his back, his four sentries were having their throats slashed, witnessing their own lifeblood pumping out onto the cool grass.

Cyrus registered their presence all too late and by the time he had leapt to his feet, there was a blade at his heart, another at his throat and a pudgy, strong hand clamped across his mouth. He fought them as best he could, stunned that his own men had not risen as one at his noise. The attackers poured a vial of liquid into a square of cloth and the heady vapour did the rest. The Prime collapsed silently into burly arms.

Rolling him in his own blanket and using none of the caution they showed before, the men carried the Prime towards the forest. He was thrown across a horse face down and tied. They took their time, for not a man in the King's Company could have woken if he had wanted to, and four others never would again.

Cyrus came to slowly. The powerful drug had left his head fuzzy and his mouth parched.

There were five of them. He could just make out their silhouettes around a small fire. From time to time one would look over at him to see if he had surfaced but Cyrus was not about to announce his consciousness. He needed to decide just how bad this situation was.

He opened bare slits in his eyes and tried to work out whether he knew who these thugs were. He thought he recognised one of them as Goron, a brutish Hatten ship-yard worker who had risen in rank to supervisor, though Light only knew why. Nevertheless, he had no grudge with Goron. As to the others, he drew a blank.

Cyrus tried to clear his head. None of this made any sense and he was concerned for his men. He had already worked out that the ale must have been tampered with, but that was impossible without some corruption on his side, or, more likely, the innkeeper. He flinched as if hit when the thought struck him.

All right, they'd drugged his men and stolen him away. Why? What could he possibly have that they could want? Everything fell into place when a familiar figure emerged from the woods. It was Corlin. This was about revenge, then. This madness centred around Corlin's hurt pride and the need to strike back at the man who had belittled him in Hatten's town square over a freakish cripple. Cyrus almost snorted aloud in disgust as the jigsaw completed itself. The man was definitely mad.

Corlin spoke quietly to the seated men before stepping around the fire and walking towards the Prime. He kicked the tied-up man violently. It took the wind out of Cyrus who grunted hard once and then struggled to breathe through the pain in his ribs, one of which was almost certainly now broken.

'Good evening, Prime.' Corlin offered his fake humility. 'This is a slight turn of situation, isn't it?'

Cyrus tried to sit up but was pushed back by a boot.

'Save your strength, Cyrus — you're going to need it,' Corlin sneered nastily. 'It's going to be the longest day of your life, Prime, and I'm going to enjoy watching you beg me for mercy.'

The man laughed loudly and Cyrus felt his bowels clench in anticipation of what lay ahead. Corlin returned to his men, and Cyrus watched them drink a small keg of ale. Apart from Corlin, who had swallowed perhaps only half a mug, the others in his band were sufficiently drunk to do anything. He figured he had only a few minutes of sanity remaining and then the punishment would begin.

This must be how it feels before an execution, he thought, but dismissed that idea. For whereas a prisoner was usually guilty of the crime and accepting of his fate, Cyrus was not. Nor was he terrified any longer. He was enraged, and promised himself that should he survive this – and there was little chance, he admitted regretfully – he would personally administer swift justice with no clemency.

Corlin was getting up from his place by the fire.

'Here we go,' Cyrus muttered to the trees. He spared a thought for his beloved wife and child, both long dead but still very much alive in his heart. He threw another thought to his men, hoping they would seek retribution. And then, ludicrously, the image of Torkyn Gynt hit him. He fancied that he saw him galloping towards him with his freakish friend at his side. Madness! The corner of his mouth twitched ruefully and he wondered why the boy had flitted into his mind.

Corlin stood in front of him. 'Get this piece of dung onto his feet,' he snarled.

Two of the group held him while a third cut the bonds from the stake then quickly re-tied his hands. Corlin spat in the Prime's face. The gob slid lazily from his forehead down the side of his nose and Cyrus knew then that he hated the man in front of him more than any man he'd known. He took exquisite pleasure in spitting straight back at Corlin, catching him unexpectedly across his lips.

'You may kiss my dunghole, you turd. I can't wait to feel my blade across your cowardly throat.'

It felt powerful to be defiant but the euphoria was short-lived. The words 'nail him' made his blood run cold.

They dragged him between two trees.

'No dulling drug to help you now, Prime Shitface.' Corlin laughed nastily and his mindless thugs laughed with him. 'Do it!'

They used a heavy mallet and thick iron nails. Cyrus felt only two exquisitely painful blows. The first made him heave up everything in his stomach and the second mercifully made him pass out. It took two more hefty blows to secure his right hand to the first tree and three to secure his left to the other. Once nailed firmly, they revived him with a dousing of chilled water for the rest of the evening's entertainment.

IO

The King's Secret

'Old man!' King Lorys of Tallinor took only a few strides to cross the large room.

Merkhud bowed deeply. 'My King.'

'Enough politeness, Merkhud – you can keep that for Court. In these chambers I expect you to take wine with me and give me bawdy tales of your travels.' Lorys gave the old man a bear hug. 'Nyria and I have missed you deeply.'

Merkhud was glad to be back in Tal. Travelling had its joys but the comforts of his chambers in the west tower were hard to beat. A page arrived with wine and marinated olives which he laid out expertly considering they could almost smell his nervousness. The lad looked up at the King and just caught the wink before he bowed low and backed away to light the sconces. The overcast chilly day hinted with sincerity at autumn's arrival. Fires would be lit around the castle in coming weeks.

Merkhud swallowed a mouthful of delicious wine – a Coriel, the grape found only in the rich lands of the south. He thought about how he had been physician to the King's father, Orkyd, arriving at the Palace only days before Lorys's grandfather, old King Mort, had drawn his last breath. No one had lived long enough to query the physic, who had spent the last one and a half centuries at the Palace.

With Orkyd away fighting battles consistently during his reign, Merkhud found himself playing father figure to the young impressionable Lorys. Where Orkyd had been a stocky, bluff sort of a man, Lorys resembled his mother: of middling height and with a swarthy complexion, dark hair and deep, soulful eyes.

The king yawned. 'Forgive me, Merkhud. My secretary is relentless with papers to be signed and papers to be read and papers to be authorised. What happened to the good old days of my forefathers when the King's word was enough?'

Merkhud knew how much the King despised the bureaucracy of his daily dealings and yet he was the best and certainly most loved sovereign Tallinor had ever enjoyed. Sipping his wine and nodding at the tirade on paperwork, he noticed Lorys was looking greyer around his temples. The King wore his hair unfashionably short yet it complimented his square face and closely trimmed beard, also peppered with grey.

'. . . and that arse-numbing throne – what possessed my grandfather to build that monstrosity?' Lorys was standing, pouring himself another glass.

Merkhud became aware of the clang of swords in the courtyard and the smell of fat candles being lit. He sighed.

'King Mort won his right to rule by battle after ferocious battle – as did your father, I might add. He took his throne above a kingdom of blood. It was important that he appear as powerful upon his throne as he did upon his warhorse. He created your birthright; the least you can do is sit upon his impressive throne now and then and look very regal.'

'Ha!' The King was always amused by how Merkhud could make him feel like the young prince again. 'Tell me of your travels, Merkhud – what's happening out there in my Kingdom?'

A large shaggy dog suddenly lifted itself from behind the desk, stretched languidly and padded over to sit by the King's physician.

'Don't you dare, Drake,' Merkhud warned. But the dog, as usual, paid no attention to the physic's protestations and flopped its backside down on Merkhud's toes. It was something the old man detested. 'Bah! You wretch.'

'He's not going to shift, Merkhud, you know he won't. Now, tell me something interesting,' the King instructed.

Merkhud wiggled his feet in vain, sipped his Coriel and made an issue of staring at the ornately painted ceiling as he pretended to sift through a myriad of items.

'Well, there is one thing worth mentioning . . .'

'Excellent. Tell me,' said the King, leaning back comfortably.

'I've offered an apprenticeship to a lad I ran across who I think will make a talented physician. He seems to—'

'What?' the King roared, his voice full of mirth. 'Don't tell me this now – after all these years?'

Merkhud feigned irritation. 'His name is Torkyn Gynt. He's seen sixteen summers and is lowborn, from Flat Meadows. Torkyn shows more intelligence and adeptness for the skill of healing than any other boy I've met in my long career. It's long overdue and he's the one I've chosen.'

'I'm delighted, old man. Just wait until Nyria hears this—'

'Hears what, my love?' A soft, spicy fragrance hit their senses as the Queen glided across the room. Neither man had heard her enter but the dog was already halfway across to greet her.

'Oh, hello, Drake.' Nyria patted the dog's large head as her husband and the only other man she had ever allowed to touch her stood and bowed.

'Good afternoon, gentlemen.'

Her gorgeous smile shone upon Merkhud like sunlight and as always his heart was warmed by her presence. He bowed again.

'Merkhud, it's wonderful to have you back.' She took his bony hand with the hand not carrying a small jar of roses and clasped it tight. He knew she meant it.

'Madam, I couldn't have stayed away another minute from your radiance.'

'Wicked old man – such honeyed words.' Nyria wagged her finger at him before settling a kiss on the King's lips and putting the flowers down on the table behind him.

As always she looked sensational, Merkhud noticed. A simple, soft velvet dress cinched at the waist showed off her still lovely figure. Her once stunning golden hair, now softening to a buttery paleness, was held neatly by two polished combs. She rarely wore it down any more.

The King was beaming. 'My love, you'll never guess the news so I won't make you try. Merkhud here has offered an apprenticeship to some lad from Flat Meadows.'

'Fiction!' Her greyish green eyes sparkled with the fun of the King's high excitement.

'It's true, I tell you. I heard it from the old horse's mouth as you arrived.'

Now Nyria stared incredulously at the old man.

Merkhud rolled his eyes theatrically. 'Oh, fuss, fuss — he's just a boy. A boy with a talent for healing, and I'm not getting any younger in case you two hadn't noticed.'

'And when do we get to meet this new apprentice of yours?'

'Within a couple of days.'

'Marvellous. Would you like me to organise for the housekeeper to clean out one of the rooms in the west wing?'

'No, madam, I can arrange it, but I thank you.'

Nyria and Merkhud smiled at one another. She knew he hated anyone meddling around in West Tower where his apartments and study rooms were located, and he knew she knew this. Her smile lingered on him just a moment longer before she turned to the King.

'I must go, Lorys. Cook wants to discuss the All Souls' Day festival menu and I've already put her off twice. I mustn't let her down again.'

The King suddenly sneezed and followed up with another four explosive sneezes. 'Nyria, you know what they do to me,' he said, gently exasperated.

'Well, put them somewhere else in the room, Lorys,' she chided equally gently. 'You hide yourself away in this stone coffin with nothing but a few ragged tapestries on the walls—'

The King feigned indignance. 'Do you hear this, Merkhud? Ragged tapestries, she says. Only the finest the Ildagarthian artisans could produce!'

She ignored him, a grin of sufferance thrown towards

her physician as she walked towards the door once more, with Drake padding softly behind her. 'I'll see you soon, Merkhud. Can you look in on the pages' quarters? There seem to be two boys unwell today.'

'I will go there immediately.' He bowed again.

'We'll have dinner in my chambers tonight, I think, Lorys.'

The message in her smile was unmistakable, and both men found themselves clearing their throats as the door closed softly.

Lorys took a large gulp of his wine. 'There is a niggling item I wish to discuss with you. Whilst you've been off around the countryside doing goodness knows what, you've probably not heard.'

Merkhud's raised eyebrow suggested he needed more information. 'Something is troubling you, Lorys?'

'It is and weighs heavy on my mind,' the King replied, scratching behind Drake's ears. The big dog grunted and rolled on his side.

When the King remained silent Merkhud gave a small shrug, his palms opened. This was not like Lorys at all.

'Tell me. I can help, I'm sure.'

The King seemed to choose his words with care, and when he spoke his voice was soft with all traces of his recent amusement long gone.

'Merkhud, that I worship Nyria with all my heart no one could dispute. Even the absence of children could not make a difference to my love for her, though it hurts my soul that we are without an heir.'

Merkhud was aware of alarm bells klaxoning in his head but he waited. Muted sounds of swordplay and someone yelling orders filled the silence. Lorys replaced his beautiful goblet on the small table and finally looked at his old friend.

'There is a woman. She lives at Wytten these days, I think. It was towards the end of last winter when I accompanied Cyrus and a small team on a hunting expedition. The castle larder needed replenishment and you know me – never one to turn down the opportunity to hunt. Perhaps you remember that trip . . . er, Nyria was quite ill with her problem?'

Merkhud nodded, holding his breath as the King's story spilled out.

'We were camped uncomfortably on our last night but the weather was mercifully mild. There were only six of us in the party and four were well soused so we had rolled them in blankets where they had fallen beside the fire. Drake and the rest of the dogs heard her long before Cyrus and I did.

'She stumbled out of the woods, eyes wide with panic and unable to talk she was so out of breath from running.'

Merkhud entwined his fingers together, gripping hard whilst Lorys stared towards a flickering candle and recalled the events of that early winter's eve.

'She had no idea who we were and we didn't bother enlightening her. Apparently she had been stolen by gypsies from her farm three miles away. They had intended to rape her – of this she seemed certain – and it was only through their drunken stupidity that she had managed to slip free and take to the woods she knew well.'

The King finished his wine, absently wiping a few drops from his beard before continuing.

'She was sore and bruised but she was a brave girl. Cyrus gave her his clothes and I found some salve for her wounds. She recovered enough to share a plate of our stew, I recall. Gorgeous thing, she was. Living with a brute of a father who beat her often and appreciated her not.'

The King stood and walked to the window, busying himself with watching the drills in the courtyard, and then the truth stammered its way out.

'I didn't mean for it to happen. We'd been away for two weeks and we'd slept rough — at my choosing — for almost all of that time. We were tired and looking forward to getting back to Tal. I offered the girl my tent.

'It must have been just a few hours before dawn when she woke me, beckoning me to the tent. In my drowsy state, Merkhud, I swear I thought she was frightened again and I staggered in, only to find her naked beneath her blanket and offering herself. She begged me to give her some affection for just one night in her pitiful life, pleading that her father would beat her badly for being away and would never believe her story.'

The King smiled ruefully. 'I betrayed Nyria with an hour of lust with a total stranger. We did not exchange names and I have not seen or heard of her since . . . until now, that is.'

Lorys pulled out a dirty sheet of paper from his pocket. He handed it to Merkhud. 'It's a notice which has been put up on the boards in the surrounding towns and villages. She knew we had Tal accents. The notice was an attempt to flush me out, I suppose.'

'And it worked,' Merkhud's clipped voice snarled as he finished reading.

'Don't you, of all people, judge me. I made an error which only two other people knew about: the girl, and the Prime of course, whom I trust with my life.'

'What happened after you bedded her, Lorys?'

The King looked sullen but continued with the story. 'Cyrus rode to Wytten at dawn and got her settled and working at the local inn. He left her with some money. We hoped, as we looked fairly rough after two weeks in the saddle, that she had not recognised us as nobles.'

Merkhud threw the paper down with disgust. 'And your horses? You don't think a country woman would recognise fine horses?' He worked hard at concealing his contempt. Nyria must never find out.

'Merkhud! There is little point in you labouring what I have already run over in my mind hundreds of times since that night. The only horse she saw was the Prime's, and he was canny enough the next morning to use one of the wagon nags. All I want to do is forget it ever happened, but this notice makes sure I never will.'

Merkhud held his anger. He re-read the simple notice that gave away very little. It was worded in such a manner that the King could simply ignore it, for it made no direct accusations, and who could care about a young woman in Wytten?

'All right. Finish this sordid tale. So, Cyrus saw the notices, put two and two together and notified you because he is worried – is that it?'

The King nodded, sagging back to sit on the stone ledge of the window.

'And the child is due shortly?' Merkhud stood and paced.

'Perhaps already born.'

'Who's to say it's yours, my King? A peasant woman gets with child. She could have shagged half the village and wouldn't know who'd fathered it. For Light's sake, man—'

As Lorys's fist banged down on the table it upended the goblet which smashed as it hit the flagstones. Merkhud was stunned.

'It's mine, damn you, old man,' he roared. 'The child is mine! She was not that sort of woman. She was barely a woman at all. I took her virginity that night and her womb quickened. Count the moons, count the tides, count the days, physic, and no matter how you juggle them you will see the child is mine. A royal bastard.'

Fuming, Merkhud stood and set his own glass delicately down on the tiny table next to him. 'Nyria must never, ever hear of this. It will kill her, do you understand?' Merkhud flapped the notice in his King's face, dangerously flouting protocol.

'I'm not dim, old man,' snarled the King.

It was Merkhud's turn to roar. 'Well, you could have fooled me! Her heart is fragile, Lorys. Shocks of this magnitude could end her life like that!' He snapped his fingers.

'I hear you, Merkhud.' Lorys had regained his composure and stood to his full height.

'Good. Leave the matter with me. Now, I must go and tend to the castle ailments long in need of my care.'

Merkhud straightened his long tunic and started to leave but the King stepped forward and grasped his arm. 'Thank you.'

The old man looked at the King and saw his eyes were glistening with tears. He loved Lorys as a son and, like any father, could not blame the man for falling under the spell of a beautiful woman. Merkhud reached for the King's shoulder and shook it gently, then he left with the ever-inquisitive Drake trailing him to the door.

*　　*　　*

Merkhud was not sure why he did so but he leaned across towards the tall woman who stood in the doorway with him and kissed her soft cheek. She flushed with embarrassment.

'Teach him well.' He bowed and left.

Entering the inn he called an order to the keeper and walked towards a dark corner, grateful the place was having a quiet morning. Marrien had surprised him. She was entirely without guile. He felt ashamed for thinking the girl had had anything other than honourable intentions when she posted her notice which flushed out a King.

Her recently born son was strong, healthy and loved, and even on the paltry wage she earned Merkhud could see she would provide a stable home for her child. She wanted nothing from Lorys. Marrien had explained to the Royal Physic that she had had no previous notion as to who had helped her that night in the woods. All she knew was that both men had been gentle and gallant towards her. The one with the short hair and beard had made her laugh when she least wanted to, and the brooding one, who deferred to the other, made her feel safe. She had not meant to tempt the first, whose merry eyes and wit had captivated her, but she had felt lonely and scared through the night. Also she didn't know how to thank them. She smiled ruefully and agreed with Merkhud that the payment she had given was magnanimous to say the least.

'It happened. What more is there to say? I was glad to give my maidenhood to the man with the lovely voice and smiling eyes. Better him than those gypsies. It would have stopped there, for I knew not his name nor from where they came and I had no need to trouble his life further.'

Merkhud, recalling that conversation, had his thoughts disrupted when the ale was banged down on the table. He did not acknowledge it, returning to his recollection of her explanation when he had asked her how she had found out who the father of her child was.

'Some friends persuaded me to use my few saved pennies to travel with them into Tal to see one of the plays in the amphitheatre. As dusk fell the word went around that the King and Queen would be attending the first half of the show. Light! We were all so excited. I had only ever heard about how handsome King Lorys is and our Queen being such a beauty.'

Marrien explained that she had nearly fainted when the royal couple arrived and she recognised him instantly, even from a distance.

'My ears began to ring and I thought I was going to return all the lovely food I'd just eaten. All I could see was the kind, wonderful man who had kept me safe and held me when I was scared and made it possible for me to begin a new life away from my father. The same man who had given me the child moving that very moment in my womb.'

She told Merkhud how everyone had clapped and cheered for the couple who looked so happy together. How they had smiled and clapped their subjects back, making everyone cheer harder. Marrien said the people around her began to discuss how tragic it was that such a fine couple had not produced an heir to the throne. Inevitably their conversation became more bawdy and they began to joke that the King might not be made of the right stuff to produce a son.

'And so you decided to tell him,' Merkhud prompted quietly.

Marrien went to pains to assure Merkhud once again that she required nothing from the King. 'I tried to think of a secret way to let him know that he could and had fathered a son. I never wanted to talk to him or meet with him. I had no intention of disrupting his life. This was the only way I could think of,' she said sadly. 'I realise now that it probably frightened him. In my mind I just saw him registering that the man I spoke of was him.'

'You thought he might ignore it?' Merkhud asked incredulously.

She nodded, clearly upset; she had not counted on bringing Lorys any trouble.

'And what will you do now?' Merkhud asked, wondering at the great list of requirements she might reel off.

But she had surprised him.

Marrien sniffed, looking up in confusion from the large red handkerchief she had borrowed from him. 'Why, nothing, sir. I shall raise the boy to love his King . . . and his Queen. Their majesties will never hear from us again but we will remain ever loyal to Tallinor.'

Merkhud remembered how her deep hazel eyes had sparkled as she confirmed her allegiance. She would take no money from him, saying she was more content than she could ever remember, that she was still able to earn their keep and as long as she could feed and clothe them, she was truly happy. Her conviction had impressed him. Finally, as though a candle had been lit in his head, he thought of a way around the growing problem. He knew Lorys would insist on the child being cared for from his purse somehow.

'Why don't you work for me?' he had blurted.

Merkhud explained that he had a small team of women around the capital who made various herbal sachets for him which he used in his medicines.

'I can sorely use a young, deft pair of hands and you can work from your home and be with the boy all of the time.'

He recalled how her eyes had lit up then, and smiled as he remembered the way she had thrown her arms around him and hugged him tight. He had insisted she would move into a tiny cottage of her own on the outskirts of Wytten, gently but firmly explaining that no son of the sovereign, bastard or otherwise, could be raised in any other manner.

'I promise that only you and myself will have knowledge of this arrangement. Not even the King will be privy,' he had said, holding her hand tightly for emphasis.

Marrien was satisfied with this and agreed to let Merkhud make arrangements for her transfer. Before he left, he exacted a promise that should she ever need anything for the boy, she should speak only to him personally.

He gave the child, the present heir to the throne, a cuddle before he left, and as he did so felt a sickness in the pit of his stomach for Nyria whom he loved so profoundly. He knew she would give her own life to bear a child for her beloved Lorys but her womb had never quickened, and though she carried her sadness with grace he saw it in her face every day.

Merkhud came back to the present with a jolt as the inn door slammed and an excited boy rushed through, yelling.

Merkhud had not caught what the boy was saying and

stopped a lass who was scuttling past him towards the kitchen. 'What's going on?'

'He says there's some huge commotion up at the castle. A rider has come in with grave news.'

Merkhud shot to his feet. 'Ho, innkeeper! What does this boy say?'

The innkeeper shrugged but could hardly contain his own excitement. 'I know not. He's newly returned from a delivery to Tal and the city is rife with some alarming news but we don't know what.' He shook his head and made a clicking sound with his tongue.

Merkhud tossed some coins onto the counter. 'Have my horse brought immediately. He's the black stallion at the village stable. Hurry, man!'

The innkeeper barked orders to one of the children outside and flipped him a penny. Merkhud paced outside the inn and scowled at the middle-aged stablehand who came cantering up on Stygian.

'A fine horse, sir,' the man said conversationally, not reading Merkhud's tense look.

Merkhud paid him without a word, took the reins, grumbled something, then mounted and urged his horse towards Tal.

'Guess you're in a hurry then, sir . . . we'll see you next time,' the slightly slow stablehand called after him.

Merkhud arrived back at the Palace sweating from the hour's hasty ride. The castle was in chaos with people rushing around and soldiers making hasty preparations to depart. He looked towards the royal wing and could see Nyria at one of the windows watching the activity. He raised his hand and she did the same. Callum, the page who Merkhud knew now served the King daily, trotted by wearing an earnest expression.

'Callum, m'boy, what happens here?' Merkhud asked, holding out Stygian's reins to an approaching stablehand. He held up his hand as the page was about to answer and turned to the stablehand. 'The horse needs a good rub down and water him gradually – he's been galloping hard from Wytten and he needs to cool slowly.'

The lad nodded and led the snorting horse away.

'Apologies, Callum. Now explain, please, quickly.'

'A rider came in an hour ago with news that Prime Cyrus had disappeared. The Company will be returning sometime today from its overnight camp at Brewis.' The boy was surprisingly concise.

'Light preserve us! Is there any more?'

'No. That's all I overheard but I must make haste to the King. He has urgent errands for me.' The boy looked overwhelmed with the excitement of the morning.

'I'll come with you; lead the way.'

Nyria met them before they arrived at the King's study. 'I presume you've heard?' She was as calm as ever and gorgeous in blue today.

Merkhud's heart did its regular flip when she laid her hand on his arm. 'I have, madam, but only that Cyrus has disappeared. Nothing else.'

He covered her elegant hand with his own and felt the familiar tingle of longing he frequently quelled in her presence.

'Come, we'll go to him together.'

She linked her arm with his and told Callum to go on and let the King know Merkhud had been found.

'Oh? Were you looking for me?' he said, surprised.

'You know how Lorys likes to have you near, Merkhud. Where have you been, you secretive old thing?' She couldn't help smiling at how she disconcerted him with such ease.

'Nowhere particular. I was recruiting a girl for my remedies, madam . . . er . . . over at Wytten.' If only you knew what I'd been doing, he thought with no little guilt.

'Oh, recruitment – is that what they call it these days?' she said laughing. She covered her lips with a hand, eyes dancing above at the innuendo in her words.

Only Nyria could unbalance Merkhud. He stopped the stammering excuse which came readily and held his tongue so his mind could catch up. 'Don't tease me, Nyria. I'm no match for you.'

Even her smile made his heart pound.

'Well, gather your wits then, Merkhud, because he'll need your clear head today,' she said, unlinking her arm and stepping lightly through the door which Callum dutifully held open.

I I

Reunion

Tor! Wake up! Tor was startled awake so violently he fell off the bed. Cloot's voice had none of its normal humour. It was thick with alarm.

Cloot, what in the name of—

Move, Tor, hurry! Cloot was shouting into his sleepy head.

Eryn was awake but groggy; she sat up on her elbows, her magnificent breasts exposed, and peered through tousled hair and half-open light grey eyes at Tor who was sitting naked on the floor.

'Tor, what are you doing?' She giggled, slightly dazed.

'Sssh . . . go back to sleep, Eryn.'

She fell back on the bed and mumbled something unintelligible. Tor picked himself up and pulled on his breeches whilst he listened to Cloot's anxious voice.

It's Lys. She came tonight. She insisted we leave immediately for Tal. She means right this moment, Tor, and she wouldn't leave my head until I'd promised on my mother's own life that I would convince you to ride tonight.

Tor was pulling on his shirt. *Did she say why we needed*

to do this? He was working hard at making it sound like a sane conversation.

Eryn moaned lightly. He hoped dearly it was a dream about him and not Margolin.

Cloot couldn't hide his exasperation. *Well, let's see now. Perhaps she thought we might enjoy an early morning ride together?*

He bit back on the sarcasm but fortunately Tor was still too groggy to be offended by it. *Tor, the moment she mentioned your name, I presumed we should both heed her warnings.*

You mean I'm in danger? Tor said, pulling on his boots.

She didn't say that. She just told me that we had to leave without a second's waste. We must ride through the night to a village called Brewis. Do you know it?

Tor yawned. *No, but I know of it. Merkhud suggested I stay there on my way. I gather it's one of the fringe villages before the capital.*

She said we must go in order to – and these are her words not mine – save him because Tor needs him. Don't waste time asking who because she did not enlighten me.

Tor's questions hung heavy across the link but he was becoming accustomed to the strange path his life was taking him along. There had to be some greater purpose to all of its curious twists and turns. He was beginning to accept his instincts were more use to him right now than his ability to reason.

I'm ready, Cloot.

Good. Where are you anyway?

Too long to explain. I'm on my way.

Tor closed the link and began hurriedly scribbling a note to the gorgeous, sleeping Eryn. He thanked his stars that his father's habitual recommendation to always keep a scrap of paper and a stick of charcoal on one's person had finally paid off. She deserved better and he wished he could leave her something. In the end he pulled off the gemstone he wore on a chain around his wrist. Merkhud had given it to him for good luck on his journey. He left the note by her bedside, kissed her lips lightly and, with hefty regret, tiptoed out of the room. He found his way to the main door, cursed the noise it made as it swung open, ignored the voice enquiring behind him, and left.

It could only have been a couple of hours or so they had enjoyed together. It was still pitch dark with several hours to dawn. Tor moved swiftly through familiar, empty lanes and in his room at The Empty Goblet found Cloot dressed as an old crone.

Don't you dare laugh, Cloot warned gravely.

Would I? Come on. We have to get the horses yet.

Tor left more than sufficient coin to cover his expenses for the room and meals then they climbed out of the small window and onto the rooftops. Gingerly they made their way to a spot where Tor knew it would be easy to climb down into the lanes, and then headed for the stables. Tor was rapidly trying to come up with an excuse for waking the stablemaster. As it turned out, they did not have to: the young boy, Bart, was emptying his bladder against the side of the barn. He leapt into the air when Tor touched his shoulder, staining his breeches. Cloot produced a coin which silenced the lad's bellows and persuaded him to open the stable.

Cloot stroked both horses' heads. He whispered to them strange words which Tor could hear but not understand.

Then Cloot pulled something out of his bag. It was impossible in the dark to make out what it was but the horses gobbled it down happily.

Cloot's sturdy stallion was called Fleet. Despite its size, he still looked ridiculous with his legs astride, wearing skirts.

'Are you sure the . . . er . . . lady wouldn't prefer side-saddle, master Tor,' said the stableboy, quietly impressed with the old girl.

'Ah no, she prefers it this way. Thanks, Bart.'

Tor couldn't steer Bess off fast enough; Fleet followed steadily. Fortunately Hatten's gates were rarely closed and they cantered through as quietly as possible onto the open road to Tal.

How long, Cloot?

Lys said to ride fast through the night and we'd make it before dawn.

All right, then . . . and she gave us nothing more on what this is about? Tor asked, easing Bess into a trot.

No, or I would tell you.

I'm not sure our horses can gallop through the night, Cloot, to be honest. Are you comfortable riding, by the way?

Don't worry about me or our horses — I've taken care of it. Just get going. With that Cloot slapped his horse into a gallop.

They arrived on the outskirts of Brewis as the deep ink of the sky was being diluted with emerging daylight. Tor knew both of them should be exhausted from the ride but he felt exhilarated from the excitement of the horses thundering along the Tal road at such speed. He had never broken into more than a canter with Bess on his way to

Hatten and had felt her incapable of so swift a pace. Cloot's horse seemed fresh enough to do it all again. It was impossible that they had ridden so far so fast.

As they slowed their mounts to walk up the same rise where Cyrus and his lieutenants had been the afternoon previous, Tor looked at Cloot. Both of them were breathing hard but the horses were not.

How?

An enchantment, Cloot answered smoothly and instantly, as though he had expected the question.

You? Tor sounded incredulous.

Why the surprise? Lys picked me for some reason and now she is equipping me, I suppose. I have no idea, to be honest. Cloot grinned and looked across towards the finger of the Great Forest.

Why didn't you tell me you possessed such magic? Tor was not sure if he was offended or thrilled.

Because I didn't know I had it until I spoke to the horses. This is all a new experience for me, and if your mind wasn't so closed perhaps you'd have felt it.

What do you mean? Tor turned sharply towards his friend.

Talking to you feels different since last night. Cloot shrugged.

Tor was puzzled momentarily, and then realised that in veiling against Miss Vylet he had almost cut himself off from the flow of power around him.

Is this better? he asked hopefully.

Much! replied Cloot, questions written over his ugly face.

Tor sighed as though disappointed. *My fault. I have so much to learn.*

Cloot said no more but as they stopped at the top of the rise and looked towards Brewis, he put a huge, reassuring hand on Tor's shoulder.

'All right, now what do we do?' Tor said aloud.

The reply in his head was sharp. *Over there.* Cloot pointed to where they could see the King's Men who had recently left Hatten. Some of them were breaking camp sluggishly; others still lay on the ground, presumably asleep.

Tor turned Bess to see better. *Are those men hurt, do you think?*

No, or the others would be raising an alarm. It's strange though.

They waited, unsure of whether Lys meant them to go on to Brewis to find the man they were searching for, or if indeed he was amongst the unit they watched.

Cloot got off his horse and removed the skirt and shawls which had covered his real clothes. *No need of these for a while*, he said, tucking them into his sack before climbing back into the saddle. *Perhaps we should——*

He did not finish for a cry had gone up. Men were running in several directions.

Let's go! Tor didn't wait for a reply; he dug his heels into Bess and they headed for the camp.

Moments later he was guiding the horses through the alarmed unit of men, making straight for the only tent, where he presumed the Prime would be. He was stopped by a grey-faced man whom he recognised as Captain Herek from the inn.

'Captain Herek, do you remember me from Hatten? I'm Torkyn Gynt. Er . . . Prime Cyrus and I spent some time together.'

'Ay, I remember you, lad, but this is no time for reunions. What are you doing here?'

Tor's mind raced. What was he doing here indeed? What plausible excuse could he give to explain this unexpected arrival before dawn?

Cloot rescued him. *Tell him we decided to ride with the Company after all.*

Herek was staring at Tor as though he were simple. 'Did you hear me, boy?'

'Yes, Captain, I'm sorry. Um, Prime Cyrus suggested I ride with you as I am bound for the Palace, but at the time I chose not to. Once you had all left, I realised it was an unwise decision and I decided to catch up with the unit.'

It was thin but the man was clearly in a state of stress and hardly heard the explanation.

'Captain . . . is something wrong?' Tor asked quietly.

Herek rubbed his eyes. A soldier raced up and saluted, his face stiff with shock.

'How many?' Herek snapped.

'All four, sir . . . er, including Lieutenant Royce.'

Tor noticed Herek's jaw clench. 'And the Prime?'

'Nothing yet, sir.'

'Thank you, Linus. Help Medlin assemble the men. I want this camp broken and the Company ready to move by full daybreak. Get the er . . . four wrapped and on their mounts. I'll want you to ride ahead to Tal. Report back as fast as you can for my briefing.' He continued to clench and unclench his jaw.

Linus snapped another salute and left. The sky was lightening rapidly around them and Tor noticed all the men were up and moving now. There was an eerie silence around the camp.

'Captain Herek, what's happened here?'

Herek barely contained his impatience. 'No offence, Gynt, but I have a lot to deal with just at the moment and I'm not at liberty to make light conversation with civilians. If you wish to ride with us, that's fine. You may join at the back of the column.'

It was a dismissal. Herek had already turned on his heel and was moving away. Tor was stumped.

Let's see if we can find Cyrus. Cloot's quiet words refocused him.

They began threading their way through the lines of men organising to depart. A heavy atmosphere pervaded the camp – *one of confusion*, Cloot said in Tor's head.

More like shock. They're hardly even speaking to one another. What in Light's name could have happened, I wonder? And what did Herek mean by telling that man to wrap the four?

At that Tor spotted Riss. He waved and was relieved to see the man lift his hand. 'Ho, Riss! Good to see you.'

The craggy soldier observed him through narrowed eyes which showed a lifetime of suspicion.

'Is it indeed? And you travel with the freak now, eh?'

Tor felt Cloot stiffen behind him.

'Yes, as you can see he healed well with the doctor's help . . . and yours.' He enjoyed unbalancing Riss with the compliment.

Golag sidled out of a group of men and came up behind his companion. 'You again!' His voiced had lost none of its harshness: it seemed to rumble rather than speak. 'How was that Eryn anyway? Bet she spread her legs wide and willingly for a young buck like you, eh?'

He laughed his horrible laugh, grabbed his crotch for emphasis and spat solidly. Tor was no longer embarrassed or shocked by Golag. It seemed that being deliberately vulgar was the only manner he knew.

'Yes, Golag, she was utterly delicious and just wild for me.' He smiled his brightest smile and heard Cloot chuckle in his head.

So that's where you were last night, eh?

Tor ignored him. 'Riss, where's the Prime?'

'Ah, so it's information you be wanting again then, boy. Last time you paid handsomely for it. Our price hasn't changed.'

Golag stretched his rotten-toothed leer behind his negotiating friend.

Tor ignored Golag and directed his conversation at Riss. 'It was just a simple question, Riss, but forget it. I'm sure Cyrus — when I do find him and can pass on the urgent message from the Mayor of Hatten — will be pleased to hear how well you helped me.'

He turned to walk away. Cloot followed, most impressed with the bluff.

'Wait!' Riss was no longer smiling. 'What message?'

Tor turned back slowly. 'I told you. An urgent message from the Mayor and I promised I'd hand it to Cyrus myself just as soon as I caught up with the King's Company. It may even be from King Lorys himself, who knows?' His eyes sparkled.

Well, you are learning fast, Cloot muttered.

'See you in Tal then.' Once more Tor walked a few steps.

'All right, Gynt. I'm not about to kiss away my wages on your behalf. What's the message?' Riss was rattled and it pleased Tor no small amount that he'd been able to do this.

'Sorry, Riss. Prime's ears only. Hurry, man, time is short and I'm moving on to Tal. This is just a favour for the Mayor.'

It was Golag who answered. 'The Prime disappeared in the night. No one knows where. Four sentries were slain also.' He stopped abruptly, as was his way.

Tor's bravado was suddenly replaced by shock. 'How could he disappear with two hundred men around him?'

'Poison is how,' Golag sneered.

'What?'

'He broke open the kegs last night and called for songs. We were all in high spirits yet most of us turned in very early and woke late, all with the headache.' Riss looked away in embarrassment.

'You mean the ale was drugged to ensure the Company was unconscious when they took the Prime?' Tor could hardly believe what he was saying. 'But what would they want with him?'

Riss shrugged. 'Search me. They killed four of our men to reach him and went to some trouble to ensure he could be taken without any interference from us.'

A small group was gathering around them.

Let's go, Tor. We won't find out any more here. Cloot took his arm.

'What about the urgent message?' Golag snarled.

'We're still going to find him,' Tor said.

Riss barked a despondent laugh. 'What, the boy and his cripple friend? We've already searched. There's no sign anywhere.'

'Dead or alive, we're going to find him, Riss.' Tor said no more but allowed Cloot to lead him back to the horses.

Let's go. Cloot was taking charge. He could see the

confusion and disturbance written all over Tor's face.

Where to?

Just follow. Cloot led his horse directly towards the forest. *I gather most people are afraid to enter this Heartwood proper?* He kept his voice light in Tor's head.

Tor had not thought about it until now. He replied absently, as though making polite conversation, whilst his mind raced elsewhere, wondering why Cyrus might be important enough that four men should die. *Yes. We're told frightening tales all our lives about the wild beasts and strange creatures which roam it. I've always thought it was just folklore.*

It may be, but people are genuinely afraid. I'd wager none of the King's Men there would venture beyond a few steps into its depths.

Now Cloot had his attention.

But surely they would have sent out search parties?

Oh, I don't doubt it. But I do doubt whether any made more than a cursory search of the Heartwood's fringe. Which is precisely why I know he's going to be here somewhere, or at least was held here through the night.

Tor pulled gently on the reins to slow Bess next to where Cloot had stopped. They were well out of range of the King's Company now and standing beneath one of the enormous oaks on the fringe of the forest.

Can you feel it, Tor?

Feel what?

My skin tingles and I hear a faint murmur. I can't lock onto it but it's there now that I'm this close to entering the wood.

I hear nothing, I feel nothing different. Tor felt almost annoyed.

That's strange but it's also good. Perhaps it means you won't be threatened by the Heartwood.

All right, let's follow that pattern of thought. If the forest terrifies most people, why would anyone take the Prime into its depths?

Cloot made a clicking sound with his mouth then spoke wearily in Tor's head. *That I don't know.*

He kneed at Fleet, encouraging him to step on. Bess followed.

Tor persisted. *Why wouldn't they just have taken him on through Brewis?*

I don't have the answers, Tor, but for Lys to become involved suggests Cyrus is important to you. And as I am sworn to share this quest I must find him.

Daylight was barely filtering through the dense trees. It was cool and serene beneath the canopy, with just the muted sounds of the odd birdsong or darting squirrel.

Do you feel or hear anything yet, Tor?

Well . . . Tor screwed up his face. *Yes . . . Now, promise you won't laugh, Cloot.* He saw his friend nod. *But it seems as though the wood is welcoming me.*

You mean it talks?! said Cloot incredulously.

I'm not sure. It's as though the branches and leaves are nodding a welcome. It feels like the forest is smiling. Yes, that's it . . . it's smiling at me, Cloot.

Light preserve us. Cloot shook his head. *My life gets stranger and stranger around you, boy.*

They walked on for a while in silence, enjoying the beauty of the Heartwood and feeling some regret at tramping through tracts of woodland flowers. The horses were unperturbed and content to meander slowly through this quiet place.

They emerged into a clearing. The sunshine was dazzling in the ring of trees and gnats flitted in the haze of its rays. Tor stopped abruptly and took a sharp intake of breath.

This is a magic place, Cloot.

I feel it. Lys is here too.

Where? Can you see her? Tor looked around wildly.

No. But I feel her.

Cloot, what—

Hush, boy. She talks to me.

Tor watched Cloot close his eyes and become very still. It was silent suddenly. No birdsong, no rustling leaves in the still morning's warmth. Even the horses stopped moving from foot to foot. His friend remained still and silent for a time, and just when Tor thought he could not bear to feel so alone for a moment longer Cloot's body relaxed and he sighed. Tears slid slowly down his cheeks.

What's happening? Tor was bewildered.

Lys tells us not to be scared. The Heartwood protects you, Tor, and those you love. But the Prime is here and is in danger. We must find him very quickly.

How? Where to start? Do we—

Settle, boy. Lys has shown me a way.

Why do you weep, Cloot? Tor asked as gently as he could.

His friend hesitated before whispering just as gently, *She required a decision of me. I've given her my answer and it made me momentarily sad to reach it.* He turned to Tor. *But it's a wise decision, and I'm glad to make it and happy to know my part in all of this.*

Tor searched his friend's face and found nothing but the large, uplifting smile he had come to love.

Don't fret, Tor. Forgive the secrecy. All will be revealed soon enough. I want you now to simply trust me. He climbed off Fleet.

I do, Cloot, with my life, Tor replied solemnly.

That's good, boy, because I pledge you mine.

Cloot, can I mention right now how much you are scaring me.

I know, Tor. But all I ask is your trust. Your life is going to be complicated and challenging and very, very important to the wellbeing of Tallinor.

Cloot saw Tor was about to object and put his hand in the air. *Hear me out. I know not what this quest is or why we make it, only that we must in order to save this land. Prime Cyrus must be found. It seems he's an important piece of this strange jigsaw surrounding you. Now I must leave you.*

'What?' Tor roared out loud.

Only for a brief time. Then I will return to you. Cloot's voice sounded shaky. *Tie up Bess and Fleet and wait until you hear from me. I promise it won't be long.*

But where are you going? Why can't I stay with you? Anger was creeping into Tor's voice. He hated the secrecy.

I'll be just over there. Cloot pointed to the sunlit clearing. *And you must stay right here until I return.*

I understand what you say, Cloot, but I don't understand what you do.

I know. You must trust me though. Cloot stepped over to stand in front of Tor. He looked into the boy's piercingly blue eyes and smiled. *I'll return. I will not leave you alone . . . ever.* He took hold of Tor and pulled him closely to his chest in a hug, squeezing hard. *I'm with you always.*

The big man turned slowly and limped heavily into the clearing. Tor was deeply disturbed. Cloot's words sounded like a farewell of sorts. That the clearing was enchanted was obvious to Tor. Every inch of his body could sense it, but it was a type of magic he did not fully understand. It was as though he could feel it but not touch it or join with it.

To Tor's astonishment, Cloot removed his garments until he stood naked in the sunlight, his strange, deformed body an intrusion in this beautiful place. Tor dared not say a word. Then his friend crouched low to the ground, pulling his head right into his knees and covering as much of himself as he could with his long, hairy arms.

The intensity of the sunlight began to increase, at first slowly and then more rapidly until Tor could barely make out Cloot's outline. He was terrified as he felt a mighty power descending. The humming sound Cloot had described was now a tangible thing: the whole wood seemed to be trembling in anticipation. Tor forced himself to keep his eyes riveted on Cloot despite the bright glare and disturbing hum. And then he heard the voice. It was deep and resonant and terrifying.

'Cloot, this is Darmud Coril, god of the forests, who speaks to you now. We accept and welcome you. I anoint you Friend of the Heartwood.'

Drips of golden sunlight appeared to smear themselves across the crouched figure. Tor could barely see against the dazzle.

The voice continued. 'This is now your home. May you never wander far from it and may you always return unharmed.'

A blaze of rainbow colours exploded from where Cloot was crouched, and Tor could see that his shape was changing. His friend appeared to be shrinking. He could bear it no longer. He yelled Cloot's name against the hum of the magic and closed his eyes against the scintillating colours which clamoured around the diminishing huddle in the centre.

Suddenly everything became silent. Tor snapped open his eyes just as a large, majestic falcon lifted effortlessly from the clearing, its wings beating rhythmically and powerfully.

Tor screamed once more, loudly and with despair, as Cloot disappeared from his sight high above the trees.

Tor had not moved. He had, however, slept. The long ride through the night to Brewis and then the numbing shock of Cloot's transformation had sent his mind scuttling elsewhere. He had drifted off to sleep and woke now to Bess nibbling his neck, perhaps hopeful of an apple. Her companion nearby seemed content enough with grass.

Why? He asked himself the question repeatedly. Cloot knew of course and that was why he had wept when Lys spoke to him. Why hadn't he run to save him? Why hadn't he tried to do something? Wasn't he supposed to be a fabulously talented sentient? So why had he not used all that powerful magic within? He felt powerless. Cloot had been changed into a falcon and had flown away.

Yet had not Cloot impressed upon him moments before that he would return? He had implored Tor to stay where he was and to wait. Yes, that's right, he had said just that. 'I won't be long' were his words. And so, with that memory charging his hopes, Tor sat very still and waited. He closed his eyes again but not to sleep. Instead he focused on the magic in the circle.

It was potent and quite untouchable to him. Tor probed around it, weaving its design and colour into his mind.

He remembered how the forest had welcomed him when he first entered it and so now he focused his mind on trying to communicate with the forest. He spent a long time casting thoughts and patterns before recalling that when the forest had smiled, as he termed it, he had been bathed in a glow of green. Tor audaciously cast out, interlacing his call with the greens of the forest. And the trees replied.

'Welcome, Tor. Be not afraid. Your friend will return and we will keep him safe, always, always, always . . .' they whispered and their words echoed softly across their leaves.

It touched him deeply that he had united himself with the Heartwood and it lifted his spirits to hear the trees reassure him. He thanked them and they fluttered their leaves in response.

He must have drifted off to sleep again but only briefly for now he felt something within him stir. His mind was being touched. A feathery touch that was barely there to begin with. The feeling of something reaching out became stronger until he was wide awake. All his senses, magical and otherwise, strained to lock onto the source. And then, as if he were right next to him, Cloot's voice boomed into his head.

Found him!

Cloot! Tor shrieked back through the link.

The one and only! And I've found Cyrus. He's here in the forest and not so far away either.

Where are you?

Here! Cloot replied and swooped down to land gracefully in front of him.

Tor was so startled he scrambled back against the tree trunk.

Apologies. Didn't mean to frighten you so, said Cloot, his head cocked to one side.

The magnificent peregrine falcon watched Tor with a large black eye, which was encircled by a luminous yellow to match its equally startling yellow legs. Tor could not help but marvel at the noble bird which stood before him, its shiny blue-black feathers cloaking a snow white chest.

Quite a change, eh, from ugly Cloot? the falcon said, cocking its head to the other side as if to give Tor a better look.

I . . . I was so frightened, Tor uttered with grave honesty.

The falcon hopped once and then leapt into the air with ease before landing on Tor's shoulder. Tor flinched.

No need to be afraid any more, Tor.

Why? Tor ran his hand through his hair and craned sideways at the falcon which clung comfortably to his right shoulder.

Because your heroic protector is back beside you.

No. I mean why the bird thing?

I'm not sure. If a bird could sigh then Tor felt that was just what Cloot was doing. *Lys wanted it this way and she begged my trust. I gave it happily. I wasn't all that fond of my body as it was anyway. This is a far more agreeable shape.*

Is this for keeps then? Will you never be just Cloot again? asked Tor sadly, very aware of the strong talons which gripped his shoulder.

I am just Cloot, Tor. Nothing has changed but the body I'm in, and I tell you, I much prefer this new one. Yes, it's for keeps.

. . . I'm not sure I can keep coping with all these strange twists and turns. You're my closest friend in the world, Cloot . . . and now you're a bird. His voice choked slightly.

Cloot's voice softened in his mind. *I know. But there is*

a purpose to all this. We must trust Lys and trust each other.

I trust you, but why Lys? She has brought you nothing but pain and grief, and now this! Tor shook his head, stood and angrily began pacing the clearing. The falcon had to adjust its grip on the boy to steady itself.

She brought me to you, Tor. That's all I know; and now she has turned me into this regal creature and I'm happy to be so. Don't feel sorry for me. If you knew what it is to soar above the land, you wouldn't. Now come, we must not tarry. Cyrus is in grave trouble. We can philosophise later on the strangeness of our lives. Right now, we must act. Follow me, he's not far away. Cloot hopped for emphasis.

Cloot . . . Tor's voice held a note of pleading.

The bird's patience was ebbing. *He's dying, Tor, and it's very ugly. Only you can help him. We'll talk later, now go!*

It took only two powerful beats of Cloot's wings to carry him to an upper branch of a tall tree. *Don't lose sight of me. We must be as silent as possible to ambush them.* Then he flew deeper into the forest.

Tor followed quietly, keeping the downy, dark feathers of his falcon's underbelly in sight as he wondered what lay ahead, and who 'they' might be. They travelled in silence for several minutes through terrain which began to thicken dramatically. Cloot became harder to follow as he swooped amongst the trees. Finally the bird halted; Tor could no longer see him but the link was open and he could feel his friend's strong presence.

Hush, Tor. You must tread with care now. They are but thirty paces ahead of you, the bird whispered in his mind.

He could hear them, rustling and moving. The voices were muted.

How many? he called to Cloot.

There are five of them. The leader is Corlin.

Corlin! Tor was relieved he had contained his yell to the link.

The same. Cloot's own voice was thick with hatred.

Revenge — is that what this is about? Tor took another few paces until he could hide behind a thick cover of saplings yet clearly see the men.

I can't imagine what else it could be. Corlin's pride took a hammering that day in the market square and he blames Cyrus for the humiliation.

Cloot dropped silently from the uppermost branches above Tor to land neatly on his shoulder.

Tor jumped. *I wish you'd stop doing that without warning.*

He looked around the scene. Two men were dozing, another two were drinking nearby. Corlin was removed from the others, sitting very still near the horses.

Where's Cyrus? Tor snarled.

Over to your right.

Tor turned slightly to peer between two branches and nearly retched. Strung pathetically between two mighty trees hung the Prime, held in place by nails through his hands. He made no sound and appeared unconscious. Blood had run in rivulets from his head, hands and body. His once white shirt was stained a dark and rusty red. They could not see his face for his head lolled away from them, chin almost touching his chest. His thick, normally well-groomed hair was matted and slicked with his own blood.

Be calm, whispered Cloot. He felt a powerful surge of magic tingle through his friend's body.

Tor's voice was devoid of emotion when he spoke. *Corlin must die for this.*

I couldn't agree more. But let's not announce ourselves just yet. We have no weapons – only your magic.

We need nothing else, Tor said in the same detached manner, his body trembling with the power infusing it and the fury which fired it.

Let them make the first move so we know what their intentions are. I'll get closer. Cloot lifted silently from Tor's shoulder, reappearing moments later on a low but well-concealed branch of one of the trees the Prime was nailed to.

They did not have to wait long. Corlin stirred himself. The men who were drinking kicked the other two awake; they said nothing but nodded towards Corlin. They all stood. Tor noted that one of the men was Goron, the brute he had helped Eryn escape from.

'My, my, this is a pleasant little group,' he muttered to himself.

'It's time,' Corlin said and picked up a pail from by the horses. He walked across to the prisoner and threw its darkish contents over the Prime's head. The others laughed drunkenly and enjoyed watching Cyrus attempt ineffectually to shake off the liquid.

'Hope he likes the taste of second-hand ale,' one of them said, nudging his companion.

'I can't say I could, knowing it's passed through your guts already,' said the other.

'Ho, you can talk Fyster!' It was Goron speaking. 'Your piss smells to high heaven but it must surely taste like hell.'

This made them all laugh again until Corlin held up his hand for quiet. Cyrus groaned, and Tor's heart lurched when he saw the blade appear in Corlin's hand. It glinted in the morning sun.

'I tire of you, Prime Arsewipe. Now look up at me, there's a good soldier, so I can slit your throat properly and with absolute pleasure.' He grabbed hold of the Prime's hair and wrenched his head back.

Tor emerged from his cover silently. Cold fury was now controlling the power which brimmed inside him. He thumped a huge bolt of energy into Cyrus, who shook uncontrollably for a few seconds, amusing his captors greatly. They read it as fear.

Cyrus took a deep breath.

'Oh, you want to say something, Prime Pigshit? Well, we're all ears,' laughed Corlin and theatrically bent down near his prisoner's face.

Tor, still unnoticed, sent another spike and enjoyed watching Cyrus open his puffy, blackened eyes and register his presence nearby. Yet even Tor could hardly believe the smile which creased across the Prime's almost shredded lips.

'I just can't wait to feel a blade slicing through your murderous throat, Corlin. Why don't you look around?' Cyrus was breathing heavily from the effort, spitting blood but eyes ablaze as the stream of life-giving energy seared into him.

The group of men were guffawing, slapping their thighs and each other's backs at their prisoner's courageous but stupid words. Corlin was not laughing though. He was turning as suggested. Turning to see Tor, alone, unarmed, standing only paces behind him and smiling.

'Remember me?' Tor asked politely.

He heard Cloot *tsk, tsk* in his head before Corlin roared his anger, let go of Cyrus's hair and charged. The other men were turning now too, and one screamed as a falcon dropped, talons outstretched towards his face, shrieking its intent.

And just as suddenly as it had all erupted, the wood went silent as all five captors found themselves paralysed.

Corlin's arm was raised, blade pointing straight at Tor. His face was contorted with rage yet his body was rooted to the spot where he stood. Only his eyes could move and they rolled wildly with confusion and terror.

Cloot landed lightly on Tor's shoulder. They both stared at Corlin for a few moments before moving to Cyrus who was struggling to hold his head up and take in the scene.

He spat blood. 'Is this a dream?'

'No. Stay still a moment,' Tor said, unable to meet the Prime's eyes. He wondered how he was going to explain this away.

Tor lifted Cyrus to take the weight off his arms and then focused on the nail holding his right hand. A simple spell eased the nail back from the tree's bark. When it came out, Tor shouldered the man's full weight to repeat the spell on the second nail. The Prime groaned when he was laid on the ground and the nails were finally removed from his numb, shattered hands.

'Untie my legs,' he breathed raggedly.

Tor stood, walked across to Corlin and unlaced the stubby fingers which gripped the knife he was brandishing. He returned to the Prime and cut the bonds which held his legs.

'Get me up, boy.'

'No, Cyrus. Please, let me—'

'I said get me on my feet – that's an order!' It took a giant effort for Cyrus to bellow this.

With Tor's help, he painfully pulled himself upright, his weak legs barely able to hold him.

'Help me, Gynt . . . please.'

Tor put his shoulder under the stooped figure of the bleeding soldier and hefted him straight. 'Now what?'

'Put that blade in my hand. You'll have to wrap my fingers around it because I can't feel them.'

'Would you not prefer to see these murderers meet their fate in Tal?'

'The four thugs over there will, but he's mine and justice will be meted by me personally,' Cyrus said through teeth gritted against his pain.

Leaning heavily on Tor, he hobbled the fifteen or so paces to where Corlin stood frozen in his charge, his breeches wet at the front from the panic he now felt. Cyrus stared at his torturer for a long time.

'The King's Company, Tor – did you meet up with them?'

Tor swallowed. 'Yes, sir. Captain Herek was in charge. He was preparing to leave for Tal at dawn.'

'Are they whole?'

Tor skirted the question. 'Most were recovering from being drugged. They feared for your life.'

'Is the Company complete, Mr Gynt? Are there any casualties other than sore heads?'

During this exchange Cyrus had not moved his eyes from the terrified face of Corlin, who was now dribbling his fear. Tor hesitated. A small flock of birds – probably wrens, he thought – lifted noisily from the canopy of trees, spooked by some bird of prey perhaps. He felt Cloot twitch at his shoulder and realised with surprise that his friend would probably now enjoy the sport of hunting and killing such game.

'Answer me, Gynt,' said the Prime quietly.

'As I understood it, sir, the four men on watch had been killed, amongst them your lieutenant.' Tor held his breath.

'Royce?' Cyrus said this as if he did not understand Tor's answer.

'I don't know his name,' Tor replied, embarrassed. He shifted his own weight to keep the Prime's tall body from falling over.

'Light! Royce! The man was just married, you worthless bastard,' he railed at Corlin, whose eyes widened at the sight of the blade dancing in front of him now.

Cyrus gathered his remaining strength. 'Your four companions will stand before the King's justice for the death of three good soldiers and for the theft, torture and near death of his Prime. But you, Corlin, you will die now in the Heartwood, before my justice alone, for the death of my newly married lieutenant, for the suffering of his bride when she is delivered the news, and for the sons and daughters he never had the chance to sire.'

Cyrus fought back tears and, with a staggering effort of sheer will, stood his full height and pushed away Tor's help. With both numbed hands clutching at the thick, short dagger, he plunged his full weight behind the blow sinking the blade to its hilt into the throat of Corlin. It was the ceremonial death of a murderer.

A fountain of Corlin's blood spewed forth over the Prime, joining his own on his torn shirt. He stood and let it flow over him, saying nothing, just witnessing the life drain from Corlin, still frozen in his steps.

'Release him,' the Prime said finally when Corlin's eyes had glazed over.

Tor snapped the spell on Corlin and his dead body thudded to the ground, sodden with his blood. Cyrus was not far behind him, collapsing first to his knees and then onto his chest, slipping into grateful unconsciousness.

It was several hours later before Tor was ready. He was shockingly tired. He leaned against a tree and looked at Cyrus, now cleaned with what water was available and bandaged with strips of Cloot's old shirt. They had dressed Cyrus in another shirt they had found in one of the men's saddlebags.

Cyrus was sleeping after Tor's powerful ministrations had mended bones and healed some of the swollen, bruised areas on his body. Corlin and his men had whipped Cyrus near to death and his back and chest were a fretwork of lacerations. Tor had weaved his magic to clean up the ulcers and prevent any further infection. He had wanted to heal the cuts too, but Cloot had strongly urged him against it, and Tor agreed it would be hard enough to explain the Prime's recovery. He had given Cyrus much of his own energy stores to stay alive but now that the major injuries were already mending Tor let him sleep so his own defences could rally. He gave him some fiery spirit they found in Corlin's possessions to help him sleep deeply, without pain.

Tor had released the men one by one from the spell, after securing their hands behind their backs and then tying them to each other with a strong rope he had dug out of their bags. They were so scared of him that they would happily have tied one another up if he had asked them to.

Cloot was concerned that although these men would

sound as though they were talking gibberish, someone might pay attention to their rantings about magic. Someone like Chief Inquisitor Goth.

Tor had pondered this whilst he went back to fetch Bess and Fleet. He recalled something which Alyssa had said to him years ago: 'Nothing is impossible with your power, Tor.' The words echoed in his head and he wondered whether it would be possible to take all memory of his intervention from Corlin's thugs.

Try it, Cloot said when Tor asked him what he thought. *Even I know that King Lorys does not suffer sentients happily. If he gets so much as a sniff of magic being wielded in his Kingdom, our days are numbered.*

What about Cyrus then?

Don't worry about Cyrus. I don't think you have anything but gratitude to fear from him, said the falcon preening itself on Tor's shoulder.

He's an honourable man, Cloot. He may feel obliged to tell the Inquisitors.

Tor was worried, but more about what Merkhud would say to him showcasing his talents than about how much fun the Inquisitors would have if a powerful sentient were revealed to them.

Cloot's calm, confident manner reassured him. *Cyrus is part of the puzzle somehow, Tor. I feel he's safe to trust.*

Tor looked over now at the huddle of men who were watching him and the falcon with frightened eyes. The empowered boy with the mad-eyed bird sitting on his shoulder. Tor could imagine the stories – it almost made him smile. There was nothing for it: he would have to try. He crouched in the shadows beneath a large tree.

Well, come on then, Cloot called impatiently from a few branches above.

Light! Give me a chance, I don't know what I'm doing, you mad bird.

For some reason, calling Cloot a mad bird made both of them convulse with laughter and it was several moments before Tor reached any level of composure. He looked at the startled men, who were now fully convinced that not only was he dangerous but insane too, as was the violent bird hopping around in the branches close by.

Just trust yourself, Cloot whispered.

Tor remembered Alyssa's words again, closed his eyes and reached out to the forest, which smiled its own encouragement. Then he focused sharply on the men, weaving a potent enchantment. When he finally opened his own eyes, their were closed and they were all slumped in sleep.

What happened?

That's it. One minute awake and terrified. The next, asleep. Do you think it worked? Cloot dropped alongside Tor.

Tor stood. *Let's see.* He walked to the men and nudged them awake with his boot. They were groggy but the fear had gone out of their eyes.

'Goron, isn't it?' Tor said.

'So what if it is?' the huge man answered, pulling at his bonds. 'Where's Corlin?'

'Dead.'

The conspirators appeared genuinely shocked.

'Who killed him?'

'Cyrus.'

'Impossible,' the man called Fyster said, shaking invisible cobwebs from his mind. 'He was nailed to the trees.'

'Well, he did it. And you fellows will be standing

before the King's justice soon for the execution of his four soldiers,' Tor replied, deflecting their thoughts from Cyrus to their own necks. They groaned as one.

'What possessed you men to do this?' Tor was determined to know.

'Money,' Fyster said flatly. 'Corlin paid each of us handsomely. Half in Hatten, half when the job was done – not that we knew what the job was. He gave us barrels of ale and kept us drunk most of the time. The only time we were sober was when we ambushed the Company, and that was easy because they were drugged. He killed the watches, not us.' Fyster shook his head sadly.

'And what about the Heartwood, were you not afraid to enter it?' Tor said.

The man who was called Chirren piped up. 'Oh, we were, but the money talked us into it and he gave us some confection to drink which he said would dull any panic. Tasted horrible but it worked. We drank it twice a day.' He was the youngest of the gang and eager to tell the tale.

Tor was intrigued. 'Where is this confection?'

'He kept it in his pack – it's in a blue bottle,' Chirren offered happily, ignoring the scowls of the others.

'We're going to face the King's justice for murder, you dope. Why don't you help him a little more?' growled Goron.

Tor was already rifling through Corlin's belongings and soon found the bottle Chirren spoke of. He unstoppered it and recoiled at the smell. It certainly would taste terrible going by its pungency. He would show this to Merkhud.

'I know you, don't I?' asked Goron.

'I don't think so,' Tor said in an offhand manner. He

hefted each man to his feet. 'Now, gentlemen, I want you on your horses and no trouble. If it wasn't for me arriving to stop the carnage, Prime Cyrus would have run you all through. He was in a blind rage and had the smell of blood in his nose.'

He heard Cloot chuckle sarcastically in his head.

'So if you want some advice, co-operate and who knows how lenient the King may be when he learns that although you participated in this heinous crime, none of you killed a man.'

They began agreeing with him. Tor got them up on their horses, which he had already saddled. Though they seemed keen to oblige now he did not trust them for a second, least of all Goron, so he tied each man to the other again so the horses would have to walk in a column. Next, he gently woke Cyrus and asked him if he could sit a horse and travel awhile.

The Prime was surprised to find he had slept, and even more surprised to find himself bandaged and feeling so alive.

'When I killed Corlin, I thought that was the end of me too, Gynt. It was the very last of my strength.' He shook his head in disbelief.

'I thought so too. We just had to pray that if we cleaned and bandaged your wounds you might live long enough for us to get you to Physic Merkhud.'

Tor felt the full weight of the piercing glare which was legend with Cyrus's men.

'You lie so badly, Gynt,' he snorted. 'And this damn bird that hangs around you like a bad smell . . . Why do I get the feeling you are covering up some terrible secret?'

Tor felt the hairs rise on his arms.

'Relax, Tor,' Cyrus added kindly. 'I have never been so relieved to see anyone in my life as I was to clap swollen eyes on you today. I am in your debt: the mere fact that I still breathe and will live to avenge the death of my men is because of you.' He held up his hand to stop Tor leaping in. 'No, wait. You must know this. When they were beating me and I sank into the black hole of unconsciousness which seemed my only escape, a woman visited me. She did not tell me her name, and I never actually saw her, but she had a beautiful voice and she calmed me, returning again and again to urge me to hold on. And do you know what she told me to hold on for?'

Tor shook his head.

'For you, Gynt. She told me you were coming and that you would save me. She said more in this black world we spoke in: she asked me to protect your secrets from all, including those I serve, and to protect you with my life. How's that for dreaming, Tor? And then you appeared.'

He used Tor to lean on as he stood slowly.

'Let's say no more now. It's all beyond my understanding anyway, other than I hope you have a damn good story for the inevitable army which will be bearing down on this region as we speak.' He laughed. 'Saying thank you seems too lame, Tor, so I won't try to express my gratitude to you and your . . . er . . . bird over there.'

'He's a peregrine falcon,' Tor said meekly.

The column set off at a slow pace: Cyrus led on Fleet, with the four prisoners in the middle, and Tor at the back on Bess and leading the extra horse. Cloot flew high above, instructing Tor on how to navigate their way back through the Heartwood in the direction of Brewis.

The prisoners marvelled at Tor's sense of direction, but the Prime looked up and saw the superb peregrine falcon flying very high ahead of them. He smiled and called back over his shoulder, 'I have a very fine Morriet in my rooms, Gynt, which I've been saving. I hope you'll share it with me on our return.'

12

A Surprise for Merkhud

The forty men of the Shield travelled in silence, their shock at hearing the news of their missing Prime still palpable.

Cyrus had two roles and was revered by his men in both. The first, and most important, was as Prime of the Shield – the small, private army of superior warriors who protected the monarch. The larger army, responsible for the security of the realm, was known as the Company and Cyrus was its head also. In the days of old King Mort there had been a man for each job but today Tallinor lived in peace and Cyrus easily handled both.

Whispered jibes from envious visiting nobles insinuated that Tal's army would not know a real battle if it came up and bit it on the backside. Yet its long history, unrivalled fighting capability, its famous Prime and intensely secret ways, made it worthy of respect.

Merkhud rode beside the King as requested. This was not work for a physic but the King needed his support. The physic felt deeply unsettled, not only because of the news of Cyrus – by his reckoning Tor should have presented himself two days ago. It was fortunate he had requested Miss Vylet's aid, for through her he had learned of the boy's safe passage into Hatten. She had kept Merkhud abreast of his whereabouts by virtue of her network of agents, but had communicated this morning that Tor had disappeared.

Merkhud had hoped with all his heart to receive word of the boy in Tal when he returned from Wytten, but no message awaited him. The meeting with Marrien, Tor's disappearance and now the misadventure of Cyrus was too much for one day.

'I said, old man, are you going deaf on me?' the King boomed in his ear.

'Light Lorys! My hearing is just fine, thank you. I was thinking, that's all.'

'Well, think on your own time, physic. I'm worried and I brought you along for your counsel, not this melancholy quiet.'

Merkhud remained stiffly silent.

The King continued, 'Don't sulk, Merkhud. You're far too old. I was asking you about the new apprentice.'

'Due any moment, I imagine, and you and the Queen will be the first people I introduce him to. You have my word.'

It was a courteous dismissal. Merkhud was not in the mood for conversation. Lorys, however, would have said more but one of his men had come abreast to tell him that the second six men would be breaking off here.

'Good, Norrysh, thank you.' The King acknowledged the salute and turned back to his friend. 'Groups of six men are peeling off at each village within ten leagues of Brewis to search for any news. These are heading to Hobb.'

Merkhud nodded. It was only minutes later though, as the main unit rounded a bend, that they saw the dust of the Company ahead. Lorys sighed with relief and picked up the pace so his Shield might meet the column swiftly.

Herek, pale with worry, brought his men to a stop, jumped from his horse and bowed with deep respect to his King.

'My Liege,' he said, on his knee now, voice barely steady with emotion. 'Did my rider reach Tal safely, sire?'

'He did and delivered his baleful tidings,' the King replied gently as he eased off his superb white stallion to stand in front of the lieutenant. 'Be easy, man.'

Herek looked distraught. Lorys became businesslike: anything else and he felt sure Herek would simply collapse from grief. He understood very clearly how the men felt about their Prime: save himself, no other person in the land had such influence over the soldiers.

'No further news then, Captain Herek?' he said.

'No, your majesty. No sign of Prime Cyrus, and I thought it best to get the Company back to Tal as swiftly as possible.'

'You made the right decision, Captain – precisely what the Prime would expect of you. Get your men safely back to Tal now, there's nothing more you can do for Cyrus at the moment. The Shield is searching the immediate area and will search the Kingdom, if necessary, to find him.' Lorys put his hand on Herek's sagging shoulder. 'You and these men need rest and some good food inside you. You've been away a sizeable part of the summer and it's time you went home to your women and families.'

'May I request permission to join the men of the Shield, my liege?' Herek pleaded.

The King smiled kindly. 'Permission denied, Captain. My orders are that you escort these men to Tal and remain there until you receive further direct orders from myself. Is that clear?'

'Yes, your majesty, forgive me.'

'Nothing to forgive, Herek. You're an excellent soldier. Back on your horse, son. The Shield will find him.'

As the column began to move off, Lorys walked slowly down the line. He smiled reassuringly, talking to the men, acknowledging their show of respect. In those few minutes he managed to lift the spirits of all around him and Merkhud had no doubt that the soldiers fully believed their King would keep his word and find their beloved Prime.

Once back on his own stallion and cantering briskly, Lorys and Merkhud fell into a comfortable silence. The next six men left the main group at the entrance to Chigley and another six followed – they would go on to Perswich, Lorys explained. And so it went, until the King, Merkhud, Norrysh and eight remaining soldiers galloped into Brewis.

'With your permission, your majesty, we'll conduct a cursory search of the village and then go on to where the Company camped.'

Norrysh waited out of respect. The King nodded his agreement.

The soldier continued. 'If Physic Merkhud and yourself would make yourselves comfortable, I'll have some refreshment brought to you, sire.'

He waited for no answer this time and one of the men disappeared into The Horse and Cart Inn in search of ale to suit a monarch. The remaining soldiers questioned the villagers. Merkhud could see them shaking their heads. He, like Norrysh, felt little hope of any leads from Brewis. Cool ale arrived with a giggling, curtsying serving girl and the two men drank deeply to quench their thirst.

The King wiped his beard. 'Something on your mind, Merkhud?'

There was no point in hedging, Merkhud decided. 'I met with the girl today, Lorys.'

'Oh, and which girl is that?' the King replied as he lifted his cup to his mouth.

'The girl from Wytten,' Merkhud replied flatly.

Lorys swung around, ale forgotten, attention keen on his physic now. 'She is well?' His voice was just above a whisper.

'She is.'

'The child?' Lorys put his cup down on the grass for fear his shaking hand might spill the contents.

'He is very hearty.' Merkhud knew it was a dagger into the heart of his King.

'A son.' Those two words spoke a lifetime of longing. A tragic look swept across the face of the sovereign.

'Indeed, my lord. He is fit and strong and very well cared for.' Merkhud was soft of speech, to ensure eavesdropping was impossible. 'I have taken care of everything and Marrien will be comfortable, as will her boy.' He stopped abruptly and waited.

'Well, that's that then,' said the King.

'It is, your majesty. I will not presume to tell you anything further on this matter.'

'And will you speak with Marrien frequently?' Lorys sounded embarrassed by his own enquiry.

Merkhud lied. 'No, Lorys.' He drained the last of his ale, the despair beside him unbearable.

'Done,' came the reply with finality and Merkhud felt relief sweep through him.

He knew the King was as good as his word. Neither Marrien nor their son would be discussed again and the Queen would continue to live in blissful ignorance of this blot on her husband's otherwise unblemished fidelity. Norrysh was back and Merkhud was grateful for it.

'We'll head on to the camp site now, your majesty — there's no information of any consequence here.'

The King pulled himself swiftly together. His voice was steady and firm again. 'As you wish, Norrysh. Lead on.'

The site of the previous night's camp was barely half a league away, and from it stretched the Heartwood.

'I know our people fear this place, Merkhud, but I, strangely, always feel reassured by it,' Lorys said climbing down from his horse.

The horse shook its head and, trailing its reins, drifted off to graze, not too close to the fringe of the wood. The other horses followed suit: these were magnificently trained steeds and would rarely wander more than a few paces from their riders. Stygian, Merkhud's mount, however, was a different beast. He kept his own lofty company and had no reservations about stepping up to and grazing calmly beneath one of the great oaks skirting the wood as soon as Merkhud had climbed down.

'All right, what are we looking for?' the physic asked.

'Cyrus has a supreme soldier's brain. He may have left us some sort of clue,' Lorys suggested, shrugging his shoulders. They began a meticulous search of the area but, as particular as they were, they all felt it was a hopeless, almost desperate measure. It was just as Merkhud was about to give up his part in this hollow activity that he thought he heard voices.

'Sssh!' he called to the group. No one else had heard anything out of the ordinary and they looked up alarmed. Merkhud cast out widely. Voices, definitely voices. Everyone was staring at him expectantly. 'I hear people coming,' he warned.

The soldiers drew their swords and reached for their horses' reins; the King followed their lead. Lorys became indignant as they all strained to hear whatever it was that Merkhud had.

'Can't hear anything but the birds, old man. Why are you startling us?'

'Because there is a small group approaching. I jest not, my King,' Merkhud snarled in a whisper.

'From where? I hear nothing.' It was Norrysh, calm as ever.

'From the wood. Trust me.'

'Our own?' suggested Lorys.

'No, your majesty, Shield men would not approach from within the Heartwood,' Norrysh said.

As the unit began to feel edgy with anticipation, Prime Cyrus emerged from the dark copse of trees at their left, blinking his eyes in the afternoon sun. Behind him came three horses with sagging riders who were gagged and bound. To Merkhud's astonishment, Torkyn Gynt appeared last, looking quite ridiculous with a falcon sitting atop one shoulder.

'The Light strike me down!' was all Merkhud could

say but his exclamation was drowned amongst yells of happy disbelief from his companions.

If Merkhud was shocked to see his new apprentice, it was small in comparison to Tor's alarm at recognising the familiar figure in black.

Oh, bollocks! he muttered across the mindlink as the column stopped.

Cloot spied the old man. *Merkhud?*

The one and only, Tor replied as he saw Cyrus lift his hand to wave.

And the others?

Your guess is as good as mine.

Cloot's voice dropped its humour. *A word of caution, my friend.*

Make it quick, Cloot — I'm working on my dazzling excuse as to what I'm doing here.

Don't tell anyone, especially the old man, about me. The bird became silent and still.

What? Why? Cloot did not answer. Instead he leapt from Tor's shoulder into the air.

A man with a closely shaved beard and fine clothes was upon them, dragging Cyrus down from his horse. Tor climbed down from his and watched the bird fly to the safety of the trees.

Don't leave me again Cloot, Tor cried across the link.

I'm not far. Heed my warning. I must remain anonymous.

Tor turned and stared into the eyes of a grim-faced Merkhud who had caught up with the younger men. They were shaking fists with their captain — as was the Shield's way — relief mixed with confusion written across their faces.

'Light, man! I thought I'd never see your face again,'

Tor heard the well-clothed leader say to the Prime.

He was speechless when Cyrus replied, 'My liege,' and tried to drop to one tired knee. Tor avoided Merkhud's icy stare and instead watched the man Cyrus addressed pull the protesting Prime to his feet.

'My King . . . there is so much to tell.'

'Later, Cyrus. These men?' asked the King, his chin jutting towards Goron and his companions.

'Scum, sire. Awaiting your pleasure,' Cyrus replied with genuine relish.

Norrysh and his men were pulling the three captives down from their horses. 'On your knees in front of your King!'

The prisoners looked terrified. The effects of the drug which Corlin had plied so plentifully had deserted them. Now they faced the reality of their deeds. They began jabbering their excuses as one.

'Take them away,' Norrysh ordered. 'We can hear their story after they have enjoyed the hospitality of the dungeon.'

Merkhud was still to utter a single word. Tor plucked up the courage to look at him again, keeping his expression contrite and full of appeal.

'Did I, perchance, see a bird of prey sitting on your shoulder?' the old man finally asked.

'Er . . . yes, sir,' Tor replied.

'I see. And what do you call your pet hawk?'

Tor wanted to explain that Cloot was a falcon but held his words. 'He is named Cloot.'

The old man flinched; he looked as though Tor had just slapped him. 'Did you say Cloot?' He seemed genuinely startled.

'Yes, er . . . he took off towards the woods when all of you approached.'

'Who named him?' the old man asked urgently.

Tor couldn't understand the interrogation over a name but recalled Cloot's warning. 'Well, ah . . . my mother used to sing a humorous song to me when I was very small about a character called Cloot. I took it from that song.' He hoped the lie had worked.

Merkhud held his eyes for a long pause then nodded.

'Lorys, may I – with no small amount of astonishment – present Torkyn Gynt, my new apprentice? Torkyn, your King,' he offered in a tight voice.

Tor bowed deeply as he had seen the others do and then dropped to one knee. 'Your majesty.'

'Hell's fire! How many more surprises today? The long-awaited Gynt, eh? And you two obviously know one another?' the King said, looking between the bowed boy and Cyrus.

'Why, yes, my King,' Cyrus replied. 'Without Torkyn Gynt my blood would be warming the grasses in the Heartwood.'

'Get up, boy. Let's have a look at you then.' Since his anxiety had dissipated at the sight of Cyrus, Lorys was now highly amused. He loved to see Merkhud unnerved, as he clearly was. 'Come on, Merkhud. You've been grumbling about his tardy arrival. Here he is, safe and sound.'

'What happened here? How could you both be here?' Merkhud could not stop the questions tumbling out.

'The . . . er . . . Prime asked me to ride with him to Tal. Initially I said no but thought better of it, and I caught up and er . . . got involved in his . . . um . . . troubles.' Tor fought his embarrassment. He knew

Merkhud could not reveal that he had been tracking his progress all along by magical means – not in front of this audience anyway. There would be time later for explanations.

The King groaned. 'What does it matter, Merkhud? He's here and the Prime lives.'

Cloot chose that moment to arrive back on Tor's shoulder.

'And the bird?' Merkhud could not hide his disbelief.

'A finer bird, Physic Merkhud, you'll not see in all of Tallinor,' Cyrus blurted. 'I watched the boy win him during a devilish hand of hari at the The Empty Goblet. He was the envy of all there.'

'Yes.' Tor picked up the lead from Cyrus. 'It was on the second night and I didn't know what I was going to do with a falcon but the bird seemed to take to me,' he said, affectionately scratching the top of Cloot's feathered head. 'I don't know why I even joined the game,' he lied smoothly.

'Too much ale, lad, but you played like a demon,' laughed Cyrus and the King joined in.

'Hari is addictive, lad. You'd better forget it and concentrate on your studies,' the King said, looking at Merkhud and enjoying the way his whiskers twitched.

'I will, your majesty, I promise.'

Lorys became business-like again. 'Good. Now, Cyrus, are you strong enough to brief me on this mysterious tale?'

'Of course, your majesty. Please, let's sit.' Cyrus pointed to beneath a nearby oak, then reconstructed the events from as far back as Cloot's humiliation in the marketplace, when he first met Tor. Cyrus was very careful not to mention names as he pieced together the story. To Tor's silent and heartfelt thanks, he remarked, almost incidentally, that the injured cripple had last been seen hobbling out of the town's gates.

'Probably died before he was a mile down the road,' Tor added daringly.

Everyone nodded with a discernible lack of interest.

Only Tor heard the falcon chuckle.

Nanak, there has to be a connection!

Never one to waste words, Nanak, keeper of the Paladin, kept his own counsel whilst he thought through Merkhud's suggestion that Cloot the Brocken, the Second of the Paladin, had re-emerged in Hatten at the same time as Torkyn Gynt, their only link to the Trinity, had arrived in the town.

I want to believe that none of the Paladin die, Merkhud, but this might be reaching. A falcon, you say?

Nanak . . . think! Cloot is a Brocken name. It is not even a common one. No Tallinese would give their son the name of Cloot. So Tor's story of his mother singing some Tallinese ballad is a sham. I don't understand it either, but very little of your or my life makes much sense, does it? You reacted with cynicism when I first mentioned Cyrus, but this is no coincidence, my friend: Prime Cyrus and this Cloot are of the Paladin.

Merkhud waited for Nanak to say something, to contradict him, to come up with something to refute this idea. But there was silence across the link.

He continued thinking aloud. *My only confusion is when and why this Cloot changed into a strange bird.*

Nanak spoke at last. *Why do you call the bird strange?*

Oh, I don't know. It's as though they communicate. I can't swear it but they work in tandem. I've tried every conceivable magic to eavesdrop but there's nothing. It could be my imagination but, Light, man, think of it. What if our Cloot and Cyrus have returned as guardians to Tor? It reinforces that he is the One.

Nanak felt his heart beating with excitement. No one was closer to the Paladin than Nanak, and his resolve cracked further each time one of them fell to Orlac's magic. He had wept most recently when Sallementro disappeared. Each death brought such heartbreak, but he had held. He had found the strength to encourage and nurture his remaining guardians.

Give me one more name, Merkhud, and I'll accept and rejoice with you.

I'll find that name for you, Nanak. You will believe it. The wheels are turning. The Host was right.

Well, where are the others? Where are Juno and Saxon and Adongo? If Cloot and Cyrus are back, why aren't the others showing themselves?

I don't know, muttered Merkhud, feeling beaten by the questions but determined he was right. *We wait. If I'm right, they will show themselves soon.*

13

Cirq Zorros

As she strolled alongside the old girl and her fractious donkey, Alyssa could not remember a time when she had felt happier, other than when she was with Tor. Initially he had rarely left her thoughts and often during those first weeks, from Twyfford towards Mexford Cross, she had thought about swallowing one of the old girl's lethal confections and ending her misery. More recently though, as the summer lengthened into autumn, she had come to think about him without tears. Alyssa had made a deliberate effort to keep Tor her own. His memory remained a tender hurt but it was his silence which was the most maddening of all; whenever she tried to cast to him it felt leaden. Alyssa believed he had simply shut her out and that had shocked her into not trying again for a while.

Now, however, as she poked around at the thick nothingness, she began to believe it was a veil not of Tor's making. It did not feel like one of Tor's shepherding tricks, as he liked to call them. Tor's were powerful, with a strong, unmistakable signature to them. This seemed infinitely more subtle; its neat, almost fastidious trace nothing she could actually get hold of. The scent always trailed away. Was someone deliberately blocking communication between the two of them? She suspected it was the old man who had made Tor behave so strangely, but how did he know of their link and why would he want to block it?

Leaving Mallee Marsh so suddenly and with a complete stranger had been uncharacteristic for her too. Sometimes she could barely believe she had done it. But if she recalled the moment when she had begged Sorrel to allow her to go with her, Alyssa knew she had been distraught. She also knew that without this distraction of being with Sorrel and hopefully embarking on some sort of new beginning, she would have fallen apart. With a father like Lam Qyn, getting through each day was hard enough, but without Tor to give her hope there would have been no point to life at all. Alyssa knew there were other young men who would happily marry her but she would not happily marry anyone but Torkyn Gynt. They were meant to be together for ever.

And so she had taken her first steps alongside Sorrel and immediately had begun to feel released from the dead weight of her own life. They walked far each day and she loved listening to the old girl's stories of life on the road. She especially liked to learn the herblore which Sorrel shared. Alyssa learned how whistlewort could calm the rage of a sore throat and, when boiled and mixed with honey, made a useful linctus for a cough. Teppenny pasted on a wound or ulcer would ensure it healed faster; nettle, mint and dandelion made the best infusion for bronchitis whilst the oil of the lemonbark mixed with that of lavender would soothe earache quicker than anything. She loved the new world which Sorrel offered to her, not just her plants but walking the Kingdom itself. Alyssa's furthest trip to date had been to Twyfford Cross once with Tor and his father.

She liked Tor's parents. They were firm but kind and so loving towards their son and indeed her. Alyssa showed more open affection for them than for her own father, though she loved him dearly. She just did not understand him. Tor was lucky. He was loved. She had no love in her life but his and she had clung to that love fiercely. How could he have left her? She knew her act of leaving the Marsh sprang mostly from anger. The fury she felt at his loss had given her the courage needed to walk off with a stranger to who knew where. She admitted quietly to herself that she was really just treating him in the same manner he had treated her. Alyssa hoped he might come looking for her, which is why she deliberately had left no word for him. She hoped he would worry himself sick over where she might be; and now he would never know because she had no idea herself where they were going.

Her mind rolled these thoughts over, day after day, as she walked alongside Sorrel, her hand resting loosely on Kythay's shoulder, while the curious trio made their slow journey north west, away from the Kingdom's capital.

'Where did you say we were headed?' Alyssa said absent-mindedly as she chewed on a grass stem.

Sorrel did not answer immediately. Her attention had caught on a cluster of small blue and white flowers nestling in the thick grasses beneath the trees.

'Aha! Jolliker petals make a wonderful tonic for belly-ache. Remember them, my girl, they're hard to come by and best picked early autumn, like now.'

She motioned for Alyssa to help. Kythay ceased his ponderous tread at the same time as Alyssa stopped walking. She had the animal totally under her control and he never needed more than a polite word from her to co-operate. It regularly frustrated Sorrel that this stubborn, grumpy animal made himself so easy to get along with where Alyssa was concerned.

'Wretched animal,' she muttered for the umpteenth time as she bent her weary back to gather her precious petals.

The two women worked quietly whilst Kythay chewed on whatever treats he could find nearby. When the midday sun began to bite into their skin Sorrel straightened with a groan.

'We're headed for Ildagarth,' she said finally, settling down to rest awhile. She eyed the girl who was still busying herself with the flowers, throwing them into a tiny sack.

'Oh? What's there for us?' Alyssa swatted at a gnat and dragged the back of her hand over her dry lips.

She had blossomed in the three weeks they had been together, Sorrel noted, filling out with the regular meals they shared. She had been such a skinny thing; now she had curves. The brisk walking along these roads had made her stronger too and encouraged a honeyed glow to her lovely skin.

At first she had been quiet; she had stayed close to Kythay and said little other than to answer Sorrel's gentle questions. Now, weeks since that afternoon when she had manipulated the girl into joining her, Alyssa was talkative and lively with reams of questions of her own. She laughed a great deal more too. Perhaps the loss of Tor was less keen . . . or possibly not – it was just that the girl had more interest in her life now, walking the roads of Tallinor. Whatever it was, it was doing her a power of good. The girl looked radiant.

She was sharp too. Sorrel noted how quickly she absorbed the lore of herbs and plants; she would easily be able to earn money alongside her. Not that they had needed any money yet, however. Merkhud had seen to it that Sorrel's purse was heavy, though she had not revealed her wealth to Alyssa. She continued to mutter that they would have to look for work soon but at each village put it off until tomorrow. Alyssa seemed to be looking forward to putting her new skills to work. So far they had spent much time gathering useful plants and herbs but they had not attempted to sell any remedies yet. All in good time, Sorrel said.

She did not want to draw attention to themselves. She needed time to get to know the girl better, especially as Alyssa had begun slowly to drop her guards, probably because of the tranquil pace and outdoor life. If they were to locate themselves in a village and begin working, it could be a different story.

Sorrel realised she had still not answered Alyssa's question about why they were headed for Ildagarth. 'Well, I've not been to that part of the Kingdom for a good many years and it seems as good a place as any,' she lied. She stretched in a deliberately casual manner. 'Besides, near Ildagarth is Caremboche. Have you heard of this place?'

Alyssa shook her head. She returned to sit beside the munching Kythay, pushing away golden wisps of glinting hair which had escaped her loose plait. The donkey turned and nuzzled her and she whispered something to him.

Sorrel continued. 'Caremboche is the ancient place where the Seat of Knowledge was located – once an opulent city filled with sorcerers and academics, artists and craftsmen, where their skills were openly encouraged and passed on. Two centuries on, it is a mere shadow of its former glorious self but the Academie remains. I'd like you to see it.'

She noted Alyssa's lack of interest and decided not to pursue the conversation further. Instead she veiled and cast.

Greetings, my love. How do you fare? replied the smooth voice.

We are both well, Merkhud, approaching Fragglesham. With luck we'll reach Mexford by the next moon.

There was a sigh of relief. *That's good news. Does she know?*

No. She is barely interested. Are you sure about this?

I am. He comes. We'll talk soon. Before Sorrel could respond, the link was sharply closed.

Sighing deeply and wondering at the seeming point-lessness of her life, she suggested to her companion that they should push on to Fragglesham which was now within a few hours reach. They did better, reaching the bustling town much sooner than planned, and immediately found themselves a room at The Wheatsheaf.

The famous travelling show, Cirq Zorros, was encamped on Fragglesham Green. Tiered benches had been erected and the wildly coloured pennants which lined the arena lifted and flapped in a lazy breeze. The northern fringe of the Green was a maze of small tents and awnings which housed the performers and their animals. At the southern end, brightly painted sideshow stalls had been set up close to the main entrance. In between roamed what looked like a town within a town: dozens of travelling performers, keepers and stall owners preparing for the evening's show.

Alyssa was enchanted by the scene. 'I've only ever heard about Cirq Zorros. I can't believe it's here!'

Sorrel was not impressed. This would slow them down for sure. In fact she was surprised that The Wheatsheaf had even had a room available. Then she remembered the innkeeper had mentioned that some of the King's men were staying at the inn. 'Inquisitor Goth,' he had whispered apologetically.

Sorrel had never feared Goth. Her ability to link was well beyond his weak senses which relied upon an enchanted stone to scry out sentients. It almost made her laugh. But Alyssa would fear him, as did most people, sentient and otherwise. She could not risk the girl becoming nervous and perhaps getting herself noticed. Nevertheless, she had taken the room and paid in advance and was now wondering how in the name of Light she was going to avoid taking the happy young woman at her side to the circus. There was no way out of it. Alyssa's heart and mind was lost to the colourful regalia, the strange-looking people weaving in and out of tents and even stranger beasts feeding and sunning themselves.

Sorrel resigned herself. 'Perhaps we could go to the show,' she said kindly.

Alyssa looked as though someone had just handed her a precious jewel. It seemed impossible her expression could show more delight and yet her smile stretched wider still, her eyes laughed their pleasure and the shriek which escaped her as she threw her arms around her friend was worth the four royals it would cost Sorrel.

* * *

Inquisitor Goth was furious. His fine stallion had stumbled and lightly sprained a leg as his imposing troop had cantered into town and now the horse was being rested, much to his disgust, in the Fragglesham stable. What a piss-poor excuse for a town this was and, to add misery to woe, the hated circus had arrived yesterday – a carbuncle on society with its flea-ridden beasts and freakish gypsies.

He banged his mug on the table in another empty show of wrath. His company was making its way back to Tal whilst he lingered in the town, refusing to leave without his prized stallion which was two days from being fit enough to travel. The noise, he knew, would get him nowhere but he liked to see the fat sod of an innkeeper sweat and, even better, it unnerved the serving girls. It might help to soften them up for his games later, he thought viciously. He leered at one young woman. She had large breasts and he imagined himself pinching them hard and making her scream. Yes, he'd make them pay all right for this delay.

The tic on the left side of his face twitched erratically but he cared little. He was powerful. No longer an orphaned, penniless noble's brat but a man to be respected. That fire which had ripped through his family's home had served a purpose. A painful one but nonetheless it had rid him of his useless parents: one a drunken skirt-chaser, the other a whimpering wreck; both headed for the debt courts having squandered his grandfather's fortune. Tallinor's Great Fire had simply sped them on their way. After their useless, pathetic lives, death must have felt like a welcome embrace, or so he liked to tell himself.

The small child left behind had been maimed by the flames but breathed still. With the inspired healing minis-

trations of the famous Physic Merkhud; Almyd Goth had
rallied, then strengthened, and finally walked from what
had seemed his deathbed straight into the arms of the
royal family, who had taken pity on the ruined face of the
boy from noble parents.

'You must rue the day you clapped eyes on my twisted
face, Nyria.' Goth giggled into his ale. 'And your despised
servant, that old man, would poison me now as soon as spit
on me. He must long to be able to turn back the years and
snuff out the life of the child he fought so hard to save.'

His mouth was twisted into an ugly smile when he
turned to see a startlingly beautiful young woman talking
excitedly as she entered The Wheatsheaf, an old woman
following her.

'Tonight then?' The girl was talking about the circus,
he realised with a snarl.

'Anything to stop you twittering, Alyssa,' her
companion replied.

They had not noticed him but he watched the old
woman push the girl towards the steps. Goth licked his
undefined rubbery lips – another legacy of the fire which
had smudged almost every feature of his face into the
other. Only the cold, slate-coloured eyes, with their icy
hatred of anything and anyone handsome or gifted in any
way, were whole. Now, as those eyes followed the shapely
rear of Alyssa Qyn disappearing up the inn's stairs, he
decided she would be his sport for tonight and help take
the edge off his crippling boredom.

Alyssa's stomach clenched as she descended the stairs to
look for Sorrel. There was only one man in all of Tallinor
with a face like that. Although she had never before seen

Chief Inquisitor Goth his reputation was legend and she had no doubt whatsoever that it was him sitting at the table between her and the inn's door.

His narrowed eyes, fixed on hers, made her feel instantly cornered. He could not be chasing her. She had used no Power since leaving her village. Her mind raced to check and double-check this fact. As she moved from the bottom stair into the main inn she felt certain he was not looking for her, so why was he staring at her so intently?

Goth grinned. To Alyssa it looked like a snarl and she stopped. Goth loved it when people recoiled from him. Yes indeed, that fire had done him a good turn. If she was scared her pale, lovely skin would flinch all the more when he touched her. She really was a beautiful creature, with her hair polished to gleaming. Beneath the battered clothes she wore he sensed a fragile body on the verge of womanhood. A virgin for sure. He shivered with delight. This would make it all the more delectable.

He licked his ghastly lips in anticipation and this time Alyssa took a step back.

'Er . . . may I help you, sir?' she stammered, looking around uselessly for the innkeeper who was nowhere to be seen. She could see Sorrel, though, through the open door, out in the street and deep in conversation with someone; as good as a league away.

He smiled horribly. 'Most certainly you can, my dear. Firstly by letting me feel between your legs and later perhaps on your knees.' It was said so sweetly.

Alyssa's bile rose at his words and sugary voice. Trapped, she watched paralysed, as he stood and slipped his cloak from his shoulders then undid the sword from his hip. *Where is everyone?* her mind shrieked. And then he was walking towards her. Though not tall he was powerfully built and she could see the cruel glint in the eyes staring out of his expressionless, twitching face.

Alyssa was unable to utter a word. She did the only thing her body was capable of at that terrifying moment. She smashed the guard she had built around herself and, raising her head, sent a terrified scream across the link she had opened to anyone who might be listening.

Goth was bemused by her strange action but grabbed her slim arm strongly, with the intention of hurting her. As he did so, he was incensed to see the girl's companion suddenly burst through the doorway screaming the girl's name. Goth had no care for what people might think of his actions carried out in private but it would be another case to answer should any commoner bring complaint to the King about him performing anything but his duty. He dropped Alyssa's arm. He had seen that look of hate which was now spread across the old woman's face many times before. It had no effect on him yet there was something more there, though he could not tell what.

'What brings you rushing in here like this, old woman?'

Goth was fuming. He had paid the innkeeper an outrageous sum to stay away until he had met with the young woman and taken her to his room. In fact, he had spread enough coin in that pig's sweaty palm to pay off all the serving staff and to ensure someone stopped the old girl in the street and kept her busy.

Sorrel was breathing heavily, more from the shock of hearing Alyssa's scream in her head than having to move so swiftly. She fought to compose herself.

'Ah. There you are, my girl.' She sucked in more air

to calm her nerves and steady her voice. 'What took you so long?'

Goth answered for Alyssa. 'She slipped on the stairs and I was helping her, madam.'

Sorrel could see Alyssa was trembling.

'Oh, how kind of you. Inquisitor Goth, isn't it?' she asked courteously, hating the very space he occupied. 'My granddaughter is such a clumsy young thing. Beautiful, yes, but could trip over a bread crumb. My thanks for your kindness, sir.'

Other people were moving into the inn now and Goth knew he had lost the moment. He would find another one though. This girl would be his.

'Don't mention it,' he replied curtly and, without looking back, he returned to the table where he picked up his sword and cloak and disappeared into the street.

An almost audible sigh of relief swept through the inn.

'How did you know?' Alyssa had finally found her voice.

'Know what, child?'

'That I needed your help. He was . . . he was about to—' She choked back a sob.

'Hush, Alyssa. Not here. Let's go now . . . it's safe outside,' said Sorrel tenderly.

They walked in silence towards the Green, both shaken. People were strolling in small bunches towards the circus tent. All around them was excited conversation and eruptions of happy laughter but the women's earlier buoyant mood had burst with the incident at the inn; neither knew quite what to say.

Just before reaching the entrance to Cirq Zorros Alyssa stopped, puzzlement creasing her forehead. 'You didn't

answer me. How did you know I needed saving from that
. . . that monster? How is it that he did not scry me out
the instant I cast? Why am I not already bridled?'

Sorrel knew she would have to be careful. 'We must
talk, Alyssa, but not now. People are watching and this
is a conversation best had in private.'

So . . . talk to me privately, Alyssa thumped into Sorrel's
head. Her eyes blazed their anger and Sorrel was caught
unguarded by the strong cast.

They moved in awkward silence to an empty bench
beneath one of Fragglesham's elms and sat down. It would
not have mattered if anyone else had shared it for no one
could hear their conversation.

How long have you known? Alyssa demanded.

There was no point in trying to appease her anger,
Sorrel decided. It was easier to allow it to spend itself.

Since the beginning, she answered.

Why the secrecy?

Well . . . I was afraid at first, she lied.

Alyssa snapped at her. *Of what?*

*Of discovering someone else empowered. I have avoided the few
sentients I've met in my life . . . we don't last long in Goth's
society if we admit what we are. Better to remain anonymous.
But you were different. You . . . well, you touched something in
me. The daughter I've never had, perhaps. I sensed your pain.
The careful way you've hidden your power all your life. Your
need for someone to love you.*

Sorrel reached out and touched Alyssa's face. *You looked
so forlorn and helpless that day I stopped by your cottage, my
heart just melted for a child I knew I could help.* She stopped
talking and dropped her hand back into her lap, despising
her ability to lie so easily.

Alyssa did not try to hide the tears. *Why did you come to my cottage?*

One of the folk in the town mentioned you dabbled with the potions and as I was low on my stores I thought I might be able to replenish some of my staple herbs.

She hated herself for hoodwinking the girl so effortlessly.

Alyssa sniffed. *And so we're going to this . . . this . . . Academie because we are sentient?*

Ah, so she *was* listening, Sorrel thought to herself. Clever girl.

We're going there to protect you, my child. You are strong with this power. I have not felt you use it until that moment when you screamed. I too am shocked as to why that butcher Goth cannot detect your or my skills but we have to be careful. In the Academie we can be safe for a while and you can find the peace you want.

Alyssa stood and looked out across the colourful pennants, watching excited Fragglesham folk filing in through the theatrical awnings. *Why are you doing this for me?* Her tone was no longer aggressive.

Sorrel paused. She took a noticeable breath. *Because I once had a son. I will not discuss him with you apart from now. He was found to be sentient. Powerful. He was punished at the start of his life for it. I lost a son I worshipped, a husband I adored and the happy life I led. Now I roam Tallinor, nothing more than a gypsy myself, offering cures for people's ailments but not getting involved with their lives. I grow older and ever emptier. Perhaps before I die I can put an end to my bitterness and open up my heart once more to someone. Maybe the gods chose you for me, Alyssa.*

The girl shivered. She recalled a saying her father had

quoted whenever he shivered unexpectedly – that the gods were walking on his grave. She understood that sentiment now as she listened to the old woman's serious words.

She turned towards Sorrel and bent to clasp her hands. She kissed the woman softly on the cheek and whispered *Thank you.*

Sorrel smiled, her sharp eyes softening. *Now let's get you to this circus, child, before we become too maudlin. We beat Goth today – there are few, if any, who could claim that. We must celebrate!*

The famous horns of Cirq Zorros which had been calling its audience to order suddenly blasted even louder, as if in answer to Sorrel's cry for a celebration. This time both women laughed as they picked up their skirts and made their way to the large tent. They pushed through the theatrically draped curtains to the main arena and squeezed into a small space still available. Sorrel silently cursed the hardness of the bench but Alyssa barely noticed it.

Her sense of the girl's power, and knowledge that her magic was undetectable by the vile Goth, confirmed in Sorrel's mind that they were doing the right thing. She fought her anxiety at blindly following Merkhud's orders as he orchestrated the capture of these two bright young people. Deep down she detested herself for manipulating the girl so adeptly, and she knew Merkhud would have toyed with the young scribe with even greater subtlety. But their purpose was far bigger than the lives of these two youngsters; far bigger than all of them. And she trusted Merkhud. They had suffered so much to come this far. He was totally committed to his quest and Sorrel believed that while his carefully plotted plans to 'own' these two people might appear cruel and calculating, his efforts were true to his cause of finding the One.

Sorrel grasped that Alyssa was important to that cause but she would have to be patient before she found out why. This girl, who was on the verge of blossoming into an astonishingly beautiful woman, would have her part to play when the time came, of that Sorrel was now sure. What that was and when it would be, no one yet knew.

She was dragged from her thoughts when the horns stopped blaring and a hush smothered the loud voices. The sconces were doused and only a few well-placed lanterns remained lit, throwing the vaulted tent into a broody dimness. Music struck up – all of it discordant which suited the first act. A troupe of oddly dressed dwarves scuttled into the arena, tumbling and twisting and throwing things at one another. They attempted to dance gracefully but it soon fell into buffoonery and their balancing acts ended just as unsuccessfully. Running through the audience they knocked off hats, stole food, sat on people's laps and made the children squeal.

As fast as it had begun, it stopped. This time all the lanterns were doused and the arena plunged into darkness. A single candle flame revealed the gleeful, painted face of one of the dwarves. Then another was lit to show the leering face of a second dwarf standing on the shoulders of the first. And so it went until ten candles were flickering and a column of eerily lit, ugly faces punctuated the dark. The audience showed its appreciation.

The dwarves, as one, put their stubby fingers to their mouths to quiet everyone and they were obeyed. A voice boomed into the darkness and six torches were lit in unison to reveal the Kingdom's tallest man, higher than the column of dwarves and balancing expertly upon enormous stilts.

He began to take great strides as he bellowed loudly: 'Welcome, good folk of Fragglesham, and our thanks for coming to our humble show.'

Ringmaster Zorros paused and was rewarded with the applause he knew would come. He resumed his striding, waving his arms and explaining what strange and colourful sights they would behold this evening.

They would see brangos, painfully shy, cave-dwelling creatures that had been tamed and taught an elegant dance routine; fearsome, horned jubbas from the north with women riding their backs; posturers who would contort their bodies into impossible positions; and strong men who could support weights that no single man should be capable of lifting.

The audience thrilled at the woman whose piercing scream could shatter a looking glass; a pair of men who, blindfolded and balanced on a spinning wheel, hurled knives at a third, their blades barely missing him. But it was the snake swallower, a young lad, who brought the most applause as he allowed the creature to slither deep into his throat.

Finally, Zorros introduced the act which most had heard about and come to witness. The Flying Foxes were a family of acrobats and trapeze artists, ranging from a scrawny five-year-old girl through to a stunning man, Saxon, who looked like the father of the troupe.

Alyssa fancied that whenever Saxon cast his eye over the audience he appeared to look directly at her . . . into her. She watched him run gracefully along a tightrope while balancing three of the smaller children on his shoulders and head. The audience loved it. He was certainly a fine-looking man with golden hair that touched his broad, powerful shoulders. His body was lean and oiled to make his muscles all the more impressive. He wore only black pantaloons, pulled in at his waist by a gold plait, and soft gold slippers.

The Flying Foxes' feats became more and more dangerous and occurred at higher and higher levels. Alyssa held her breath each time any one of the family leapt into the air, trusting that Saxon would catch them. He was deft and confident. He never missed. To Alyssa they looked like angels flying around in their sparkling costumes with their wild blond hair streaming behind them.

The music changed to become more dramatic and the elder members of the family began to climb a scaffold high into the peak of the tent. There came a drum roll as Saxon swung strongly on a swing. He launched himself into the air, turning somersaults before catching his colleague who came flying from the opposite side of the tent in a huge arc. The three males performed a number of death-defying passes, their movements becoming more complex and frightening. Then Zorros reappeared in the arena's centre.

'And now we require someone from our audience tonight to fly with the Foxes,' he invited.

Hands flew eagerly into the air, desperately trying to catch the maestro's attention, while parents desperately tried to ensure they went unnoticed.

'I think we should ask Master Saxon to choose, don't you?' asked Zorros.

'I wish he would choose me, Sorrel,' Alyssa yelled, recklessly throwing her own arms into the air with all the other would-be trapeze novices.

'Sit down, child, I beg you. Truly that's the last thing we need. I don't think my heart could bear any more excitement today.'

Saxon descended, graceful and strong, down the ropes which his wife – as Alyssa guessed she must be – began to spin harder and harder from the ground. In doing so the woman moved him in an ever-widening arc around the tent until he was circling wide and low above the audience.

'Choose!' commanded Zorros.

The audience picked up the chant. 'Choose . . . choose . . . choose . . .' they chorused.

Alyssa was yelling along with everyone; she dug Sorrel with her elbow to encourage her to join in, and drummed her feet on the boards.

Saxon Fox continued to fly through the noise. With almost imperceptible adjustments the woman slowed the rotation of the ropes until he skimmed just above the audience's heads. Just when it seemed unthinkable that he could slow down any more without falling out of the air Saxon made one final, impossibly low pass and grabbed Alyssa's outstretched hand, lifting her smoothly with him. Alyssa knew it was Sorrel shrieking below.

'He chose!' bellowed Zorros and the audience roared its approval.

Alyssa looked down and almost gagged.

'Don't look down. Look ahead, or at least at me,' Saxon said. And when she turned to look at her captor's handsomely lined face with its dark violet eyes, he smiled widely and whispered across a link he sliced open in her mind. *Don't be scared.*

Then they were climbing into the highest reaches of

the tent. Alyssa was disorientated by the height and the fact that Saxon had slung her over his back like a sack of flour. She must be mistaken. Surely he had not spoken using a link? She must have imagined it in all the excitement.

Saxon plonked her next to his two strapping lads and then swung off towards a distant platform. *Trust me!* he called into her head.

She was not mistaken. Fox had linked with her. Goth was sitting in an inn five hundred steps away and this madman was using magic on her.

'Don't look down!' Oris, the eldest, repeated, steadying her as she swayed.

His brother Milt, who looked disarmingly like his father, squeezed her arm. 'He won't drop you. Just make your body go slack and look forward to wild applause.'

Alyssa's fear caught up with her. 'Are you all mad?'

Both boys laughed. Just like their father, she thought.

'We do this in every town. There's always one empty-headed victim like you who wants to fly. Just don't panic and he . . .' Oris pointed to Saxon, who was some way below them now and swinging furiously on his beam, '. . . will catch you.'

'Catch me?' Her voice had become squeaky. 'You're going to throw me to him?'

'What did you think we were going to do?' they said in unison, each grabbing one of her arms and jumping off their platform on a large swing.

Alyssa screamed her protest. Below, the audience echoed her terror. The drums were rolling loudly and she could smell the wax of the candles and soot from the sconces. She dangled from the boys' arms, feeling them

pulling her hard and forcing her body to swing to precisely
the right momentum.

'Get ready!' Milt called to her ominously.

Come, Alyssa, whispered Saxon oh so gently in her head.
Trust me, I've been sent to protect you.

Alyssa wondered in that sharply held second what he
meant but before she could reply Oris and Milt swung her
hard, upwards and outwards. They let go. Her body began
to spin into helpless somersaults and so she tumbled,
shrieking and plummeting to certain death she was sure.

Tor! She cast out wildly but the noise of the audience
lifted towards her, she felt strong arms plucking her from
the air and cradling her, then she and Saxon were swinging
back and then forwards together.

He was upside down, hanging onto his beam by bent
legs. She had no idea which way up she was but she looked
into his eyes and the terror stopped.

Who are you? she pressed into his mind.

I'm yours, he replied, deliberately vague. *Now take your
applause, my lady.*

Miraculously Alyssa found she had been lowered to the
ground and watched Saxon being pulled back upwards,
hanging now by his feet.

Curtsy for the people, he reminded as he drew away.

It was true, the crowd had gone wild. Even Sorrel was
on her feet and clapping. Alyssa curtsied but when she
looked up all she saw was Goth's ruined face twisted into
a scowl. He knew she had seen him so he licked his lips
deliberately. She felt a chill crawl across her body and all
the excitement shrivelled in her stomach.

She cast, no longer afraid of him scrying her out. *Goth's
here, Sorrel!*

Sorrel was careful not to whip her head around too quickly. *We'll be careful to get lost in the crowd. Calmly come back here now*, she said.

Alyssa nodded. As she turned to watch the family taking its applause, Saxon caught her look and winked, making her blush. In her embarrassment she did not notice the three people pushing into spaces behind Sorrel, eyeing Alyssa rather than the entertainment.

'Let's steal out now,' Alyssa whispered as she found Sorrel again.

'Once we're through the curtains put this on,' the old girl said, handing Alyssa a large shawl. It was drab and brown. 'Cover up as much of that dress as you can and hide your hair with this.' She gave Alyssa a thick leather thong and a bonnet.

'Where did you have all these hidden?'

'In my bag of tricks.' Sorrel patted the battered cloth bag she habitually carried. 'Now, let's go.'

Alyssa felt less nervous once her hair was safely hidden beneath the bonnet and the surprisingly large shawl was draped to disguise her yellow skirt. She stopped trying to glimpse that terrifying face and allowed herself to relax and walk amongst the crowd, even chatting to strangers about the evening's entertainment.

Sorrel too began to feel less threatened now that they were anonymous in the crowd. At the yell of 'Fire!' though she felt a claw of fear grab her. She turned to see the sumptuous awnings of the circus tent, just steps behind them, licked by flames. People began to scream and those still trooping out from the tent began to panic, and then they all began to run, shoving and trampling those in front. In seconds the southern entrance was ablaze and in the space of a heartbeat Alyssa's hand was torn from Sorrel's grip and the girl was pushed sideways in a surge of people.

Get to the inn! was all Sorrel could think to say across the link in the panic, though she realised that Alyssa's retreating back was being carried away from the town as people desperately tried to escape the fire which was eating its way ferociously towards the tent's peak and across its ropes. The crying of terrified animals joined the panicked screams of people. Sorrel saw a child fall; when she tried to grab the small girl she was pushed over herself. Feet trampled her.

Light preserve you, Alyssa was her last thought before something hit her head and she plunged into darkness.

Sorrel awoke groggy. She looked around and could not place where she was. It took a moment or two before she recognised the concerned face of Saxon Fox peering into hers.

'Welcome back,' he said gently. There was no bright grin on his face any more.

She sat up as quickly as her old bones would allow and was rewarded with pain. She winced.

'Easy, old woman. I'm Saxon Fox, from Cirq Zorros. What's left of it anyway.'

'I know who you are,' she croaked. 'Where's my granddaughter?'

'I hoped you'd tell me.'

She shook her head gingerly. 'We became separated in the panic. What happened?'

The performer sighed. 'Who knows? One minute we were taking our bows, the next the tent was on fire.' He shrugged in the distinctive manner which could belong to only one race of people.

'You're Kloek,' she said, now recognising the height, golden hair and light eyes so common to that race. Hearing the gentle brogue in his voice, she felt sure.

He looked offended. 'Of course. Which other race is this handsome?' It was an attempt at humour he did not feel. 'We've lost almost everything tonight. Many of our exotic animals perished. The tent is ashes, though our caravans are safe. A small generosity from the gods. Six of our troupe are dead.'

He stopped talking as Greta — the woman from the act — arrived with a tray of cups.

'Here, drink this.' She was angry, which, under the circumstances, Sorrel considered fair enough.

She took the cup. 'What is it?'

'It will soothe,' was all the woman said before turning and walking away.

Sorrel looked around. There were many people sitting or lying on the ground, dazed and confused. She could see one of the beautiful brangos lying dead, its body twisted and charred. She sipped the concoction and recognised the herb rimmis within the fiery liquid. It was the right choice and would help.

'Is that woman your wife?'

Saxon laughed harshly. 'No. She is my dead brother's wife.'

Sorrel sat up properly. 'She makes a good tea. I must leave to find Alyssa.'

'I will help you,' he said firmly.

'Why? You seem to have enough chaos here to deal with.' She looked hard at him. What was his interest in Alyssa?

'She is a beautiful girl . . . and she flies nicely,' he replied with no guile in his voice that she could detect. 'I am no use here for a while. Let me at least walk you back to your dwelling.'

'We don't live here, Master Fox. We are travellers. But you may walk me back to The Wheatsheaf. I would be grateful for the assistance.' Her head hurt horribly.

'I prefer Saxon,' he said, helping her to her feet.

At the inn, people were milling around in confusion. Fragglesham was in shock. Nine townsfolk had lost their lives in the fire as well as the six circus performers. Alyssa was not in the inn nor had anyone who might have recognised her seen her.

Sorrel noted that Goth was nowhere around either. That alarmed her most of all. She cast to Alyssa but there was nothing. It did not surprise her. Like most sentients, she could only communicate on a link if she was relatively close to the person she wanted to talk with – unless she was bonded, of course, as she was to Merkhud. She had never heard of anyone other than them casting over great distances.

She pulled the circus man aside. She would have to trust him.

'Saxon, are you familiar with Inquisitor Goth?'

The man spat through two fingers onto the ground. It was another peculiar habit of the Kloeks. 'Who isn't!'

'Well, he's in town and has shown more than a passing interest in Alyssa. This afternoon he contrived to . . . er . . . well, shall we say, compromise her.'

Saxon's violet eyes blazed and told his companion more than he wished. So, she thought, there is more to this than just helping a stranger find her family.

'You think he has her?'

It was her turn to shrug. 'Perhaps.' Sorrel could not allow herself to believe Alyssa had been killed in the panic, though that had already crossed her mind. But with no body as evidence she clung to the hope that her precious cargo was alive.

'Then I will find him. Stay here, old woman, I'm faster without you.'

'Find her! You must keep her safe,' she said harshly as the rimmis took its effect and her mind began to blur.

She did not hear Saxon mutter under his breath: 'That's what I've been sent to do.'

When the panic began and Alyssa was pulled from Sorrel she realised it was no use fighting against the tide of people. It was easier to run with them. She was shocked by the flames which jumped so rapidly, consuming the tent they had all been sitting under minutes ago. She heard Sorrel telling her to go to the inn but for now that was impossible. She would have to run to the safety of the fields surrounding Fragglesham first and then walk back around them into town. She slowed to a walk within the small group around her; although dazed they seemed to know in which direction they were heading.

She heard a single rider cantering up behind them. The four people she was walking alongside parted and stepped back to the side of the road. As they did so the rider came into view and stopped.

He looked down at her. 'Is this her?'

Alyssa's brow wrinkled as she tried to make sense of it. One of the men she had been walking with moments earlier stepped up and, before she could react, pulled her arms behind her back where a woman tied them together. Struggling, she yelled but they ignored her and addressed the rider instead.

'The money?'

The rider tossed a pouch of coins at the man who then turned to face her. 'Enjoy your night,' he said. His mirth was infectious for they were all laughing now.

She swung around to the woman she had been talking with. 'Help me . . .'

The woman smirked. 'She needs help, Fil.'

The man grabbed Alyssa by her waist and hoisted her up onto the horse behind the rider. Then they were moving fast as he whipped the horse into a gallop, riding not back towards Fragglesham Green but out into the darkness of the countryside.

It suddenly became clear to her. Alyssa knew that Goth would be waiting for her at the end of this journey.

'Welcome, my dear.' His voice made her feel ill. 'Thank you, Drell.'

The rider nodded and left. She listened to the sound of his horse disappearing, along with her only hope of escape. Alyssa felt the cold touch of despair and allowed it to consume her before she turned it into hate. Hate for this filth, who poured himself some wine as he contemplated what horror to visit on her for his pleasure.

He sipped, allowing the dry wine to roll around his deformed mouth. 'Come, drink with me. We have a long night ahead together. Why not make it enjoyable?' The mouth contorted into its hideous sneer.

She found her voice and was proud it did not sound thin. 'Is this the only way you can ever get to touch a woman, Goth – tie her up and force yourself on her?'

She surprised herself at how strong she felt. Her contempt was powerful. 'You pitiful, scarred wretch. Get on with it then and kill me or I will surely kill you for it.'

She watched the twisted flesh twitch and the eyes become black dots. Goth was confused. This was not how it was meant to be. Usually they snivelled and begged and then tried to be charming, hoping it would make it easier on them. That made him all the more cruel. He loved to see them terrified. And he did not like his sport being spoiled like this. So yes, he would rape her and then kill her, but not before hurting her and soaking up the agony in her eyes. Then, just to lay rest to any doubts about the depth of his hatred, he would hunt down the grandmother, who was probably scurrying around the smouldering town right now hopelessly searching for her beloved girl.

The firing of the circus had worked well. He loved fire. It had been an inspired piece of skullduggery. In one move he had singled out the girl and had devastated the circus-dwellers he despised so much. If he could kill every gypsy he would, but they were protected by the stupid ancient law of sanctuary.

He realised his mind was wandering and that she was smirking at his apparent hesitance. That would never do. She must die knowing fear, not triumph.

'As you wish, my sweet young thing. I shall certainly take my pleasure from your delicious, ripe little body. And if death is what you lust for rather than me, then you shall have it. It is the least I can do as thanks for your services.'

He put down his glass and was glad to see her flinch. 'And afterwards, Alyssa – that's your name, isn't it? Afterwards I shall torture and kill your beloved grandmother. I owe her some special thanks for her interruption this afternoon.'

He wanted to howl with laughter when he saw her resilience crumple. What a silly young fool she was to lock swords with him.

'Now let's get those peasant clothes off shall we, my dear?'

In two strides he was across the room, pulling a blade from his belt. He sliced through her blouse and everything beneath it, including her skin. Blood oozed from the wound. It was a surface cut but it hurt and he knew it. Alyssa bit down hard on her lip to prevent herself crying out loud and instead cried out silently across the link she opened to the one person she knew would hear it.

Leaving The Wheatsheaf, grim-faced and ready in his anger to tear the head from Goth's shoulders, Saxon Fox heard Alyssa scream into his head. It stopped him dead in his footsteps.

Where? he bellowed into the night, sweet relief at hearing her panicked voice mixed with dread.

While Goth expressed fake sympathy at the blood and stooped to lick the trickle between her breasts, Alyssa told Saxon, as best she could, how to find her.

Be quick, flying man, I'm as good as dead.

The searing pain as her captor bit into the soft flesh surrounding her nipple snapped the link shut and she forced herself to go in search of the Colours.

Tor had taught her how to do this. He could put himself

into a trance-like state, delving deeper into himself until the blinding Colours surrounded him. Though she had never achieved more than floating in a serene, sensual Green, Alyssa loved going there and she fled there now. She had to escape Goth. It was no use hurling her powers at him; he was protected by the scrying stone on his ring which deflected the magic back to the sender. Yet it seemed he had not been able to detect her powers. She did not understand it but now was not the time to ponder it. Instead she floated through the Green, praying that Saxon would reach her before Goth tired of her. She spared one last thought for Tor, wishing it had been him there to share the loss of her virginity.

Goth had become excited at the taste of her blood. He had thought to make a long night of teasing and torturing the girl but she had annoyed him and the blood-letting ensured he was lost to lust. His own desires allowed no further time for games. She was beautiful in her naked-ness though, he had to admit that.

He ripped off the band which tied her hair and let the golden locks fall every which way as he pushed her down onto the straw mattress.

'Now, my lovely,' he said, irritated beyond belief that he suddenly found her limp, with no fight to titillate him further. Her eyes were closed. He slapped her hard.

Somewhere in the Green Alyssa knew her body was being hurt but her senses were mercifully disconnected and she floated on, hoping for delivery one way or the other.

'Bitch!' He punched her hard in the stomach. He stood and kicked her repeatedly, his boots inflicting terrible blows. But the girl did not wince. She was as dead to him as if he'd choked the final breath from her. The violence Goth delivered made his body throb all the more with lust. He must do it now. Risk waiting a moment longer and he would lose that lust onto the grimy coverlets he had her slumped on.

He pulled off his clothes hurriedly, smiling as his badly burned chest was exposed. Women hated the sight of it. He wished this bitch had seen it too. The fire had not touched what throbbed between his legs though. He grabbed it now and slammed himself deep into the girl's body, hardly noticing the token resistance. He poured into his sexual frenzy the fury he felt at being robbed of her screams.

As Goth stole her virginity, the safe Green dissolved and Alyssa found herself staring at a scene.

There were two creatures − not quite men, not quite beasts − something strange in between. They were laughing. One was reaching into . . . what was it? A woodland? No, a brilliantly beautiful glade where exquisite flowers bent in a soft breath of wind and sunlight bathed their petals. She could almost smell their sweet fragrance. A brook, its waters catching on smoothed stones, sparked with light as it gurgled around the mighty trunk of a tree. And to one side there was a man and woman holding each other close. They were beautiful. One pale-skinned and flaxen-haired, the other darkly handsome.

One of the man-creatures was lifting something from the ground; as it pulled its hand back she could see it held a baby. She flinched. The baby squealed. Its pitiful cry tore into Alyssa's heart. The thieves were laughing and running away, the baby was shrieking.

She watched as shock registered on the couple's beautiful faces, but they did not give chase. Why not? Alyssa tried to run after the baby but her legs were pinned. She began to scream and scream and scream.

Ah, now that's more like it, thought Goth, pushing himself still further into the girl. Now she could really feel what a powerful man he was. He enjoyed hearing her calling out in fear like that. It excited him more.

Goth should have heard him. Instead, his first indication that someone else was there was when he was lifted off Alyssa and flung savagely against the wall. His body slumped there, weakly pumping its liquid as he wilted with shock.

Alyssa was back in the safe Green when she heard it, as though from a great distance — someone calling her. It was a voice she trusted; it belonged to the one who had been sent to protect her. She rushed towards the voice. She knew she would be safe if she could reach it.

Her eyes opened and she looked into the face of Saxon Fox, then saw the crumpled brute splayed against the wall. Saxon buried his head in her hair and held her tight as she shook with fright.

You're safe now, he spoke gently into her mind.

Saxon covered Alyssa with his cloak as she clumsily pulled herself to her feet. Confused, she watched Saxon pull a mask over his face then she backed away as the Inquisitor shook himself slowly to consciousness.

'I'm glad you're awake. I did so want you to see this,' Saxon said.

Goth had no time to protest. Saxon grabbed between the man's legs and a blade swung and blood spilled across the floor. Alyssa ran out of the hut, away from the chilling screams and the sight of what Saxon had done. She dragged in air with deep sucks as the evidence of the Inquisitor's lust slid down her legs.

Inside, Goth whimpered and drooled in a pool of his own blood. He was as good as dead, he was sure, but dared not spit out what had been stuffed into his mouth by the enraged madman towering above him. He could take a terrifying guess at what the soft bundle was. The only hope he held in his dimming, dying mind was that through the doorway he thought he glimpsed a distant, swinging lantern.

'Die slowly, Goth. May you rot in darkness eternal,' spat the stranger.

Saxon had also spotted the lantern. He made his escape without being seen, galloping the borrowed horse into the black of the woodland behind the hut before beginning the journey back towards town. Alyssa sat in front of Saxon, his long arms wrapped around her body. She was naked still, save for his cloak.

'Did you kill him?' she said aloud.

'Yes,' he answered, his voice flat. He could feel her trembling beneath the cloak. 'We must disappear tonight. You and your grandmother must travel with us.'

'She's not my grandmother.'

He kissed the back of her head. 'I know.'

'You killed him?' Sorrel's eyes blazed her shock. 'The gods preserve us . . .'

She had been frantic until their return and now paced the tiny room while Alyssa wrung her hands and Saxon maintained a stony silence.

Alyssa had washed herself as best she could behind a

screen while haltingly explaining to the old woman what had occurred. She felt herself failing now.

'This is why we must move ourselves as far from this town as possible,' Saxon finally said.

'To where, you fool?'

He flinched at Sorrel's fury.

Alyssa shushed her, speaking gently. 'Sorrel, we can't stay here. They will start looking for Goth's killer soon and who knows what might implicate us. My shawl was left behind, my shoes . . .'

She looking imploringly at Saxon, pleading with him to try again, unsure of whether she could stand a moment longer.

Saxon did try but was not gentle. 'Listen to me, old woman. Your only hope is to disappear into this night now. Knowing Zorros, he will be salvaging everything he can this very moment, with plans to head out as fast as he can move everyone.'

'It's you who committed murder, friend Fox. Not I and not this girl. We have nothing to be frightened of.' Sorrel hardly believed it herself.

Saxon spat. 'Then it's you who is the fool! If you won't save yourself, let me save Alyssa from his companions. They will track you down and they will hang or stone you both. And no magic will save her!'

Sorrel looked as though someone had punched the wind from her. She swung around on Alyssa, a look of genuine fear and disbelief on her face.

'I . . . I told him,' the girl admitted, covering Saxon for his indiscretion.

Alyssa didn't see it coming. Sorrel's hand slapped the side of her cheek so hard she stumbled and fell. 'Then you are more of a simpleton than he,' Sorrel whispered in a frail voice, all the fight gone from her suddenly.

Saxon was at Alyssa's side in one step. He picked the dazed girl up and lifted her into his arms.

His voice was cold with anger. 'We leave now. You can come with us or you can stay here but I'm taking her from this place.'

He turned and climbed nimbly through the window with Alyssa clinging weakly to his neck.

Sorrel watched as he ran sure-footed along the rooftop of the inn before disappearing behind another roof. She shook her head to clear it of the anxiety and fear. Alyssa, a critical piece of this frustrating jigsaw puzzle, had just been removed. How could it have happened so fast? Merkhud would kill her himself, she felt sure.

No, she must go with them, and whoever this strange Saxon Fox was, he was part of them now. He was privy to their secret.

It took her just a few minutes to gather their few belongings before paying the innkeeper. She fetched Kythay from the stable and let him carry her back to the smouldering ruin of the circus.

Even Goth had to marvel at his ability to thwart death, which had now made two visits and failed. As the rimmis drug was slow to perform he took another sniff of the krill pod to dull the pain. The physic, pale and perspiring, worked on his patient's mauled crotch. The man's voice shook from fear at the atrocity of the wound.

'You are fortunate, Inquisitor Goth . . . er, if that is possible under these circumstances. A while longer and we would not have been able to staunch the bleeding.

You will be weak for many days but you will live.'

The doctor nervously began to clear away his instruments.

'And my—'

'I can't save it,' the physic interrupted, his tension spilling over.

Being in the same room as this man was frightening enough. He was known to kill without conscience. Still, he was being paid well. All he needed to do now was to finish and leave swiftly; but his nervousness betrayed him.

'Your days of siring are over.' And then his nerves betrayed him and the frightened thoughts tumbled out before he could stop them. 'You'll have to squat like a woman to piss.'

Goth felt the fury course through his body. The bitch and her accomplice, whoever that strong bastard was, would pay for this. He would hunt them down and he would kill them. In spite of his weakness, he reached over and grabbed the sweating doctor by the throat, squeezing just hard enough to choke the breath from him.

'If you breathe a word of this to anyone I'll slice you into small pieces, after you've watched me slice open each member of your family and feed them to the town dogs. A handsome wife and two pretty daughters, I believe?'

The doctor stared into the mad black dots of his patient's eyes. He felt his bladder release as Goth let go of his throat.

'I have nothing to say to anyone, sir,' he croaked, hoping it was the right choice of words this time.

Goth's stare gave no quarter to the petrified man.

'Go now, doctor, and find yourself some fresh breeches. Is my man out there?' The rimmis was finally beginning to make him fade. He must hold on just a while longer. He saw the man nod tentatively. 'Send him in immediately. And remember your promise, for I am a man of my word.'

The physic fled. Moments later an Inquisitor appeared at Goth's side. It was Rhus. He bent low to hear his chief.

'Those people who brought me here . . .' The man nodded. 'Do you know who they are? How many?'

'Yes, Lord Goth. There are four who saved you. A family named Horris. The parents laid you out and the son was sent to fetch that physic. His baby sister remained here. They await your pleasure.'

No wasted words; he knew not to raise the Chief Inquisitor's ire.

Goth sighed with relief. 'Good man. Kill them all, including the doctor and his family. Do it now and let there be no trace.'

14

Saxon the Kloek

Sorrel could hear Alyssa's laughter coming from a small clearing near the camp. They had recently set up within the northern region of the Great Forest which stretched almost the length of the Kingdom.

She had been surprised when young Caerys had scuttled up to the cart they had hitched to Kythay and given the message to break for camp. Like most Tallinese she was respectful towards the Great Forest. It was said to be enchanted and although it did not terrify her – as it did many people – she had not felt comfortable at spending a night, perhaps more, here. It seemed the gypsies of Tallinor were oblivious to the long-held notion that the forest was a world unto itself.

Zorros had ambled back up the line of wagons, as comfortable as if they were unsaddling their horses outside a decent inn. Sorrel had decided to follow suit. The gods had protected her for too many centuries already to kill her off now, before her job was done. She had swallowed her disquiet. Now, with a stew gently simmering over a fire, she relaxed against an old tree and reflected on the past days.

When she had returned to Fragglesham Green on that terrible night it was already deserted and she could just see the swinging lanterns of the disappearing caravan of Cirq Zorros. She had cursed her luck and urged Kythay to hurry but he had characteristically refused to go faster than he chose himself and it had taken a long time to draw level with the wagon in which Alyssa sat huddled close to Saxon. Neither seemed surprised to see her.

Sorrel noticed Alyssa had a sickly pallor and her eyes were dimmed. At first she thought they had drugged the girl and felt a flare of her old anger towards Saxon, but before she could say anything he explained that Alyssa was ailing from the blows she had received from Goth. He was worried, especially as he knew Zorros had no intention of stopping the caravan but would travel through the night to get as far away from Fragglesham as possible.

Together they laid her down in the wagon and when Saxon picked up the reins again and they had some privacy, she stripped Alyssa. Even in the watery light of a trembling candle flame the sight of the girl's abused body was still a terrible shock. It had taken Sorrel several days of tireless care to bring her through the dangerous first stage of recovery. Her fevers were high, leaving her shaking and delirious, crying out in her fretful sleep.

Sorrel treated the worst cuts and put warmed poultices on the severely bruised areas. It took all of her knowledge of herbs to treat Alyssa's internal wounds and she had made her drink the black tonic to flush out Goth's hateful seed. Fortunately, the girl's bleed arrived not long after. That seemed to be a turning point and from then Alyssa had started to mend fast.

Sorrel noted that Alyssa's friendship with Saxon had also deepened. Saxon was not romancing the girl as Sorrel had originally presumed. Instead he seemed more a father figure. She was glad of him in their lives now and she enjoyed his intelligent, witty company as much as Alyssa did.

On Saxon's advice they had continued to travel with the circus to the far north-west. He suggested they stay with the caravan as long as possible before leaving its security to head further north still to Ildagarth.

Sorrel stirred the stew again. It was almost ready. She heard Alyssa's voice and looked to where she could see the girl squirming while Caerys demonstrated the rudiments of snake swallowing. She listened in on their chatter and smiled at Alyssa's squeal when her friend pulled a bright green snake from the hessian sack between them.

'Ooh, I hate this one – what's his name again?'

'This is Jinn. 'E's my favourite – as you well know – and 'e does 'is trick neatly and gives me no grief.'

Alyssa grimaced again.

Caerys continued. 'Now shall I go through it again and then you might want to 'ave a try,' he offered.

'Yes, please. All of that except the part about me having a try.' She giggled.

Sorrel knew Caerys was as much under Alyssa's charm as the rest of the younger men in the troupe. Who could blame them?

Caerys sighed. ''Ow will you ever learn this if you don't try?'

She gave him a murderous look and he capitulated.

'I've already cut the stinger out of Jinn 'ere 'cause 'e's more than capable of 'urting me. 'E does taste queer.

Draw'd the roof of my mouth the first few times. Rough sort of a taste and the scales scuff you a bit when you pull 'im back.'

'Ugh.' Alyssa shuddered. 'What do you mean?'

'Well, you see a snake will go into ever such a little 'ole and they are smooth one way but rough the other when you pull 'em back. Jinn's 'ead will go about this much down my throat . . .' he said, showing her the distance between thumb and first finger in the air, 'and the rest of 'im curls around like in my mouth. You've seen me 'old 'im by 'is tail but what you don't know is that I gives 'im a little pinch like this and that makes 'im go all the way in.'

He could see she was still puzzled.

'So why doesn't he just keep going down your throat?'

Caerys beamed. 'Clever Alyssa, you are! 'E would do that, 'e would! But I'm cleverer. I nip 'is tail with my nails like a pincer because 'is tail is slippery and I musn't let 'im go.'

He demonstrated. Alyssa felt queasy to witness it so close up. She thanked him but did not wait to watch him drag the hapless Jinn back out of his mouth. Instead she hurried to Sorrel by the fire and took over stirring the pot.

'That's some fine trick which Caerys can do with the snake,' Sorrel said, tossing seasoning into the stew.

'Oh, he is clever, that's for sure. You know he can swallow blades and knives too. I've even seen him swallow a sharpened sword.' Alyssa said it with pride.

Sorrel handed her their clay bowls. 'Is Saxon joining us?'

'No, he's eating with his family,' Alyssa said, ladling stew into each bowl and handing one to Sorrel.

'That woman's jealous of you, you know.'

Alyssa nodded quietly. 'Yes, I do know. I've heard her talk unkindly to him about me. He's very good to her and the boys since his brother was killed in the accident but she can be very hard on him.' Her voice trailed off.

Sorrel was pleased Alyssa was opening up a little for she was normally very guarded in her discussions about anything personal. Perhaps now might be a good time.

'You know, when you were sick and I sat with you day after awful day in that wagon, you called out someone's name time and again in your fevers.'

'Did I?' Alyssa seemed amused as she dipped a small hunk of bread in her gravy.

'Mmm, yes. You called him Tor. You kept begging him to talk to you.'

'I don't remember.' She answered the old girl cautiously.

Sorrel was determined to know more.

'Who is he?' She kept her voice light, trying to look more interested in her food.

'A friend.'

'Do you miss him, my girl?'

This time Alyssa paused for a stretch of time. 'More than he will ever know.'

'Will you tell me about him?'

'Some time I will.'

As Alyssa's large eyes rose to meet Sorrel's, Saxon strode into view and broke the awkwardness of the moment. He pulled a flask from his pockets and took a sip, then passed it to Sorrel who accepted. They began to talk quietly around the fire as night set in and the camp settled down.

'Zorros is headed for Ardeyran in the far north. You will need to farewell them at Bebberton on the edge of

Ildagarth. We'll do a show here and there, whenever he thinks it's safe. We need to earn enough funds to cover our food and that of the animals. No profit, just survival for now.'

Alyssa shifted to a more comfortable position to enjoy the fire. The nights certainly were cool now.

'How can Sorrel and I do our bit?'

'Well, I've been thinking about that. We can teach you a few tricks. I've been working on a new routine with the boys which was always going to require a fourth. Young Maze is not strong enough to handle it, but with some training I believe you can.' He continued quickly with his idea for Sorrel. 'Perhaps you could prepare some of your medications; teach some of the women about treatments and infections. I know Zorros would view this as a very special consideration on your part.'

Sorrel shrugged. 'It's the least I can do but I'm not sure about Alyssa joining the act, Saxon.'

Alyssa refused to be spoken about as though she was a child or, worse, not there. 'I think I should, Sorrel, if just for the protection these people are giving me. I can do it. Saxon will be there and I'm not scared by it at all.'

If anything Alyssa felt elated that he had included her in his plans. 'How does Greta feel about this?'

'She has no choice,' he replied evenly. 'Good, I'm glad that's settled. Tomorrow we begin your training.'

Sorrel opted to leave well alone. She knew Alyssa could always fall back on her power if Saxon's stunts proved too challenging, but in a society which had experienced centuries of persecution towards the Power Arts she still felt daunted by Alyssa's casual use of it. She drifted into a restless sleep, knowing she would have to tell Merkhud the latest turn of events but that it could wait until tomorrow.

Safe in the Great Forest the circus folk were in no hurry to leave.

'Count, damn you! Don't jump on five, jump on the sixth beat.' Saxon's voice boomed. They had agreed to speak out loud in front of the Fox family.

'I thought you meant me to go on five,' Alyssa hurled back angrily as she stood between an amused Milt and Oris, balancing on their linked arms.

Saxon took a calming breath. 'No. Five. Then jump.'

She did as she was told.

'That was a fine jump, Alyssa,' Milt offered.

Saxon snorted. Anything Alyssa did was fine by Milt. 'It was hopeless. She has to nail it over and over and over or it could cost her life. Do it again!'

'Saxon, I've had enough for today.' She tried hard to keep the anger from her voice this time.

'You'll keep doing it until I – not love-struck Milt – tell you it's fine.' He turned his back, ashamed that he had hit out at harmless Milt who had reddened instantly.

Oris whispered close to her ear. 'It's not worth arguing. He always wins. He's just like our father was.'

This last he said wistfully and when Alyssa looked into his eyes she saw his sadness. She missed a father too.

'Let's try again,' she said, bending her knees slightly as their arms slackened to create a bouncing platform.

After a count of five, the boys threw her upwards; in that same moment she somersaulted but landed badly on Saxon's back, misjudging his shoulders.

This time he swung around, rage in his face, hands clenched into huge fists. She had seen that bleak look before and she knew the person on the receiving end of it had been left broken . . . dead.

'For Light's sake, Alyssa! You have to land on my shoulders *every* time, not once every now and then. I can't see you so I can't catch you. You need to make this jump on your own.' His eyes glittered with unspent anger.

She slid down to the ground, past anger herself, perplexed at his hostility.

She opened the link. *I don't want to do this any more.*

'Go back and repeat it,' he said aloud, challenging her to disobey him. The forest fell silent whilst the two of them eyed each other like predators.

Alyssa, seething, capitulated and clambered back onto the arms of the patient boys. She would show him.

This time when she jumped she closed her eyes and let go with just a small push of her power, feeling where Saxon was. As she somersaulted high she relinquished all fear and trusted her senses.

Sorrel felt the thrum of magic as she bent to pick some scaffer leaves and Saxon felt it too, as he stood with his back turned, waiting for the girl's feet to thump into his shoulders.

When they did he reached quickly behind to grab her ankles and prevent her falling backwards, although he knew this time she would not fall. The two boys were cheering and whistling and some of the others who had gathered to watch grinned and clapped, wondering what the fuss was about.

Saxon was pleased and Alyssa could sense the silent praise which he played right down when he spoke. 'Now that was good. Soon you will be able to land this jump from anywhere at any time, blindfolded if necessary.'

The four of them continued to practise to Saxon's precise instructions over the next two days, until Zorros remarked that the caravan would be moving on the next evening. They would aim to give their first performance at Shockleton Marsh two nights hence.

When the caravan did move on Sorrel travelled with Greta for a change. Alyssa and Saxon found themselves alone for the first time in the weeks since he had dealt with Goth. They travelled in comfortable silence for an hour or so before Saxon broke it.

'Sorrel keeps a close eye on you.'

Alyssa laughed and he realised how much he loved the way her nose wrinkled when she did so and just how beautiful this girl was.

'She does. I think she thought you had designs on me.'

It was his turn to smile. 'I do. But not in the way she suspected.'

Alyssa was not sure whether she was relieved or disappointed by his remark. He was a most handsome man and there was certainly a curious intimacy to their relationship. She loved to be close to him and he could make her laugh, make her furious, make her cry. Most of all he made her feel safe. It was frightening to realise they must part soon and then she and Sorrel would be alone again, making their way to Ildagarth.

She shifted closer and felt his warmth through her own shirt. 'I wish I knew what you mean by that, Saxon. We've never talked about why we're here together. Tell me.' There was a plea in her voice he could not ignore.

'I will tell you what I know.'

Holding her breath, she focused on Kythay's ears which were flicking backwards and forwards as he plodded alongside their wagon. The caravan was moving steadily but not fast and she allowed Saxon's now soft voice to enter her head as he linked with her and began his tale.

He had been born to a carpenter father and a mother who took in washing from surrounding towns. Theirs, Hertsey, was in the central southern area of the Kingdom and the family, though hardly more than 'comfortable', lived happily there.

The two boys, although born in Tallinor, were not allowed to forget their Kloek heritage. The tiny island's culture was taught to them by their father of an evening as he sat by the fire, smoking a hand-carved pipe and rocking gently in a chair of his own design. He had come to Tallinor as a child with his family who, despite their desire to escape the poverty on their ancestral island, was rich in the Kloekish traditions.

Saxon and his brother, Lute, older by one summer, were close. They argued and fought like any brothers but disagreements were swiftly forgotten. According to Saxon, Lute showed an early talent for tumbling and was spotted by visiting gypsies. Word somehow got back to Cirq Zorros and he was offered a decent wage to join a new troupe of acrobats.

It was no surprise – though still heartbreaking for their parents – when Saxon, seemingly incapable of happiness without his elder brother, joined up also. He was not as supple as Lute but possessed more daring and dash; always prepared to try out ever-more dangerous stunts to impress audiences.

The two very quickly established themselves as more

than handy discoveries and when Lute met Greta, and married her soon after, it seemed a small miracle that she too was impressively supple, fast and daring. Lute and Saxon taught her all they had learned and when they were blessed with five children in the marriage, including the twins, these too were taught the skills and the Flying Foxes rapidly found fame wherever the circus travelled.

What happened to Lute?

It was the first time Alyssa had interrupted Saxon's quiet narration.

He died. There was pain in his voice.

An accident?

No. No accident. It was destined to happen but could have been avoided if his brother had not insisted on taking such risks. The wound was gaping in his raw voice.

She hated pressing him but somehow this seemed important. *Tell me.*

Saxon was silent for a long time. When the silence became uncomfortable Alyssa resisted the urge to fidget or speak; she stole a glance at him and saw he was struggling with tears.

It was a piece I called Flight. Very dangerous. Lute was a brilliant flyer and tumbler. He was so skilled he could find my arms, my legs, my shoulders anywhere it seemed. I was always the better balancer. He made me do the more spectacular acts on the high wire because of this.

Flight combined both our skills but it needed us to be so perfectly in tune that if I were to stand a hair's breadth away from where he expected, or Lute were to over-jump minutely, it spelt serious injury . . . or, as it turned out, death.

Alyssa let his pain consume her and shared his tears.

He continued. *We had practised it so many times but Lute never wanted to perform it because the risk was too high and so we let it lie.*

But one summer's night we were honoured by the presence of King Lorys and Queen Nyria. The whole circus was abuzz at their unexpected attendance. Cirq Zorros had been performing in Tal for three moons — such was our popularity — but this was the first time the royals had joined the audience.

And so you thought you'd put on something spectacular for them, she concluded.

Exactly. Lute refused, as he always did, and I persisted, as was my way, until he relented. He gave a brittle smile and shrugged.

He waited until we had almost completed our act, so strong was his reluctance. Zorros was already striding out into the arena to join the applause for the Foxes and to announce the next act. To this day I don't know why Lute suddenly gave in and stuck his thumb in the air.

Alyssa felt as though she did not need to hear any more but the floodgates had been opened and Saxon was going to finish this story.

I was still on the high wire. Greta realised what Lute had signalled and was screaming at us from the ground not to do it. I clearly remember my brother smiling at me from all that way up. It was the gentlest, most affectionate grin and I loved him so much for allowing me to show off this trick to the King and Queen. We took off the red bandanas we used to wear in those days and, just before we tied them around our eyes, he mouthed 'Don't miss me, little brother, or you'll miss me very much'. I laughed at him for we had become clever at lip-reading over the years.

Alyssa wondered if this was the first time he had ever

recalled this reckless event other than in his own painful thoughts. She took his hand as he spoke.

Lute had begun to swing. Even blindfolded I knew this because the drums had started a roll. I think we all knew as soon as he let go that it was going wrong. I yelled out so loud to him and yet, despite the noise of the audience and my own voice, the sound of the sickening thump his body made as it crashed to the ground will never leave me. He missed by . . . well, a hair's breadth, so close were we to doing it perfectly. One of his legs caught my shoulder and I toppled together with him and down upon him.

They were both crying freely now.

The gods showed a small kindness. There was no pain or suffering. He was dead the moment he hit the ground.

His voice fell silent in her head and his hands dropped from the reins. Still the horse and Kythay kept plodding forward. Alyssa reacted instinctively, reaching her arms around his wide body and hugging him fiercely. She stroked his hair, amazed at how soft it was, and then found herself gently kissing his stubbled cheek which was damp from tears. Without knowing why she did it, Alyssa turned his face and kissed him tenderly on the lips.

She sensed his surprise but when he did not immediately pull away she could not help herself and added the passion and grief and loss she felt for him.

Gently, ever so gently, he cupped her face in his large hands and pushed her lips away from his. With a great sadness in his handsome face, which she intuitively knew was nothing to do with his brother, he shook his head.

No, my lovely Alyssa. I am not the one, he whispered.

Alyssa felt as though she had been slapped.

Sensing she was on the brink of a rush of embarrassed, angry words, Saxon closed the link and put his fingers to the lips he could still taste.

He spoke aloud but softly. 'I love you, Alyssa, but I am not allowed to love you in the way that you would like me to just now. There is another. He will come to you one day and you will know he is the right one.' Saxon's voice was steady and firm.

She brushed her hand across her mouth to wipe away his kiss. She felt juvenile and inadequate.

Saxon could sense this. 'There is more to my tale, Alyssa. May I finish the story?'

When she looked down and said nothing, he continued.

He explained how, from a very young age, he had experienced a recurring dream about a particular woman. Even though he never saw her, he knew she was very beautiful because her voice was like a crystal-clear brook, her fragrance like a spring meadow. She visited him frequently through his life and it was she who told him to follow Lute even though his inclination was to remain and continue in his father's trade. He admitted he could not remember a time when the lady had not been in his life, telling him in his dreams about a curious group of ten people known as the Paladin. They were protectors, guardians; chosen from the most ancient people of Tallinor.

'Who did they protect?' Alyssa asked, fascinated now.

'They guarded a dangerous prisoner. They protected the people he wanted to hurt.'

Alyssa frowned. 'And why did this speaker of dreams tell you all this?'

'Because I am one of them,' he said, a faraway look

drifting across his face. Even his voice sounded clouded.

He shook himself and continued with his story, explaining how after Lute's death the dream woman had insisted he remain with the circus and take on responsibility for Greta and her children.

'And you just did as she said?'

'I had no reason not to, and nowhere else to go, Alyssa. Greta was newly widowed with five young children to care for. I felt responsible for Lute's death. They had no act without me; even with me it was nothing special, but we worked hard on it. The boys especially gave everything after their father's death and in a year or two we had a popular act again. Better perhaps than the original because I refused to take any risks and so we relied on theatre in our pieces.'

'Go on,' she said.

'Well . . . that was it for several years. We travelled extensively around the Kingdom, performing and turning ourselves into a family. I became a father to the children—'

'But never a husband to Greta?' She hated the jealousy in her question.

He flashed a smile and rubbed at his chin, self-consciously. 'Once. But it didn't feel right.'

Alyssa felt a snarl of anger. So she had been correct. There was more to Greta's hostility than just having another couple of mouths to feed.

Saxon hurriedly pressed on. 'We decided just to live alongside one another and not try to pretend anything. I admire and respect Greta and love the children and that's how it should be. I will always consider this family my own.'

'Well, hurry up and get to the bit that matters, Saxon. I'm no longer interested in who you have lain with.'

'Are you not?' The wicked glint had returned to his eye.

'No! Tell me the rest or just stop talking.'

His brows knitted as he told the final part of his story.

'I can pass over all those intervening years to just recently when we were approaching Fragglesham. I began to have the dreams again, each night rather than just now and then. I have never seen this woman, you must understand, but she has travelled with me since I was a young lad so I trust her totally.'

He was looking intently at her now. Alyssa felt the hair rise on the back of her neck.

'Her name is Lys. In all the years she has roamed my dreams, she has mentioned a young woman whom I was to look out for. I had heard it so often and for so long I had begun to stop paying any attention to it. She said this person was critical to the land's future – I never understood it.'

Alyssa wanted to stop him talking. Stop his voice and stop where this conversation was heading. It was no longer fascinating; it had become frightening. But he wouldn't stop. Saxon's voice continued slowly as the wagon rocked gently forwards in the night.

'Just before we entered Fragglesham she appeared brighter, for want of a better word, in my dreams. I could almost swear I dreamed of nothing else but her and you, Alyssa. She told me you were close, that this meeting was what my whole life had been heading towards.'

'Stop! Don't say any more, Saxon. I don't want to hear this.'

Alyssa moved as if to jump down from the wagon but he grabbed her and linked.

You will hear this because you must and you will not turn away from your destiny, as I haven't turned from mine.

You're frightening me yet you say you love me.

I do love you, Alyssa. And you must trust me.

She sat back down on the wooden plank.

There is not much more, he said, picking up the reins again — not that their horse or Kythay needed anything more than the wagon in front to follow.

In the early hours of the day of the fire, just as I was stirring, she came to me. As usual I could not see her but her perfume was stronger than ever and her voice clear, as though she was lying beside me.

Lys said that you would enter my life that night and I would know you immediately. Somehow, in that strange world between asleep and awake, she exacted my promise that I would protect you . . . with my life if necessary. I am one of the Paladin, she reminded me.

He stopped talking and Alyssa took a much-needed deep breath. What in Light's name did this mean?

And did you know me, Saxon? I mean immediately?

The instant I walked into the arena and glanced around the audience. There you were: your cheeks flushed with excitement, your hair shimmering, that yellow dress. I knew who you were and I felt at peace that I had found you at last.

He shrugged again as if to say, the rest you know.

They said nothing for some time.

Finally she spoke. *Did you know about Goth?*

No.

She shook her head. *Well, what are you supposed to protect me from . . . apart from him? I mean, you cannot expect me*

*just to accept that your life has been dedicated to waiting for me
. . . surely?*

But it has . . . and you must accept.

Alyssa felt her anger rising. Was he being deliberately
obtuse? Up ahead they could see a few of the others
jumping off their wagons to walk alongside them and
stretch their legs. It would be barely a minute or two
before someone sauntered up to their wagon.

Is there anything else you think I should know? she asked
quickly.

He squeezed her hand affectionately. *You now know everything I do. From here on I have no idea what to expect or what
is expected of me.*

He turned to the sword swallower who had dropped
back to their wagon. 'Ho, Caerys, why don't you take over
here for a while? I should check on my family.'

Saxon hopped neatly off the wagon and strode ahead.
Alyssa covered her confusion at the complex tale she had
just heard and the rush of jealousy towards Greta by
smiling sweetly at Caerys, who seemed overjoyed to be
riding next to her.

How do you fare, friend Nanak? Merkhud asked across the
link.

*I fare well, Merkhud. You sound almost jolly for someone
who carries such an enormous burden,* ventured the Keeper.

I am very, very happy today.

*Will you share your glee, Merkhud? The Light knows we
could use some gladness in this forsaken place.* He sounded
tired.

Merkhud brought news of such import he knew it
would send Nanak's spirits soaring. It was everything the

Keeper of the Paladin had given his life to hear.

Nanak, he said gravely, *Saxon has shown himself!*

Don't toy with me, growled the normally quiet voice.

I jest not, my friend. I promise you, Saxon has emerged.

Tell me, the Keeper whispered in awe.

Saxon the Kloek — to us, the Sixth — is now Alyssa's travelling companion. You need not know the details; only that he has been reborn and is with her.

Saxon . . . Nanak wanted to repeat the name over and over. The brave, mighty Kloek who had withstood the pain so long; withstood the onslaught of Orlac's whisperings and powers over decades . . . only to fall.

Merkhud gave him silence for a while. He knew what this meant to the Keeper.

Then he said, *Saxon is in a circus. Apparently he's very good.*

It was the first time, Merkhud thought, he had ever heard Nanak laugh. It was a lovely sound. He prayed he would hear it again someday.

They're coming back, Nanak. All of them — I promise you this. I understand it now. They flee Orlac to surround those who will save us. You must hold strong. Beg, cajole, command that Figgis and Themesius and especially Arabella hold for me. I have work to do yet; I must have the time to shape this plan.

I will give you that time, Merkhud. We all will. And promise me — you will speak to this falcon they call Cloot and you will tell him that Nanak is proud of him. Tell him the Paladin are proud of him.

But, Nanak, he does not speak. He has shown no sign of any power.

*Say the words to him, Merkhud. He will understand if he
is Cloot of the Paladin.*

The link closed but this time with a sense of true hope
for the first time in several centuries of despair.

15

Goth's Revenge

It was two moons before Cirq Zorros arrived at Bebberton on the fringe of the famed city of Ildagarth. It had been a happy and uneventful journey; they had performed in some of the smaller towns and enjoyed a new level of success wherever they appeared. The shock of the fire was not fully behind the troupe but the healing had begun and the spirits of all were lifting. Word of their losses had spread around the Kingdom swiftly and audiences had been generous.

Zorros was convinced that the circus would be able to replace some of its precious animals by Newleaf and he had already commissioned new canvases and awnings to be created, such was his optimism. Everyone was thrilled when the Mayor of Ildagarth welcomed the circus and insisted it must stay as long as it pleased – at the city's expense – in the area known as the Crook, a beautiful meadow barely an hour's journey from the city centre. This was an unheard-of generosity.

The Mayor presented the circus with a letter from King Lorys himself, who had been made aware of the tragedy at Fragglesham and was adding his own personal welcome to Ildagarth.

Saxon was astonished by all the goodwill. 'He's a good man,' he said of the King.

'Oh, you've met him?' Alyssa teased. Her comment even brought a brief smile to Greta's normally pinched expression.

'No. But I know it. I've seen him, watched him. He cares about his people and this proves it.'

They were watching Zorros make formal acceptance of the King's letter. People had turned out to cheer them and they were forced to shout over the applause.

'I'd consider him a far better King if he'd stop persecuting people,' Alyssa yelled.

Some of the others nodded. 'He could so easily overturn the ancient law which allows people like Goth to rampage anywhere they want in the Kingdom, maiming and killing anyone he thinks doesn't fit into his idea of society. There has been no sanctuary offered for such people.' More people nodded. Alyssa continued. 'If Goth and his thugs decide your family's talent on the high wire is magically inspired, he could hide behind that law and disband you at best and kill you if he pleased. Is that a good King who allows this?'

Alyssa knew she should stop. Sorrel had touched her arm in a gesture meant to prevent her saying any more so she was relieved when Saxon backed down.

'Well, you're right of course. I don't understand that law.' He switched to the link. *Hopefully, with Goth dead, his troop of cowards may be disbanded.*

Then I would think highly of our King. She smiled to let him know she held no grudge but added: *Until then; I despise him.*

Alyssa's mood was low. The moment she had been dreading had arrived: she just did not know how to say farewell to Saxon and the circus she had called home these past months. Sorrel had explained they would part company with Cirq Zorros this morning. Their final destination at Caremboche was just a half day's walk from Ildagarth but it might as well have been an eternity away for Alyssa. Even if the circus stayed in the city for many weeks, she knew this was probably the last time she would be close to Saxon.

'Well, my girl,' Sorrel said matter of factly, breaking into her cloudy thoughts, 'we must continue our journey now. Better not prolong our farewells.'

Sorrel beamed at those around her and began her goodbyes; hugging those she had come to know well and thanking others for their kindness. Alyssa felt sick. She followed Sorrel, trying to put on a brave face. She could see their few belongings piled on Kythay's back. He was flicking his ears, anxious to leave the noise and smells of Bebberton.

People hugged her and even Caerys finally plucked up the courage to kiss her. She didn't have to look to know where Saxon was. Alongside Greta was where she knew he would be; standing at the back of the crowd, grinning his wide smile, encouraging her to be brave.

Then it was the turn of the Fox family. They all stood quietly, facing one another, not knowing quite what to say. Alyssa was sure that if she had to look Saxon square in the eyes she'd lose her little remaining composure.

'Goodbye, Oris.' She gave him a tight squeeze. Milt bent to take his hug but she impulsively kissed his cheek. 'Thank you, Milt, for being so good to me.' She was surprised he did not seem as overwhelmed as she felt at this moment, particularly as she knew he carried a torch for her. He grinned shyly.

Sorrel and Alyssa gave the younger children bear hugs and made them squeal and then thanked Greta genuinely for her various kindnesses to them at a time when they had no other place to turn. Alyssa hugged her warmly, despite her misgivings, and again was surprised at the almost smug manner in which Greta accepted their parting.

Finally, there was only one person left to thank.

She could not help herself. Raising her eyes she looked at Saxon, wanting to hate him for the broad grin and his insensitivity to how hard this was for her. She shielded, refusing to allow him to enter her head.

Sorrel spoke to him instead. 'Saxon, you've been our saviour. Alyssa and I—'

'Don't.' He stopped her with a hand in the air. 'No need.'

He bent low and picked up the little old woman in his hug, making her shriek and beg to be put down. It melted Alyssa's resolve and she despised her eyes for betraying her as they loosed their tears. By the time he had turned to her she was sobbing.

'By the Light, girl . . . what's all this?'

'Come on now, Alyssa. A quick farewell is the best sort,' Sorrel grumbled, making tracks towards Kythay.

Saxon watched Sorrel push by and looked back at Alyssa.

'Why are you crying?' he asked her.

She could not help but notice Greta's smirk. She cleared her throat and started to follow Sorrel. 'I'm just sad, that's all. I'll miss you all very much.'

She hurried to Kythay and helped the old woman to climb on the donkey. She could do this, she knew she could. She was already moving Kythay forwards when she chanced her luck by turning back to wave once more. He was still smiling broadly; tall and handsome, his eyes blazing mirth. She tore her gaze from him and flashed a fake grin at the others.

But he called out, 'What, no hug for me?' and clasped his hands to his big chest theatrically. His family burst into laughter.

This was the final straw for Alyssa. She dropped Kythay's rein, ran back towards Saxon's outstretched arms and began punching him. She tried her hardest to hurt him but, laughing, he quickly tied her in knots, pinning her arms behind her. There he kept her until her fury was spent and she stopped struggling. She was breathing hard, tears coursing down her cheeks.

He put his mouth close to her ear. 'I'm coming with you,' he whispered, then let her go.

She spun around. 'What?'

'You heard. I've been sent – remember?'

Alyssa heard his words but it was as though she could not understand their meaning. It was dear Caerys who shook her to her senses.

'It's true. 'E's given up 'is position at the circus. 'E says 'e 'as to stay wi' you.'

Now everyone was laughing. Sorrel heaved herself back down off Kythay to find out what the delay was. She hoped like fury that Saxon was not suggesting he go with them. She looked at Saxon then back at Alyssa and did not need an explanation to work out what had passed.

'He says he's coming with us,' Alyssa said, still full of disbelief.

'With your permission, Sorrel?' Saxon looked at her but she knew that couched behind the polite words was something far from a request. He was simply paying her the courtesy.

'Well, Saxon, this is a shock. We are going to Caremboche and I have no idea what the situation will be there for us, let alone for a male companion. Um . . . I'm not sure we can—'

'Let's worry about that later. May I accompany you to its gates at least?'

Sorrel's eyes narrowed. 'You know of Caremboche?'

'Yes. Anyone who has travelled this Kingdom as widely as I has heard of its stories, its legend.'

All her old anxieties about his intentions resurfaced. It was Alyssa, though, who raised the most obvious objection.

'But what about Greta and the children? You can't possibly leave them.'

'We don't need him,' Greta chipped in, not unkindly. 'We have someone who will take care of us.'

She grinned mischievously. Alyssa had not thought she had such playfulness in her.

'I don't understand any of this!' she cried.

Caerys couldn't help himself. 'Greta's marrying Zorros. 'E's loved 'er for ever!'

'It's true,' Greta confirmed when she saw the disbelief in Alyssa's face. 'He has loved me for many years but I've always refused his affections, clinging too tightly to memories of a dead man.' She sighed.

'But the children need a man in their lives and it's not

fair to make Saxon live his brother's responsibilities. Lute made his own decision; he knew the risk and took it. We lost him. No one is to blame. At last Saxon has found what he wants in his life – can't say I blame him, you're very beautiful – and I've decided to give in to Zorros and his romantic notions about us. The children adore him so I know that part of the arrangement will work well.'

Alyssa could hardly believe the gorgeous smile which suddenly lit Greta's face.

'But what about the act?'

'With the circus owner for a husband, who needs to perform anywhere but between the sheets?' Greta winked. 'Milt and Oris may want to continue but the little ones will live a life outside of the arena if I have my way.'

Zorros had arrived. He put his arm around his wife-to-be. 'I gather you've been told. Are you not going to offer us congratulations?'

'Of course!' Alyssa said, still wondering when the dream would end and she would wake up walking next to a donkey and an old woman along a lonely road bound for a strange sanctuary.

They covered the few miles to Caremboche quicker than they had expected. Sorrel rode Kythay whilst Saxon and Alyssa walked briskly beside her. The time passed uneventfully and it was a beautiful journey as they could see one of the fingers of the Great Forest in the distance.

Sorrel had decided to accept Saxon's presence. From his travels he must already know that this was not a place for men but something could be worked out, she was sure. Thinking about it during the ride, she realised his companionship could actually be a blessing. Alyssa was clearly thrilled that he was still with them, which boded well for the difficult adjustments which might need to be made to fit into life at the Academie.

Sorrel had explained to Alyssa that it was a place of sanctuary and would bring them complete security for a while. If she enjoyed her time there, she might like to become an acolyte. This decision would be left entirely to Alyssa. She had been told of the archalyt disc and what it meant to accept it. The girl was bright. She understood and had even said solemnly that she would consider such a future once she had lived it for a while. For now the Academie meant rest and recuperation. They had been on the road for a long time. Sorrel knew too that the solitude of the Academie would suit Alyssa. But, more than this, there was friendship awaiting her there. Girls of her own age would probably welcome her warmly and perhaps Alyssa could start to build the new life she talked about.

Walls appeared along the side of the road with orchards spreading behind them. They had arrived on the outskirts of the Academie.

Kythay obligingly halted for Sorrel to speak. 'All right now, the gates are not far from here. What say I go on ahead and make our introductions? You can follow later, when your shadows lengthen before you.'

It was not a request; they both nodded at Sorrel who gave Kythay a gentle prod with her foot to speed him on. For one of the rare times in his life he obeyed her and was soon kicking up dust.

They moved to the hedgerow. It had been a mild day and their dusty walk from Ildagarth had brought a light sheen to their faces. Alyssa wiped a kerchief across her forehead and looked around her.

'Do you think they'd mind if we took some of those plums?' She was already climbing over the stile nearby.

'Would it matter if they did?' replied Saxon, amused. He followed her.

'You'll miss them dreadfully won't you, Saxon?' she asked, finally saying out loud what had been gnawing at her.

He chewed on a plum, the juices running down his chin and into its slight cleft.

'The family? Yes. But Greta has made a wise decision and Zorros loves her, that's for sure. He will take excellent care of them, particularly the youngsters. It's true, they really don't need their dead father's brother hanging around.'

'Oh, don't. I'm sure you're more memorable than that,' she said, throwing a plum stone in his direction.

'Aye, perhaps. I do worry about the older lads though. Milt and Oris are at that awkward age and they need a firm hand, a father's time and wisdom. I wonder if Zorros will provide that.' He shook his head. 'I had to threaten them with a whipping if they tried to follow us.'

Alyssa was taken aback. 'They wouldn't, would they?'

'No doubt at all.' He laughed briefly. 'Either that or die of broken hearts at being separated from the lovely Alyssa.'

She smiled sadly. 'But how would they follow us?'

'Love can be a cruel master, Alyssa. They would not hesitate to steal a cart and follow our trail. They even know roughly where Caremboche is from previous travels.'

Alyssa did not want to think any more about the boys and their loss of the man they loved as their father. 'Shall we go?' she said.

'Er . . . let me go first, Alyssa.'

'No! Why? We go together.'

'Oh, call it an old man's hunch. I'll just check all is well before you arrive. I won't take long, I promise, just enough to look around first. You can pick some more fruit,' he suggested hopefully.

Her eyes narrowed. 'Has your friend Lys warned you of something?' She felt the first tingle of fear creeping up her spine.

'No, not exactly. Just something she mentioned has made me cautious, that's all. It's nothing, Alyssa, really. But I feel safer taking the precaution, that's all.' He stood.

'All right but I'm already counting,' she said, beginning to count aloud as he broke into a run.

She stood and walked slowly to the edge of the orchard. A long, high wall ran well into the distance, as far as her eye could see, down the length of the orchard and beyond. It was built from the same pinkish stone and she presumed it must enclose the Academie.

Sorrel had not divulged much about the Academie; probably because Alyssa had not shown much interest. All she cared was that it provided the haven Sorrel had promised. There was the question of taking the archalyt disc. The way Alyssa felt today she could do it, even though it meant giving up all hope of a man. There was only one man for her and he was no longer in her life. She loved the idea of the chance to study, to learn more about her abilities. Sorrel said there was a fine and expansive library at the Academie with archives of ancient parchments and books. That excited Alyssa. She could lose herself there and hopefully bury Tor's memory amongst the dusty tomes.

Looking along the line of pink stone, Alyssa worked out that she could save herself a longer walk if she cut across the meadow and climbed the wall. Had she waited long enough yet? No. She had to keep her promise to Saxon. To pass a few more minutes, she climbed a nearby pear tree and began selecting fruit. If she had not withdrawn into herself so much, enjoying the peaceful surrounds and even begun humming absent-mindedly, she might have caught the sound of distant horses.

Putting three pears into various pockets she set off, happy that she had given Saxon long enough to check all was safe. What was he afraid of? Goth was dead. He had been her only threat, surely? Alyssa refused to spook herself any further. She dismissed her own fears and strode on for half a mile towards the part of the wall which was relatively near to the roadside.

There was a huge tree on the orchard side. That would do perfectly to scale the wall. Sorrel would be furious with her for such an entrance. As she reached the wall, she could hear men's voices. She assumed they must be men from the village or perhaps orchard workers. Lifting the cotton skirt which Sorrel had insisted she wear, she began to climb the tree. It was easy. Just like the old days at home with Tor.

Alyssa found herself in unbearably happy spirits. This was a new beginning for her and Sorrel. Finally a place to settle down and she had Saxon with her still. Hopefully he might be permitted to live close by or work for the Academie. She felt carefree for the first time in ages and almost released from Tor's pull. He flitted through her mind less often now and the pain had dulled to a hard, shiny stone — as she liked to think of it — in her heart.

She had decided some time ago to lock it away and only examine it from time to time. Those times were getting further and further apart; she had even given up her infrequent castings to Tor. All she met anyway was the thick, bleak, disappointing void.

With some effort she hauled herself up onto the top of the high wall. She swayed with dizzy disbelief at the scene below. She was looking into a large courtyard. There were horses and men with purple sashes across their chests — at least ten of them. In one heart-stopping glance she took all this in, including the women who were watching fearfully from the parapet above, on the safe side of the Academie. Sorrel was with them; Alyssa could see her bleak expression.

And there in the centre of the courtyard, forced to his knees, with blood running from various wounds and matting his golden hair, was Saxon. His clothes were torn as was his beautiful body. The men were beating him with clubs but he refused to fall fully to the ground.

Alyssa's scream echoed shrilly around the yard. When Saxon dragged his head up to look at her, she saw gaping holes where his striking violet eyes had been; blackish blood flowed wildly down his face.

His lovely voice cut through her terror and into her head.

I know you're there. Be calm, my girl. Please, please save yourself. Use whatever your powers are now. Kill us all if you have to but save your life.

Then, incredibly, the voice she hated most in the world echoed out across the courtyard, its unnaturally high pitch unmistakable. There he was. Standing to one side and gloating.

'Ah, there you are, Alyssa. We've been waiting for you and amusing ourselves with your friend here. I really took offence at the disrespectful way he looked at me so I poked his horrible eyes out. I wish he had screamed and brought you running but the courageous fuck simply groaned. He's no fun at all for us. I'm sure you'll be far better sport.' He laughed his hideous, girlish laugh.

Alyssa swayed dangerously, hanging onto the over-hanging branches. This could not be happening! Goth was dead.

Saxon tried to rise but they clubbed him mercilessly, smashing their weapons down again and again on his back. He made no sound but he also did not rise again.

Saxon, don't . . . she begged him across the link, her tears salty on her lips. *Save your strength, save yourself.*

His voice was barely a whisper. *To the death, my child. I must protect you to the death.*

She snarled at him. *I'll throw myself on his mercy if you move again, I swear it.*

Another familiar voice. It was Sorrel screaming her anger at Goth. It bought them some time.

'Oh fuck me, now it's the old bitch. I'd hoped you'd burned in Fragglesham, you old whore. Why won't any of you die when I want you to?'

The Inquisitors laughed. Goth was enjoying himself hugely. His prey was completely cornered: she had nowhere to escape to and no way of getting inside Sanctuary, the one place where his influence had no juris-diction.

The Academie at Caremboche was an untouchable place, protected by the King and ancient decrees, surrounded by mystery. Even Goth would not risk flaunting the law of Caremboche. But then he did not have to. Alyssa was trapped outside while her stupid, screeching grandmother was inside and her beefy, broken friend was at his feet. He would have her within the next few minutes but, for now, this was high fun and a lovely part of his payback for the hideous maiming he had endured that night. He would visit full revenge on her later.

Impossible though it seemed, at that moment Milt and Oris turned into the courtyard. Alyssa guessed they must have stolen a cart after all, in order to follow them. Light knew, she understood why: Saxon was their father to all intents and purposes and they had obviously refused to allow him to leave them.

Their lovely smiles died as they saw the scene before them and they shrank back in fear. Alyssa yelled for them to run. But, frozen at the sight of the humbled, bleeding Saxon, they clung to each other, not knowing whether to flee or just stand there.

'Milt, go!' Alyssa screamed again through her own tears.

Saxon called weakly into her head, the pain obvious in his voice. *The boys are here?* His face reflexively turned towards the entrance to the courtyard.

Fools! Yes, they're here.

Saxon's voice was ragged with the effort of holding the link. *Alyssa. Listen to me now. There's only a few seconds. Climb as high as you possibly can in that tree.*

What are you talking about? she shrieked. She could see Goth waving his horsewhip towards the boys, giving his second-in-command an order.

With huge effort Saxon yelled into her mind. *Climb now, damn you, Alyssa!*

With what was surely his final reserve of spirit he yelled out to the boys: 'Flight! You must perform Flight, boys. Do it now, my lovely sons. Make it perfect.'

Alyssa screamed with fear and despair. She knew what Saxon was going to make them do. And she knew it was her only hope but, in saving herself, those men below her whom she loved would probably die. But there was no more time to think; she scrambled higher and higher in the tree. She saw the boys following Saxon's orders; they linked their arms and walked into the centre of the yard.

'What the fuck are these halfwits doing now?' asked Goth.

As he spoke, the Academie gates burst open and out thundered Kythay, snorting, squealing and kicking madly. He laid out four of Goth's men before they had realised what was happening; the others scattered, Goth included.

Saxon linked again. *Now, Alyssa, fly. Fly for me, girl. Don't let me fail again.*

Alyssa let go of all her thoughts, closed her eyes, felt the Green gathering around her and leapt. She pushed out with her powers and, like a ruptured fountain, they spewed magic and she flew, dropping and tumbling towards Milt and Oris who were waiting. It seemed an eternity. While Kythay terrified the Inquisitors and Goth screamed his disbelief, Alyssa landed on the boys' braced arms which acted like a spring. They tossed her up towards the parapet and her powers lifted her impossibly high in the air, spinning like a top. She finally landed into the strong grip of Sorrel and other women around her.

Alyssa had never felt such combined fear and power before. The impact knocked her almost unconscious; she lay in the safety of Sanctuary, pear juice oozing through her garments like blood.

In the panicked seconds which followed, Kythay miraculously found his way back through the gates, which were slammed shut behind him.

The boys, as if coming out of a dream, began to laugh as they realised what they had done and how high Alyssa had flown. Sorrel watched, sickened, as Goth's fury turned wild. He picked up a club and bashed Saxon until he lay prone in the dust of the courtyard. He was bleeding, it seemed, from every inch of his broken body. When he offered no more resistance, Goth turned to the boys.

On his hysterical command, arrows were loosed into their slim bodies. Milt was slayed by four and Oris took three. They collapsed against one another, their arms still braced together, the barest smile of wonderment at their achievement still evident on each face.

Goth screamed up at the parapet. He sounded deranged.

'I am a patient man, Alyssa!'

She did not hear him. She had disappeared into the Green and fled to its darkest spot to hide.

16

Tor's Journey

The girl played with the thong which held his breeches on his hips and pouted.

'Why so soon?'

Tor kissed her softly. 'I am expected back at the Palace for my duties.'

'You have duties here, physic.' She pouted even more.

'Cassandra, I'm ashamed for you.'

He continued to fasten the black glass buttons of his white collarless shirt which marked him as a man of medicine. Cassandra continued with her attempts to undo them just as quickly.

'Now stop!' His voice crackled with humour. 'I'll see you again soon but I must away now, my sweet lady.'

Tor twisted away and looked around the room for any stray belongings which might have got cast into some corner during the evening's pleasures. He spied his black jerkin.

Cassandra's voice had hit a whine. 'You always say that. Yet I must wait and wait and queue behind Dorothea or Shally, and Betsy even told me you made a promise to Sissy Beaton. I'll kill you if you lay with Sissy!'

Tor laughed. He found his hat, pecked her cheek and squeezed her young breast gently. 'Just remember, Cassy. I love you best of all.'

She picked up a cushion and hurled it towards the door as he opened it.

'You are irresistible, you know.' With a parting wink, he closed the door and took the stairs two at a time.

Girls in various stages of undress called their farewells, most reminding him it was their turn when he was next in the city for a night of fun. Tor stepped from Madame Grace's brothel and winced at the sharp daylight. A large falcon landed soundlessly on his shoulder. No one reacted. All were used to seeing Tor and his majestic bird.

The falcon preened its feathers and linked with him. *Carousing with the ladies is your business but being late for your Palace rounds will raise Merkhud's blood to boiling.* The bird stopped just short of clicking its tongue with exasperation.

Tor's success with women was well known in Palace circles; in fact he was something of a mascot for the King's Guard. Tor did not mind this reputation one bit. Ever since that night with Eryn he had derived immense pleasure from the company of women. He was a generous and considerate lover and the girls at the brothel, like Cassandra, often felt jealous if he did not spend his whole evening with them. His manners and gentle ways enamoured them of him quickly; it almost did not matter that he had matured into an extraordinarily good-looking man. For the working girls, this was a bonus.

Tor's dark, thick hair was now worn longer. Whilst his face had hardened and thinned to make him a handsome man, it was his eyes which caused most comment. They were a remarkable blue, their brilliance often unnerving for those meeting his gaze for the first time. Not intimidating though. Tor's smile lurked within his eyes constantly and his hearty laugh was infectious.

The last few years had seen him mature into a confident man. Those blue eyes no longer looked awkwardly down. Now he held his head high. Years of training with the Guard under Cyrus had developed his muscles and bulk and now Tor had the body to match his great height.

He absorbed his training under Merkhud with the greatest of ease and Tor's ability as a healer was unrivalled. Now he was the first to be called to any ailing courtier and remained on permanent duty to the King and Queen. He deferred only to Merkhud, who quietly recognised that the young man's skills often surpassed his own these days. People said he had taught his apprentice well. Merkhud knew better. He had hardly taught him anything. Tor had developed his own talent and his audacious use of the power continued to trouble the old man, who fretted constantly at the threat of discovery.

The falcon, Cloot, was talking but Tor's thoughts had fled elsewhere that bright morning. He was thinking of Alyssa and wondering what she would make of his success. Tor had never stopped believing that one day he might find her again. For all the women who loved him and for all the women with whom he found his frequent pleasures, none could match Alyssa.

He found himself in a pensive mood as his friend lectured him about responsibility on the way back to the Palace.

Tor was consumed by an unrest which had been

creeping up on him since Newleaf. He had pushed it to one side, reassuring himself that his life was enviable and that he should not pursue these other nagging concerns. His good sense rarely prevailed in this contest though.

He interrupted the bird. *Cloot, has it ever occurred to you that people must think we're strange? Me walking around with a mad bird balancing by my ear?*

Cloot blinked. *No. Never. I think I make you look rather dashing. In fact it's probably because of me that all these women fall at your feet. I make you look a little dangerous . . . certainly romantic.*

Tor grimaced. *I'm being serious.*

Cloot knew precisely what Tor meant.

I've promised that I will tell you if Lys comes to me again but she has been quiet these past five years. Since coming to the Palace I have not dreamed of her at all. If she still has tasks for me I'm yet to hear them.

Tor strode on, his long legs making easy passage of the distance from the brothel to the more salubrious part of the city. He acknowledged almost all those he passed with a wave, a nod, a smile. His real attention, though, was elsewhere.

But what does she have in mind for me, do you think? His tone echoed the frustration gnawing at him.

Cloot scolded gently. *Most people can only dream of the privileges you now take for granted. Forgetting the comforts you enjoy, every man likes you, every woman falls in love with you . . . I think even our Queen is a little smitten. You have a craft to practise and you are not just good at it, you are the best. You have nothing to want for!*

Tor's frustration bubbled over. *Except an explanation for Lys, for you, for this insane power and for Alyssa. Where is she? Why can't I reach her like I used to? Am I supposed to just forget her? Is that all part of the plan?* he slammed into Cloot.

Aha and so now we have it. I thought we had laid this to rest, boy. You chose your way and Alyssa chose hers. It's been five summers since you left Flat Meadows; don't you think that if she wanted you she would have answered you? Written perhaps? Sent word through another? Why do you chew old gristle?

Tor took a moment to consider Cloot's answer and to calm down. He lifted his hand to wave to a mother and her son on the other side of the street. He had saved the child's life not long ago from the green fever. No one had ever heard of anyone recovering from the condition; it had caused quite a stir at the time. Railing against everything Merkhud had instructed, Tor had used his powers rather than his now extensive knowledge of herbcraft and medicine, but then he had already known no herb could save the child.

Whilst the cityfolk claimed a miracle had visited the household, Merkhud had seethed for days before he could even look at Tor. When he had finally confronted him, Tor was glad the West Tower of the Palace was so isolated since he felt sure Merkhud's fury could have been heard even in the East Tower. Merkhud had spat out his rage, berating his apprentice for ignoring his order to never, ever make use of his magical powers during his duties as physic.

Tor had surprised his mentor by meeting the fury with calm but deliberate resistance and the claim that he would use his powers as he pleased. Something then had broken between them. Tor knew at that moment he needed to be free from the stifling control Merkhud held over him and begin to lead his own life as he chose.

He did not fear Inquisitor Goth or discovery and he refused to accept that his powers should not be used to aid people in need. What else use were they? And then there was Cloot. He had learned to accept his friend in the guise of a bird but who would ever believe such a tale? Who would believe that the magisterial falcon had once been a crippled freak of a man?

He sighed. Cyrus would believe it. They had never discussed the episode of his rescue from the Heartwood, yet from that moment Cyrus had become an ally at the Palace.

He made Tor take up sword lessons and the fighting arts, in which he relentlessly drilled the King's Guard daily. Though Light knew why, Tor often thought, for he needed no weapons. His powers were more than equal to any aggressor. Cyrus also taught him about fine wine, everything he knew about women and about loyalty and respect to Lorys. Tor knew the Prime had become something of a big brother to him but it had occurred with such subtlety and over so many years that he had barely noticed until now how close he was to the King's Man.

Cyrus had accepted the falcon from the day Tor and Cloot had turned up in the forest and saved him from an ugly death. He had even lied to the King for him. Why?

And who was Lys? Why had she sent Cloot to him? What was she protecting Tor from? These questions circulated in his mind endlessly. This was not the first nor the last time he would taste them on his tongue.

Cloot had not said anything. Tor knew he had still to answer his question.

Because, Cloot, I love her. Looking back I could almost believe Merkhud took me away from her. I can't even feel her presence any longer. Tor reached up and stroked the bird's head. *I want to find her.*

He heard Cloot sigh.

And I want to leave here for a while and find out what my life is meant to achieve. I want to speak to Lys, I want the Heartwood to talk to me again and I want to eat one of Goody Batt's pastries!

Cloot chuckled at his friend's attempt to lighten the moment. But both of them knew there was nothing light about this decision.

Tor walked alone through the cool corridors of the Palace, musing on his outburst to Cloot and his extraordinary decision. He did not feel like work today. It would be the usual offering of sores, sparring injuries, sprains and toothaches which afflicted the Palace's population on a regular basis.

From around a bend in the corridor, a young lad with straw-coloured hair and freckles came charging up to him. He burst in on Tor's thoughts of bunions and the very choice carbuncle on Peggy Weltsit's neck which might be ripe enough for him to deal with today.

'Physic Tor!' The boy's face was pale. He was shouting. His breathing was hard and he had obviously been on the move for a while.

'Whoa, young Peagon. What's the hurry?' He bent down to look Peagon in the eye. Tor surprised himself sometimes at how tall he had become.

'Please, sir, we've been looking for you. It's the Queen, sir.'

Tor continued to be surprised that anyone would think to call him sir. He frowned. The Queen had been well when he saw her yesterday.

He cocked his head to one side. 'She's ill?'

'Yes, sir.'

'Bad?'

Peagon took a big pull of air. 'Yes, sir. I believe very bad . . . er, sir.'

'Quick, lad. Is she in her rooms?'

He caught the nod of the boy's head and then lengthened his stride into a run, leaving the panting page well behind. Tor knew his way to her majesty's apartments. He could have found them blindfolded, or walking backwards, from any part of the Palace. His long legs took the stairs into the East Wing three at a time. He did not bother with the courtesies of being announced. The guards knew him anyway and stepped aside briskly when they saw who was thundering up the stone stairwell. He could almost smell their relief at seeing him.

Inside, he strode past two ladies-in-waiting, their faces pinched. They registered shock at his impolite arrival in their Queen's rooms but the look on his face was sufficient not to be argued with. One of them pointed a manicured finger towards the bedroom.

Tor pushed through the doors and his eyes went straight to the Queen. She looked serene as always but as pale as he could ever remember; even her lips were as colourless as the cream silk nightgown she wore.

Nyria was propped against pillows in her large gilded bed. Her eyes were closed. King Lorys, still in his riding clothes, was struggling with her embroidered bed canopy. His broad shoulders and the confined space in which he stood seemed at odds. It would have looked comical if not for the stricken, ghostly expression on his face.

Tor could tell immediately the Queen was fatally ill. He needed no magical powers to know this. Around her were crowded other high-ranking courtiers and Chief Inquisitor Goth. No doubt here in his laughable role as the Palace priest, Tor thought. The Inquisitor privately hated the Queen but publicly went to great lengths to be as obsequious as possible to her. Tor was not fooled and neither was Nyria. Goth was certainly not here to wish her a speedy recovery.

Tor picked out Cyrus who was muttering in a low voice to the King. Lorys nodded and Cyrus withdrew to the back of the room.

Standing by the large picture window, which over-looked the surrounding valley in which the capital sat, was Merkhud. The old man stared out over the lush hills of the beautiful Southern Downs. His normally erect shoulders were hunched today. He must have sensed rather than heard Tor's arrival. He looked up and Tor saw he was chewing his lip. It was something the old man did when he was angry or distressed . . . or both.

Lorys broke the thick silence. 'Tor, lad. You're our last . . .' The King choked on whatever else he was going to say.

Merkhud stepped quickly back to the bedside and whispered something to Lorys. The King coughed lightly.

'Yes, of course. Gentlemen, please. Let's allow our healers here to have some peace and space for their minis-trations.'

The King motioned towards the reception room but Cyrus was already at the door herding people out.

'We'll be outside,' the King said and shot a look at Merkhud who nodded.

The Queen had not opened her eyes in this time and her breathing was shallow.

The others moved to follow Lorys but not before Goth could level one of his sneers at Tor. Their mutual hate was rarely disguised by either of them.

'Quick as you can, Inquisitor.' Tor couldn't help but needle him. He saw Cyrus lift an eyebrow which said plenty.

'Priest, if you please.' Goth's cold eyes flickered in the tortured, twitching flesh of his face.

Tor sensibly let it rest and closed the two doors softly behind those departing. He turned back to face Merkhud.

The old man's voice was soft but accusing. 'We've been searching for you for hours, Tor.'

'Cloot found me, sir.'

'A bird? What good is that?' Merkhud was angry.

More good than you'll ever know, Tor thought but not unkindly. How could he? He owed this man so much. More than that, he loved him. Merkhud's agitation was palpable and Tor knew he must tread carefully. He became business-like to disguise the guilt he was being made to feel.

'Tell me what we know,' he said firmly. It got the desired result.

Merkhud sighed. 'Very little. It's her heart of course. As you know, it's fragile. Perhaps Cyrus should tell this. He was there.'

Tor looked towards Cyrus in the shadows. The Prime cleared his throat. He did not move but his voice was clear and he told his tale like a military debriefing.

'Their majesties had enjoyed an uneventful ride and were on their way home. It was only when they stopped for a draught of wine that the Queen mentioned she felt weak. I believe King Lorys recalls that she used the word "breathless" to him. It passed quickly so we continued on but soon had to stop again. This time it was serious enough that the King listened to my advice. He and the small company we rode with remained with the Queen whilst I sent runners to find either Physic Merkhud or yourself.' Cyrus fell silent.

Tor looked back at the old man. He was not surprised as much as distressed to hear the old man's voice shaking whilst he told of his arrival on the scene. He knew Merkhud was extremely fond of the Queen – everyone did – but it was not until this moment that the thought kindled that perhaps the old man was actually a little in love with her. It seemed preposterous and yet, why not? She had been an elegant, engaging and attractive woman. Tor checked himself for thinking about her in the past tense.

He put his hand on Merkhud's arm. 'And then?'

Merkhud shook his head. 'By the time I reached them Nyria had passed out and was beyond my reach. Now she lies here, beautiful and dying.' He looked away quickly.

'We won't let her die, Merkhud . . . I promise.'

The old man's voice was thick with emotion as he linked with Tor. He obviously didn't want Cyrus to hear this exchange.

How can you promise me that, boy? We can't breathe life into the dead or even the dying.

Tor took a deep breath and gestured at his Queen. 'May I?' he said aloud.

The old man nodded. He looked tired and resigned to the inevitable. *We should try anything we can . . . for the sake of Lorys.*

Cyrus reached for the door. 'Would you prefer me to leave?'

When both physics shook their heads, he let the latch drop silently and returned to the shadows.

'We've lost her, Tor,' Merkhud said sadly.

'Allow me a few moments, Merkhud. Here, please . . . sit down.'

Tor was very respectful. This needed a delicate touch for what he was about to attempt would shock his mentor of the past few years.

Tor bent over Nyria. His hands moved over her body though not touching her; they hovered instead as close as was possible. Tor was lost. Suddenly Merkhud and Cyrus, the people outside, the Palace and all sound disappeared; all he could hear was his body's senses communicating with Nyria's.

Merkhud was right. It was her heart. There was a blockage. She would die. Hours at worst; maybe a day or two at best remaining of her life. He could see it all clearly. He could feel the failing pulse struggling to keep a rhythm. He could almost read her thoughts: muddled, frightened, scattered. And then the Colours roared up inside him. They took him completely; bright and pristine, they were so intensely distinct and so sublime when combined. He laid his hot hands against Nyria's chest.

Merkhud and Cyrus were calling him but Tor did not hear. He heard nothing but Nyria's body. The Colours passed from him into her; into her heart through his hands. There they weaved themselves about the troubled organ.

His own pulse began to slow until it matched Nyria's weak, irregular pace.

Gradually, so very gradually, Tor's pulse forced the Queen's heartbeat to gather momentum. It pulled her, faster, faster and more steady. It was matching him now, beat for beat, push for push. The Colours worked furiously, repairing what nature could not.

As Tor's body rocked back and forth silently over his Queen, Merkhud watched, fascinated and almost demented by Tor's defiance. He could not see the Colours which were blazing around the young man but he felt Tor's power. Felt it like a massive pounding against his own senses. It was mighty and yet he sensed this was still hardly tapping the source.

He was right to have chosen Tor. This young man was the Trinity. How and in what form was still beyond Merkhud but he was secure that his role was almost over.

He tried talking again to Tor but the man seemingly heard nothing. He touched him and flinched at how hot he was. In all his years Merkhud had never witnessed anything like this.

The voices outside were restless. There was a gentle knock and the King whispered through the door. When Merkhud failed to reply – he struggled to know what to say – the King's enquiry became more insistent.

Others joined in. The knocking turned to bangs, which turned to thuds and ultimately a determined thumping.

'Merkhud, what in Light's name do you do in there, man?' Lorys asked, despair thick in his voice.

Merkhud felt helpless. Cyrus made to open the door but Merkhud knew Goth must not see this. He shook his head. Thank the Light the Prime was not on the side of

the Inquisitors. Merkhud knew the soldier was as dedicated to Tor as Merkhud himself was. The old man never
really understood why, could only guess that something
must have happened during that time when Cyrus was
captured in the Great Forest. He shook his head again.
The air was crackling around the room, thick with a potent
magic he himself did not understand, and the grumbling
voices outside had risen in pitch.

'Not long now, my King.' He failed in keeping his
voice natural. His words sounded contrived and they saw
straight through them.

'Open up, damn you!' The King must have kicked the
door.

'Guards!' It was Goth yelling. His high-pitched voice
was laden with menace.

This time they must have put their shoulders to the
tall, double doors. Merkhud heard the wood crack, then
splinter. It would not take much more to smash them
through. Cyrus yelled through the doors to his guards to
stop but they had been whipped into a frightened frenzy.
A direct order from their King overruled all other
commands.

Merkhud opened a link in desperation and threw it
hard at Tor to bind them. Suddenly he was suffused in
such bright colours that he felt blinded, weakened. He
had no idea what this was but he tasted such power as
he had tasted only once previously. It so shocked him that
he pulled away, slamming the link shut and staggered
back to his seat.

As the door finally gave way and guards, followed by
Goth and King Lorys, tumbled through the door, Tor
lifted his hands away from his Queen. Merkhud sensed

the magic dissipate to nothing in the blink of an eye.

'You bastards!' Lorys was beyond courtesies, even to his dearest friend and the apprentice he admired.

'Your highness!' Cyrus said, cutting off the King's tirade.

All turned to see the Queen's eyelids fluttering gently. They opened. Her gaze was as clear and brilliant as they all remembered it to be. A blush of colour had returned to her cheeks and her face broke into a soft smile.

'Lorys . . . my love. What occurs here?' Her voice was strong. 'Hello, Cyrus. Merkhud, my old friend? And Tor.'

The guards dropped as one to their knees. The ladies-in-waiting covered their mouths to stop themselves crying out and sank to the ground too. Merkhud pulled himself out of his seat, suddenly exhausted from his long, strange life. Then he too knelt.

'Welcome back, your majesty,' he whispered, relief and joy flooding his body. He hated himself for loving Tor for giving her back life and hated himself even more for the fury he felt towards the boy for using his powers so.

Tor collected himself and knelt beside Cyrus who looked at him with intense curiosity. Only Goth flouted protocol and remained on his feet. His face betrayed nothing by its incessant twitching but his darting, angry eyes told plenty about his disgust that this woman was alive. Worse, she looked healthier than ever.

The King hugged her close with the same disbelief that was visible on the faces of all the witnesses present.

Tor was slumped on a seat in Merkhud's silent rooms. The West Wing of the castle was a lonely place which was how Merkhud liked it. Tor lifted his head from his hands and looked around at the dark bottles, heavy jars and boxes, each with their own mysterious contents, which lined the shelves along the walls. Competing for space with them were dusty books and weighty tomes relating to ancient herbcraft. He had studied them all, knew their secrets intimately.

Only a small number of people ever ventured into the West Wing and barely a handful had been invited into Merkhud's private quarters; the King and Queen amongst that privileged few. None of them, however, knew of the other books Merkhud kept hidden. Written centuries previous, these volumes concerned themselves with another sort of craft. The craft of magic and the wielding of the Power Arts.

In his five summers with Merkhud, Tor had viewed these special writings only on rare occasions, such was the old man's anxiety that anyone should discover the talent he had kept secret for so long.

Tor felt tired. A combination of the night's activities with Cassandra and then the healing of Queen Nyria had left him weary. A sound at the open window would have startled anyone else but Tor knew it was Cloot. The falcon shook his handsome feathers and fixed his friend with yellow eyes.

Embarrassment twitched at the side of Tor's mouth. *You've heard?*

Cloot made a clicking sound before replying. It was his way of showing the irritation that parents reserve for children who keep repeating the same mistakes.

I didn't have to. I felt it.

Really? I didn't feel you with me, Tor said, genuinely surprised.

No? Too busy perhaps. Bringing queens back from death can be demanding, I imagine.

Don't, Cloot. Not you as well.

What do you think, Tor? Do you reckon that Goth is going to let this pass? The whole Palace is buzzing. Everyone knew she was dying. The King knew it; he'd even begun his grieving. Even the old man had accepted it. Why couldn't you?

The falcon hopped around the sill in agitation. What Tor had done was miraculous but stupid. How in the name of Light could this be explained away?

Goth's had you marked for years. Now you've given him the excuse he wants to—

To what? Accuse me of magic? What proof will he bring? He has nothing on me – nothing! His stupid orb doesn't even flicker around me, much as he'd love it to. How many times do I have to tell you and Merkhud – he does not frighten me.

Cloot sighed. *All right. Calm down. I know you are correct in what you say. But you court danger, I fear. He will find some way to hurt you, Tor, I just know it and you had better start to watch your back. How is she anyway?*

The Queen?

No, Peggy Weltsit and her ripe carbuncle! Who do you think?

Their laughter halted as Merkhud re-entered the room.

'Ah, I see the bird has found you again, Tor. He's quite remarkable at seeking you out.'

Tor had already decided he would not be goaded by Merkhud. He knew the old man would be spoiling for a fight after this morning's performance. He remained quiet. Cloot knew when he was not wanted and dropped off the ledge to glide gracefully into the woodland at the bottom of the royal gardens.

'Wretched creature seems to know exactly what we're

talking about,' Merkhud muttered in exasperation. 'Here. Drink this.' He held out a cup.

Tor's nose wrinkled. 'What is it?'

'Do you want the complete recipe or would me saying something to relieve the effects of too little sleep and too much activity suffice?'

Once again Tor ignored the barb. He took the cup and drained it. Nettle, larkspur and a pinch of orris root he ticked off in his head. Merkhud had trained him well.

He put the cup down. 'Thank you.'

Merkhud sat at his table. 'Let's talk.'

When Tor did not respond but chose instead to stare out of the window Merkhud spoke again. 'Let's talk about what you did today.'

'I healed her.'

'I want to know how.'

'I don't know how I do it.'

'This suggests you've done it before. Ah, yes, there was the boy . . . the one with green fever. I remember now. Was it the same then?'

Tor shifted uncomfortably. 'Similar.' He had never mentioned Cloot or Cyrus.

'And can you breathe life into the dead?' There was sarcasm in Merkhud's voice but also a tinge of awe.

'I have never tried, sir.'

Before Merkhud could respond Tor stood. He wanted to get this confrontation done with.

'I thought you would be happy. I know how much you love Lorys and Nyria. I thought everyone would be pleased.'

It was not the right move. It gave Merkhud the chance he needed to vent his anger. He seized it.

'Pleased because they now know we have a warlock in the Palace? Pleased because we can now torture and bridle you and send you off to some work camp in the middle of nowhere to live the rest of your wretched life as a maimed, pathetic outcast?'

Spittle flew from Merkhud's lips he was so angry. He too stood now and strode around the room, his steps punctuating his angry words.

'I have forbidden you to use your power on the sick. I have forbidden you to show that power at any time outside of these four walls. Is that not so?' he bellowed but did not wait for Tor's response.

'I have forbidden you to welcome any undue interest from that butcher Goth and his merry band of halfwits. He is just looking for an opportunity to get you, Tor. He hates you. You don't need magical powers to know that. You could slice up his hate for you and serve it on a plate, it's so real. And if he can't get you, he'll get to others — those who love you. What about your parents? Your friends? Your damn bird? Alyssa?'

That was an error; he saw Tor's body stiffen. He poked his bony finger at him. 'And I forbid you further freedom to disappear into the brothels of our city. You will never again arrive late for your Palace rounds because you will not leave the Palace without my sanction. I forbid you to flaunt your skills and I forbid you to disobey me again.'

Merkhud knew as he looked into those disarming blue eyes that he had made a terrible mistake. The voice that spoke back to him was so cold it chilled the old man's blood. It felt as if icy water was running through his veins.

'You will not forbid me anything, ever again.'

Tor looked ten leagues tall and ten years older. His

expression matched his voice. 'I take my leave, sir.'

'I won't allow it!' Merkhud spluttered.

Tor's words fell like ice splinters. 'And how will you stop me, old man?'

'I'll have you put under guard if necessary.' Merkhud knew this was a ridiculous threat but he was clutching at fragile threads of authority. Tor was beyond him now. He had pushed the boy too far. He should never have mentioned the girl.

Tor's finger twitched and he became invisible. A link opened in Merkhud's mind and Tor whispered, *How will they find me?*

Merkhud was shocked at the ease with which Tor performed a trick most wizards could not achieve in several lifetimes. He had not realised Tor had reached such a level of competence. He composed himself quickly. 'I can sense you, Tor. You forget, I am sentient too.'

But not this good, I fear, said Tor, more unkindly than he meant. He shielded his presence with a magic Merkhud had never felt before; it sent a new wave of terror through him. Merkhud reached out with his powers but could no longer sense his apprentice. He scanned, confused and angry. This was not right. Merkhud knew he was the most powerful sentient alive in the land today. He had never doubted it for his magic had been deepened further by the gods. Yet his apprentice was making a fool of him.

Tor reappeared. He had surprised himself too; that was a wild trick he had tried for the first time in that moment and it had worked. He turned and made to leave.

Merkhud stretched out a trembling hand and grabbed his arm. This latest performance had shaken him to the very core. He must not lose the boy completely or the Trinity would be doomed to fail.

His voice sounded ancient. It was heavy with despair. 'Tor, I . . . please . . . I'm sorry. I have no place talking to you like that. Forgive me, son, I'm so frightened for you.'

Tor turned back. He hated what he had done to the old man. He remembered what Alyssa used to say to him: *Showing off will always bring you grief.* His expression softened and he covered Merkhud's hand with his own. Gone was the bitter chill; his voice was as gentle as soft summer rain now.

'Merkhud, I love you but I must leave here now. I must find out more about who I am and what my purpose is. You've given me a privileged life but my heart tells me this is not what my life is about. I know you keep secrets from me. Why do I sense that you have a purpose for me; that it was no accident you found me?'

Merkhud had to stop himself from crying out. The boy must not know yet. It was not the right time.

Tor continued, his brow creasing into a frown as he searched his thoughts. 'It's been niggling me for as long as I can remember and I have only just put it into words, Merkhud. It's as though you had been searching for me and then you found me. You took me from my parents – perhaps you even took away Alyssa – and you brought me here and made me a clever physic. But you have more in mind for me, don't you?'

Merkhud pulled away from Tor's hand. He dug his own nails into the arms he now crossed firmly and defensively in front of himself. He must not tell Tor anything . . . not yet.

'You have a very high opinion of yourself, boy, if you think my life has been spent looking for you.' His voice sounded hollow.

'Then why have you never taken an apprentice before?'

'I have not needed one before. Death is not far away from me now, I fear. The years have caught up with me and it is time to train a successor.'

Tor considered this. It was plausible. 'Alyssa?'

'What of her?'

'Where is she?'

'Why do you think I know?' Merkhud said, avoiding Tor's gaze.

'Do you?'

'No,' he lied, offering no further explanation.

Tor stared hard at him. 'Well,' he said matter of factly, 'it doesn't change my decision. I am leaving here . . . today.'

'But why?'

'Because of this, Merkhud,' he said, waving his hand slowly around the room. 'This is not what I am meant to do. I know this now. I'm good at it because you are a good teacher. You say I have a high opinion of myself – that is not true. I have doubted myself and my abilities for too long. I have not trusted my powers; I have been scared of them for too many years of my life. I need to know what my destiny is now – and there *is* a destiny. I feel it.'

There, it was out and said, Tor thought with a sense of relief. He had finally admitted what had been gnawing at his mind for so long. He had crystallised the thought at last: destiny.

Merkhud sat down. He felt dizzy with fear and his

mind raced towards controlling whatever damage had been created by this conversation. He needed time to think, to plot, but he did not have it. Tor was preparing to walk away. To walk away from all of Merkhud's carefully laid plans.

'Tor, would you fetch me a drink of wine, please?' he asked.

Tor snapped out of his thoughts and realised how fragile Merkhud looked. He disappeared into the back room. It bought Merkhud a little precious time. His agile mind raced. An idea bloomed and he poked at it tentatively. It could work, he told himself.

A cup was held out to him and he drank unsteadily. This unnerved Tor who asked him if he could do anything else for him.

A chance. Grab it!

'I haven't eaten since yesterday morning, I realise,' said Merkhud, adding a tremble to his voice. 'I think I must be faint with hunger . . . all this anxiety is taking its toll on an old man.' He allowed his hands to shake too.

Tor felt like the young apprentice again, leaping to his master's whim. He adored Merkhud and though he knew this was his time to seize now, his moment to define himself and choose his own path, he worried about the old man.

'Can I go to the kitchens and fetch you something?'

'Yes, my boy. I'm sorry but I will have to ask you to get me a small bowl of Cook's soup, or whatever is going.'

Tor left. As soon as the door closed Merkhud was on his feet and pacing, tossing over and over in his mind the plan which was beginning to take shape. He opened a link and shielded it expertly. The acknowledgement was immediate.

Things are happening faster than we expected. The boy leaves today.

What? Are you going mad, old man?

Not yet, my love, he said softly in her head. *How is she?*

She is a wonderful child. A woman these days, came the reply, full of warmth and fondness. *What can I tell you? She studies hard. She's capable, talented, very beautiful. Keeps to herself. She has one special friend, another student.*

Can we make this work do you think? Merkhud asked. For the first time she heard him uncertain.

Of course. She forced herself to sound confident but she had always taken her lead from him. It was unnerving to hear him confused about this terrible journey they had been on for so long. *We are in the hands of the gods now.*

He shivered as her words came into his mind. *I suppose you're right. What about the Kloek?*

Same as before. Devoted.

Will that be a problem?

I won't let it be one, she said defiantly. *We've come too far now.*

Merkhud could hear Tor's tread on the stairs. *I must go, my love. We'll talk again later.*

He closed the link as Tor opened the door. He was carrying a tray with a bowl loosely covered by muslin. What Merkhud didn't expect was Cook herself bursting in behind Tor.

'Now what goes on here, old man?' she boomed.

Cook's answer to everything from a runny nose to aching limbs was food. She had a dish, she said, to ease every ailment in the land and most people, including

Merkhud, could not help but believe her. Her chicken soup was legendary in the Palace and he could smell its delicious aroma right now as Tor placed the tray on the table. The bowl steamed through the muslin and the tantalising smell of fresh bread combined with it to make a heavenly brew. Cook, the only person who could get away with such treatment, began to berate Merkhud.

'Get this down you, you silly old fool, and if I catch you skipping my meals again I'll beat your bony body myself.' She thrust a napkin into his lap before gathering up her skirts and huffing back out of the doors.

They could hear her laboured breathing going down the narrow stone stairs. Tor laughed. Merkhud had to stifle one as well.

'Remind you of anyone, Tor?'

'My mother!'

'She's wonderful, isn't she?' Merkhud said as he heard the tower's main door slam closed. He imagined Cook striding across the courtyard, slapping at young lads and scattering chickens. 'What would we do without her?' he added with reverence.

'I'd suggest you hurry and eat up, or face her wrath.'

'Will you stay with me, Tor, whilst I eat? I have something to tell you.'

If Tor had looked at his three stones – those Merkhud had called the Stones of Ordolt – he would have seen them blazing into colour.

This time it was the colours of warning.

Merkhud was not hungry but he had to go through the masquerade of eating like a starving man. Besides, Cook's chicken soup was not to be sniffed at. Tor joined him at the table and chewed on some dried fruit and nuts he'd grabbed from the kitchen.

'Have you heard of a place called Ildagarth, Tor?'

'Yes. The Queen has told me that her tapestries and bed canopy were embroidered by the craftsmen of Ildagarth. I know that it is famed for its artists and artisans.'

'Very good,' said Merkhud between mouthfuls. They had resumed teacher and apprentice status. 'And have you heard of a place within Ildagarth called Caremboche?'

'No, sir, I haven't.'

Merkhud swallowed another mouthful of soup and took a bite from the bread. It was delicious.

'Caremboche is a sort of convent, for want of a better word. Over centuries it has become a haven for women who show the slightest sign of possessing magical powers. It was set up to protect sentient women from the Inquisitors. Of course, most gifted women never make it to those secure, closeted halls. They are butchered by Goth and generations of torturers before him. Those that do, however, are protected from society.

'They are treated with the highest of respect. It's curious, Tor. They are no different from any sentient woman in a village but for the fact that Caremboche's weighty and revered tradition through the ages has resulted in its inhabitants being honoured like priests. Our own King, who would see a sentient woman bridled, would allow a Caremboche woman to eat at his table.'

'So why don't they all run away to this place?' asked Tor, his interest piqued. He had not known what to expect from Merkhud but this conversation was certainly a surprise.

'Well, exactly.' Merkhud nodded. 'But it's not that accessible located as it is in the far north-west and many prefer to hide their talent and try to live a normal life with a husband and family rather than live a cloistered existence. Also, over centuries of Inquisitors, such gifts have gradually been bred out of our people. Fewer and fewer show the talent. Now I would say that most sentients posses only the wild magic, not the sort from times past which was passed through generations.'

'Is that what I have then?'

'Most probably. Neither of your parents have the power, do they?' Merkhud looked suddenly aghast; perhaps he had missed this crucial point. But the Gynts had given no evidence of being sentient.

'No,' Tor said quickly. As his father had advised, he had never mentioned to Merkhud the tale of how he came to be with Jhon and Ailsa Gynt. He maintained the charade that he was their true son.

'Then you are simply blessed, Torkyn Gynt.'

They exchanged glances acknowledging this was said with a certain amount of irony. Having magic at one's disposal was not a blessing in these times.

'Why are these women given such privilege if they are no different to other sentient women?'

'Well, they embrace their time at Caremboche almost like a religion. They study, they teach, they practise very advanced herbcraft and pass on this knowledge to our communities and their physics with generosity. They become servants of the land; I can't think of a better way to put it. They are not permitted to marry, not even permitted carnal knowledge. It's a great pity, of course, because these are often very young women who flee there to escape persecution. Often they do not realise what they are giving up for their safety.'

'What would happen if they were caught with a man?'

'They would be crucified and stoned.' Merkhud's voice was harsh. Tor sensed there was a message there.

'Fairly final then.' He grinned.

Merkhud did not return it. 'They have made their choice and must abide by the rules. This is why I began by telling you it was run almost like a convent. In the same way that some women give up their lives to the gods, these women give their lives in service to the land.'

Tor ate the last of the nuts. He nodded slowly. 'All right, I understand. Why are you telling me this?'

'Because you and I were meant to be going to Caremboche.'

'What?' Tor sat up.

'Yes, it's true,' Merkhud lied. 'Every ten-year cycle there is a special Festival held at Caremboche. It is a marvellous event. Usually the royals attend but obviously that is out of the question now. I have been fortunate to be invited every year since I've served this family.' Merkhud smiled as he recalled how long that had actually been.

'When is the Festival?' Tor asked.

Merkhud puffed his cheeks and then blew the air out. He scratched his beard. 'Oh . . . let's see now. The next full moon the festivities will commence. It stretches over several days and people arrive at various times.'

'What are they celebrating?'

'Survival mostly, I'd think,' Merkhud answered on reflex. 'No, that's not quite right. Its true meaning has long been forgotten but the Festival is so steeped in tradition that it is very important to the folk of the north.'

'And we were supposed to attend?'

'Well, yes. I thought it would be good for you to experience something as special as this. So few people would have the opportunity . . .' He let his words trail off deliberately.

Tor looked miserable.

'But look here, Tor,' Merkhud began brightly, as though a wonderful idea had struck him. He could hardly believe he was able to sound so jolly as he laid his trap. He hated doing this to the boy. If the truth be known, he felt as though he should bite off his own tongue to prevent this innocent being entangled any further in the horrible web of deceit which had been woven five years ago.

'I don't fully understand it but I do appreciate the passion with which you've expressed yourself today. Perhaps I've been too hard on you; if that's so, it's because I love you, boy. I feel like a father to you.' He smiled and then added, 'Well, grandfather perhaps.'

Tor shrugged. This was awkward for him.

'I haven't hidden anything from you, boy, but I have always wanted you to be the very best. Your talents are astounding; I don't know either what this world has in store for you but I certainly had hoped I'd always be able to protect you from squandering that talent. Handing yourself over to the likes of Goth amounts to the same thing.'

'But, Merkhud, Goth cannot see it. No one but you — and perhaps others like you or me — can. So what do you fear exactly?'

Tor was right of course. Goth was completely unaware

of the powerful magic which was being wielded in front of his ugly face. That gave Merkhud small satisfaction.

'Child, Goth has sufficient authority to kill you first and have the questions asked later. He hates you. He does not need much of a push to cook up a reason to have you despatched.'

Tor laughed. It was full-throated and filled with genuine mirth. Merkhud was shocked.

'You think he's a match for me?' Tor was not being arrogant; there was too much honesty in him to bother with such folly. 'How would he ever hold me long enough to kill me, Merkhud?'

All true, Merkhud accepted silently.

'You forget what I said earlier, Tor. He doesn't necessarily need to hurt you personally. There are far more subtle ways to inflict damage on you by hurting the people you care for.'

Tor nodded. Merkhud was right. Goth was unscrupulous and would not hesitate to contrive the death of someone like Cyrus if it meant he could hurt Tor by doing so.

'Well, that's another reason for me to leave here,' Tor said.

Merkhud jumped in. 'But not like this. Not stomping out, never to be seen or heard from again by people who have shared your life and care deeply for you.'

Tor was puzzled. 'You have another suggestion?'

'I do. Go to Caremboche for me. Represent Lorys, Nyria and myself.'

Tor was astonished. 'Go alone?'

A flapping sound at the window alerted them that Cloot had reappeared.

Merkhud made a sound of disgust. 'Do you agree with

me, boy, that that bird listens to everything we say? I'm
sure the falcon will accompany you but essentially, yes,
you will go alone.'

'I don't know what to say.'

'Don't say anything; you have my leave to go. We will
provide you with a horse, food, money. You will be representing the royal family. I hope you will consider it an
honour.'

'I won't let you down, Merkhud.' Tor wanted to hug
the old man. How could his world spin one way and then
another in a matter of hours?

Merkhud suddenly reached out and took both Tor's
hands in his. He squeezed hard. 'I want you to promise
me that you will mind my warning. Be aware, be very,
very sure of this,' whispered the old man in earnest. 'These
women at Caremboche are not called "Untouchables" for
no reason.'

Tor nodded but Merkhud squeezed harder. 'Tor, this is
serious. You have a reputation. I know how much you
enjoy the company of women. Not a hair on the head of
any woman at Caremboche must be touched by a man.
It spells ruin for the girl and the perpetrator.'

He paused. 'They won't hesitate to deal harshly with
the couple in question.' He stared hard at Tor, impressing
his words on the young man.

'I hear your warning, Merkhud. I promise you, I will
conduct myself impeccably.'

Merkhud relaxed and smiled warmly. The trap was set
and the bait was luring its victim. He felt contempt for
himself as he turned away from the boy whose death knell
was already sounding.

It would haunt Merkhud's dreams from this day on.

17

The Heartwood

It had been five days since they had departed Tal and the countryside had hardened from the lush vineyards of the southern counties into the rugged hills of the mid north.

Tor was filled with a sense of optimism. He had no regrets about leaving the Palace, though he did feel hollow at not wishing his great friend Cyrus farewell. That thought haunted his happiness like a cloud but he managed to push it away most of the time, reassuring himself that Cyrus would get his note and understand.

Cloot thought otherwise.

Well, what would you have had me do? Wait around 'til Sixthday when he may have ridden back into the city? No one knew when that camp of theirs would finish.

He deserves better, the falcon persisted.

They had endured several similar tetchy exchanges during the journey so far and Cloot usually ended their conversation by snapping shut the link and flying off for a while. Tor quietly agreed with the falcon's sentiments but had no idea what he could have done differently. Having had it out with Merkhud there was no choice but to leave and, anyway, the old man had insisted that he make haste if he was to reach Ildagarth by next Fourthday.

Tor heard a squeal and pulled his thoughts back to the present, noticing that Cloot was circling high above him. He watched with awe as the bird hovered effortlessly then suddenly dipped its head and went into a dive. Cloot seemed to fall out of the sky, gathering speed with his wings shaped like an arrow.

Must have seen another rabbit, Tor thought, his stomach lurching at the notion of his friend gorging on entrails.

He allowed his horse to follow her nose along the narrow path they were treading and he returned to his musings.

Queen Nyria had known, of course. Tor recalled how she had looked at him when saying goodbye. They both knew she was more than well enough to be standing in the Palace courtyard but she played along, allowing her maids to wrap a heavy shawl around her shoulders. He remembered how she had held onto the King's arm and tottered, as though weary after the effort of getting up from her sick bed. Her expression had communicated something entirely different to him, though, as she wished him an uneventful journey and speedy return home.

'Don't be away too long, Torkyn Gynt.'

He had bent to kiss her outstretched hand and could not resist sending a gentle spike of love through his lips as they touched the back of her hand. He saw it register in her eyes; they blazed with recognition of his magic.

'Madam.' He had bowed low then, not daring to look at her again and she had not uttered another word to him.

The King, however, was unable to look him in the eye at all. Tor sensed that his sovereign was suffering. Lorys knew nothing but magic could have saved the Queen from death. Light knew, she had been barely clinging to life. Lorys, because of his devotion to Nyria, had ignored what had occurred; even though it went against everything he stood for and believed in, he allowed it because it meant saving that which he loved more than any other. It made Tor's stomach turn as he thought of all the poor wretches who had been punished, tortured and banished in the name of sentient cleansing.

The hardest part for Tor was knowing that Lorys was indeed a good man. An excellent King. Lorys had proved it over and over again in just the short time Tor had been at the Palace. Such compassion for his subjects; such a love for his Kingdom. If only, Tor thought once again, the King could find the courage to deal with Goth and the whole misfounded fear of sentient people. This was another reason why he had to leave. He had to get away from Lorys and the hypocrisy he now ruled under.

Countless other well-wishers had gathered to bid him a safe journey. Deep down Tor wondered whether he would ever see them again. He was not so sure he would be back, though he played along with the supposition.

They had all been such good friends to him. Even the young pages were there. The older soldiers, who were not on the camp with Cyrus, saluted him. He realised then, with just a little pride, that every face in the Palace bailey was a familiar one. He had treated and healed each of them at some stage during his time in Tal. Their presence today, he was reminded by Cook, was a rare sight usually reserved for the King or Queen. The gathering of so many acknowledged what a popular figure he had become.

Tor forced himself to search out Goth. It was not hard. There he was, standing not far from the King and wearing his usual smirk. Here was one person who would be thoroughly glad to see the back of him and Goth was probably amongst the throng just to make sure he really did leave. He wondered how Goth was dealing with the restored health of the Queen. He surely must have known she was on her death bed and that it should have been simply a matter of time. However, it was one thing to accuse a peasant of wielding forbidden powers; it was quite another to accuse the most well-loved person in the royal circle, bar the sovereigns themselves, of the same crime. Goth would be required to justify such a claim and proof would be difficult to provide. His sneer was directed at Tor and both knew they had a score yet to settle. It could wait. It would have to.

Finally Tor had embraced Merkhud. Their affection for one another was genuine but, like any father and son, parting was necessary – essential even.

Once Tor was through the city gates and the throng of waving well-wishers was behind him, Cloot had joined him, flying low alongside him. Both had laughed as Tor encouraged his new young filly, Timara, a gift from the King, into a gallop. He slowed her down only when they were well into open countryside and the sense of leaving Tal behind was complete.

Now, guiding his horse with his knees as Cyrus had taught him years previous, Tor pulled out the small pouch which he had kept secret since Jhon Gynt had given it to him. He was shocked to see that the Stones of Ordolt, which had remained dull and lifeless for the past few years, had begun to burn with vibrant colours again.

He did not understand any of it but he had taught himself to follow his instincts. The orbs which his parents – his real parents – had left for him were all he had to link himself with his past and somehow he knew they should be trusted.

Three days later Cloot and Tor arrived at the small town of Saddleworth. Tor found a modest room for the night at The Horse and Lamb. The falcon decided to remain in the nearby woodland.

Tor was tucking into a tasty stew when Cloot linked with him. *By the way, what excuse would you give Cyrus for walking out on him without a proper goodbye?*

Tor continued chewing. *Why do you ask?*

Oh, only that I think you may have the opportunity, Cloot replied.

With that, the inn's door was flung open and Cyrus barged in, his expression grim. If Tor had not been sitting against a wall he would surely have toppled backwards off his chair.

Cyrus looked saddle-weary. His usually immaculate clothes were dusty and his grey eyes were flinty with anger. 'Why?' His voice was edged with danger.

Tor knew there was no point in being glib with Cyrus. Only honesty worked when the Prime was in this mood. He covered his shock by swallowing and taking a moment to compose himself.

'Will you join me?' he finally said, self-consciously.

The Prime ignored him. The room had become quiet;

its occupants sensed a confrontation and had stopped to watch.

Tor cleared his throat and held his cup in the air towards the innkeeper. He raised two fingers and the innkeeper nodded, busying himself with pouring an ale for the lad and the soldier who had just walked in. The simple chore eased some of the tension and forced people to return to their own conversations.

Tor, relieved, looked back at Cyrus whose expression had not softened in those moments. He wondered whether the Prime might hit him; he looked angry enough.

'It's something I have to do, Cyrus. I don't really understand it myself but life at the Palace is no longer . . .' Tor searched for the word, '. . . enough.'

He held up his hand as he saw Cyrus was about to leap in again, his anger ready to spill over.

'No, wait,' Tor said firmly. 'Let me try to explain . . . and please, sit, have an ale with me. You look terrible.'

A girl banged down two mugs on the table and Tor gave her some coins. Cyrus sat down stiffly. Tor sensed that Cloot had settled in a tree opposite the inn.

Is everything all right? the bird asked.

I'm not sure. Cyrus wants an explanation.

Good luck. Cloot fell silent.

Cyrus swallowed most of his ale in one thirsty gulp. He looked across the table, gaze unflinching. What he said next took Tor by surprise.

'Has your leaving anything to do with what happened in the Heartwood between you, me and the falcon?'

Tor blinked. It was an involuntary reaction to an extraordinary question but it was enough for Cyrus to know he had hit his mark. He continued.

'We've never discussed what actually occurred, Gynt, but I think we should, don't you?'

Tor found his voice. 'Why are you so angry?'

Cyrus nearly leapt across the table. He fought to control his temper. 'Because you had an important role in Tal,' he spat. 'My men need your skills nearby; you are just beginning to handle a sword and, dammit, man, you didn't even give me a reason . . . just a terse note. Why in the name of Light would you squander everything and disappear on some mad journey to the other side of the Kingdom to dance around in a mask and pay homage to a crank festival no one even understands?' His words built into one long shout.

'That's not it,' Tor said in a low voice, embarrassed by the renewed stares from the other patrons. 'You're not just upset, you're scared of me . . . of not having me close, I mean.'

Careful, Tor, warned Cloot.

'Out!' Cyrus stood up so fast and suddenly that his chair toppled with a loud clatter. Onlookers gasped.

'We want no problem tonight, you men,' called the innkeeper.

'Out now!' Cyrus bellowed.

Well, at least he's shouting, Cloot said. *Cyrus is far more dangerous when he speaks quietly don't you think?* Cloot cleared his throat awkwardly. Perhaps this was not the right moment to discuss character traits.

Tor needed no further encouragement. He stood and meekly followed the Prime to the door. Some of the other men, mostly farmers, took a few steps forward as if to block Cyrus's path. Tor was touched by their efforts to save his skin. It must look bad but he did agree with

Cloot: shouting was good; a silent Cyrus was dangerous.

Cyrus pulled off his cloak to reveal his uniform and badge of office. The men instantly became passive, two of them blurting apologies.

'It's all right,' Cyrus said. 'We're friends.'

It was a comical thing to say under the circumstances. The Palace dined on stories of Cyrus's legendary temper and Tor had no desire to see it unleashed on him. At the same time, he did not want to humiliate his great friend by using the magic he could feel, ever potent, at his call.

'Hold this!' Cyrus said to one of the farmers and handed him his cloak.

The man obeyed. Everyone watched in silence as the Prime strode out of the door with the tall young man loping behind. Once outside, Cyrus rounded on Tor. He had the sense to speak normally now but it sounded just as ugly to Tor.

'You're damn right I'm scared. Do you think I don't know you go around wielding magic on your patients? Do you think I'm as stupid as Goth? He might not see it with his scrying stone – the Light knows why! – but you forget you touched me, boy, a long time ago in the forest and since then I can feel your magic!'

'You do?' Tor spoke before he could check himself.

'Yes.' Cyrus's eyes blazed.

'Why haven't you said anything before?'

'Why would I? Your powers saved my life. I was dead for sure, just like our Queen. And, miraculously, we both survived to tell our tales simply because you chose for us to live!'

Cyrus shook his head. As quickly as it had kindled the

angry spark went out of his eyes. He looked beaten. The soldier sat down on a bale of hay. Cloot dropped silently out of the dark and onto Tor's shoulder.

Listen now, boy. This is important, the bird said.

Tor had no idea how Cloot would know this but he lost the thread of that thought as Cyrus began to speak.

'I've begun to dream. The woman whose voice I heard in the forest – the one who said you were coming to help me – well, I've heard her again.'

'Lys . . .' Tor breathed her name.

'Yes, her. She warned me that you were leaving Tal on a long journey. When I returned the whole Palace was abuzz with news of your hurried departure.'

Cyrus stood again and walked over to stand in front of Tor. He seemed to struggle with what he was about to say. 'What does it all mean?'

Tor was as confused as Cyrus.

'Cyrus, let me tell you something. That day we came to you in the forest, we rode there through the night. You know it's impossible to ride from Hatten to Brewis in a single night but we did it.'

'You mean you and the bird here?'

Tor felt uncomfortable. 'Yes.'

He was suddenly fixed with the stare he had been warned about by the soldiers of the King's Guard. Tor had not felt the weight of that look since Cyrus had first gazed at him in The Empty Goblet.

'Tor, I'm just a soldier but it does not pay to underestimate even the lowliest of men. Has it occurred to you that you mentioned the name of the cripple whose ear was nailed to the post at the time we met?'

Tor look confused. Cyrus reminded him. 'When I called

him a halfwit, you gave me his name. I did not mention it at the time; I just allowed you to gabble on.'

Tor's eyes fell to his feet. He had been skilfully trapped. He remembered his mistake clearly now.

Cloot spoke. *Tell him.*

Tor could not believe what Cloot had said.

This is no time for games, scolded the bird.

Cyrus, not privy to this silent conversation, was intent on Tor. 'Tell me the truth, boy. Is this falcon the freak Corlin was torturing?'

'Yes,' Tor mumbled.

'Well, fuck me!' The Prime clapped his hands. He even began to laugh. It sounded demonic. 'I knew it. And you did this to him?'

Tor shook his head miserably. 'No. It happened in the Heartwood before we found you.'

'How then?' Cyrus circled Tor and stared at Cloot with wonder. The bird obliged, offering his best angle, even lifting his wings to show off the gorgeous colours hiding beneath.

'As soon as we arrived in the Great Forest he was transformed.'

Cyrus stopped circling. He was serious again. 'Is the woman involved? This Lys?'

Tor nodded. 'Yes. I don't know any more than you now. I was telling you that we were in Hatten. I was actually in a brothel at the time—'

'What a surprise!' said Cyrus, some of his humour returning.

Tor ignored the jibe. 'And suddenly Cloot screamed into my head that you were in dire trouble and we had to leave immediately for Brewis.'

Cyrus cut in. 'The falcon was allowed into the brothel with you?'

'Er, no . . .' Tor took a deep breath and plunged on. 'Cloot can speak to me . . . in my head.'

'And you can speak with him.'

It was not a question but Tor answered it as if it was. 'Yes.'

The soldier sighed with wonder. 'So, have you seen or met this Lys?'

'No. She has never come to me. I have never heard her voice or dreamed of her existence. She had only ever visited Cloot . . . er, and yourself.'

Tor could tell that Cyrus had already decided to suspend all normal understanding and beliefs. He had accepted Cloot, the magic, the link, even Lys and was behaving as though he was receiving a briefing from one of his men. He could not help but admire him.

The soldier continued in a matter-of-fact manner as he paced. 'So what is this all about – this running away from the Palace?'

Tor pressed on. It was a relief to share this with someone he trusted.

'I disagree with the whole Inquisition thing but, like you say, Goth and his band have nothing on me – well, perhaps suspicions but I'm well protected.'

Tor ran his fingers through his hair. He was a little confused himself now. It had seemed so clear a few days ago.

'The King suspects I'm using the Power Arts but has hypocritically ignored this because it suits his needs. I couldn't stand to be around him any longer. The Queen, like you realise now, can feel it. She has said nothing but then I know that if she could she would execute Goth for the murderous thug he is and dismantle the Inquisition immediately. The King, however, seems to fear the ancient past so upholds those antiquated laws. I had to get away.

'Furthermore, you might as well know that Merkhud knows what I am. He is aware that I'm sentient and using my powers to heal. He is terrified I'll be caught. We've had words . . . unpleasant words. It really was best to leave. Instead he suggested I should take the chance to learn more about the history of the Kingdom. He believes that if I understand how the Inquisitors came to be then I may be more careful, perhaps more tolerant. I think he hopes I may be more cautious.'

Cyrus looked unconvinced. 'So he's sending you off on this wild errand to Ildagarth?'

Tor considered this. He knew in his own heart it was a thin premise.

'Actually, it's probably a good idea. I could use the change of scenery. I want to go back to the Heartwood and I want to try and find out more about Lys. Somehow she seems to be at the centre of all this.'

Cyrus nodded. 'Now that's something on which I do agree. That's why I'm coming with you.'

'You're what?' Tor was shocked.

'You heard. She's already told me I have to, so don't start blustering. Save your energy. I'm as much her puppet as you and the bird are. Plus, I didn't ride for six days, nearly killing my horse to catch up with you, only to ride back again!'

'But how can you leave? How will the Palace cope without you?' Tor was almost babbling.

'In case it has escaped you, boy, I've already left. And

everyone will cope without me in the same way they will without you. I don't understand any of this and I don't understand you but I know we are joined, Torkyn Gynt, and I know I must travel with you on this strange journey.' He stared hard into Tor's bright blue eyes. 'Let's not fight it. Let's just accept. I'll be back shortly.'

Cyrus left, his strides long and deliberate.

Tor looked at Cloot and blew his cheeks out, his mind completely confused now. *So, what do you think?*

I don't think, Tor, I do. Cyrus is right. If Lys has talked to him then she is making all the decisions for us.

But what does it mean?

Don't ask me questions I have no idea how to answer. All we know is that the three of us are linked somehow. We both knew as much anyway. We must follow her will. What other choice is there?

Tor thought it over. *You're right. One thing, though, and I've given it a great deal of thought since we left: I expected more of a fight from Merkhud. He seemed to give in too easily about my leaving. I think he knows more than he tells me.*

Cloot agreed. He was deeply suspicious of Merkhud and his motives.

After a night's rest the odd trio set off, heading north. After several hours Cloot flew back to Tor, landing on his arm.

'Something wrong?' Cyrus asked Tor casually, who shook his head as if to say he did not know. It was not usual for Cloot to sit on his arm.

Cloot perched quietly for a short while. *I didn't tell you this earlier because I needed to think on it.* The falcon fixed Tor with a single yellow eye. *Lys came to me last night.*

Tor pulled harshly on Timara's reins and she obediently stopped her gentle canter.

'Something *is* wrong,' said Cyrus, halting his own horse.

Tor spoke aloud. 'Cloot's only just decided to mention that Lys paid him a visit last night.'

Cyrus did not seem overly surprised. 'And?'

We're waiting, Tor said to Cloot across the link.

The bird ignored his tone. *A few miles to the west of here is the fringe of the Great Forest. She wants us to head that way.*

And I suppose there was no explanation why as usual, Tor snapped.

Well actually, now you mention it, I think she thought we might like to take a woodland picnic with her. The falcon flew off, his sarcastic reply burning Tor's cheeks red.

'Tell me,' said Cyrus flatly.

'Apparently our lady friend would like us to head west for a while until we reach the fringe of the Great Forest.'

'And?'

'That's it. That's all we know.'

Something in the young man's troubled expression warned Cyrus not to press it further. 'Fine. I know where we're supposed to go. The forest curves around about three or four miles slightly west of here and then it bends back around sharply. We should be able to get there by this evening if we ride briskly.'

He sounded like a true soldier. There was no emotion in his voice and no longer any query in it. Tor was grateful for that much.

Hours before their first glimpse of the Great Forest, the three of them sensed its strange pull. Cyrus felt it more strongly than his companions and, as they began to skirt the fringe of the woodland, he became quieter. By the time the afternoon had sunk into chilly late evening, he was completely silent. Tor was concerned. Since they had decided to obey Lys, Cyrus had kept up a much needed narrative on Palace gossip to distract all of them from more sinister thoughts of where this strange adventure was leading them. Now that Cyrus had fallen into this mood it stirred new anxieties.

What do we do? Tor asked Cloot.

We shouldn't enter yet, I don't think. Lys had a particular spot she wanted us to find. We're close though – I feel it.

Well, how will you know it?

Trust me. She'll show us.

Cloot landed on Tor's shoulder. He had ranged high and broad from his friends all day and it was comforting to have him back, Tor admitted silently.

Right now, I'd say we make camp for the night and tackle the forest in the morning. Cyrus is behaving oddly and the dark can play tricks on men. This place is enchanted enough without one of us turning strange.

Tor nodded. 'Right,' he said aloud and rather too cheerily, hoping to snap Cyrus out of his brooding. 'I'll collect some firewood.'

I'm off to find some dinner, Cloot called, already way above the treeline. *Stay alert*, he added.

Tor busied himself with setting and lighting the fire but he too felt the forest around him, almost calling to him. He remembered the first time he had sensed its power, that day when Cloot had transformed. At that time he had felt unnerved by its power; now he felt protected by it.

He looked over at Cyrus who was going about his

chores more out of habit it seemed rather than out of any conscious thought.

When they were comfortable, warm and had finished chewing on their dried meat and hunks of cheese and bread, Tor began to hum an old song which his mother used to sing. It felt comforting amongst the sensations of the forest's constant calling and the strange disquiet that troubled Cyrus. His voice was pleasant enough and he continued to hum the lullaby as he readied himself for sleep. When he looked up to wish Cyrus a good night's rest, he was surprised to see the soldier was weeping softly. He stopped his tune.

'That was my wife's favourite song.'

'I'm sorry I—'

'No. Don't be sorry. It's lovely to hear it again. I think I pushed it so far from my mind during those early years that I'd forgotten it.'

'Do you still miss her, Cyrus?'

'Deeply. Every day,' he replied.

'And there's never been anyone else for you?' Tor could have pulled out his own tongue for his bludgeon-like directness.

'Plenty. Like you, I enjoy women and just like you, I keep it casual. No, there never will be anyone else I'll share my life with. When you've known perfect love, as I have, you don't even bother to look again.' There was no regret in his voice, just resignation.

Tor shook his head. 'It must be terrifying to love someone like that.'

'It's the only way to love someone. Have you never been truly in love, Tor?'

'Once. But I lost her.'

'Dead?' Cyrus sounded shocked.

'No. Well, I don't think so. That's another reason why I left the Palace. Somehow I have this feeling I might be able to find her, if I look hard enough.'

Tor shrugged and held out the wineskin to Cyrus who took and raised it in a toast.

'To lost souls then and to finding love again,' he said, smiling at last.

Tor seized the moment. 'Cyrus, do you mind if I ask what happened today?' He hoped his sense of timing was sharp this night. 'I mean, why you've been so withdrawn?'

The Prime let out a long sigh and lay back on his bedroll. He turned on his side, his back to the deep shadow of the forest which loomed in the distance.

'Didn't you feel it?' he asked.

'Feel what?'

'Perhaps it was just me then.' Cyrus was almost whispering. His eyes were closing.

'What did you feel, Cyrus?' Tor kept the fear at bay by warming his hands against the happy, dancing flames of the fire.

'I felt a great sadness wash over me. It seemed as though all the grief I'd held over these years, all that melancholy, passed through me again . . . and then it was gone.'

'Gone?'

'Cleansed. Now I feel nothing except a burning desire to re-enter the forest and I'm scared of the feeling. I'm frightened of what it means.'

Tor snuggled into his bedroll too. 'Cloot's certainly glad to be back here,' he offered in consolation.

'There's more though,' Cyrus mumbled. 'I have this overwhelming sense of . . . destiny.'

It had been a full Eighthday since the Prime was last seen. Herek was used to Cyrus's shifting moods; there were occasions when he sensed it was best just to leave the man be. He was complex, could brood for days — sometimes on the past, often on an event which had just occurred. He was a deep thinker and his decisions were rarely rash.

This had seemed to be one of those times when Cyrus needed to be alone and Herek had not thought to question it. He was the Prime, after all. They had returned from the south to the news that Physic Gynt had left the Palace bound for the great Caremboche Festival. He was representing the royals this year in the stead of Physic Merkhud who was ailing.

It was a logical notion to send Gynt. But Cyrus had reacted strangely to it. He had fallen into a foul humour upon hearing the news and this had spiralled into one of his famous black moods where the entire Company knew to give him a very wide berth. Two days later he had announced to Herek that he had some personal matters to see to up north and ordered Herek to assume command until he returned. Well, now that time had stretched into eight days without any word and Herek was worried. Cyrus had looked drawn during the patrol. He had complained of sleeping badly and dreaming constantly. Herek had not thought much about it at the time but now realised Cyrus had definitely been out of sorts.

Perhaps the Prime had taken himself off on a brief

sabbatical? But being the professional they knew him to be, he would have mentioned it to his second-in-command. He was not a man to disappear without any follow-up word and yet this was precisely what he had done. He had taken his horse, a few provisions, packed lightly and even left without formal word to their majesties; again totally unlike the Prime's normal protocol. Herek would be lying if he did not admit he was worried, which was why he had requested an appointment with the King this morning.

He waited in the antechamber until he was announced. Drake met him at the door and sniffed at his heels as he walked across the room to bow low to King Lorys.

'Ah yes, Herek. Welcome. Are you thirsty, man? I was just thinking of a cool ale.'

'No, thank you, your majesty . . . er, not on duty.'

'Good, right. So, you wanted to see me?'

'Yes, sire.' The soldier stood to attention.

'Herek, please sit, man. At ease.' Lorys offered him a chair.

Herek preferred to stand but he sat to please the King. The dog wandered over and sat on his feet which was an altogether unsavoury and uncomfortable experience. He cleared his throat.

'Tell me . . . how can I help you today?' the King asked while signing papers at his desk.

'It's about the Prime, your majesty.'

The King looked up. 'Cyrus? What's wrong with him?'

Herek suddenly wondered if this was such a good idea. Cyrus would probably arrive back any moment and have a few fiery words to say about Herek tattling behind his back to the King like a worried old aunt.

He cleared his throat again.

Lorys eyed him. 'Speak, man. What's troubling you? What's happened with Cyrus?'

'He's gone, sire.'

'Where? Why?'

'That's it, your highness. I don't really know.'

The King put down his quill. 'Disappeared, you mean? Like the time before?'

'Yes . . . er . . . well, no not exactly, your majesty.' Herek was very uncomfortable and pulled at the collar of his uniform. The dog was making his feet hot and he really wished he had not come here. 'He left of his own accord on personal matters he mentioned.'

'How long ago?'

'Eight days, sire. But it's not like him to leave without providing information about where he could be reached or without sending word.'

'I agree, Herek.' The King scratched at his short beard. 'He has always reported to me before going on any mission away from the Palace. You are right to be concerned.'

At that moment Goth was announced. Herek made to stand but the King waved him back. Drake had not made any effort to move; in fact the huge dog grunted at being disturbed.

'Send him in,' Lorys told his secretary.

Goth entered immediately and bowed obsequiously to the King and nodded at Herek. Herek despised the man. He enjoyed the fact that Drake had stood and was now sniffing the Chief Inquisitor's crotch, much to the man in black's discomfort.

'My liege,' he said, pushing at the dog's enormous snout.

Drake, satisfied with the unnerving routine he visited upon people he did not like, wandered away.

'Good day to you, Goth. You're early.'

'Have I interrupted your majesty? Shall I return shortly?'

'No, no, you're here now, man. I was just having an interesting conversation with Herek here. Apparently Prime Cyrus has disappeared.'

Goth's piglike eyes looked at Herek. Dark and small, they gave away nothing.

'Oh dear, we lose two in one week. First Gynt and now the Prime. Perhaps they are together?'

Lorys stood and walked to the window. Herek was pleased for the chance to stand as well.

'Unlikely I'd say, Goth,' the King replied.

'Well, they were quite close. And it seems those two have a habit of disappearing then finding one another,' Goth suggested.

The King grinned at the soft jest. 'But Gynt was going to Ildagarth and on to Caremboche and Cyrus . . . er, where did you say he was headed?' the King asked Herek.

Herek did not want to reveal anything in front of the Inquisitor. 'He simply said he was heading north, your majesty. He gave me no details.'

'Well, north, your highness – how much further north can one go than Caremboche?' said Goth.

The King shook his head. 'No reason to though, Goth. But I agree it is a strange business. Look, thank you, Herek, for bringing it to my attention. Perhaps if we have no word in the next two days you will arrange for some of your men to see what they can find out, eh?'

Herek bowed, relieved. 'As you wish, your majesty.'

Goth interrupted this exchange. 'No need, my King. I myself am heading north shortly. My men and I will gladly keep an eye open for any sign of the Prime; in fact I will make it my purpose to ask questions and discover his whereabouts.' He smiled sweetly at Herek but the soldier could almost smell the guile beneath it.

'There you are, Herek,' the King said brightly.

Through gritted teeth Herek thanked both men and left. Cyrus would not forgive him for this. He prayed the Prime would return before Goth had the pleasure of officially tracking him down.

The fire's embers offered weak light and warmth on a cold night but both men had drifted into a dream-free sleep. Cloot, though, was restless and kept himself amused in a tree above his companions by watching the busy and erratic travellings of a tiny vole. However, a movement at the forest's edge caught his attention. The miracle began.

Tor! the falcon called into his friend's blurred mind. He dropped like a stone from his perch and made a commotion with wing and voice.

Cyrus came to instantly and sprang to his feet, a wild look in his eyes. 'What the –!' He did not finish what he had intended to say; he too was caught in amazement.

Tor climbed from his bedroll, dazed, and together the three of them watched in astonishment as a slender pathway lit itself from the fringe of the Great Forest to where they camped.

Tor recalled the golden drops which the god of the forest had rained down upon Cloot during his transformation. Here they were again, even more beautiful against the backdrop of an inky night. Their keeper, Darmud Coril of the Heartwood, was present. He stood, arms outstretched, and from his fingertips flew his drops of gold. The air was filled with chimes, like glass tinkling in a breeze.

'It sounds like heaven,' Tor said.

'It sounds like home,' Cyrus replied dreamily.

We must walk the path, Tor, Cloot said quietly, his voice tinged with awe.

Cyrus had already begun to do so, a faraway expression on his face. Tor, with Cloot steady on his shoulder, caught up and rested his hand on Cyrus's shoulder. It seemed right that the three of them entered the Heartwood together, as one.

None of them knew what to expect, though every ounce of Tor told him that magic of the most powerful kind was surrounding him. It made his flesh tingle. The last time this had happened he had lost his friend. He pushed the thought from his mind and focused on the magic, committing its unique scent to his memory.

The golden drops continued their beautiful chiming and when they finally drew level with Darmud Coril he towered above them, much like a tree himself. He wore the colours of the forest, his robes an ever-changing patina of greens and browns. His long beard, which almost trailed along the forest floor, sparkled with the iridescence of flowers they had never seen before, as did his silvery long hair. The overwhelmed visitors entered the canopy of his forest and instinctively dropped to their knees, heads bowed.

Darmud Coril reached over and stroked Cloot. When he spoke his voice was soft and deep.

'Our hearts are glad that you are home, Cloot.'

He moved silently to rest his hand on Tor's bent shoulder. 'Welcome back to us, friend of the forest.'

Tor forced himself to look up into those gentle green eyes. 'Thank you' was all he could whisper.

Walk safely amongst us always, Darmud Coril breathed into his mind like the touch of a falling leaf. Tor was so filled with emotion he wanted to weep. He resisted the urge to follow the trace of magic back to the god but his memory adeptly embraced its signature. He would never forget it.

And then it was the turn of Cyrus. Tor could feel him trembling.

The god spoke again. 'Ah . . . Cyrus. The Heartwood celebrates your life and your spirit back amongst us. Do you hear the Flames of the Firmament? They sing for you, Kyt Cyrus. They welcome you to your home.' His voice, so kind and sincere, sent a wave of sadness towards Cyrus who found himself weeping softly.

'Hush, hush,' soothed Darmud. 'You are home and safe, my son.'

None of them understood Darmud Coril's words but each realised something critical was taking place. Later Tor would curse his own stupidity and Cloot would reason with him that neither of them could have guessed. For now, the three companions felt safe within the love and joy of the Great Forest and the Heartwood itself.

They slept deeply. When they woke Cloot explained to Tor some of the rules of the forest as the two men marvelled over the plentiful food which lay nearby.

Everything will be supplied. We are not to kill its creatures or pluck fruit from its trees or bushes. We may not fish its streams nor burn its wood. He paused for Tor to repeat his words to Cyrus.

'Who provides all of this?' Tor asked.

The forest, Cloot replied flatly.

Tor turned to Cyrus again, who waved his hand. 'No, don't. I can guess what he said. Let him get on with it.'

Cloot ruffled his feathers importantly. *Gentlemen, meet Solyana.*

A huge wolf, its silver fur flecked white at the tips, moved with the graceful silence of its kind into the clearing. But, unlike other wolves, her eyes were shiny black and fathomless. She loped towards them. Both men trusted Cloot but Cyrus nonetheless groped for his sword, which he discovered was no longer at his side.

The wolf spoke into all of their minds. It was a new experience for Cyrus and he felt as though an icy blade was slicing into his head. He took a sharp breath at the sensation.

Her voice was velvety. *I will be your guide. Together we will travel the forest and in a few days we will emerge within a day's ride of your destination, Torkyn.*

But that's not possible. We are still a four-day ride from Ildagarth surely?

If a wolf could smile, Solyana would have. Her intelligent eyes reflected her mirth.

In the Heartwood there is no need of horses to ride nor distances to measure. Trust me, Torkyn. I will take you where you want to go many times faster than traditional means or routes.

Tor nodded. He understood that he must trust the magic of the forest and besides, he liked Solyana already and wondered at the notion of travelling alongside a wolf . . . such a large one too.

Cyrus spoke. 'So this is how you talk to one another?' His amazement made Tor smile.

'May I try it?' Cyrus asked the wolf.

She responded in silken tones back into his mind. *I would caution that you can only use the link if you are bonded. You are not bonded, Kyt Cyrus. However, strange magics prevail in our Heartwood. You are welcome to try.*

Cyrus made a polite bow to the wolf and then squeezed his eyes shut. He looked like he was in pain. Tor laughed.

'Go ahead, you bastard,' Cyrus said aloud but with good humour. 'You have no idea how frustrating it is knowing all of you are carrying on conversations without me.'

'Cloot thinks he knows what you were casting to us.'

Cyrus stopped his efforts and looked at Tor expectantly.

'He said that you were telling us how easy war would be if you could communicate with your men using the link.'

Cyrus looked amazed. 'How he did he know that? Could you hear me, you wretched bird?'

'He says lucky guess,' Tor said shrugging his shoulders.

Solyana briefed them further. *Please, eat plentifully. We have a long journey ahead of us today but we will take it at an easy pace.*

What about our things, Solyana? Should we lighten off so we can carry them?

Thank you, Torkyn. I almost forgot. No. Please leave everything. They will be taken care of. You require nothing for your wellbeing. The forest will feed, bathe, warm and rest you. It is your host and you are its guests.

She noticed Cyrus was about to say something and

answered before he could. *Your horses are well cared for and will be returned to you, Torkyn, when we reach the northern fringe of the forest.*

Cyrus found it vaguely irritating that the wolf seemed to address only Tor about the journey but he let it pass. They all nodded their agreement and answered the grumble of their hungry stomachs instead of worrying about the strangeness of their situation.

Tor cooked the fish over a small fire Cyrus made with the kindling and branches provided. They ate luscious berries none of them had tasted before, dried nuts and a strange drink which Solyana told them was milk of gurgon.

'Let's not even ask,' Cyrus said, draining the thickish, buttery-coloured liquid.

'This is good,' Tor said, licking his lips. 'What do you suppose a gurgon is?'

Don't even suppose, Cloot joined in as he cleaned his beak from the fresh meat which had been left for him. *Ah dormouse, delicious!* he said deliberately to Tor who gave him the extreme satisfaction of squirming.

Solyana bade them not to worry about the mess. *I know, I know*, said Tor to her, *the forest will take care of it*. He enjoyed hearing her laugh deeply in his head.

They set off in high spirits with Cloot swooping deftly amongst the branches and Solyana padding at a slow lope between the long strides of Tor and Cyrus. They exchanged stories along the way. Solyana told them about life in the Forest and for the first time Cyrus heard Tor's story from the moment he had witnessed his first bridling at Twyfford Cross.

Even though the days had cooled considerably now they

were so much further north and the beginning of winter was fast approaching, neither man required warm clothing. Within the forest they walked in a perfect warmth where butterflies, long dead by now in even the southern counties, flitted joyously amongst the undergrowth. Dusk took a long time to arrive but when it did it fell hard and fast, swiftly turning the forest into a more brooding place.

Would here be suitable for your camp tonight? Solyana asked politely.

Cyrus saw the food laid out beneath one of the trees. He snorted and shook his head in amazement. 'Tell our wolf it's perfect, thank you.'

She seemed to understand without Tor interpreting and wished them all a pleasant evening before disappearing into the woodland. Cyrus busied himself with making a fire whilst Tor sorted through the provisions for their evening meal.

They did not need their bedrolls. The spongy floor of the forest was comfortable enough and this time Cloot relaxed completely, drifting into a bird's doze whilst the two men chatted quietly after eating. Tor agreed to sing and chose a lusty ballad about a man who loved every woman he met. This amused Cyrus and it was good to hear him laugh again. Soon enough they slept deeply.

The second day followed a similar pattern with Solyana arriving as they broke their fast. They enjoyed an uneventful and peaceful day of walking, the wolf guiding them northwards along a path which seemed to build itself a few steps ahead of them.

They did not feel tired, as they had done the previous

evening, and were in excellent spirits when they finally fell asleep amongst the security of the trees.

This night, however, both men dreamed.

18

The Story of Orlac

Tor could feel the presence of Lys as he slept. When she finally made herself known to him he was neither shocked nor surprised; he was glad. He had many questions for her.

She did not speak at first. Still asleep, he could sense that the stones tied in the pouch around his neck were blazing dazzling colours. Tor could feel power. Immense power.

Hello, Lys.

I'm impressed you know me, said the voice which was as delicate as snowfall.

I've been expecting you, he continued, surprising himself at how calm he sounded.

I'm sorry I took so long to make myself known to you, Tor.

He liked her calling him Tor. *Will you enlighten me?*

As best I can at this time, she breathed softly. *Ask your questions, Tor Gynt.*

How long have you known me?

All of your life. Before you were born even.

He ignored the obvious protests he wanted to make.

The people who raised me, Jhon and Ailsa Gynt, are caretakers, not my real mother and father.

Is that a question? she said gently.

He felt a flush of embarrassment and tried again.

Who are my real parents?

Your father's name is Darganoth and your mother is Evagora.

Are they sentient?

Indeed. Her voice betrayed the humour she found in his query.

I was told they are dead. Are they?

Now she was more serious. *They live.*

That shocked him. He decided to leave that topic for now.

But they love you eternally, she added.

He pressed on. *Is Alyssa alive?*

Lys seemed keen to answer this; he could hear her enthusiasm. *She is alive. She is a most captivating woman.*

Does she ever think about me? He had not meant to ask this.

She used not to be able to get through a day without you filling her head. Now she thinks on you rarely. She finds it painful. Alyssa has a new life now.

So she loves another? Even after five years the pain was hard to endure.

I did not say that. Alyssa has not loved any other man romantically since you. However, she is happy in the life she is living.

Can I find her? Will you help me?

Yes to both questions. Tor, there is something we must share before you wake.

Knowing he still had so much more to learn from her

and no guarantee they may speak again soon, or ever, Tor
hurried on.

Why am I so special, Lys?

We are all special, Tor.

Fool! He was cross with himself for this clumsiness.
Am I destined for something special, Lys?

Most certainly.

Will you tell me what?

*Let's make that your last question for now, child. Instead of
me answering it, allow me to show you something.*

As he slumbered, a breeze blew across his face and
mists swirled about him. It felt suddenly cool. As the
scene cleared, he found he was looking at a palace; more
sumptuous a place he could not imagine. He travelled
its marbled corridors and saw into its grand halls and
rooms. Everyone in the palace was supremely beautiful,
all shapes and sizes, all colours — these people were
magnificent. But although he saw much, Tor could hear
nothing.

Now he was staring into a light-filled room with many
arched windows, a glorious mosaic floor and tall columns
of marble. He saw a woman who had just given life to a
golden-haired son. The baby was crying and the woman
wept with joy, the pain of birth already forgotten as she
held her perfect child. Tor watched a tall man rush into
the room. The midwives quickly covered her unwashed
body and all of them were on their knees within seconds,
heads bowed to the man.

He had dark wavy hair and brilliant blue eyes. He knelt
by the bed and stroked the woman's flaxen hair and gently
held the tiny hand of his newborn, pride etched across
his handsome face.

Suddenly Tor was outside. He saw trumpeters but again could not hear them. A multitude of people had gathered. The couple emerged onto a balcony; their son — slightly older now — was in his father's arms. The people below cheered and clapped. Tor watched the couple become increasingly tense as the constant stream of visitors and requests to show off the boy showed no sign of abating.

Tor guessed the babe was a prince. The king and queen obviously had no other children which explained the hysteria surrounding this child's birth.

Good, he heard Lys whisper in his mind.

He saw the mother crying. She was explaining something to the king who was nodding. Next, Tor saw the royals strolling in a lovely, sunlit wood. Just the three of them, no entourage; they were happy, peaceful together at last. The child had grown. Now he was an infant, gurgling cheerfully in his mother's arms.

Ahead, shimmering into new existence, appeared a glade even more beautiful than the wood in which the royals walked. They stopped. Their astonishment turned to curiosity . . . or at least, for the king. The queen was cautious.

Tor wished he could hear their conversation but he could only watch. There was a stream, its sparkling waters impossibly bright. Flowers he could imagine existing only in a dream bobbed gracefully in a light breeze; he imagined he could smell their heady, exotic fragrance.

The king pulled his queen gently towards the glade. Tor sensed danger; he wanted to shout at them not to go there. Lys soothed him. It was a feathery touch; there one moment and the next, gone.

I'm showing you something which happened a long, long time ago, Tor.

Why?

Because you must know this.

Well, how—

Hush. Watch . . . she urged.

The royals were in the glade now. The boy sat between his father's legs. Tor stared at the contrast between them; no one would imagine them to be of the same flesh and blood. The child had golden hair in soft curls and violet eyes whilst the king's hair was so dark as to be almost black and his eyes blue.

Lys, something bad is going to happen. Tor hardly dared to watch.

Lys said nothing. Tor's stomach tightened as he watched the queen lie down. The king was already dozing and it was not long before her lids finally closed too.

Tor's attention was now riveted on the child who had drifted away from his parents, gathering flowers. He was a very beautiful child and Tor imagined he would be a striking man. No wonder the parents were proud of him. He was the perfect prince and heir to their throne . . . wherever that was.

Tor could not tell who owned the arm which reached from the shadows behind the child. The boy did not see it; he was busy. His mother awoke with a start and looked around wildly, waking the king as she called out his name. Just as the queen turned to look at her son, who was holding out a bunch of three brightly coloured blooms to her, the intruder gripped the child. And then the arms were pulling the prince back through a grey misted hole.

Tor found himself on the other side of that hole and watched in horror as the thieves, half men, half beasts, came running out of a small copse and off down a dusty road. They jollied each other along, the prince in their arms.

Tor had a moment for only one brief glance. Beyond the rent in a transparent, shimmering sheen he could see them: the queen slumped to her knees; the king, his handsome face a mask of anguish.

Now Tor saw the thieves dressed differently and in a new location. They placed a bundle behind a bush and then walked quickly to a nearby inn. They were clearly not locals but no one in the inn seemed to notice anything out of the ordinary. They each downed a cup of ale quickly and then one pointed to a man slumped at a table. The other grinned. They walked over and must have asked if they could join him. He seemed not to answer but they sat anyway. Something about the man tweaked at Tor's consciousness. Through sunken, grief-ridden eyes the third man watched the newcomers. He appeared to have been drowning his sorrows at the inn.

The three talked for a while and the man's body language suggested to Tor that he was taking greater interest in what the two thieves were saying. The three looked around self-consciously then the third man knocked knuckles with one of the thieves. Tor recalled this as an ancient practice used in centuries previous for everything from a welcome to agreeing on a deal.

It seemed a deal had been struck.

The man followed the thieves. In the dark they all glanced around again nervously. The bundle was handed over. The familiar-looking man pulled back the blanket and Tor watched his face soften into a smile which he knew well but could not place.

The man fumbled as he pulled out a pouch. He tossed it to the thieves who disappeared swiftly.

Now Tor saw him entering a house. A woman came into view. Her hand went to her mouth to stifle a yell. The man was talking fast and the child was scooped into her arms.

Something about the man niggled again at Tor's mind. He did not recognise him but he looked so familiar. He watched the couple caress the child lovingly and kiss him, just as he had watched the boy's real parents do minutes earlier.

The vision faltered as the mists returned and Tor was alone with Lys again. He desperately wanted to see what happened to the child.

You were right, Tor. The boy is a prince. But no ordinary prince. He is a prince of the Host.

Of the gods? Tor said incredulously.

Yes. There is a phenomenon, Lys continued, *known as The Glade. It chooses when it appears, where it appears and to whom among the Host it appears. It is a highly magical place for it has the ability to touch other worlds. The Host warns its people never to be enticed into The Glade. The king should have known better . . . did know better.*

They're gods, Lys — why couldn't they save their son?

Because gods and their vast powers are not allowed to enter other worlds. It can unbalance both worlds involved and destroy their very fabric.

Why did the child not create havoc then?

Oh, he did, she sighed. *But let me explain. A newborn is not aware of his powers. He is also too small to have much effect.*

When the child was taken through he hardly disturbed the land he entered. If the king or queen had done anything other than watch, their world would be dying now — and yours, she explained.

And the thieves who reached through to snatch the boy?

They are called Scavengers. Members of a race who lived off the crumbs of others. Drifters with no land to call their own. Petty thieves. Over the centuries they have died out.

So, what happened to the boy?

She sighed. *He grew up oblivious to his history, as were his new parents. They also chose not to tell him that he was not their true son.*

Was he empowered?

Mightily so, Tor. Fortunately these people were sentient; the father was a particularly gifted wielder. You must understand these were times of extraordinary harmony and tolerance when sentient people lived happily alongside the non-empowered. No Inquisitors in those days.

Tor could not imagine a world without Inquisitors.

Lys continued, quickly now. *He grew up an angry young man but never really knew why. His parents decided the best place for him was the Academie at a place called Goldstone. You know it today as Caremboche. He was enrolled as an acolyte under the Master Wizard Joromi. All seemed fine for a year or two but the prince became bored, restless with his tasks. He was far more powerful than anyone had ever imagined and as soon as he was old enough to grasp this he began to use that power against the harmony of the Academie.*

They had no answer to it. The boy had become too unpredictable, too dangerous. The elders decided on a dangerous scheme to link and use their combined power against the acolyte to stem his flow of power. It had never been tried before — it had never been needed before — but if they could draw on ancient theory and Quell the boy, then they would have time to consider what should be done permanently.

The boy learned of the plan. Years of anger manifested themselves in the most horrific devastation of Goldstone.

He levelled a city? If Tor had been awake his eyes would have been shining with awe.

And killed more than two thousand people in moments, Lys replied sadly. *I have dwelled too long on this tale, Tor. Allow me to bring it to a close quickly. I visited the boy's earthly father and nearly killed him with the shock of my story.*

I told him about his son, that he was the prince of gods, trapped in a mortal life. We devised a plan. It was audacious. The father lured his son to a place not far from Goldstone called Rune, a rare portal through which we could communicate with the Host.

The father told the boy his story and compelled him to talk with his true parents. It was a terrifying betrayal on our part. There was no talk. Instead, the Host linked and, using the father as a medium, they weaved a most astounding and complex Quelling.

I will never forget the way the son screamed his despair when he realised what was happening to him.

Could he not just . . .

Go back? Lys said.

Yes.

Tor heard her sad sigh. *As I explained, transference between worlds is too dangerous. Instead, the Host placed the mightiest of enchantments upon their prince. In their own way, they were protecting him.*

Tor frowned. *Lys, who are you?*

He thought he could sense her smiling. *I roam between*

the worlds, Tor. I do not belong with the Host, nor am I one of your people. I am a sort of caretaker of worlds. I help to keep the balance.

Tor could tell there was more but she was choosing her words with care. She continued.

I assembled ten guardians, one from each of the major peoples alive in the Four Kingdoms at the time. This group became the Paladin. They took their cargo, in his enchanted prison of light, to a secret place.

You mean he's still alive?

He is alive. The Paladin guard him still but they are failing. For centuries he has pitched himself against the magics of the Host and the stamina and powers of his guardians. Slowly he is winning the duel. He knows no mercy. He feeds off his own hate, his own despair of betrayal by both his fathers and his determination for retribution.

Tor swallowed hard. *Will he break free?*

Almost certainly. And he will return to Tallinor to finish what he began.

Lys, Tor breathed hard as panic gripped him, *why are you telling me his story?*

Because you must stop him, Torkyn Gynt, she said, fading.

Wait! he cried. *What is his name?*

In your world he goes by the name of Orlac.

Tor felt Lys pulling away from him. Consciousness tugged at the fringe of his mind. He was waking.

Lys . . . please. Tell me the name of his earthly father. I must know it.

From very far away she whispered into his mind. *His name is Merkhud.*

Tor awoke.

*   *   *

Cyrus also dreamed. Lys came to him and spoke as tenderly as a lover.

Solyana will come for you soon, my brave soldier.

Must I follow her? His voice was edged with grief.

It is your destiny, she replied.

I would wish to stay close to Tor.

No, Cyrus. Your time with Tor is finished for now. He has his path to follow and you have yours. You have a far greater task ahead of you now. It is the most precious of gifts we bestow on you.

I'm scared, Lys. I have faced death many times but this time I'm scared of it.

Your destiny is not to die, friend of the Heartwood. You must live long. The forest embraces you as its own. It loves you. You held strong and sincere for the Paladin. Only three of them hold now. Soon Orlac will break free and we have other tasks to perform before he does. Yours is the most important task of all.

Cyrus had no idea what she was talking about though something stirred distantly in his memory when she spoke of the Paladin.

Lys . . . Cyrus was astonished to hear the fear in his voice. *Who am I?*

You are one of the Paladin. You are a guardian. She is here, Cyrus; be calm. She too loves you.

Cyrus looked across the clearing. He could see Tor curled on the ground nearby and all around familiar things including Solyana who stood silently. Her eyes regarded him with abiding friendship.

Will you join me? Her smooth tone reassured him.

Farewell, Cyrus, Lys called.

He had forgotten what he needed to know. It had fled from his mind when Solyana spoke. Instead he followed her slowly, as if his feet hardly touched the soft earth of the forest floor. Solyana padded silently just a step or so ahead. Cyrus rested his hand on the thick silver fur of her back. She did not mind. The wolf led him along a special path which unravelled in front of them and soon led him far from Tor. Cyrus hoped Cloot was paying attention but somehow he knew the bird would not witness his departure.

He sighed as his dream-walk led him into a clearing. The air was perfumed. It seemed a thousand flowers had suddenly released their fragrance to welcome him.

The clearing was overhung with a canopy of thick foliage and lit enchantingly by the Flames of the Firmament which flickered and danced, chiming softly. In the middle of the circle they created stood Darmud Coril. Around him had gathered the beasts of the Heartwood, each of them magical and each to bear witness.

Cyrus felt calm tracing through his body. His heartbeat slowed and his breathing deepened. He realised his eyes were open and he looked down at his hand buried deep in Solyana's fur. Her serene face as she turned reassured him further.

Welcome to our family, Cyrus, the beasts said into his mind.

He wept with the joy of belonging.

Darmud Coril waited until the soldier had composed himself. When Cyrus found the courage to look into those soft eyes he no longer felt scared. He felt elated. Cyrus smiled and the god of the Heartwood returned it.

You have shed your blood amongst us, Kyt Cyrus. You are a brother to the creatures of the Heartwood and you are chosen by the goddess Lys as protector. Darmud Coril spoke quietly but clearly.

There was silence. Even the chiming flames had quietened. No leaf stirred.

Protector of what, Almighty One? Cyrus asked, his brow creasing.

Protector of whom, the god corrected gently. *You will know more in time, my son. Know now only that you have been chosen. You are precious. For now, the Heartwood protects you.*

Darmud Coril spoke to his creatures. *Gather him to your hearts, my children.*

Cyrus watched as the flames burned tall and more brightly than ever, their chimes ringing clearly again in the still night.

The creatures closed on the circle of light and Cyrus, his fingers still tightly gripping onto Solyana, was welcomed and absorbed into the Ring of the Heartwood. His last thought was one of comprehension.

Ah, Solyana, this is why you only spoke to Tor about our journey through the forest. I go no further.

Sadly no one heard his thought for he was not bonded . . . yet.

Tor awoke with a start. He remembered everything from the dream scenes Lys had shown him, including the chilling revelation about Merkhud. He shook his head with disbelief but knew it was useless. Lys had no reason to lie.

Cloot dropped to the ground in front of him. The bird looked dishevelled.

Cyrus has gone.

Tor glanced around. *What do you mean, gone?*

Gone. Departed. Absent. No longer here.

Gone where? Tor couldn't help himself.

Tor, if I knew where, I would not have spent most of the hours since dawn flying all over the forest. Cyrus is no longer with us.

Tor pulled himself angrily to his feet. *But that's ridiculous. Why would he go? Why would he leave us without saying anything? Where would he go?*

Indeed. All the same questions I've asked myself a hundred times already.

The truth was, the falcon could hardly believe it himself. Cloot was sure he had been alert for most of the night and his hearing was sharp; even if he had dozed he would have woken at the slightest sound.

Tor raked his hand through his hair and looked around helplessly, as though his anxiety alone could conjure Cyrus back to them.

It was timely that Solyana appeared. Her voice soothed their immediate barrage of questions.

Please don't fret, Torkyn. Kyt Cyrus is safe now. He is where he belongs.

And where is that, pray? Cloot saw Tor glare at his sarcastic tone.

He belongs in the Heartwood, friend Cloot. Last night we welcomed him formally.

Tor bit his lip; tasted blood. Another friend lost to Lys. He was a fool. He should have sensed it from the Flames' first greeting of them and Darmud Coril's initial welcome.

Solyana, are you telling us that Cyrus will remain here? He will not journey further with us?

You are correct.

Anxiety coursed through his body. *Why?*

Because he must. Because Lys has chosen him. Because Darmud Coril welcomes him as a member of the Heartwood. Because, she said wistfully, *it is his destiny.*

Tor linked with Cloot, knowing Solyana could not hear him.

Cyrus spoke of this before we entered the forest. He was afraid. He said he sensed his own destiny.

Cloot flew to Tor's shoulder. It felt safe to be touching one another. *Then we must go on. If Lys has chosen this path for him, it is part of the complex web she spins.*

How can you be so accepting of her, Cloot? He looked at Solyana who was patiently waiting for them.

Because of what I am. I was a crippled freak of a man. She turned me into this falcon. I believe in the enchantments of the Heartwood. It offers nothing but sanctuary and love to us. I trust it. If it welcomes Lys, we have nothing to fear from her. We must trust her . . . and we know Cyrus is safe.

The wolf spoke. *Perhaps you would like to eat,* she said politely, her eyes glancing at the food laid out on leaves nearby. *And then we must continue our journey. It will be our last day of travelling together. Tonight you will reach Ildagarth.*

19

Xantia

Alyssa stepped past Xantia as they left the dining hall of the Academie. As always, the noon meal was a noisy affair and she far preferred the sanctuary of the library.

'Back to the crypt?' Xantia called after her. 'Too much sunlight?'

Alyssa looked back at the young woman who had become her tormentor. She knew Xantia and her sidekicks were just baiting her, yearning for the excuse to give her today's nasty medicine.

She could not recall when or why their friendship had gone sour. They had made a glorious pair: Alyssa, golden-haired with soft green eyes and a reserved demeanour was the perfect foil to Xantia's raven-haired, dark-skinned looks and fiery temper. Both had matured into beautiful women and before the curves of womanhood had settled on their bones they had been friends.

When Alyssa made her dramatic arrival on the rooftops of Caremboche five years previous, Xantia was an angry girl of similar age. She had no friends at the Academie and her loneliness fuelled a lofty attitude. That afternoon

in the early autumn most of the women were in Ildagarth.
Each Eighthday the Academie allowed its members to do
their marketing and most took advantage of the freedom
it provided. Xantia was rarely asked to accompany the
others for it was accepted by all that she was generally of
bad humour and destined to ruin a pleasant escape from
strict routines. Strolling through the markets alone whilst
the others enjoyed their day out together merely rein-
forced Xantia's feeling of isolation and so she often chose
to remain at Caremboche.

And so Xantia was one of the first to hear the commotion outside that day and easily the swiftest to get to the
roof. She was joined there by a stranger, the visitor who
had met with Elder Iris that morning. The old woman
was distraught, babbling that her granddaughter Alyssa
was trapped outside the Academie's walls.

Others arrived, breathless but not fast enough to send
the youngster away from the terrible scene below and so
Xantia had witnessed the reviled Inquisitors and their
despised leader torturing a helpless man. She learned from
the grieving newcomer that he was Saxon Fox of Cirq
Zorros and that he had been travelling with the old woman
and her granddaughter as they fled the Inquisitors.

Many times during her years at the Academie Xantia
had been accused of being cold; some would even whisper
heartless. She hated her life of imprisonment – as she saw
it – and the daily, uneventful routine and any change to
it, bloody as it may be, was exciting. And so she watched
Saxon being tortured, noticing how he made little sound
save a low, animal-like growl, and she witnessed the
murder of the boys. Their smiles of wonder at Alyssa's
enchanted acrobatics were still curiously evident when

their lifeless bodies were dragged into the compound.

Everyone was shocked by the violence but the newcomer had remained that way for many weeks. Alyssa just stared straight ahead, glassy-eyed, and reacted to neither words nor touch. Even food seemed a trial. Nothing more than brochen – the thin porridge of the region – would she take and that had to be massaged down her throat. Xantia, who was fascinated by the strangers, was sure Alyssa would have died had Sorrel not persisted with such dedication.

It was only when the man the Inquisitors had left for dead had hobbled into Alyssa's tiny room that she had returned to some normality, first trembling then weeping for hours.

Xantia had requested very early that she be allowed to assist these newcomers. The Elders had agreed, glad to see the young acolyte showing some compassion and interest in life outside of herself. And so she had spent many afternoons watching the Kloek and Alyssa. She sensed a bond between them yet no words were ever said. Xantia desperately wanted to know more.

Saxon had clung to life through the tireless attentions of Sorrel and the Elders but the cost was immense. The Inquisitors' attack had left him with neither eyes nor tongue; the latter had been hacked out and fed to the scavenger dogs. His smashed arms had healed awkwardly and no longer hung normally at his sides. His legs were so badly deformed by the beating that he could barely walk and even Xantia could see that his spine would never straighten again; he would hobble like an old man for the rest of his life. As for speech, rather than grunt he chose to remain silent, communicating with a nod or shake of his head, perhaps a shrug. That he worshipped Alyssa was clear, though, and this intrigued Xantia all the more.

The weeks lengthened from autumn to winter and as the newcomers showed no intention of leaving, the Elders suggested that Alyssa become a member of the Academie. They had spoken with Sorrel and learned that the girl was empowered. Only the Academie could offer a sentient woman absolute protection.

The old woman had accepted the gracious offer but on the proviso that Saxon be allowed to remain also. They had agreed but he was not allowed within the Academie's hallowed halls. Instead, he tended the Academie's animals and handled errands and odd tasks around the complex. He slept in the hay loft and ate his meals alone in one of the many small courtyards.

As she looked at Alyssa now, Xantia remembered how it had been only her dogged persistence that finally brought the girl out of her shell. Saxon may have kept Alyssa sane but it was Xantia who had retrieved her spirit. Five years on and you would hardly believe this to be the same timid creature; except for the odd moments when one could tell she carried scars. She refused to discuss her life and the very mention of Goth could stop her in her tracks.

Alyssa answered Xantia's attack. 'I've got a lot of work to complete in the archives.'

Xantia would not let her off as easily as that, especially with an audience of young, impressionable acolytes listening in.

'Alyssa, are you soft in the head? Did you hear what Elder May announced? There's a visitor from Tal arriving any day now. You heard the story of Queen Nyria's illness and so neither she nor that handsome King of ours can attend.'

'I'm really not that interested,' Alyssa said.

Xantia nudged one of her friends. 'You're so pious. We know we can't touch but we are still flesh and blood. We are allowed to . . .' Searching for the right word, she settled on 'lust' and said it with her eyebrows arched.

As Xantia expected, it won the response she wanted from her two companions, who laughed.

Alyssa tried not to sound condescending but these days whenever she spoke with Xantia she felt like the eternal Miss Do Right. 'You're courting danger, you know that. Why torture yourself over a man when you will never be allowed to enjoy one?'

Xantia ignored the comment and grinned at her colleagues. For just a moment, Alyssa glimpsed the friend she used to adore.

'You know they usually send us this ancient physic who is no fun at all. I know it's not him this time because I've checked. It might be someone young, someone tall and devilishly handsome.' Xantia pretended to swoon.

'Yes, and it could also be someone middle-aged and podgy with nasty breath,' one of her companions countered.

Even Alyssa had to smile at that but she still wanted to leave. Soon Xantia would feel compelled to twist the conversation back into a nasty dagger levelled against her and Alyssa did not want to wait around for it.

Xantia folded her arms theatrically. 'It won't be. Not this time. I refuse to believe it.'

'What are you getting yourself into such a state for anyway?' asked another girl.

'Because it's the only time in ten years we'll be allowed to dance with a man, you fool. They relax rules for the Festival! And our Alyssa here . . .'

Here we go, Alyssa thought.

'. . . is such a beauty who could resist dancing the night away with her?'

Alyssa fixed Xantia with a look of disdain. 'You'd do well to keep your mind on your work and away from men. You do recall your status?'

She regretted her words instantly, knowing they were exactly the lead Xantia needed.

'How can I ever forget?' she spat. 'I wish I'd never been brought here. I would rather have taken my chances against Goth.'

Xantia watched Alyssa's controlled expression turn cold before she disappeared down the corridor. She shrugged, delighted that she had scored another cruel blow.

Xantia hated being a prisoner of the Academie. She was not scared of Goth, not even with the knowledge that her own sentient mother had been dealt with by the Inquisitors. If she ever found the well-meaning villagers who had delivered her into the hands of the Academie, she would destroy them with every ounce of her power. That old anger never waned in Xantia. She resented everything about the Academie: its pious attitude, its inflexible routines, its unnatural attitude towards men and especially its forced warding of each individual's power. Unlike the majority of the other women there, she had not chosen Caremboche. Xantia knew she was far more powerful than her mother and would have preferred her freedom.

She touched the archalyt disc on her forehead. She never

stopped thinking about how to remove it but it was impossible. She had tried everything. It was an impregnable shield. As a youngster, she had frequently drawn blood trying to prise it off. On each occasion the Elders had sombrely reminded her that once an archalyt stone is touched to the forehead of a sentient girl it attaches for eternity.

'There is no power in the Kingdom, brute strength or enchanted, which is potent enough to remove it. Consider it part of you, my girl,' Elder Iris had counselled.

Xantia would never get used to it though and grew obsessed with the idea of escaping the life of an acolyte.

Then, about twelve moons ago, after Helene died, it was announced that a new Elder would be appointed from the senior acolytes. Xantia could hardly believe it. There had been no Elder status awarded since she had come to the Academie seventeen winters previous. This was her chance. Finally, the opportunity to break the shackles; achieve some measure of freedom, status, authority. Even the chance to travel the Kingdom.

Xantia began to daydream. She could see herself in the future as Chief Elder; now that was something to aim for. The idea of power appealed to her so strongly that she began to think of nothing else. Before long she had convinced herself that there was no one better for the position. She had been at the Academie the longest of all the acolytes; she was extremely intelligent – that was acknowledged by even her greatest critics. Most importantly, her specialty was a subject no one else cared to study. She had made the Dark Arts her own domain and no one could hold a candle to her for her understanding of these powers or their history.

Her writings on the Dark Arts had no equal in the land.

And then the blow had fallen. Taking a short cut through the gardens one bright spring morning she overheard two of the most respected Elders chatting. They were discussing the most likely choice from the four candidates under consideration for the new Elder position. To Xantia's despair both had resoundingly supported Alyssa. She knew their voices had weight in the Circle of Elders. If Alyssa was getting their vote, then her own chances were seriously damaged. Worse, she was well aware that the Chief Elder held nothing but admiration for Alyssa.

Without meaning for it to happen, during that spring, Xantia had gradually turned against her close friend. At first it had manifested in petulance and the ever-patient Alyssa had put up with it. By summer's arrival it had deepened into Xantia finding fault with almost every aspect of their friendship.

Her latest strategy was to look for ways to make Alyssa look bad in front of her peers. So far, however, none of the mud had stuck; Alyssa always managed to come out of it clean. Then, one day at the beginning of Deadleaf, Alyssa's tolerance had snapped. She accused Xantia of scheming and lying. Xantia turned on Alyssa, suggesting she was suffering from a sad case of self-persecution.

At that point Alyssa gave up and accepted there was no friendship left for them. And now, for the past three moons, she had maintained a distant politeness whilst Xantia seized every chance she could to needle her.

Which was where Xantia found herself this morning.

She did not even like the two younger girls who were hanging around her but they made her look popular and they laughed when she needed them to. Suddenly tired of the twittering novices, she asked them to leave her. They had served their purpose.

She walked aimlessly down the exquisitely hand-painted corridors of the Academie. She saw none of it. Her mind was elsewhere and her gaze blank. When she brought herself back to the present she was in the grandly arched entry hall. Marble throughout, it never failed to impress visitors. Xantia had spent most of her life surrounded by such beauty but she rarely paid it a scrap of attention.

Her attention was caught by Saxon who was hobbling across the front courtyard towards the gates. What was the blind fool up to? It was not one of the delivery days and, besides, stores were usually received through the back gates. She watched him pull back the catch on the peep-hole and put his ear to it. Hearing was all he had left she thought cruelly. He listened then opened a very small door to receive a roll of parchment. It was not sealed and it fell open.

Xantia's sharp vision glimpsed the royal crest in wax. She saw Saxon touch it, his fingers travelling over its distinctive pattern.

'Oh Light! He's here,' she whispered.

Xantia watched as Saxon unbolted the gates and, nodding humbly, allowed a tall man to lead his horse inside. Saxon felt for and took the reins, handed back the parchment and pointed in the direction of the reception lobby, where she stood. Embarrassed, she fled behind one of the magnificent arched pillars, hoping she had been quick enough. She took another peep; he was breathtaking.

The most extraordinarily blue eyes scanned the shadows

where she hid. Xantia felt as though all her prayers had
been answered. Here was one glittering chance to enjoy
the company of a man. The next opportunity would be a
decade hence, by which time she would be an old woman
of almost thirty summers.

She was not going to waste this chance.

As he walked towards the lobby Xantia breached all
protocol. She took a deep breath, smoothed her robes and
stepped out from the shadows.

'Good afternoon, sir, welcome to the Academie.'

She bowed deeply, glad that the cut of the acolyte's
robes actually suited her slender frame and especially
pleased that she had worn her glossy hair untied today.

He stopped. 'Ah, I thought I saw someone here a
moment ago. Thank you . . . er. . . . ?'

'I am Xantia. My apologies that you have not been
given the welcome we reserve for our royal guests but we
were not expecting you so soon.' She smiled at him, using
the moment to absorb his imposing presence.

Tor was amused. He was tempted to enquire how she
knew he was the royal representative but it had been too
long since he had clapped eyes on such a beauty. Not since
Eryn in fact and his mind naturally wandered from her
to Alyssa. He could not resist the temptation to enjoy
this moment, though Merkhud's warning hovered. She
was politely waiting.

'Yes, I travelled much swifter than I expected. I hope
my prompt arrival presents no inconvenience, Xantia?'

Even his voice was delicious.

'Not a bit. A welcome distraction for all, I'm sure,' she
flirted, enjoying the effect of her coquettish remark in his
sparkling eyes.

'My name is Torkyn Gynt. I'm Under Physic to the royals and most honoured to be here.'

A gaggle of urgent voices preceded the disgruntled arrival of Elders Iris, May and Ellyn and prevented their conversation going further.

Xantia curtsied, blushing.

'Acolyte Xantia!' Elder Iris admonished.

She would have to face their wrath later she was sure. She kept her face turned towards her toes. The rules may well be relaxed for this special festival but Xantia had broken strict protocol. She could see it written over their stunned faces when she stole a glance.

'Elders,' said their visitor, bowing low.

He made his formal introduction again.

'I am Under Physic Torkyn Gynt, representative of their majesties King Lorys and Queen Nyria and here on behalf of Physic Merkhud who is a little too frail to travel this year. I must apologise for my unexpected early arrival.' He did not wait and gave them no time to respond. 'I believe I misunderstood the blind man out there. He did not actually say anything but when he pointed, I thought he meant for me to wait here.'

He allowed a pause for the full weight of his smile to soften the pursed lips in front of him. They remained determinedly pinched.

'And your most polite Xantia, who happened to be passing, greeted me so courteously. She was keen to find you but I fear I kept her talking about your beautiful architecture here.' He turned to wave his hands at the auditorium. As he did so he winked at Xantia.

She held her breath to stop herself getting into any further trouble. He had winked! She adored him.

'Perhaps during my stay Xantia might be allowed to show me around the areas of the Academie I'm permitted to see?'

She had to clench her teeth to stop disbelief washing away her contrite expression. The Elders could hardly decline him publicly. Now he was formally kissing each of their hands and gravely handed to Elder Iris the rolled parchment he had carried from the King.

Her voice was still hard but Xantia sensed the old girl was warming. 'Well, Physic Gynt, we're glad your journey was safe and speedy. How is the Queen?'

'I saw her just a short while before I left the Palace and she was making an excellent recovery.' He waited, those blue eyes wide and disarming.

'That is good news.' She twitched with an attempt to smile. 'And our dear friend, Physic Merkhud?'

'He is much improved, Elder Iris. Still fragile from a recent illness but certainly mending. Extremely disappointed, of course, that he could not be with you for this special celebration.'

'He will be missed,' Elder May chimed in.

Xantia could feel the thaw and was glad to see she had been forgotten for the time being.

Ellyn, the least crusty of the Elders, was smiling at last. 'Has Saxon taken your belongings, Physic Gynt?'

'He has, thank you. Maybe I could wash away some of the dust of the journey and join you shortly? I have news and gifts from Merkhud.'

They bowed.

Elder Iris spoke briefly to Xantia. 'Show our guest to his rooms.'

Xantia was surprised and delighted to be given such a task. She bobbed a quick bow to her Elder.

'And Xantia . . .'

She turned back to the stern face. 'Yes, Elder Iris?'

'The free hour is almost complete. Straight back to your duties, please.' There was enough in the Elder's tone to warn Xantia against flouting the rules further.

'Thank you,' she muttered to Tor as they took their leave.

'Don't mention it. Are they always that much fun?' he asked.

'I don't understand you – Elder Iris was in high spirits.' She laughed at her jest. 'Did you mean what you said about me being your guide?'

'Of course! But I'm not sure if the Sisters of Mirth will permit it.'

Xantia had to stifle her delight at his irreverent dig at the women she found so tiresome in her life. Torkyn Gynt was a brilliant breath of fresh air and she was going to make sure she relished every moment of his stay. She took him the longest possible route she could devise to reach the small building not far from the stables which the women had readied weeks ago.

'Here already?' he said.

She would later repeat that over and over in her mind, searching for whether she heard regret in his lovely voice.

'I hope you'll be comfortable here, Physic Gynt,' she said, opening the door and stepping aside.

Saxon hobbled over. Tor found it hard not to stare at the ruined orbs of his eyes. He tried to imagine how such a gruesome injury could have occurred. Saxon pointed to Tor's saddlebags, already deposited in the rooms and disappeared to the stable.

'Now there's a man of few words,' Tor commented.

'Well, that might be because he can't speak. Goth stabbed his eyes and cut out his tongue, amongst other atrocities.' Xantia saw the shock pass across Tor's smooth, open face. 'Oh, of course, you would know the Chief Inquisitor.'

'And I wish I did not,' he said coldly. 'I'm very sorry to hear this tale.'

'Oh, it's far worse. But it's a long story and I'll be skinned if I don't get back to my study.'

'Xantia, thank you. I have enjoyed this time and hope we'll get an opportunity to talk again. Perhaps you can tell me Saxon's full story?'

He took her hand and kissed it lightly. She felt a thrill pass through her.

Tor, be careful, cautioned Cloot over the link. He sat on the rooftop of the Academie.

Oh, fly away, bird and find something else to prey on, Tor replied.

You're playing with fire, Cloot warned. *Actually I am hungry. I'm off to hunt, though I think you should give up the hunt!*

He did his usual trick and closed the link before Tor could respond.

Xantia had every intention of seeing the physic again whether she was permitted to or not. She blushed, embarrassed by her own thoughts, and hurried away, taking the precaution of going the long way via the study of Elder Iris to make sure she was seen scurrying past alone, busy about her duties.

Helplessly drawn back through corridors which might catch her a glimpse of Gynt, she paused when she spied him at the well, his shirt off and his face and hair dripping. She knew he could not see her so she felt safe, hidden behind another convenient pillar, to stare at his body which was lightly sculpted with muscle.

Tor knew she was there, of course. He smiled inwardly and stretched for her benefit, shaking his hair free of the water. She might as well enjoy the sight of a man. He hated that such a lively young acolyte might be shaped into the brittle women the Elders seemed.

Xantia dared not tarry any longer and tiptoed away. Tor sensed her leave and thought of Alyssa, who would be about the same age as this lovely young woman. He cast from habit, not expecting anything after so many years of silence. He reached the usual void but this time did it seem just slightly less dense? He stopped drying his face and followed the trace back. He was right. It was different; definitely not as dull as usual.

He felt a spark of excitement. Lys had told him Alyssa was alive and that she would help him to find her. Perhaps this was the beginning. Perhaps she was even somewhere close by.

Alyssa was not furious as Xantia had hoped but she was unsettled. Talk of Goth always unnerved her. She could hardly remember the weeks after the attack and she did not want to. The sight of Saxon in such pain; those young boys . . . No, even now she preferred not to recall any of it.

In those first weeks, floating in the Green had been her only sanctuary. So it was a shock to hear Saxon's voice reaching for her, searching for her. He was dead. How could he talk to her? She thought she was imagining it but she chased it anyway, racing towards his voice and finally opening her eyes to see that it was true. He lived.

He looked so different now. But the black ruin where his bright eyes had been did not frighten her. The twisted limbs, which had once been part of a fine body, did not offend her. His voice across the link was still the same and that was enough; she had curled into his gnarled, crippled arms and felt calm again.

Alyssa had not been aware of Xantia for a long time though she realised later that the young woman must have been there from the beginning; always watching, ever helpful. Alyssa spoke to Saxon and Sorrel via the link, until that power was taken away from her a few years back when she was accepted as an acolyte at the Academie.

Sorrel had confirmed that the Elders had accepted them; that they knew Alyssa was sentient and had offered their protection. When she was summoned, Alyssa had gone to the grand hall where everyone from the Academie was gathered. After a brief ceremony, Elder Iris had taken a beautiful green disc from a velvet pouch and pressed it to her forehead, where it remained to this day. She was a full member of Caremboche now, an Untouchable. And it did feel safe.

Xantia had filled the gap of friendship for her. The girl was fun. She made Alyssa laugh and they became very close quickly, though Alyssa never revealed her past. This was a new beginning for her. She liked her quiet existence at the Academie and she soon showed an adeptness in the archives unrivalled by any other.

'Not since Elder Amie have we had someone so dedicated and talented in our archives,' she had heard Elder Iris comment.

It was true. Alyssa felt completely at peace amongst her books and she spent her time devouring their contents. She had learned much and just recently had stumbled across a small trapdoor in the library which no one else seemed to know was there.

It was covered by bookshelves and only discovered because Alyssa had begun a committed 'clean up' of the library. An enormous task. It had taken her almost a year of toil to get this far – not even halfway. With Saxon's help she had moved this particular row of shelves and found the loose flagstone.

A search beneath the trapdoor had revealed nothing exciting, just some very old, dusty tomes. To Alyssa it was treasure; to the other acolytes, who had been expecting a stash of gems or similar, it was a disappointment. And to the Elders, who had merely hoped not to find crumbling skeletons, it was a relief to give the books into Alyssa's care.

'It's in a language I've never seen,' commented Elder Ellyn, probably the most learned of all the Elders.

Alyssa had never seen the complex characters before either but was astounded to discover that she could understand them. She had no idea how or why.

She had just finished reading the first of the carefully hand-inscribed books when the luncheon bell had forced her up from the tomb of the library. Alyssa was not much interested in food but she had promised Sorrel she would attend each luncheon, not just to eat but to mix with the other women. Sorrel felt this was important but Alyssa had found it increasingly difficult since she and Xantia had fallen out. It was too sad. Such a great friendship in tatters and for what? Too many times to count Alyssa had turned over in her mind why Xantia behaved so aggressively.

Now, back in the library and still angry with Xantia for throwing Goth's name in her face, Alyssa did not feel in the mood to embark on the second book, though her fingers itched to open its leather cover. Startling revelations in the first had convinced her that the old folklore stories about the warlock Orlac, who had devastated this place many centuries earlier, were not all legend. It was a terrifying notion and she had decided not to mention it to anyone yet.

She had laid the books aside and was preparing to transcribe a parchment for Elder Ellyn when she felt a nudge in her mind. She knew she had to be mistaken. She had not been able to open a link or even feel one open for years now. Her last communication in this manner had been to bid farewell to Saxon's voice.

She frowned. She felt it again; almost familiar but very indistinct. If she was not concentrating so hard, she would hardly even know it was there but something was definitely niggling at her. Alyssa touched the disc on her forehead. The archalyt was there. No link could open with that in place. She shook her head; she was getting fanciful in all this silence.

The sensation made her think of Tor, though. She briefly wondered what he might be doing at this exact moment and allowed herself just a fleeting satisfaction that perhaps he had tried to link with her. Then she chided herself. Tor was a memory now and she should not dwell on him. She would never see him again.

Alyssa forced herself to return to her ancient parchment and got lost in her transcribing.

*   *   *

'Acolyte Xantia is impressionable. She has never been . . . shall we say, comfortable . . . with her status at Caremboche.'

Tor knew he was being given a shrouded warning. 'Do the women not make a choice to be at the Academie?' Tor asked, deflecting where this conversation was headed.

'Not always, Physic Gynt. Xantia, for example, was delivered here as an infant, just four moons old. Her sentient mother had been bridled by the Inquisitors and the folk from her village feared for the child's safety.'

'That's understandable—'

'Ah, but wait,' she interrupted. 'When Xantia was old enough to grasp that she had relinquished freedom she objected and she has not stopped objecting since. Of all our acolytes, Xantia is the one most fiercely opposed to this life of sacrifice. She could make a fine Elder, but sadly never will. She is very intelligent and has an amazing grasp of the Dark Arts. Not that we use them,' she added quickly, 'but she has a fine understanding of how people fall prey to that darker side.'

'Is this what Xantia studies?' Tor was intrigued.

'Oh, yes. She knows all the ancient incantations – spells and enchantments long vanished from common use. She is forbidden to use them; our job is simply to record history. Xantia's work in this area will be priceless to Tallinor in centuries to come.'

'I see,' he said, sipping at the warm lemon tea they were sharing in one of the many beautiful rooms at the Academie. He pressed on. 'The Academie is breathtaking, Elder Iris. I am genuinely keen to see more of it but I realise I cannot wander its gracious halls alone . . . that I must have a guide.'

Her voice hardened once more. 'Physic Gynt, I will permit Xantia to act as your guide for I see you are determined to have her company. I cannot blame you. I can imagine that the thought of one of us ancient Elders accompanying you may feel more like a chore —' She held up her hand to prevent his protestations.

'It will be good for her too. You have three days to spend with us before the festivities begin and I like the thought that you might give them over to learning more about Caremboche. But allow me to remind you of the law which governs us here.'

Tor leapt in this time. 'Elder Iris, forgive my interruption. Physic Merkhud went to great pains to impress upon me all that the Academie stands for and the rules surrounding its privileged and protected members.' He sat forward, an earnest expression stealing over his face. 'I have come here to learn. I have absolutely no intention of so much as bending your rules let alone breaking them. I do understand your caution. Trust me, Elder, I have nothing but education on my mind.'

She nodded sagely. 'Then I will instruct Xantia. She may well benefit from the experience and I hope you will use this opportunity to speak with all the Elders. You will find this a fascinating place, Physic Gynt.'

'Thank you,' he said, elated. 'I shall take back marvellous stories to tell at the Palace.'

'You must visit our archives too. In there you will find the most amazing stories of all. Be sure Xantia introduces you to our archivist.' Elder Iris smiled sadly. 'She won't suggest it herself, I might add. They are rivals for the position of Elder which we will appoint shortly and I'm disappointed to say that a great friendship between these girls has soured as a result.'

Tor felt dismissed but was glad to escape the crusty old girl's sharp scrutiny. Xantia met him not long after in the main courtyard.

'Good morning, Physic Gynt.'

Tor could not help but admit this was a woman to turn heads. She wore her shiny dark hair artfully braided today which revealed her striking features set in an oval face. He noticed in the sunlight how the olive tone of her skin made her perfect teeth and bright eyes all the more brilliant.

He realised she was looking at him now with a bemused expression.

'Pardon?'

She laughed. 'I said, how did you manage it?'

'The Sisters Grim fell for my charms,' he offered.

'I don't think so somehow. The Elders would not recognise a man's charm even if it came up and bit them on the—'

'Ah, Elder May. Xantia was just explaining that your work in the herbals is exceptional.' Tor addressed the older woman who was crossing the courtyard behind them.

She replied that he was most welcome to visit her rooms and he graciously accepted, throwing a look towards his companion warning her to be more careful.

The morning passed too quickly for Xantia. Tor, as he had suggested she call him, was fine company, witty and intelligent. She enjoyed strolling through the halls of the Academie with him and felt proud that he was impressed by her knowledge.

When the dinner bell sounded she resented its intrusion.

'Will you join us? I'd love to show you off to the other acolytes.' Her laugh was seductive.

'It's very tempting and Elder Iris has insisted I meet the archive specialist. I believe she has some fascinating stories to tell?' He saw the smile leave Xantia's face. 'I assure you I have every intention of meeting her but I won't come to the dining hall today, Xantia, thank you. I have some letters to get away to Tal. I imagine life will get fairly busy for all of us shortly and these should not wait.'

Tor figured that if Elder Iris was eating in the dining room this afternoon she might be impressed if he distanced himself from socialising too keenly with Xantia.

'I'll look forward to seeing you this afternoon,' he finished and left.

As Tor walked back to his room Cloot landed lightly on his shoulder.

And how many sacred rules have you broken this morning? the falcon asked.

None.

Well, it's early days, the bird said, ruffling his feathers.

There was a small fire going in Tor's room, which he attributed to another quiet deed from Saxon, and a tray of food. A note on the tray was from Elder Iris who hoped he had enjoyed his morning's tour and wished him a quiet dinner. Tor smiled to himself knowing he had made a sound decision to eat alone.

Sorrel was quick to inform Merkhud of Tor's arrival. The old man was surprised at the speed with which his Under Physic had crossed the Kingdom. He went so far as to ask whether she was quite sure.

Sorrel snapped with irritation. *Of course it's him. His name is Torkyn Gynt, is it not?*

Yes, yes. I don't understand though. It should have taken him at least seven or eight days at the earliest to cross so many counties and traverse the mountain passes.

Well, all I can say is he's here and I imagine your carefully planned meeting will occur tomorrow.

Who is with him?

No one is with him, she replied tartly.

No bird, no soldier?

Merkhud, I think you need a rest. No bird? No, of course there's no bird with him. There is no one else with him.

Strange . . . His voice trailed off and so did the link.

20

A Rude Awakening

Alyssa could not sleep. Since her formal welcome into the Academie she had been treated like all other acolytes and moved into a room which she shared with Xantia and two others. She could hear them all now, breathing slowly and deeply; she envied them their rest.

Something was bothering her.

She could not stop her mind flitting between thoughts of the secret books and that odd sensation of a link trying to open in her mind today. And now, in the stillness of night, she was plagued by thoughts of Tor. Irritated by her restlessness and the contented sleep sounds of her companions, she threw back her blankets and felt the frosty air. Slipping into a robe, she grabbed her boots and tiptoed from the room.

Alyssa loved silence and the dark did not disturb her as she hurried through the warren of corridors which led her towards the crypt. Her thoughts were firmly on tackling the second book but when she scurried across an open hallway spanning one of the courtyards the flickering glow of candlelight from the window of the small rooms near the stables distracted her.

She paused to consider who could be in there; Saxon slept in the hay loft. Then Alyssa remembered the royal visitor from Tal. How could she have forgotten after Xantia's mind-numbing description of how handsome he was, how beautiful his voice, how blue his eyes, and his charming manner and wicked wit. The narrative had claimed most of the dinner hour and Alyssa had been thrilled to escape the babbling.

She hugged her robe around her more tightly as she stared at the glow from the room. She felt a small shock as a shadow passed briefly across the window before the candle was extinguished. The tall stranger's profile could have belonged to Torkyn Gynt, she thought. Or was her mind playing tricks? She continued to stare at the dark square where the light had been. It was not him, of course. She was thinking too much on Tor these days.

'Get a hold of yourself, Alyssa,' she whispered as she stepped lightly down the curving staircase which led into the archives.

This area was dimly lit by infrequently placed sconces which the Elders kept burning permanently. She was glad of this practice now as she progressed deeper into the building where it was cooler still and smelled faintly and pleasantly of the earth.

Alyssa lit two candles and carried them to a chair she favoured in a nook which was well secreted between tall bookshelves and a cupboard. She was happy to see she had left a rug there and, after fetching the books, she curled herself into the chair and tucked the rug around her. She yawned. Now she felt sleepy. Well, too late!

She opened the second book but did not read. Instead she began to wonder why anyone would hide the books in the first place. If the story of Orlac was pure fancy, a tale to scare the little ones around the fireside at night, then why had it been so carefully scribed in what she now knew was ancient script? But if what she had read so far about this stolen god was true, then there certainly was good reason to protect these books.

Alyssa believed that the events described were indeed a narrative of the day. Her guess was that some dedicated member of the ancient Seat of Learning had recorded for generations to come the horrific events which had unfolded centuries previous. This disturbed her. So did the unsettling coincidence that a man called Merkhud was named as the mortal father of the boy god, Orlac.

It was a far-fetched notion but somehow she could not help bringing into focus the other man called Merkhud: Royal Physic, beloved healer and revered sage. The same man who had stolen Tor from her. The name Merkhud was uncommon; nay, it was rare indeed. She had been studying these books for years and such a name had never appeared in any context other than as father to Orlac.

Surely it was too much of a coincidence that a Merkhud had tracked down a young man whose sentient powers had gone undetected by the Inquisitors?

Many years had passed before Alyssa learned that the old man she had feared at Minstead Green on that fateful day of the Floral Dance was the famous Royal Physic. She had never understood why the old man had sought out Tor and why the sight of him had created such fear in

Tor that day. But how could he be the same man? The Merkhud mentioned in the old books would have to be centuries old to be alive today. Impossible! But then her agile mind slipped around the idea.

Why not? If she and Tor were able to hide their powers from those devoted to tracing magical ability, then why could a man not possess such magic as to make himself live for centuries?

Alyssa finally allowed Merkhud to slot neatly into the jigsaw in her mind. He was Orlac's father. So why was he still alive and what was his interest in Tor? It had to be Tor's powers; even she knew they were vast.

She steadied her mind now and thought about what she had learned so far from these strange but marvellous writings. She had discovered that the scribe's name was Nanak. Alyssa felt sure he was not just a scribe though. The elegant hand, the intelligence in his words, the precision of his narrative, suggested he was far more than a simple writer. She could be wrong but she wanted to believe he was one of the Masters himself.

Nanak told how a vastly talented lad had been brought to Goldstone by his parents. It was only much later that the father, Merkhud, was actually named. Orlac and his powers were more potent than any who had lived previously. He was a stunning discovery and Nanak had recorded how excited the Masters were to have such an accomplished wielder in their midst. They had such high hopes for him.

Orlac was described as 'beautiful' which Alyssa found curious, but the more she learned of him the more she could believe it. It took only a couple of summers, she read, before the young man realised his potential. Nanak explained in his careful words that Orlac was an angry person; he was filled with resentment and bitterness for no apparent reason.

Alyssa recalled how briefly Nanak had summarised the events which led to Orlac's downfall. How he had shocked Goldstone by challenging the Masters, then learned of the cunning plan to Quell him. Great sadness came through Nanak's words as he described the fall of the great Seat of Learning as Orlac, gifted with extraordinary powers, had razed the glittering, mighty city to rubble. How he had murdered more than two thousand people in his wrath before fleeing to the catacombs beneath the city. There he had hidden for days.

The few Masters remaining had summoned the young man's parents and learned that Orlac was not their true child but adopted. A child who had been sold to them by Scavengers. And this was where Merkhud was first mentioned, Alyssa remembered, although the mother's name was not given. Nanak had described how the Masters had sent Merkhud to track down the truth of his son's birth. There the first book ended.

Alyssa rubbed her eyes. She was tired and still had not read a word from the open second book.

A mere horror tale did not take this long in the telling nor would it require the services of a professional scribe, perhaps a Master of the Power Arts, to write it down. It would be told simply and passed from family to family. No, Alyssa was convinced that this was no piece of folk-lore. This was truth. She was reading about real events which had taken place centuries previously when the Academie had indeed been the Great Seat of Learning in a thriving city. She presumed that the author, Nanak himself, must have hidden his writings. Why? What was he afraid of? It had to be Orlac that frightened him.

And old man Merkhud must have plans for the great power he had found in Tor. But why? What did he want? His own son had been as empowered and yet all of that had gone terribly wrong. Orlac had been imprisoned and Merkhud was still wandering the land several centuries on.

Perhaps Merkhud wanted to use Tor's power to release Orlac. Alyssa snuggled deeper into her chair as she turned these thoughts over and over in her mind. And gradually, without realising it, she drifted into the heaviest of sleeps in which she dreamed of a silver wolf welcoming her into a forest.

Apologies, my love, for the late hour.

Sorrel heard a tightness in Merkhud's voice. *Are you well, Merkhud?*

Tired.

She felt her former snappiness towards him dissipate at his fatigued tone. *Are we near the end, dear one?*

You know, I feel we are drawing close. Tor and Alyssa will meet soon. I am unsure what will happen next but, however this unfolds, you must stay close to Alyssa and follow their path.

And what of you, my love? she whispered across the link.

Oh, I shall wait. You will be my eyes and I shall wait for your news. He sounded terrible.

Merkhud, it's been so long now. Will I see you again . . . ever?

I'm not sure, Sorrel, but I love you dearly. I hope I shall see your lovely smile again. There was no conviction in his voice.

The Festival is in two days, she said, changing the subject.

Sorrel, Goth may be at Caremboche.

What? Her alarm pulsed across the link.

Fear not. You are warned. Take the necessary precautions, he said firmly. *Show no fright to the girl. She must be allowed to make her decision without the threat of Goth skewing her choice. I have no idea where this is headed. We must trust them now to take the right course.*

But Merkhud, they don't know anything. They don't know who we think he is and even we have no idea how Alyssa fits into this.

That's right, we do not. All the more reason to trust them and the forces guiding them. We have to, Sorrel. There is nothing else. I have no more plans, no more schemes. It is up to Tor now. He must show us who he is and what he is capable of. Why he was sent here.

What if he isn't the One?

He is, came the short reply. *Remember my warning.*

Merkhud shut the link.

The following morning Xantia woke early and dressed carefully. She was irritated to see that Alyssa had obviously been up for ages; her tousled bed sheets were cold and unslept in. There was no sign of her at breakfast either but that was not unusual and by then Xantia was too consumed with seeing Torkyn Gynt again. Today she would have to introduce them; Elder Iris had insisted. Xantia decided she could turn it into something amusing by flaunting this man she was smitten by in front of Alyssa.

She left the dining hall with the other chattering acolytes but, as usual, held herself apart from their conversation. This time she was happy with the arrangement as her thoughts were elsewhere. How she could leave the Academie and travel with Torkyn Gynt was already a well-chewed idea. Would he accept her? She doubted it because of the archalyt and what it signified. Her Untouchable status made even his revered status look lowly. But Xantia was way past needing Tor to love her back. All she could think about was being with him.

She spotted Elder Iris but would have pretended not to have noticed her if the older woman had not beckoned.

'Good morning, Xantia.'

'Elder Iris, I hope you slept well,' she said, bowing with the respect accorded all Elders of the Academie.

'Like a log. And you?'

'Peacefully, thank you,' Xantia said, ignoring the Elder's slightly lifted eyebrow.

'I hear you gave our esteemed visitor a most engaging tour of the study halls yesterday. What do you have planned for today, child?'

The emphasis on the word 'child' was not lost on Xantia. Her blood boiled but her countenance remained composed; her voice humble.

'With your permission, Elder Iris, I thought I might take Physic Gynt to the archives.'

'An excellent idea, Xantia. I'm sure you and Alyssa will keep him enthralled.'

There it was again; irony lacing her polite words. Xantia ignored it and continued. 'And later I hoped you might give me permission to take one of the wagons to show Physic Gynt around Ildagarth.'

'I'll give that some consideration but you might check whether Saxon is free this afternoon to take our guest into town.'

'I'll do that now,' Xantia said sweetly, hoping she kept the sneer from her expression.

Xantia found Saxon loading logs into baskets on either side of Kythay. It was certainly cold enough now to be lighting the fires in the Academie. She repeated her request and refused to leave until she was sure the man's dumb nod meant he understood and he would make himself available. The silly old fool had done the journey so many times now, as had his equally dumb donkey, that both could make the trip blind.

'Good,' she said, feeling that perhaps everything might fall into place.

Xantia was confident that Elder Iris would give her the permission she so desperately needed to leave the Academie and spend some hours with Tor away from the scrutiny of the Elders. She found him speaking with several of the youngest acolytes in the arched reception lobby. They were giggling as silly young girls do and a pang of jealousy tingled through her. She saw Tor flash his broad smile and then whisper something to them, making them all squeal with laughter this time before accepting his magnanimous bow as he excused himself. He had sensed Xantia's arrival but pretended to notice her only at that instant.

Xantia forced a smile to her lips. 'I see you are already a success with our youngsters.'

'They are delightful girls. A credit to the Academie,' he said disarmingly.

'Quite.' She suppressed her jealousy, shocked by her longing to touch this man. She could not stand anyone – not even ten years olds, sharing him even for a moment. She balanced herself and banished her desires for the time being. Brightening her expression, she migrated to safe ground and asked him how he had slept.

'Incredibly soundly, thank you,' he replied.

She blushed furiously at the thought of him lying naked in his sheets and changed the subject again.

'Do you know one of the Elders mentioned during breakfast that she saw the most glorious peregrine falcon this morning circling above the Academie?'

'Really?'

'Yes, she was most excited. A peregrine hasn't been spotted in these parts for decades.'

Tor grinned. 'He's mine.'

She did not believe him for a second and assumed he was teasing. 'Fiction!'

'I swear it. He is mine and a finer falcon you will not see in all of Tallinor.'

'He's tame?'

'Indeed. You must meet him.'

Xantia took joy in the flippancy of this conversation after a lifetime of suppression in these halls. 'Oh? A formal introduction! And can this bird of yours speak?' she said, pointing towards the corridor they needed to follow.

'Of course. But only to me.' He winked and took her arm.

Xantia had never known such a thrill. It was a simple, courteous movement but his gentle touch made her blood rush to her head for the second time in almost as many heartbeats. She felt giddy. This was a new and rare experience. She dared not speak for fear of breaking the spell but Tor broke it anyway.

'So, what is your plan for me today, my pretty guide?'

he asked. He unlinked his hand from her arm when he saw Elders approaching.

Her disappointment at the loss of his touch was immense. 'I would like to take you to our library in the crypt where you will meet the Academie's archivist.'

'Ah, yes. She sounds like quite a woman.'

Xantia did not reply for fear of saying something regrettable which may get back to the Elders.

Tor continued, oblivious to the consternation he was causing. 'Elder Iris was telling me that she's not only extremely learned but also very beautiful.'

Xantia nodded reluctantly and pointed left into a new warren of corridors which would lead them to the crypt.

'A deadly combination,' he said behind her.

Alyssa woke sharply to the sound of her books slipping from their precarious perch on her curled lap and slapping loudly to the flagstoned floor. She jumped at the noise and realised she had spent the night in the crypt; now, in its gloominess, she had no idea of the time. She glanced towards her candles. Both had burned out. If it had not been for the thicker ones still courageously burning elsewhere in the library, she would have been plunged into darkness. Her stomach told her that breakfast was long finished but her hunger concerned her less than being missed at breakfast by Xantia, Sorrel and, more importantly, Elder Iris. The head of the Academie preferred that all of its community broke bread together at least once daily.

She rubbed her eyes and tried to smooth her unkempt hair. Now she would have to creep through the less-used corridors and make it back to her room the long way. No use lingering, she told herself.

As she bent to pick up the spilled books, she froze. The voices were muffled and sounded as though they came from the top of the stairs to the crypt.

She listened. It was Xantia's voice she could hear.

How awkward this was going to be. Discovery by an Elder would be tricky enough but Xantia would make sure everyone knew. What did she want in the crypt anyway? She hated the place. Alyssa figured Xantia must have another acolyte in tow so did not hurry herself. She retrieved the books, set them on her desk and had just returned to her nook to fold the rug when her visitors arrived.

'Hello?'

'A moment,' she called from behind the bookshelves.

'Where are you?'

'Right here,' Alyssa said, stepping out behind them. She was surprised to see not only Xantia's back but that of a very tall man.

They both turned at her voice. In an instant the man's heartbreakingly familiar smile fled from his face. She saw dull shock replace the brightness of those impossibly blue eyes she remembered all too well.

Xantia noticed only the untidiness of the usually immaculate acolyte. 'Good grief – don't tell me you've slept in the library again.' She laughed harshly, delighted now by the embarrassment she could see on Alyssa's face.

'Let me introduce you to—'

'Torkyn Gynt,' Alyssa said.

Xantia was miffed at the interruption. This was her

shining moment to show off. 'Good guess,' she said smoothly. 'Physic Gynt, this is—'

'Alyssa,' he said softly.

Xantia moved her confused glance from him to Alyssa and then back again. The silence between them was thick.

'You know each other?'

He nodded, not daring to glance away from the astoundingly beautiful Alyssandra Qyn. Even with her hair tousled, blotches on her cheek from where she had slept against the chair and in a most unflattering night-shirt, she was more lovely than he recalled.

Alyssa regained her senses first and took a step forward. She bowed, as courtesy demanded, but she refused to look into his eyes which were riveted on her.

'Forgive me, Physic Gynt. You have caught me by surprise. I have indeed passed the night in the library and you must allow me a moment or two to tidy myself.'

She turned to Xantia. 'I shall return shortly.'

And then she fled, running up the stone stairs as fast as her long nightshirt would allow. She zigzagged down various hallways, more in fright than with any purposeful direction, though it did not surprise her that she found herself at the stables. Breathless, not from her flight but from shock, she collapsed in a corner, terrified he had followed her.

She almost screamed when a figure loomed from the shadows. She should have recognised Saxon's distinctive hobble but for Alyssa nothing was as it should be.

Alyssa had finished her ablutions and was dressed for the day in her acolyte robes; her hair was neatly plaited and pulled into a thong. Going through that routine may have stopped the shaking but her unease was far worse.

That was his silhouette she had seen last night and she was now convinced it was Tor who had attempted to link with her earlier yesterday. Confusion, anger and fear was the unnerving brew coursing through her when a young messenger arrived to request that she go to Elder Iris's study.

As Alyssa crossed the courtyard Saxon approached. He handed her a note, squeezed her arm and moved on. She lingered a moment to look back at him but there was no time to read the missive now. The young acolyte had obviously been told to fetch her immediately and she was not to be held up in her mission.

Elder Iris welcomed her warmly; she was fond of Alyssa and her committed way to life at the Academie. This young woman would make Elder far sooner than most; she would be a remarkable superior for the youngsters to look up to and emulate. Elder Iris watched her now as she politely bowed; there was something so contained and controlled about her. Something . . . she searched for the word in her mind. Regal. Yes, that was it.

'Come in my girl and sit,' she beckoned. 'Are you well? I missed you when we broke our fast this morning.'

'Yes, I'm sorry, Elder Iris I—'

'Slept in the crypt again?' offered the older woman kindly.

Alyssa nodded, wondering how she knew.

'Alyssa, I gather you met our royal visitor earlier and that the two of you know each other from a long while ago. Now, we have learned little of your past and I have no desire to pry so we will leave it at that, though Physic Gynt has been to see me.'

'Oh? I have to admit I was embarrassed and rushed off rather swiftly . . . What did he have to say?' Alyssa tried to keep her voice as neutral as possible.

'Oh, not much really. He mentioned that you two grew up on opposite sides of a valley, him in Flat Meadows and yourself at Mallee Marsh.' Elder Iris laughed, surprising Alyssa. 'Physic Gynt mentioned that you used to tease him a great deal when you were both younger.'

Alyssa forced a bright expression onto her face.

'I imagine you two have plenty to catch up on,' continued the older woman.

'Elder Iris, I haven't seen Tor for many years now. I hardly remember those childhood days. In fact I can hardly remember him.'

'Now, Alyssa, don't be coy. You have one of the sharpest minds in the Academie and I don't believe for a minute that you forget any detail.'

Alyssa blushed. 'It was an unpleasant surprise to meet Xantia and our visitor in the archives and me barely awake.' She smiled, hoping it was artful enough. 'Have I let you down, Elder Iris?'

'Not at all, my dear. In fact, you have helped me with a prickly situation. Please sit and let me explain.'

Alyssa took the herbal tea and biscuits on offer. The activity of pouring and sipping gave her precious time to think. The old girl was far too sharp to be hood-winked.

'Alyssa, Xantia made it clear she wanted the task of entertaining Physic Gynt during his stay here. You probably don't know this, buried in your books as you are, but he arrived almost three days earlier than expected and

I've been at a loss for what to do with him. It was against my better judgement but he seemed more than happy to have Xantia as his guide.'

Alyssa coughed and smothered her feelings by sipping tea.

'Yes, indeed,' said the Elder, reading the younger woman's thoughts completely. 'I have no doubt as to why Xantia manipulated the situation and I also have no doubt that he is relishing the company of such an exuberant member of our Academie.'

Alyssa nibbled a biscuit as her mind raced. Elder Iris was no fool.

'Anyway, Physic Gynt has assured me he is here purely for his own education. Curiously, he came to me a short while ago to request that Xantia be relieved immediately of her duties on his behalf.' The old girl noticed Alyssa's surprise. 'Now isn't that an amazing coincidence? He bumps into his childhood friend, now a beautiful young woman, and suddenly has no more interest in the less intriguing acolyte.' She raised her hand to prevent Alyssa's protests.

'It's quite all right, Alyssa. There's nothing wrong with the admiration of men but as Untouchables we must always be aware that that is the point where it must stop.'

Alyssa nodded. 'I've always respected our rules, Elder,' she said dutifully.

'But I'm not so sure Xantia will continue to do so. Thankfully, your friend the physic is smart enough to realise her interest is becoming too . . . ardent, shall we say. It is dangerous to his career at the very least. And so he is keen to avoid an awkward situation – as I am.'

'And he has requested that I assume the role of guide for the rest of his stay?' Again Alyssa kept her voice deliberately flat.

'Yes, my dear, you've presumed correctly and I can't think of a better person for this job. You are so reliable. We can rely on you to make sound judgements.'

Alyssa put down her cup for fear of it falling to the floor. Elder Iris liked to drink from the very best Ildagarth porcelain and it would not do to smash her prized china.

'Elder Iris, I'm so busy with my transcriptions. Perhaps acolyte Shelley could step in?' she said desperately.

'Oh tush, Alyssa. There is no one in the Academie more in awe of your fine work than I, but even a crusty old lady like myself knows there must be some relief . . . some playtime. You work too long and too hard. I hope you won't make me insist. I'd like to think that you will take up this task because it might be pleasurable. It's only until tomorrow night, after all. What can it hurt?'

Just my whole life, Alyssa thought but she realised she would not win this argument. 'What would you like me to do with him?'

'Thank you, Alyssa. I knew I could count on you. Saxon will be available this afternoon to drive you and our visitor into Ildagarth. Xantia had an idea to give him a walk around the streets where the festivities begin. I agree with her and it will kill plenty of time. I don't expect you to rush back. Stay in town until this evening, if it pleases. I trust your integrity completely.'

Alyssa looked up anxiously. 'Saxon will stay with us?'

'Of course.'

'And Xantia?'

The older woman shooed her out the door. 'I'll deal with Xantia.'

Xantia sat on her cot; she had been waiting for Alyssa to return to their room. She watched her hurriedly throw a few items into a small sack as she prepared for her day in Ildagarth.

Alyssa could not bear the seething jealousy hanging heavily around them. 'Xantia, aren't you supposed to be in your study room?'

'Don't be condescending to me, Alyssa! You're not an Elder yet!' She punched her pillow. 'You don't even go into Ildagarth much.'

'And neither do you so we know about the same amount. I'll muddle through.'

Xantia sat up angrily. 'Why has Elder Iris done this to me? She has relieved me of my tasks to spite me and picked her favourite acolyte to step in. Now you are relishing the thought of going off with him.'

'Oh, stop it, Xantia! You're acting like a child. Do you think I want this task? Do you think I asked Elder Iris if I could do this? Does it sound to you like the sort of day I would enjoy?'

Xantia's mouth twisted. 'How am I to know your whims, Alyssa? You're such a closed book to all of us,' she said sourly. 'I want to know about the two of you.'

'I'll say this once only. Tor and I were raised in the same district. We met occasionally. That's it.'

'I can't help it, Alyssa.' Xantia did not mean to spill this to the person she despised. 'I love him. I want him. I have to be with him.'

Alyssa felt sick; she was not sure whether it was from Xantia's yearnings for Tor or her own hidden love.

'Xantia, on your forehead is a pale blue disc of archalyt. It is not a piece of jewellery. It marks you. You will be an Untouchable until released by death. You will never be loved by a man. You will never feel a man's embrace.' Alyssa's voice was icy.

Xantia had not witnessed any emotion in Alyssa since she had first seen Saxon again after his torture. But there was something burning behind those cold words now, a fact she stored.

'Alyssa, you don't need the archalyt to make you Untouchable. You do it so well all on your own because you're as cold as death itself, which is perhaps the only embrace you'll ever welcome. You wouldn't know what it is to yearn for a man's touch. I fear Goth must have done a great deal more to you than just beat your lapdog senseless and cut out his tongue.'

The shock of these words hit Alyssa so hard she felt winded.

Xantia was not finished. 'Oh yes, I hear you talk in your dreams. I am no fool. You've been touched by the monster of all men. It is a lovely irony!' She barked a bitter laugh. 'Go about your duties. Run to your friend. Be the self-assured, aloof Alyssa the Academie expects you to be. And whilst Tor's wondering how he got stuck with you, I'll be remembering the way he kissed my hand with longing and how he looked at me with desire.

'Tomorrow night at the Festival, when all rules are relaxed, I'll have my moment with your childhood friend, Alyssa, and whilst he's caressing me as we dance,' she touched her cheek, 'I'll remember how much I hate you.'

Alyssa felt the years of despair and her own unrequited love bubble up and boil over.

'Xantia.'

Her friend turned, eyes glittering with her win.

'Elder Iris did not relieve you of your duty. I must have failed to mention that the man you love so very much and can't bear to live without, the same man who apparently desires you so much, personally requested that you no longer accompany him during his stay. He was playing with you, Xantia, because you're so easy to impress. You did precisely what he knew you'd do – you fell for his charms and now he's laughing at you.

'Oh, and Xantia – Elder Iris did not choose me and I did not request it. Physic Gynt asked for me specifically.'

The face of the girl in front of her darkened like a gathering storm. Alyssa knew she had a new enemy to accompany her nemesis, Chief Inquisitor Goth.

'I hate you, Alyssa.' It was all she could think of to say.

Alyssa did not even look at her. 'Close the door behind you, Xantia.'

21

Aczabba Veiszuit

Alyssa could see him standing next to the cart. He said something to Saxon whose shoulders moved with laughter for the first time in years. Tor was all grace and charm it seemed.

She stayed in the shadows and watched them, digging her hands deep into her pockets to stop the nervousness. Her fingers felt a scrap of parchment; it was Saxon's note. How had he managed to write it blindly? She unfolded it and glanced around to see if anyone was nearby. She was alone. Alyssa read.

Do you remember when I told you that I was not the one for you . . . that there was another? I said one day he would come. He is here now. Follow him. Believe in him. He is the One.

Alyssa read the note three times. What in the Light was Saxon talking about? She did recall that day in the forest; remembered very well how her kisses had been gently spurned.

She hurriedly put the note away; she would have to think on this later. Stepping into the thin sunlight of the winter morning, she regarded the two men. One crippled and humbled; an older man with the life beaten out of him. The other in the very prime of his life, looking like a beautiful god on loan to the world. Self-assured; clearly used to the worship of women and the easy companionship of men.

He looked towards her, straightened himself to his glorious full height and waved, only to look embarrassed at his own enthusiasm. She liked him for that. Not so self-assured after all perhaps. It was a good feeling to know she could still unbalance Torkyn Gynt.

She arrived in front of him but spoke first to Saxon. 'Saxon, thank you for doing this.'

He shrugged and she turned her attention to Tor, hoping he did not read her deep breath for the nervousness it was.

'And hello again, Physic Gynt.'

He held her gaze, staring much too intently for her comfort. She gestured towards the cart. 'Shall we?'

'Only if you call me Tor and not Physic Gynt.'

Alyssa nodded.

Both men offered their hand. She took Saxon's calloused one and stepped up lightly. Tor joined her on the back bench. Whilst Saxon clicked to his horses, two of the Elders obliged with the gates. Soon they were out of the compound and trotting at an easy pace past the orchard.

Tor could not help himself. He reached across and took her hand but Alyssa snatched it back.

'Please don't,' she said, frightened by the emotion she saw in his eyes. She pushed her hand into her pocket for extra security and she felt the note again.

He is the One, she repeated in her mind as a difficult silence fell.

Tor suddenly looked up and a moment later a majestic falcon swooped out of the skies and landed on the wooden bench next to Saxon but facing them. *This is impossible!* Alyssa thought in alarm and let out a short squeal. She was surprised to see Tor grin.

Good timing, Cloot, he said across the link.

It looked as though you needed rescuing. Don't rush her, Tor, the falcon counselled. *She doesn't know the man. She only remembers the boy.*

The bird gripped the bench with sharp talons and cocked his head to one side. Alyssa felt as though she was under serious scrutiny. Tor turned. There was no avoiding those blue eyes now, she thought. He spoke aloud.

'Cloot, I would like you to meet the woman I have told you about. This is Alyssa.'

The large bird moved from foot to foot as it regarded her intently from bright yellow eyes. Alyssa stared at it in wonder.

Tor nudged her. He cleared his throat and nodded towards the bird. Alyssa found her manners.

'Er . . . how do you do, Cloot,' she said, completely in awe, then turned back to Tor. 'Is this your hawk?'

'Peregrine falcon if you don't mind,' he corrected. 'Cloot gets very put out if one refers to him as a hawk.'

Her eyes sparkled. 'Indeed. And he understands what I'm saying no doubt.'

'Every word, so be nice.'

She looked back at the bird. 'In that case, you are the most handsome falcon I have ever seen, Cloot.' She was delighted to see the bird bob his head.

Tor translated. 'He commends your excellent taste.' And enjoyed hearing her laugh at this.

Saxon, unperturbed by the bird of prey next to him, pointed to the small brook they were passing.

'Yes,' Tor said. 'Why don't we stop here for a moment?'

He wagged his finger when Alyssa pulled a face at stopping so soon. 'Your job is to be my guide. Here is where I wish to stop and admire Ildagarth's beautiful scenery.'

Saxon motioned that he would stay with the horses. Tor and Alyssa walked in a more comfortable silence now to the brook's edge while Cloot flew ahead to the small copse of trees. She marvelled at his grace.

'Tell me about Cloot,' Alyssa said as they sat down on the spongy grass.

She watched Tor's face battle through a series of private conflicts. He finally sighed. 'Where to begin?'

'Well . . . how about after the Floral Dance?' she said softly, pain lacing her words.

And so he did. He told her everything. Merkhud's sensing of their link, the Stones, the fact that his mother and father were not his real parents, and how he had felt he must follow Merkhud to Tal. He explained how he had ridden two days later to Mallee Marsh to find her, to beg her forgiveness and her hand, to ask her to go with him; only to discover she had gone away. No note, not even an indication of where or why. Tor ran his hand through his hair; she remembered that trait. Then he told her how alone he had felt without her; the countless times over the years he had tried to link, always in vain but never giving up hope.

It was then she took his hand in her own. Tor felt a strength from her touch.

He described finding a gentle giant of a man – a cripple

– nailed to a post and how this stranger, who could link with him, had begged him to stay close. When he told her the stranger's name was Cloot, Alyssa, intrigued, looked at the falcon which was preening itself on a branch nearby. Tor knew the bird was doing this for her benefit. He told Cloot to stop showing off. Cloot ignored him, stretching his powerful wings wide so Alyssa could appreciate his fine, broad chest. She laughed, but not for long.

Tor detailed how badly injured Cloot had been that day; told her of Prime Cyrus and Doctor Freyberg; of the ant dismembering the cockroach and his healing of his new friend. He spoke of the little he knew of the Paladin. He chose not to mention being crowned King of the Sea, or Eryn. This was perhaps not the moment, as Alyssa began to caress his hand, to be talking about making love to another woman.

His story gathered momentum: chasing through the night to Brewis; Cloot shapechanging into this glorious falcon; Cyrus nailed to a tree and how they had saved him; the King and Queen; Merkhud; life at the Palace and his growing obsession to find her.

Her tears fell onto his hand which she clasped close now.

Tor brought his life over the past five years to a rapid close for her, detailing his healing of Queen Nyria and subsequent falling out with Merkhud; his suspicions of the old man; the Prime's disappearance in the Heartwood and of Darmud Coril and Lys. Tor did not speak of his dreams, though, and what he saw in them. That he would tell her later.

Right now he looked at her earnestly. 'Do you believe me?'

Alyssa looked into his eyes and beyond. 'All of it, Tor. Saxon has spoken to me of this same dream woman, the one you call Lys. She is the one who guided him to me.'

He nodded. 'That makes sense. He is your guardian.'

It did not make much sense to her but before she could say more he was talking again.

'Will you forgive me for Minstead?'

She put her cool hand to his mouth and stopped him trying to continue. She nodded.

'And Xantia?' she asked quietly.

'Xantia?' he said, as though not understanding the word. 'She is no one, Alyssa . . . a distraction.'

'Really? Well, that distraction has been my closest friend for years. More recently she chose to make me her enemy.'

'Because of me?'

'No. It's complicated. Two sorts of jealousy have her entirely in their grip. A new Elder is to be named soon; Xantia believes the role should be hers. There are four candidates and as I'm one of them she feels threatened by me.' Alyssa did not elaborate further but Tor guessed Alyssa was the first and obvious choice to all. He kept his thoughts to himself.

She continued. 'More recently she has become enamoured by a man. You. She hears no reason. And in me, already someone she despises, she sees only a rival for that man she has known for hours and now claims to worship. Tor, Xantia thinks we are lovers!'

He smiled. 'Let's not disappoint her then. Let's make your falling out earn its grief.' He meant it. She could see it in his blazing blue eyes.

The falcon must have said something because he grimaced sharply at it in rebuke.

'Tor, I'm not sure why but lately I seem to be reminding people rather too often what this circle of archalyt on my forehead means.'

'What – this?'

When he touched the disc it fell soundlessly into the well of fabric formed by her robes as they draped across her crossed legs.

Alyssa was speechless. Even Tor looked bemused as he picked up the disc between his long fingers and held it up, the green gem glinting fiercely in the weak sunshine.

He sliced a link into her mind, *Welcome back to me*, and slipped the disc into his pocket as he leant to kiss her.

Numb, Alyssa permitted the kiss but did not return it. It was as though she had been seeing the world through blurred vision these past years; hearing it through a gauze. As soon as she was released from the archalyt, every colour, scent and sound – and probably taste, too, she thought – increased in intensity.

Tor pulled back from her mouth. How long had he dreamed of that? He did not even care that the affection was so one-sided on this occasion.

Saxon! Alyssa called across the link.

He came as fast as his hobbling gait and blind eyes would allow, his face contorted by emotion.

You're back, his lovely, deep voice said into her mind; a voice she had missed so much. *How?*

Tor did it.

Saxon smiled his torn and ragged grin; a ghost of its former radiance. *That's because he is the One.*

*   *   *

The ride to Ildagarth proper would take them until midday and Saxon took the horses slowly to ensure the precious couple he escorted had plenty of time to say what needed to be shared between them.

'So, what about you?'

Alyssa looked at Tor quizzically to buy herself a few more moments before she had to relive what she had tried to deny every day of her life since.

'It's painful for me, Tor.' She looked at the purplish hills in the distance and the different greens of the grasses which stretched out towards them. She swore she could catch on the breeze the fragrance of the lavender on those hills.

He took her hand and kissed its palm tenderly. *Tell me*, he spoke into her mind.

And so she did, sparing him none of the brutal details. She watched him smile at her tale of flying with Saxon Fox and she watched grief form in his eyes when she described her first ordeal with Goth; then watched those blue eyes deepen into despair and then hatred when she told of her second, more physical encounter.

Her voice shook in the telling but his own trembling touch steadied her so she could finish the story. Perhaps he had thought it could not get worse but she felt his body stiffen at her description of what Goth had done to Milt and Oris, the injuries he had inflicted on Saxon and how he had promised he would wait for her.

When she had finished her telling, silence claimed the slim space between them. Finally Tor nodded.

'I understand why you would choose the Academie. I even admire the archalyt now for how it protects you. I did not protect you.'

'Tor, don't. You weren't to know any of this would occur. You forget – it was my choice to leave with Sorrel. I control my life, not you.'

She realised she had forgotten to tell Tor about the dream she had experienced while floating in the Green as Goth claimed her virginity but there was no time now. Saxon opened a link to tell her they were almost at their destination.

Alyssa reminded herself to tell Tor later about the stolen child and the books. Perhaps he might know something of the story or be able to make the connection with Merkhud.

She squeezed his hand. 'Come on. Let's make this a good day.'

Normally Tor would have revelled in the opportunity to explore a new city, particularly one of such historical note as Ildagarth, but his attentions were fixed firmly on Alyssa. Just watching the way she moved her hands as she spoke was far more fascinating for him than the glorious architecture, albeit in ruins, which surrounded him.

Ildagarth, or so the tale went, had never fully recovered from being razed by the warlock Orlac. All around were ruins of sad beauty which looked as though they had reared through the ground from another world. Around them had sprung a new city but the old one still peeped through.

The locals' eyes slid easily past the exquisite columns of marble; the decorative floors, of which perhaps only a corner remained; the achingly beautiful carvings. In the oldest and most inspiring part of the city thrived a new community dedicated to commerce and learning of a less philanthropic nature. To a visitor, however, Ildagarth was a place of unrivalled magnificence where one could almost hear the ghosts of centuries gone if alone in one of the dozens of empty, ruined buildings.

Right now, though, the city was filling rapidly with masses of the living. They had travelled from throughout the Kingdom of Tallinor and beyond from the Four Kingdoms to celebrate the most famous of all festivals: Czabba. Literally it meant 'Death' but the occasion was anything but solemn. The Festival dated back centuries to the time of the folklore legend of Orlac but its original meaning had become muddied as the times marched on. In truth Merkhud was right. It had evolved into a grand masquerade of gigantic proportions in which every street of the city reverberated to the merrymaking of its guests.

Everyone wore masks during the night of the Festival itself. Tradition dictated that if you covered your face then Death could not see who you were. So there was always an assortment of death masks as well as strange beasts and animals from the wildest imagination. Obligatory, however – and far more interesting for no one could ever explain why – was the tradition for eleven particular masks to always be present. They were created by the finest craftsmen in the Kingdom and the chance to wear one of the eleven was considered one of the highest privileges bestowed on an Ildagarthian.

One of these masks was Death, which took the shape of a handsome man who was meant to be Orlac. The remaining ten depicted the most ancient of races of people from around the Kingdom of Tallinor, or so scholars suggested. Truth or fiction? It meant nothing to the present-day revellers but merely added to the pomp and intrigue of the Death Festival.

Alyssa now realised that the ten ancient races referred to the Paladin. Another piece of the jigsaw slotted into place.

She was giving Tor a tour of the streets she knew from her infrequent outings over the past few years. He drank in her calm voice, studied the way her lips moved, recalled how she used to fiddle with her honey-coloured hair the same way as a child. Her long hands with their perfect almond-shaped nails kept his attention rapt far more than her description of life in the city of Ildagarth, famous or not.

They found themselves wandering in a street known for its excellent watering holes, as Alyssa called them. Here they served every herb tea imaginable and a drink called zabub which was a heady, delicious brew served thick and sweetened. It was a local specialty and Alyssa suggested he try it.

Tor listened to her order in the language of street vendors of the north. He could tell Alyssa was a gifted linguist.

He spoke aloud. 'This must be your first Czabba Festival too.'

'It is, yes,' she said, then frowned. 'Do you think Saxon is all right . . . and what about Cloot?'

He grinned. 'Cloot can take care of himself. He doesn't like crowds or cities much. He'll stay close and he's always in my head.'

She sighed. 'It used to be that way with Saxon too, before the archalyt.'

'You've no need to worry on Saxon's behalf. He's a wise

man. He'll stay with the horses on the fringe of the city.'

'It's always in my mind that Goth will keep his promise. He means to destroy me because I've escaped his clutches twice.'

She saw his jaw clench at her words.

'He will lay no finger on you ever again, Alyssa. I promise you. The man is a fiend. He must pay for what he did to you.'

She was about to say something when the drinks arrived. Instead she whispered across the link. *It's past. Let it be.*

She thanked the young serving woman and then clinked her mug with Tor's. 'Zabub is served heated to take the chill off a winter's day. Be careful it doesn't burn your mouth.'

He blew on the steaming contents and sipped. It was rich and laced with an exotic liquor.

'Mmm,' he said with genuine pleasure. It made her laugh. 'So what do you think of all this festivity?'

'It doesn't mean much to me, Tor. In truth I prefer to celebrate life.'

'Or perhaps survival,' he said gently. 'Czabba – is that Ildagarthian?'

'Yes, but very old, a dialect dead for a century or more.' Alyssa suddenly became still, her mug lifted halfway to her mouth and a frown creasing her forehead.

'You'll catch a fly if you keep it open like that,' he said, using a favourite phrase of his mother's.

'Tor . . .'

'Yes, I'm still here . . . hanging on your every word.'

'It doesn't mean Death.'

'Should I be following this?'

'Czabba . . . the Festival . . . it doesn't simply mean Death.'

'Oh?' Tor said, confused and totally uninterested in anything but the thought of kissing her sweet lips again.

Alyssa's voice was suddenly excited. 'Listen to me — this is really important. I've been reading two ancient scripts I found buried beneath the crypt in a place which was no casual hidey-hole. These books had been carefully concealed.'

He nodded. The temptation to tease her was great but she seemed very intent on this. He kept his expression serious.

Alyssa continued. 'In those books I have read what I believe is a true commentary, written by one of the Masters of Goldstone. His name was Nanak. He told a story — too long in the re-telling for now — but it roughly goes that a child was stolen. No ordinary child, Tor, but a god.'

She saw him swallow very slowly. He placed his cup gently on the table. 'Go on,' he said carefully, all flippancy gone.

'He was stolen from the Host and sold to mortals by—'

'Scavengers.' He completed her sentence.

It was Alyssa's turn to put her mug down. Her skin paled before him. 'You know?'

'Please, go on,' he encouraged, giving no eye contact now.

She felt compelled. 'I . . . I meant to tell you this earlier. When Goth raped me I used the Green to escape his touch, the pain. In the Green I had a vision. I watched a baby being stolen from its parents. They were beautiful and they stood in an exquisite glade. They did nothing to help him, simply watched as the thieves ran away with their child.'

'Tell me more,' he said urgently.

'Nothing more from that vision. Only what I've read in this book. The child grew amongst mortals, not knowing who he was. His mortal parents, who were sentient, also had no knowledge of his background. He was gifted, an extraordinary talent with the magics. They enrolled him at the Academie where his powers surpassed those of the Masters and they became scared of him.'

She paused. It was Tor who continued as his own dream vividly came back to him.

'When they hatched a plan to Quell him, the young man razed the city of Goldstone – the Ancient Seat of Learning – and killed two thousand people. That city is now known as Ildagarth and the Ancient Seat, Caremboche, is where today's Academie now sits.'

Alyssa shook her head in disbelief. 'Tor, you must tell me how you know this.'

'I dreamed it.' He rubbed his hands over his face in consternation.

Alyssa's words tumbled over one another in her excitement. 'I have only read the first of the books. It is written in the most ancient of languages and I don't understand how I can read it. No one else can. I have never encountered that language before; how do I know it? How do I know that this Festival is not Czabba but Aczabba Veiszuit?'

Tor shook his head in silence, waiting for her to explain.

'Czabba is Ildagarthian for Death all right but I believe it might be a poor translation, a bastardisation if you will, from this more ancient language which the books are scribed in. Aczabba Veiszuit means Death of a God.' She clapped her hands in wonderment. 'Tell me what else you dreamed.'

Tor felt a chill crawl over his body as he began to recall for Alyssa all that he had seen in his dream. When he had finished they sat in silence for several moments.

'This Lys you speak of – she told you that he lives and would return? That you must stop him? Tor, what folly is this?'

'No folly. His name is Orlac.'

Her knees felt weak. Tor spoke the truth.

'There's worse.' He finished his drink. 'Want to take a guess at his mortal father's name?'

'I don't need to. It's written in the book. His name is Merkhud.'

'One and the same.'

'But, Tor, that would make your Merkhud centuries old.' She wanted to use this impossibility to dismiss everything.

'Why not? Nothing makes sense in my life any more, or yours come to that. There is potent magic surrounding us; coursing through us. We go undetected by Inquisitors and yet Merkhud finds us. He seems to be at the very core of all of this. Alyssa, I could almost believe he contrived to have you leave Mallee Marsh because he suspected I might try to bring you with me to Tal.'

Tor's face creased in thought as he tried to gather together threads of ideas which had lain on the fringe of his mind for years.

'It would not have suited him to have you with me but he knew you were sentient and that you also had escaped notice; you were too valuable to ignore. I know it sounds like a wild notion but I could even believe that he veiled you from me!' He leapt to a new thought. 'Alyssa, why did you leave? What made you wander off with a woman you had never met before?'

She thought hard. 'After the Floral Dance I hoped that you might . . . well, you know.'

He nodded, knowing all too well.

She sighed. 'Instead you scared me with your harsh words and angry voice. She was so kind to me on that first day when I felt alone and scared. But now that I think about it as an adult, I recall that Sorrel's conversation was cleverly directed at informing me of your leaving. Now I hear that you had not left at all. Sorrel wanted me to get angry at you, perhaps. I don't know. Why would she lie otherwise?'

'Exactly! I'll bet all the gold in Ildagarth that Sorrel is part of this elaborate web which Merkhud weaves. Alyssa, if Merkhud is the mortal father of Orlac then why not—'

'Don't say it, Tor, please. She's been my guardian for five summers. She has protected me and nursed me and watched over me.'

'Of course she has! That's her task. She may well love you, Alyssa, but she's controlled by Merkhud, her husband. And why? I'll tell you. Because she's the mortal mother of Orlac. They have controlled us from the start and deliberately kept us apart.' There was no elation in his voice as he weaved his threads together.

Alyssa felt hollow. She knew she had accepted Sorrel into her life all too easily and that the woman had come along at just the right time to help a hurting young girl find her feet and a purpose. Tor's summary was very painful because it rang of too much truth. The jigsaw piece hovered, then snapped into place.

Merkhud and Sorrel, mortal parents of Orlac, working together to manipulate events.

'Did you choose to come north when you left Tal?' Alyssa asked carefully as she frowned again in thought.

'No, Merkhud suggested it.'

'So, if we follow your plot, then they have contrived to bring us together; they knew we would have to meet again. Why?'

Alyssa never did hear Tor's reply for at that precise moment a familiar figure caught her attention. Suddenly she was cold to the marrow. Over Tor's broad shoulder she glimpsed a flash of purple; a colour she had not cared for since Fragglesham when she had lost something precious to a man she hated more than any other. That same man was now strolling down the street in Ildagarth where she sat twisting over a theory and sipping zabub.

Tor watched her expression flip from puzzlement to terror. He turned and immediately saw what had created the fear. He felt his own bile rise but fell into the practised calm he had taught himself that night when he felt Cloot's life slipping away from him. That was the very first time he had banished fear and replaced it with power – his own power from within. Tor had called upon the calm many times since then and he called upon it now for he knew fear would draw the enemy to them.

He opened a link to Alyssa and told her to look at him. She turned with effort away from the purple and stared into the blue she trusted.

Pull your hood up over your hair, he said calmly. *Do not look at Goth.*

Then he sliced open a link to Cloot and warned his friend of the turn of events. The falcon was in the air before Tor had turned back to Alyssa.

Link with Saxon. Tell him you are coming. He must be ready to flee straight back to the Academie.

She did as she was told.

Good. Now, my beloved, I must do something I regret deeply but it will save you once more. He reached into his pocket and withdrew the pale green archalyt disc.

Cloot, circling high above, spoke a warning. *He's about forty steps from you, Tor, but is engaged in conversation with a storekeeper. He is not looking your way.*

Tor pressed the archalyt onto Alyssa's forehead and it adhered. She felt herself back in dullness, cut off from Saxon or Tor. It was a keen sense of isolation and renewed terror she now experienced but Tor stood and gripped her elbow, lending her his strength. He turned her from Goth and spoke quietly but firmly, releasing her arm so they drew no attention.

'You are going to hurry but not run. You will move straight past Goth.' He saw her flinch. 'It is the shortest way back to Saxon. Goth will not notice you because I will distract him. I promise you will be safe.'

Alyssa did not believe him, he could see it in her frightened eyes, but she had courage and she would do as he asked.

Cloot?

He's still busy haggling over some trinket. You had better do it now or not at all, my friends.

'I love you, Alyssa,' Tor said tenderly; then firmly: 'Go now.'

Alyssa had heard him utter those words before, on a

sunny day at Minstead Green. She left him against her will once again; this time walking away from the man she loved towards the man she hated.

Tor hid himself and watched her progress. He would not act until she was safely past Goth, whom he could now clearly see arguing with a shopkeeper.

Goth had had a pig of a day. None of his soldiers were with him at present and although he could not force a bridling without his men, he could certainly pick an argument with a grubby storekeeper who was fleecing people of their hard-earned money.

From the corner of his eye the Chief Inquisitor saw the robes of an acolyte of the Academie moving briskly past him. His practised observer's technique registered that within them was a petite and slender woman. He could not see her face for she had it turned aside. And then she was out of his view and he was back with the story about eight mouths to feed as well as an ageing mother to care for.

At that moment the storekeeper stopped and looked up in wonder at the sky. Goth looked up too and noticed a falcon circling high above. The storekeeper and those around him were marvelling at it and commenting that no falcons had been seen in these parts for years.

It took only a second for Goth's sharp mind to put it together. He had been following in the bastard physic's footsteps for weeks now. He had lost all trace of him at Saddleworth; had hoped to catch up with him at the pass through the southern fringe of the Rorky'el Mountains – the only way to the north-west – but had found no sign. However, that was unmistakably Gynt's bird flying above.

The physic was here for sure. Goth dropped the item he had been haggling for and looked around wildly for the man.

His powers of observation served him well once again. Just about everyone around him was looking up towards the bird; everyone except the retreating acolyte. She, he saw, kept her robes pulled tightly around her – as if she did not want to be noticed – and was hurrying.

Goth had always led his life instinctively and his instincts had never let him down. Now they suggested strongly that he should follow that small, slender figure. His mind raced to the conclusion that his prey was close: Gynt was here. However, his gut feeling demanded he follow the woman as the only Caremboche woman who would flee from him was Alyssandra Qyn. Granted, he admitted as he walked away from the pointing crowd, he had not expected her to be an acolyte for she was not sentient. Perhaps it was a guise or perhaps it was not her at all but he followed all the same. He knew the women of the Academie were protected by royal decree but he could not care a damn for such rules. He would find a way around them.

She would lead him to Gynt for sure. He would have the physic soon . . . and he would have the trembling, frightened Alyssa Qyn in his arms once again.

Tor ran out into the street and felt his stomach turn. Goth was not approaching as he had hoped; he was moving away and in the direction of Alyssa.

I sense I'm something of a novelty in these parts, Tor, said Cloot. *I'm going to follow Alyssa; see she gets to Saxon safely*.

Tor quickly caught up with Goth but kept out of sight

behind whichever person, animal, store or pillar presented itself. He could not communicate with Alyssa but he could see she was no longer giving care to stealth. She was running.

Alyssa risked one look behind her. She did not expect to see anyone but glimpsed the contorted face of Goth, possibly fifty steps away; close enough to make out the lumps of his ugly face. He was chasing her. She threw off her hood and dropped the cloak which was slowing her down and ran. Her golden hair flowed free and Goth yelled out in delight.

'It is you, Alyssa! Oh, I am looking forward to our reunion.' He broke into a run.

Goth was short but he was also fit and powerful. Tor, loping fast behind them now, could see it was a matter of moments before the Inquisitor ran Alyssa down. He had to do something but could not strike directly against Goth who was always well shielded by the same archalyt which protected Alyssa. Tor thought fast. He had only a matter of moments.

A man was leading two horses towards the stables ahead. As Goth ran towards them Tor spiked the animals with sharp pain. As he had hoped, both reared up, squealing. One ripped itself free from the shocked stable-hand and the other kicked out furiously and struck Goth on the shoulder.

It was not much more than a glancing blow but it was sufficient to knock Goth to the ground. People came scurrying to assist him. He shook them off and grimaced, not from the pain of his shoulder but from the agony of watching his quarry disappear around a corner and out of his sight.

Alyssa heard the horses but did not turn; she just kept running towards the edge of town where she knew Saxon would be waiting for her. She glanced above and, despite her fear, felt elated to see Cloot flying with her. She loved the falcon for this and even dared a wave.

The falcon cast back to Tor. *Alyssa will be fine. Now you must get back to the Academie too. He knows you're here because he's seen me.*

He's heading back to the stables, I think, to get his horse. Are you sure Alyssa will be all right?

Saxon has her and they are already heading home at full gallop, came the reply. *Just keep Goth busy for a few minutes more.*

Think! Tor screamed to himself. He doubled back towards the stables.

Cloot spoke again. *Remember that Aspecting charm Merkhud mentioned which all those Masters found so impossible to wield? I know you never bothered with it but now might be as good a time as any.*

It was as though a shaft of sunlight had burst through dark clouds. *I love you, Cloot.*

What would you do without me? the bird said and closed the link.

Aspecting was an extraordinarily difficult charm; it and Shadow-walking seemed to exist only in theory for not even the great Master Joromi had wound his talents around either of the tricks. Nevertheless, as Tor watched Goth disappear into the stables he centred and felt the Colours surround him. Against his chest he felt the thrum of the Orbs as they vibrated with their and his power; he wished, yet again, he knew their true purpose.

He focused on a man standing to his right and cast

the complex glamour. Goth reappeared, slapping his thigh with the whip he would use on his stallion to thunder down the road to Caremboche. He glanced around, his small boar-like eyes scanning the crowd swiftly and penetratingly. They were arrested by the profile of a man he knew. The tall figure noticed him and turned away to walk down a side street.

Goth's pudgy face arranged itself into a nasty smile. 'I have you now, Gynt.'

He was surprised not to see the physic when he too entered the side street but this was one of the maze of streets which comprised Ildagarth's famed bazaar. Goods were strewn on makeshift tables under awnings and there was everything on offer, from boots to confectionery.

He took his time, watching closely. There he was! Talking to someone. Now he was moving off under the cover of the awnings. Goth followed.

He had lost him once more. Goth began to whip his thigh again in frustration. Surely Gynt was playing with him. Suddenly he saw him again, this time carrying a tray which he handed to a woman. Whatever was the physic doing? Goth watched him say something to the woman and then walk into a shop.

By the time Goth arrived at that shop it was empty, save for the storekeeper and the same woman buying rice.

Anger welled and control capitulated to rage. Goth was no longer thinking clearly. He wanted Gynt; wanted to hurt him for years of avoiding his wrath. He wanted to punish him for all those women who fell at his feet. Most of all, he wanted to break him now whilst he was away from the protection of Merkhud, the King and that arrogant Prime.

He stomped out of the shop and, to his surprise, found Gynt directly in front of him, offering him a quartered orange. His frustrations spilled over.

'No more games,' he said nastily. Gynt did not seem to recognise him and addressed him in Idagarthian, suggesting Goth try his fruit.

This enraged him. Goth struck Gynt across the face with his whip, then fell on him in a frenzy. He wanted to tear him limb from limb. He had lost Alyssa again and here was someone upon whom he could vent the anger of that loss. He felt hands frantically pulling at him but he was strong; he clung tight and banged the physic's head again and again against the cobbles.

He heard himself giggle. My, my! This would take some explaining back at Court. But explain he would.

When Goth was finally wrenched off the body he saw it was a child who lay lifeless in the street, her blood mixing with the juices of crushed oranges. It did not make sense. What had happened to Gynt? Goth's anger subsided.

People were whispering around him but most were too shocked to speak aloud. Many had known the child since she was born. None had known she was sentient. Why would the Inquisitor beat her to death?

It was fortunate that Tor did not witness the result of his Aspecting charm. He had waited to see the first two work beautifully and then had ducked and weaved through the cobbled streets of Ildagarth to put as much distance between himself and Goth as possible. He made his escape, out across open fields, running in the direction of the Academie.

Cloot, however, saw it all. He chose not to re-open the link and share with Tor the high point of his handiwork in adding a new dimension to the charm by making it pass from person to person through touch. No, he would keep this to himself and accept the guilt of the child's death as his burden.

Nanak's voice broke as he sliced the link open. *Arabella, the priestess, she has fallen to Orlac.*

Merkhud's face twisted in a grimace of despair. *Too soon. This can't be.*

It's true.

Did she say anything?

She just called out that her time had come.

And she disappeared like the others?

Yes.

Merkhud paced his study. Nanak said no more.

Then she will show herself somewhere, my friend. She will re-emerge. We know that now. Her life as a guardian of Orlac is ended. Her life as a protector of the Trinity has begun.

He received no reply. The link closed.

22

Sanctuary

Tor returned to the Academie and, after hurriedly tidying himself, went looking for Alyssa. He found Xantia.

'Back so early, Physic Gynt? I thought even Alyssa could have kept you amused for slightly longer.'

Tor was in no mood for her. 'Do you know where she is?'

'I don't, sorry.' She took a few steps towards him, even dared to trace her finger across his hand. 'Perhaps I could show you whatever she hasn't got around to yet?' The innuendo was not lost on Tor.

'I'm sure I can find her,' he said and walked away.

'I'll look forward to that dance tonight, Torkyn,' she called after him. He ignored her and made his way to the crypt.

It was a good guess; Alyssa was there. She appeared calm but colour was burning her cheeks. There were other acolytes in the library and her look told him to be careful.

'Are you all right?' he whispered, desperate to hold her.

She nodded. 'Did you just get back from the city?' Her tone was clipped. It was his turn to nod. 'And our mutual friend?'

'Thrown off your scent,' he whispered again. He saw the pulse at her temple pound. Goth's hold over her was monstrous. 'We must talk.'

'Not here,' she cautioned. 'I'll meet you by the fountain; you can have a tour of the gardens this afternoon. I'll be there shortly.'

A feeling of foreboding had gripped Alyssa. It was not just that Goth had returned to her life, though the sight of him giving chase had terrified her. Tor's return had stirred up emotions she thought she had long buried. Somehow she had convinced herself that life as a member of the Academie was enough; it was not. Now she understood Xantia's sentiments. All Alyssa wanted now was to be with Tor. But life could never go back to how it had been yesterday. She remembered her angry words to Xantia; how hollow they sounded now as she struggled to take the same advice.

She was an Untouchable. The disc of archalyt was her sole protection against Goth but it doomed the love she held for Tor. And yet Saxon had pressed her to accept him as the man she must follow. She walked through the Academie's corridors, confused, and only realised when she saw him standing in the courtyard that she had actually come looking for Saxon. In her hands she carried the two volumes of Nanak's writings.

'Keep these safe for me, Saxon,' she said, not exactly sure why she was doing this. Like Goth, Alyssa was led by instinct. Right now it told her to hide the books once again but to keep them close. Saxon nodded. He took the

books and put them under a cloth in the back of the cart
he was mending.

The revelations she and Tor had discussed today were
yet more reasons for her dark mood. He was waiting at
the fountain for her.

'We must be very cautious. The Elders' watchful eyes
are everywhere.'

They began to stroll along the paths and Alyssa kept
up a narrative about various plants, the history of the
gardens, about the herbs and special potions they made
at Caremboche and new remedies they had discovered.
But beneath that they also talked.

'What did you do?'

'A trick.'

'. . . shalack is one of our most versatile herbs . . . He'll
be back. He'll be here tonight when I'm vulnerable.'

'Then don't come out into the open.'

'. . . made into a paste which we then warm . . . I have
to. It's part of the ceremony . . . but just gently,' she
continued.

Tor ran his hands through his hair. 'Listen to me. A
mask will be delivered to your room today. Be sure Xantia
sees it. Be sure that's what you are wearing when you
leave your dormitory.'

'. . . good for all forms of pain within the body but is
particularly effective for stomach cramps. Over here is a
tiny pink flower we call strap . . . I already have a mask
organised.'

Tor gestured to a bench. They sat. 'You must be wearing
the one which is delivered.'

'What is it?'

'A fox,' he answered. 'I'll be the pig.'

'That's appropriate,' Alyssa said, unable to help a sad, fleeting smile. She stood again and continued talking about herbals.

'Alyssa, our time is short,' Tor urged.

She stopped to pass a few words with two Elders Tor had not met before.

'And did you enjoy our famed zabub, Physic Gynt?' one of them asked.

'Immensely,' he said.

They nodded politely and moved on.

'You were saying?' she said. 'About time being short. So when do you leave?'

'Tonight.'

'Ah.' Alyssa tried to think of something to say to cover her shock but Tor spoke rapidly. 'Except I won't be leaving alone, Alyssa. This time you will be coming with me.'

He put his finger to his lips to hush her when she swung around in alarm. 'It is no longer safe for you here. Untouchable or not, we were meant to be together. Even Merkhud wanted this. So let's not disappoint. I have a plan.'

A small troop of acolytes passed them and one said good afternoon to their esteemed visitor. Tor and Alyssa forced polite smiles to their faces.

'Just wear the fox mask and do as I say, when I say.'

'Saxon?'

'Is coming with us, as is Sorrel. They're as deeply involved in this strange puzzle we're putting together as you and I. I will speak with Sorrel this afternoon. Leave everything to me. Play innocent to all questions but make sure Xantia sees you put that mask on.'

'I understand.'

'I love you, Alyssa.'

Her spirits soared to hear him say it out loud, even though it was barely above a whisper.

'Likewise,' she replied and they parted.

Goth had to use all of his powers of guile and persuasion to climb out of the sticky hole he found himself in. Fortunately a small band of his Inquisitors had finally caught up with him in Ildagarth and the strength of numbers lent weight to his argument that the gypsy child had been sentient. He told the city fathers that the young girl had blazed with magic and had cast it against him; he had feared for those around him. He apologised for the manner in which he had dealt with her.

The mother was distraught and calling for his blood. The authorities knew this would never happen of course but they explained that they needed to placate the woman somehow. After all, she had lost a child.

Goth had no mercy for gypsies at the best of times. In fact, sitting here now in the Mayor's office, sipping zabub and listening to the twitterings of the city fathers, he had almost convinced himself it had been the decent thing to do. To deny life to a gypsy child meant yet another drifting pickpocket had been dealt with. He knew he could not express this publicly but his twisted mind loved the right-eousness of that thinking and he knew many people would applaud it.

'I will make good with the family, of course,' he said magnanimously. 'Is it a large one?'

'I believe there are seven children; well, six now,' said one of the men uncomfortably. 'No father but there are two grandparents as I understand.'

As he had guessed – a whole filthy sackful of the thieving rats! Goth banished the sneer which came easily to his lumpy face. He must not show his true feelings.

'Mayor Jory, how about I send my men around to their dwelling tonight with a filled purse? They will express my sincere sympathies and explain my position. It's most unusual of course, considering the child was sentient and had to be dealt with, but I feel badly that we did not bridle appropriately.' His manner was courteous and humble.

Goth had already worked out that the Mayor cared little for these lowlifes who fleeced the Ildagarth community. He tolerated them at Festival time when hordes of gypsies flooded the city to make money from the thousands of pilgrims and revellers. They served a purpose then but the Mayor wanted them gone straight after. Perhaps this would be just the right encouragement.

'I think that should cover it,' the Mayor said. 'Thank you, Chief Inquisitor Goth, for your patience in this matter.'

Goth waved the genteel words aside as if to say it was the least he could do under the circumstances. He called his man over and spoke in a low tone.

'Have two cases of Morriet sent over to Mayor Jory's house with my compliments,' he whispered, pressing a purse into the man's hand at the same time. 'Give him this too.'

The man nodded. 'Ask Rhus to see me, please,' Goth added before the Inquisitor departed.

Rhus appeared. Goth made a show of standing and pulling out a large and clearly heavy purse of gold.

'Give this to the family of the child, Rhus,' he said

loudly enough for the city fathers to hear. He watched them nod their approval and then turn away to discuss other matters. Rhus looked at his chief, knowing more precise orders were about to be given.

'Six children, a mother, two grandparents. Apparently they are presently residing on the fringe of town under canvas with the rest of the gypsy filth. With luck though, Rhus, they may also be waiting downstairs for the outcome of this meeting.'

The Inquisitor turned to leave. He understood the orders totally.

'Oh, and Rhus . . . the mother's not a bad-looking sort. You and the boys may have your fun but be discreet and dispose of all bodies with care.'

The man smiled darkly. 'No trace will be left, Lord Goth. I shall return your purse later.'

'Thank you, Rhus.'

Alyssa was nervous. There had been no time for Tor to explain this plan of his but she knew he was right. Life would not be quite so safe for her any more. Goth had her cornered. The only hope was for Tor and her to try and disappear. She clung to this thread, knowing it was fine indeed. She was a marked woman and Tor was so well known in prestigious circles that disappearing would not be easy.

Her other confirmation was Saxon's note. Saxon had been sent to protect her and he had not let her down. Now he was telling her to follow Tor. She was making the correct decision, how ever dangerous it seemed. The books, this strange dream of Tor's, even her own dream in the Green – she was beginning to feel as though it was all part of some grand scheme. She was too frightened not to stay with Tor.

Alyssa had managed to avoid Xantia all afternoon but had followed protocol and reported to Elder Iris. She had explained that the crowds in the city were thick and it was hard to see much in that sort of merry throng. The Elder had accepted this reason for her early return quite happily. Alyssa explained that she had given Physic Gynt a tour of the gardens and he was now writing letters to the Palace and preparing for his departure tomorrow morning. He would be busy enough for the remainder of the day.

'Did someone remember a mask for him, Alyssa my dear?' the Elder asked anxiously.

'All in hand,' Alyssa replied then took her leave and escaped to the crypt. Sorrel found her there. They were alone and free to talk.

'Physic Gynt visited me this afternoon.'

Alyssa decided it was no use hedging. 'Did he tell you about Goth?'

'He did. However did you get away?'

'By running fast. Did the physic say anything else?' she asked almost shyly.

'You know he did,' Sorrel said. She sat and fixed Alyssa with a stare. 'Are you sure about this?'

'I am. Sorrel, do you remember asking me what I was running away from at Mallee Marsh that day?'

'Like yesterday,' the old girl replied.

'Well, he is who I was running from.'

'I gathered as much,' said Sorrel, not enjoying the fact she had helped to manipulate the reunion. 'I remember now; he's the young scribe who left Flat Meadows to train at the Palace.'

Alyssa nodded. Deep down, though, she wanted to scream at Sorrel. When Tor suggested Sorrel may be Orlac's mortal mother the notion had made complete sense. She thought back over all her conversations with Sorrel; seemingly innocent at the time, now she felt they had all been contrived. Everything about Sorrel's arrival, where she had brought Alyssa, how she had stayed close, had been a series of manipulations. It occurred to Alyssa that the only unknown was Saxon, which is probably why Sorrel had been so aggressive towards him initially.

But she needed Sorrel. If Tor was right then Merkhud was communicating directly with this woman – perhaps his wife – and she may yet guide them. Sorrel was empowered so it was perfectly feasible that everything she and the old girl had done since leaving Mallee Marsh had been fed back to Merkhud, who had timed his release of Tor perfectly. It made Alyssa feel ill to think on it.

'My dear, are you unwell?' asked Sorrel.

Play along, Alyssa told herself, be the innocent as Tor suggested. 'I'm all right . . . just thinking about Goth makes me feel weak. Tor hasn't told me yet of his plan.'

Sorrel had heard it already. She enlightened Alyssa. 'He aims to escape tonight during the festivities. Saxon is preparing a cart. The physic has kept it as simple as possible. Under the shield of darkness and the obvious mayhem of the Festival, who will notice an old cart rolling out from the back gates? Simple.'

It certainly sounded easy but Alyssa was no fool. 'But where do we go?'

'Well . . .' Sorrel sighed. 'He seems to feel if we can make it to the fringe of the forest, we will be safe.' She tried to hide her own doubt.

Alyssa agreed. 'Sorrel . . . do you really care?'

'Light strike me, girl! What an odd question for you to pose. What would make you ask such a thing of me?'

Sorrel looked shaken and Alyssa regretted her hastiness.

'Oh, I don't know. I'm sorry I said that. I just feel threatened.'

'Know this, Alyssa,' Sorrel said gravely, 'I would give my life for you. Perhaps one day soon.'

Dark fell swiftly in a northern winter. There was promise of snow in the icy air but not for this night; tonight it would hold off as the merry fires burned from Ildagarth city to Caremboche and torches lit the main road connecting the two.

Chief Inspector Goth, his group now swelled to almost two dozen men on horseback, was filled with anticipation. The thought of holding Alyssa's sweet body against his own tantalised beyond even his own understanding. He had no idea why she had such a hold over his senses. Now that she was a woman, her body filled out and offering so much more promise, the excitement he felt was even more exquisite.

Everything had gone to plan. The gypsies had been dealt with quietly and his heavy purse was back in his pocket. Goth was feeling invincible this cold and clear night in an Ildagarth which throbbed to the sound of music and festivity.

He touched the demon mask on his face. It made him smile that its ugliness was actually less intimidating than the grotesque face behind it. He thought again about the Prime, wondering briefly where the soldier might have disappeared to, but the thought vanished when he caught sight of a young woman with golden hair, dancing.

She wore the mask of a cat. It could almost be Alyssa but Alyssa would not be here so boldly. No. She would conceal herself for as long as possible in the sanctuary of Caremboche; but she would have to show herself at some point. Then he would have her.

Perhaps he might have Gynt too. Now that was a satisfying thought. The great Torkyn Gynt at his mercy. He would soon wipe that arrogant smirk from the physic's face. How convenient that the person he wanted most and the person he hated most were both in the same place at the same time. He congratulated himself once again on his perfect timing.

While Goth was shivering with anticipation, Alyssa shivered with gloom. It was as though she could feel Goth thinking about her. She touched the disc on her forehead and drew strength from its pledged security.

She looked again at the fox mask lying on her cot. She was ready, dressed in the traditional crimson robes worn by the Academie women every decade at Czabba. It occurred to her now that perhaps the deep red symbolised the blood shed on that terrible day centuries ago when many dozens of the Masters of Goldstone were felled by the angry god Orlac. A few days ago such a thought would have been fanciful; now she could easily believe that the story behind these robes was embedded in the tale of Nanak.

Alyssa's palms felt moist. Her nerves were betraying her. She smoothed her hands against the thick fabric of her robes and begged herself to remain calm. The other girls had long gone to the scenes of festivity outside. They would not be missing their chance to dance, even flirt a little with the men.

As Alyssa's thoughts turned to Xantia, the door opened and in she walked. The awkward silence between them was broken as Alyssa deliberately reached for the fox mask.

'Really, Alyssa, I thought you would come up with something more sophisticated than that. It's so common.'

'I like it. I think foxes are intelligent and handsome,' she countered.

'That's interesting because most people think they're just vermin. Far too cunning and best seen hung out on fences to discourage other foxes from pursuing what isn't theirs. Actually, it suits you perfectly,' she said sweetly. She pulled on the mask of a beautiful maiden with overly rosy cheeks and full red lips. The hair cascading around it was flaxen.

She posed for Alyssa. 'Well, aren't you going to comment on my mask?'

Alyssa would not be drawn but the likeness to herself was not lost on her. Xantia was behaving like a fool. Not wanting to risk further confrontation, she was relieved when a couple of acolytes their own age knocked on the door and asked if they were ready. Both squealed with laughter at Xantia's mask.

'The Righteous Virgin. Oh, Xantia, you're wicked! It's perfect,' said one.

Alyssa pushed past, pulling on the fox head as she went. She tried to keep her voice even and friendly. 'Come on, girls. Let's not miss the fun.'

The four girls emerged into the cold night and Alyssa instinctively scanned for any sign of Goth. Xantia immediately assumed her wide-eyed search was for Tor.

'He's over there,' she said, pointing towards a brazier in the corner of the main courtyard where Tor, obvious despite his pig mask, was talking with a group of excited young acolytes.

'I was looking for someone else,' Alyssa replied coolly.

'Good. Then you won't mind if I keep my promise to seek out your friend.'

Alyssa's patience snapped but her calm voice belied her irritation. 'Do what you will, Xantia. I'm tired of you.'

She had no idea what Xantia felt at this dismissal. The mask of the virtuous virgin remained serene. Alyssa briskly walked away in the opposite direction towards where the main gates were flung open for the first time in a decade and city folk, curious visitors and pilgrims walked freely between them. She could see fires burning and around them people twirled to a frenzied series of steps known as the Cleffyngo. Hard, furious and noisy, they banged their feet and clapped to the rhythmic sound of drums and cymbals.

It would be a while yet before her participation in this Festival became necessary so for now she kept herself as inconspicuous as possible and watched carefully for Goth or any of his men. By joining a large group of revellers she was able to stay on the fringe of it, in shadow, but still have a good view of the proceedings. She watched Tor.

Just looking at his tall, broad stature which towered above most of the people he stood with made her heart-beat quicken. She wanted to hold him; to lay with him. Alyssa smiled ruefully behind her fox mask. She had never thought she would have the urge to be touched by a man again. Older and wiser, she realised the incident with

Saxon had just been her way of reaching out for affection. She had been so young back then; inexperienced and terrified by her introduction to the ugliness of an unwanted touch. Perhaps Saxon had represented safety.

His encouragement of her relationship with Tor was curious. Saxon keenly wanted them to pursue it; his note said so. It occurred to her that he must have had it scribed in Ildagarth for her. What did Saxon know that she did not?

She turned things over in her mind. If Merkhud and Sorrel had orchestrated the reunion, then clearly they too expected something to happen between herself and Tor. And if Merkhud and Sorrel were being manipulated by some higher magic, as Saxon had been all of his life by Lys, then should Alyssa also accept Tor as her destiny?

And what about Cloot? Alyssa figured out that the falcon must have a similar role to Saxon: Cloot had been sent to protect Tor. How else could one explain his transformation unless by powerful magic?

Her thoughts were suddenly disturbed by a wolf, grinning from ear to ear, who asked her to dance. No one was permitted to refuse a dance on the night of Czabba and she allowed herself to be led to one of the braziers to join the twirling figures. Her wolf partner shouted above the noise to reveal he was a local shopkeeper at the bazaar. He sold sugars, he told her, rather impressed with himself. She smiled politely, just pleased he was not the real wolf who wore the purple sash.

There were no purple sashes to be seen, in fact, and Alyssa danced twice more, not without fear but safely. Escaping back to the gates and into the shadows, she almost screamed when someone grabbed her waist.

Spinning in alarm she saw the face of a pig.

'Well, how about once around the bonfires for me?' Tor asked.

Relief turned to laughter but the arrival of the Virtuous Maiden brought back all of the tension.

'You two seem to be hogging one another today, don't you?' Xantia's voice was laced with hatred, or so it sounded to Alyssa who knew her well. She wondered again at how their friendship had come to this and in such a short time.

'Hello, Xantia. Having a good time?' Tor was all politeness.

'You promised me a dance, Mr Pig.' She emphasised her last word so it sounded as an insult.

'You two go ahead. I'm exhausted anyway and in search of cool water,' Alyssa offered.

She was surprised that Tor made no protest.

'Well, if you'll excuse us, Alyssa, this young maiden cannot be refused,' he said, turning on his charm.

Alyssa watched Xantia's eyes widen behind the mask; it was as though she could hardly believe what she was hearing. Suddenly she was girlish and coy. Alyssa turned away so as not to say anything she may regret.

'Why, Tor,' Xantia cooed, 'I'd be delighted.'

'The pleasure is truly mine. Meet me by that bonfire,' he said sweetly and pointed towards the largest fire outside the gates. 'I must fetch my trusted guide a cup of water and I'll be with you in a moment. Be quick, don't miss our position. I love to be at the front of the Cleffyngo, don't you?'

Xantia's mask gave away nothing but her eyes narrowed behind it. 'I do. You will come straightaway then?'

'I promise. Chivalry calls, though. My King would be

disappointed if I showed anything less towards Alyssa.'

There was nothing Xantia could do but head towards the gates. The second she turned her tall, slim shoulders in their direction Tor gripped Alyssa's elbow and forced her to sit on an old tree stump, conveniently in the shadows.

'Wait here,' he said urgently and ran off towards the long tables where pitchers of water were regularly replenished from the Academie's well.

He returned swiftly and handed Alyssa a cup. Before she realised what he was doing, he had pulled off her mask and touched her forehead. Immediately a familiar, almost unbearable rush of colours, sounds and smells came to her. He had removed the archalyt disc and dropped her mask back down before she could say anything. No one had noticed, he had been so deft and had deliberately blocked anyone's view with his broad body.

Alyssa felt the welcome, gentle slice of Tor's link.

Now, isn't that better? he said walking away without looking back at her. *No one will suspect anything as your mask covers the truth. Behave normally and keep the link open. I need to be able to speak to you from now on.*

Hurry up and get that dance done, she replied. *And remember who you're promised to.*

Her lightness of heart was short-lived; she caught her first sight of purple silk. It was not Goth but it meant he was not far away.

I see it, Tor said, hoping to calm her. *Goth is not here. You must remain steady, my love. You will draw more attention if you do not act normally.*

Alyssa watched as he took Xantia in his arms and said something to her which obviously made her laugh for the maiden's head flipped back coquettishly. Then the thunderous beat of the Cleffyngo began. Alyssa rejoiced that it was too loud for conversation between dancers and within a moment Tor's voice was back in her mind.

Whilst I keep Xantia happy, make any excuse you have to go to the crypt. Go fast. Beneath the stone where you found the books is a new mask. I have moved the stone. No one knows about it. Do it now.

She wasted not a moment but Elder Iris caught her hurrying into the Academie. Alyssa's expression turned to one of terror beneath the safety of her fox guise.

'Is that you, Alyssa my dear? It is. What are you hurrying for, child? Our ceremony begins in a few minutes.'

Alyssa thought fast and steadied her voice. 'I know, Elder Iris. That's why I'm hurrying. This fox mask has something sharp inside which is hurting me. I thought I might see if I could adjust it a little but I know we mustn't take them off during the Festival so I thought I'd better do it in my room.'

The woman nodded. 'Be quick then.' The Chief Elder could not think anything bad about Alyssa and it would never occur to her to question the acolyte's integrity. She moved on and Alyssa ran for her life.

In the crypt she was amazed to find the mask of a ghoul with a wig cunningly attached. She was impressed that Tor had not selected raven hair which would be the obvious disguise for her bright, fair hair. Instead the wig was crafted from the dullest of light browns; completely unspectacular and cropped without any regard for vanity. His note told her to tie up her own hair and fasten it tightly to the back of her head with the clips he had supplied. She found a new crimson robe which he told her to ensure she wore. It swamped her petite frame but this was deliberate on Tor's part and he insisted she tie the garter very loosely. To complete the hideous ensemble he had provided boots with an amazingly tall heel. She had never seen boots like this before and when she pulled them on, apart from finding them uncomfortably tight, she was sure she would be unable to take more than two steps in them.

Are you ready? he boomed into her head. *I'm feeling dizzy from twirling Xantia around this wretched fire!*

What are you thinking about, Tor, with all of this?

Your beautiful head still attached to your slim neck and resting against my shoulder, at which time I shall kiss it and be glad that you are safe.

I can't walk in these things.

You will walk in them and you must promise me to do it confidently. Remember, Goth is looking for a small, slim, golden-haired woman. You will be a saggy, overly tall ghoul with dun-coloured hair, which is real, by the way. I paid a fortune for it!

His humour helped but only a little. Her palms, no longer just moist, felt permanently damp. She stuffed all the unwanted things back into the hole and managed to cover them with the stone. Where she found the strength she would never know but put it down to extreme anxiety. As she teetered off towards the crypt stairs, she wondered how in Light's name she was going to carry off this bizarre disguise.

Tor had just finished telling Xantia what an extraordinarily fine dancer of the Cleffyngo she was when Cloot sliced open a link.

Goth is about to arrive.

Tor could tell Cloot was nervous. His plan was simple but audacious and even his loyal falcon was questioning his sanity.

He went through the checklist in his mind. *Is Saxon ready?*

As ready as he's ever going to be. Sorrel is with him. So is a donkey.

Tor was making polite sounds about fetching Xantia a cup of wine. He stopped when he heard the last part of Cloot's message.

A donkey?

Yes, you know – long ears, strange beast, not quite a horse, makes an odd braying sound.

Tor bristled. This was not a good time for Cloot's sarcasm.

'Xantia, allow me to fetch you a glass.' Without waiting for her reply, he stalked off. *I know what a donkey is*, he snarled across the link. *What is he doing with a donkey? It will slow us up.*

Search me. I'm not sure you've noticed this, Tor, but Saxon's a strange fellow. Perhaps the donkey's important to him and at this stage of your precarious, dangerously underplanned plan, I think it's the very least of our worries, don't you? Cloot snapped closed the link.

Tor saw the falcon lift from the cover of the trees and circle high above them. From the corner of his eye he also saw the ghoul appear but he refused to look at Alyssa squarely.

You look lovely, he whispered across the link. *The Spinsters of Minstead would be proud of you.*

She did not give him the satisfaction of a verbal response

but he felt a spike in his ribs such as he had not felt in years. It was classic Alyssa trickery and he had to cover up his 'oof!' by pretending to drink some of Xantia's wine and then coughing theatrically.

Getting slow in your old age, Tor? You should've felt that coming.

He agreed. He winced and walked to where Xantia patiently waited and handed her the wine.

'Won't you share a cup with me, Tor?'

'Of course. But I just have to speak with Elder Iris who is looking for me. If you'll excuse me briefly, Xantia, I'll be right back.'

She nodded and he made his escape with barely a moment to spare before Goth and his main party of riders arrived at the gates.

Tallinese horses from the King's stable were well disciplined and rarely needed to be tethered. The Inquisitors let the reins fall as they dismounted, knowing their horses would content themselves with nibbling at the grasses at the roadside and remain where they left them.

A distinct hush spread itself amongst the happy mob at Goth's arrival. Many had witnessed his despatch of the young gypsy girl earlier that day and almost all the townsfolk had heard about the despicable deed.

Goth smiled behind his demon mask. He did so love to ruin the fun. As the music struck up again and people forced themselves to return to their dancing, drinking and conversations, Elder Iris met Goth at the gates. She wore a stern mask of a bull. Her mood at seeing him matched the bull's expression.

'Inquisitor Goth. I can't stop you joining us, though I wish I could.' She paused.

Fucking witch, the demon thought as it bowed courteously.

The bull continued, just as sternly. 'Though I can prevent you and your men entering these gates. The last time you visited the Academie you left it strewn with bodies. I heard about the gypsy girl. It grieves my soul that I look into your cold eyes and see no remorse.'

As well you might, you old whore, he thought.

'Elder,' he said, 'my men and I come simply to enjoy the festivities. We will be gone directly after the main ceremony, I assure you.'

'Good,' Elder Iris replied. 'Then please remain outside these gates.'

'Actually, there is something you can help me with right now,' Goth said, unperturbed by her attitude.

'And that is?' she said curtly.

'I have a friend here at present. Physic Gynt is representing the Palace, as I understand it. Perhaps you might ask him to step outside. But please, Elder Iris, don't tell him I'm here . . . let me surprise him.'

A woman in crimson stepped forward. She wore the mask of the Virtuous Maiden. 'He wears the pig head, Inquisitor,' Xantia said, delighted that this man of such legendary cruelty, and strange connection to Alyssa, was here. 'I'll find him if you wish.'

Elder Iris turned on her. If Xantia could have seen her expression beneath the bull's head, she would have shrivelled. But there was no going back now. This was a chance to hurt Alyssa.

'Oh, and Inquisitor Goth,' she said sweetly, 'Alyssa is wearing a fox mask if you're looking for her too.'

'Xantia!' Elder Iris admonished loudly. 'Hold your wicked tongue, girl.'

'Alyssa . . .' Goth turned the name over his rubbery lips.

If Xantia had not been standing in front of the raging bull, she would have hugged herself. Alyssa's secret early years were shaping themselves in her head now and she was sure that before the night was ended she would have the full story. She revelled in the thought of her former friend's downfall. She would peel away the layers of lies which she was now convinced Alyssa lived beneath and reveal her closely guarded past to the Elders. She would see to it that Alyssa never became an Elder. She came out of her reverie to hear Elder Iris addressing her.

'Be gone, Xantia. Prepare yourself for the ceremony, after which you will return immediately to your rooms and await my summons.' She turned to Goth. 'Excuse us, sir.'

'Oh, by all means,' Goth said, bowing again. The moment the women left he ordered his men to go in search of pigs and foxes. He could already see there were many but his prey were distinctive; they could not conceal themselves with masks alone. He would have them both before dawn.

Whilst Elder Iris was admonishing Xantia, Tor had slipped away. He returned now for the ceremony. He could see Alyssa lurking at the back of a big crowd of people; she was well hidden for the time being. He followed suit, slinking deep into the shadows away from Xantia's prying eyes. The girl's freedom was limited, however. Elder Iris had given firm instructions that she remain at the side of another Elder, who had no intention of allowing the acolyte to disobey orders. Tor could almost smell Xantia's frustration and allowed himself a brief smile of satisfaction. They had won a small battle there but the war was still to be fought.

Now the Elders and the key masked figures were preparing for the formal part of the festivity. Many hundreds of people had gathered, spilling into and out of the famous Caremboche gates. So many people milling around would aid Tor and Alyssa's chances of disappearing amongst them.

So far Goth's men had been kept at bay; they mingled amongst the crowd, pulling at the masks of the countless pigs and foxes they encountered. Tor had chosen well. They were easily the most common headwear.

Goth did not participate in this humiliating exercise. He left that lowly task to his men. Behind his demon mask, his sharp eyes never stopped moving, briefly resting from time to time on tall, dark-haired men or young women with golden hair. He would know his prey immediately. He had already guessed that Alyssa may hide her hair so he also carefully checked every dark-haired woman who passed across his line of sight. And Alyssa could not disguise her slight build. He knew it all too well, having touched it so intimately. After seeing her only today he knew she had not put on much height, just become slightly curvier perhaps.

The acolytes were being summoned to form the lines which represented some event from legend centuries earlier when the sentient Masters of Goldstone had been murdered. Goth cared nothing for legend and even less for any empowered people, myth or not. He thought about

Alyssa instead. He would have only moments to talk to her. He briefly wondered if he could snatch her away, but the Untouchable status she now possessed cowed even his devil-may-care attitude.

He would make do with forcing her to engage in the Death Dance with him. It meant he could hold her against him. She could not refuse, of course; even the old witch could not refuse it for this was high tradition. He wished he was still whole and could push that part of his body against her which would frighten her. He desperately wanted to see the fear in her eyes again.

Goth shook himself free of these thoughts. He had almost forgotten the physic. He must find him and deal with him. He gave orders to Rhus to step up the search. He needed Gynt found and taken.

A cart edged its way to the fringe of the mob, stopping as close to the Academie gates as possible. It was small, drawn by two nags. Beside it was tethered a donkey. The driver was a tall, broad man with longish dark hair and the mask of a pig. Despite the poor light and deep shadows, he looked familiar to Rhus who began fighting his way back through the crowd towards Goth. He knew this would make his chief very happy.

The solemn chimes of a bell sounded as the ten characters of the Czabba legend began to make their slow way, chanting words none of them understood. Behind them walked the figure of the handsome young man in his prime; the one responsible for all the devastation.

Women's voices were raised in beautiful harmony as all the members of the Academie erupted into song. Xantia felt Elder Li pinch her, forcing her to sing the song they had practised for months; nevertheless, she studied all the girls around her, searching for Alyssa. It infuriated her that she could not see her. Not a fox head in sight; not even her giveaway small frame and light hair.

Custom dictated that the acolytes must be registered on the night of Czabba by answering to their name when called. The Elders took this part of the ceremony very seriously and the group was counted and checked to ensure all were present. Both Goth and Xantia clearly heard Alyssa answer to her name. Goth smiled but Xantia, knowing it was Alyssa's voice but not being able to see where she spoke from, became more frustrated.

She found her chance when the acolytes were required to walk out of the main gates through the crowd which parted for them. There they would meet with the eleven characters, their songs intermingling to a crescendo of voices. The finale would be the Dance of Death, which began slowly but gradually increased in intensity. Everyone would join in. Xantia was sure Goth would take the opportunity to reunite himself with Alyssa.

In the move towards the gates, Xantia was able to slip gradually further behind until she could see all her companions. Alyssa was there but not there. Where amongst this group had she hidden herself? Somebody tripped ahead and caused several of the girls to stumble. In that moment of confusion Xantia caught sight of a boot with a heel she had never seen the like of before. It was gone in a second, covered by crimson.

She stopped her singing and wildly searched the figures. She locked onto a person wearing very loosely fitting robes. The lifeless hair was unfamiliar and the figure wore the head of a ghoul, a mask she had not seen on any of the acolytes earlier in the evening.

'Alyssa,' she whispered and then she yelled as loudly as her voice would allow, 'Alyssa!'

The ghoul turned then broke from the group of women. Pandemonium ensued.

At the same moment Xantia spotted Alyssa's boot, Rhus finally reached his chief.

'I have Gynt, sir. Over there.'

Goth looked over and saw the physic standing on a cart just ahead of him. The pig mask swivelled, as if on cue, and then Gynt whipped the startled horses who wasted no time in galloping off. As Goth watched with disbelief, he heard someone yell 'Alyssa!' Emerging from behind some bales of hay at the back of a cart, he saw a figure throwing off a blanket to reveal the head of a fox and golden hair cascading behind.

'After them!' he shrieked.

Despair that he had allowed her to slip away like this, and that bastard physic with her, fuelled his anger to breaking point. He was the first man mounted on his horse and whipped its flanks mercilessly as they gave chase.

Tor, hidden just inside the gates, raced out onto the road. He removed the horse's head he had changed into and watched the Inquisitors disappearing through a haze of dust. Alyssa pushed through the crowd and ran to his side awkwardly on her tall heels. Xantia was close by, screaming from behind her Virtuous Maiden's mask and Elder Iris arrived just moments later.

'Physic Gynt . . . what occurs here? Alyssa, Xantia . . . what is this behaviour?'

No one answered. Xantia began to pull at Alyssa's mask but Alyssa held onto it firmly, determined not to show her face.

Above the confusion Cloot spoke calmly to Tor. *Stop the horses and you will stop the men.*

Tor, his arm around Alyssa, gathered the Colours within him. He knew the glamour would be wearing off by now but Saxon did not have far to go before reaching the fringe of the Great Forest. He and Sorrel would be safe there. Cloot was right: all it would take was to slow down the horses.

He cast.

Saxon was laughing wildly although his eyes saw nothing. Kythay and the nags were under one of Cloot's spells and seemed to know exactly where to gallop and in which direction.

It was one of the few times since Saxon's disfigurement that Sorrel had heard his voice. She pulled off the fox mask and noted Saxon had already thrown off his pig's head. She could hardly believe it when she saw Kythay leading the gallop in pace with the horses. The donkey's eyes were as wild and wide as Saxon's.

She clung to the side of the cart, frightened of being tossed over the side, and looked behind her. She did not need to see Goth's men; she could hear them and they were closing fast. She swung back and looked ahead to see the Great Forest; one of its long fingers was reaching towards them. Tor had said they only had to make it to the woods and there they would find sanctuary. He had also warned them that Goth must not recognise Saxon. Once the trick had worked, he was to be well hidden.

Saxon was no longer holding the reins; there was no need. The horses galloped as though possessed, following Kythay who seemed to have no intention of stopping until he had reached the forest's cover.

'Get behind the bales,' Sorrel yelled at Saxon. She pushed Saxon's head down and looked behind them again. Just in time. She swore she could see the whites of Goth's eyes. In sudden defiance of his menace, she echoed Saxon and his wild laughter.

The ruse had worked; all the filth had followed. Sorrel heard Goth curse when he finally saw his prey close up. The Inquisitor realised he had been duped superbly and there was murder in his eyes.

Sorrel felt her knees weaken. There was no laughter in her wrinkled face now; only fear.

'I will make you suffer.' The effeminate voice sounded clearly above the din and she prepared herself for death. As she closed her eyes Sorrel suddenly felt the thrum of powerful magic being wielded.

The horses carrying the Inquisitors were almost close enough to leap aboard the cart but suddenly the beasts began to slow; the riders could do nothing. It made no difference whether they whipped or kicked at their mounts. As one, the horses slowed to a walk. Aghast, Goth guessed that magic was being wielded.

Sorrel just laughed louder as the cart swung into the safety of the trees of the Great Forest, which seemed to part and then close behind them, surrounding them with peace.

Saxon climbed out from behind the bales and looked around in wonder as the Heartwood's sanctuary welcomed another of its precious Paladin.

*　　*　　*

At Caremboche, the crowd milled in confusion. The ceremony had come to a halt and it did not look as though
the Chief Elder was going to re-start it. She was busy
demanding information from the trio in the road.

Tor hardly heard Elder Iris's questions. Alyssa clung
tightly to him. Xantia was hysterical, first directing a
torrent of obscenity at the pair of them before turning
her wrath on Elder Iris.

What Tor wanted to hear finally came. *They're safe in
the Forest. Saxon was not seen*, Cloot said.

Tor felt elation. *Goth?*

*Fuming on a horse which won't go faster than a limp. Good
luck with the next bit — I'll be waiting for you, my friend.*

And I'll be with you soon, Cloot.

Tor turned wearily to the others. 'Elder Iris, it's time
for us to leave.'

The older woman pulled off her mask, finally realising
the Festival would not be progressing much further
tonight. She fixed him with a baleful stare.

'Xantia, shut up, please,' she said, tired of the young
woman's abuse. 'It's probably appropriate for you to leave,
Physic Gynt. Please explain what you mean by "us".'

Tor had not let go of the Colours. What he planned
to try was loaded with risk and no certainty of success.
He pulled Alyssa closer still. She felt like a rag doll in
his arms.

'Alyssandra Qyn was forced to remain here because of
Inquisitor Goth but she does not belong here.'

Elder Iris stifled her exasperation. 'Her name is Alyssa
to us. And where *does* an Untouchable belong, physic?'

'This one belongs with me and I am taking her to a
secret and safe place.'

At his words, Xantia began a fresh stream of abuse but this time in another language – an ancient one. Tor felt Alyssa stiffen next to him and then she began to tremble.

What's happening? he spoke gently into her mind.

She's invoking a curse on us. She's speaking in the language of the books.

We go, he said, knowing Alyssa's fragile control would not hold much longer.

Someone in the crowd shouted out and Tor looked up to see Goth running towards them. Baffled by the actions of the horses he had resorted to his own legs. Tor felt a brief moment of respect for the man's powerful determination and watched, amazed, as the short man's legs brought him closer disturbingly quickly.

'Physic Gynt, release Alyssa immediately!' commanded Elder Iris, who still believed she was in charge of proceedings.

Tor shook his head. 'I'm sorry, Elder.'

He gathered the Colours, intensified their brightness and focused. The last sound he heard was cries from the crowd.

The last sound Alyssa heard was Xantia's voice invoking a terrifying spell. It was connected to the release of a dark and vengeful god. The words frightened her more than anything she had ever experienced before. Her mind fled to the story of Orlac and how Tor's chilling revelation that the god lived and would return to Tallinor for revenge.

And then she felt it. It was very distant. Something opened its eyes and smiled in answer to the ancient invocation. Alyssa's body became cold as she felt its feathery touch on her senses.

Tor should have felt it too but he was immersed in recalling the exact scent, colour combination and minute details of Darmud Coril's power. The feathery touch of one god passed his notice as he called upon the power of another god.

He demanded the power answer him and link with his own magic; he opened himself to the God of the Forest and beseeched his help. He felt an enormous surge as Darmud Coril heard and responded.

Onlookers watched in terror and awe as the entwined couple suddenly blazed in a rainbow of colours which arced from them towards the Great Forest beyond. It burned so brightly that all were blinded momentarily, and in almost the same instant all was dark again and the couple were gone.

Xantia was silenced. Elder Iris fell to her knees; she had never been in the presence of even a fraction of such power in her life. Others followed suit.

Chief Inquisitor Goth arrived, panting; a mist evaporating off his hot body in the cool night air. He refused to believe what his eyes had just witnessed. He too fell to his knees but not out of respect or even fear but cold, dark fury.

His fists began to pound the stony earth until his blood ran freely on the spot where Alyssa had stood.

23

Forbidden Lovers

Silence surrounded them. Tor opened his eyes and triumph surged through him when he saw the brooding darkness of the forest. He had done it! He had wielded the magic of a god; used Darmud Coril's power to transport them.

Welcome, Alyssa, to Sanctuary.

Alyssa turned to see a huge silver wolf standing not far from them. Her mouth opened in surprise.

Solyana, Tor said softly. *Thank you*, he added humbly.

The wolf's liquid eyes did not shift to him; they were firmly on his tentative companion. Tor took Alyssa's hand and walked her closer.

My love, meet a very special friend of ours. This is Solyana. She is an enchanted creature of the Heartwood which protects us.

Finally sure that she was safe from Goth, Alyssa crumpled slowly to the ground. She wrapped her arms around the wolf's huge neck and cried with relief. Neither Tor nor the wolf moved.

Solyana whispered comfort into her mind. A message, just for Alyssa. *We have waited so long for you, Alyssa. And we are ready now to serve the Trinity.*

Alyssa looked into the wolf's fathomless eyes, the tears still wet on her cheeks. *Who is 'we'?* she asked. Their link remained private.

We are the Paladin.

So, Saxon had not lied, Alyssa thought. She was already drawing strength and peace from this noble creature. She looked again into the wolf's face.

You have my loyalty, she cast directly back.

Tor wondered what had passed between the two of them.

Solyana knew his next question before he asked it.

Two people entered the Great Forest not long ago. She replied to both of them. *Saxon and Sorrel are well. Fret not, the Heartwood protects and heals them. Please, follow me.*

They walked either side of Solyana as she led them to a large pool. Steam lifted gently from its surface and, even by night, they could tell this was a beautiful place.

You may wish to cleanse yourselves in this warm spring, she said. *And there are fresh garments for you over there. Food has been laid out beneath the tree. I will leave you now. The Flames of the Firmament will light now and later guide you to a resting place.* Solyana padded away, then turned and added, *Take your pleasure in each other.*

They looked at each other, embarrassed by her final remark. This was the first time they had been together in privacy. Tor knew he must lead; cast away self-consciousness and all doubt. He loved Alyssa and he knew she loved him. This was their time.

'Shall we take a dip?' he said, hopping on one leg as he pulled off a boot.

Alyssa was shy. 'We're completely alone?'

'Yes.' He walked barefoot to her and leant down. Even

with her special boots on, he still had to bend slightly to kiss her softly. 'I'm sure you want to get those heels off.'

'I never want to see them again!' She sat on the spongy forest floor, relaxing as she marvelled at the warmth surrounding them. 'I thought it was winter.'

'It's never winter in the Heartwood,' Tor said. He pulled off his shirt without looking at her. He must not rush her. Alyssa's first experience with a man had been so painful and vicious.

'You are beautiful, Tor. You have the body of a god.' She stared unashamedly at his broad, strong chest. 'I remember you skinny.'

He laughed. 'Prime Cyrus spent years changing that.'

'Do you miss him?'

'Yes. I had to lose him to find you.' Tor saw hurt flit across her face. 'That came out wrong. What I meant is – he is a true friend but that could not stand in the way of my love for you. I had to find you or die trying. But I do miss his counsel, his gruff way, his strength.'

'Tor, isn't he here? Can't you ask Solyana—'

'I don't believe she'll tell me any more about him. The Heartwood seems to have claimed him. I don't think he's dead; there will be a purpose for him, I suppose. But we won't see him.' He sounded very sad.

Cloot's arrival was well timed. He landed next to Alyssa.

'Cloot!' She was delighted to see him and he allowed her to stroke his head.

My, my, I must stay away from your lady love more often.

Tor was glad to have Cloot nearby again. *Where have you been, you rogue? What news of Saxon and Sorrel?*

Oh, they're tucking into a feast and should be snoring soundly not long from now. Saxon seems deliriously happy. Can't stop smiling. Sorrel's anxious about you two.

Tor brought Alyssa up to date with this news. She loved hearing that Saxon was happy. 'Why would that be so?' she said.

Oh . . . you'll see, the falcon replied evasively to Tor's query on her behalf.

'How do we get word to them?' she asked.

Cloot began preening himself. *Oh, I'm sure Solyana will find a way to reassure them. Right now the night is yours and you must not worry about them . . . ahem . . .*

What are you up to, bird? Tor asked.

Oh . . . nothing. It's time I was going though.

You've just arrived!

Cloot flew to his shoulder. *And now I must leave. The Heartwood wishes it.*

Tor hated it when Cloot was secretive. He recalled the last time, when his friend had shapechanged to a falcon. Cloot sensed his anxiety.

Nothing to fear, my friend. This is a private place for Alyssa and yourself. I'll see you both in the morning.

Alyssa had remained quiet whilst they spoke across the link, not minding that she was excluded. She had got as far as undoing the loose belt and the crimson robe hung in huge folds around her. She looked at Tor.

'Apparently we're to be left alone,' he said, explaining Cloot's departure. 'Well, I'm ready for a warm bath. How about you?'

She nodded. 'You go first.'

Tor stepped out of his remaining clothes and slowly walked to the pool. He could feel her eyes travelling with him. As he paused at the edge of the water, hundreds of tiny flames flickered into existence. They sang for him as he waded into the water and submerged himself in its welcoming, warm depths.

Alyssa was entranced. She was standing now, captivated by the dancing flames which moved and chimed all around her. She reached out to them and at each feathery touch she heard that flame talk to her, welcome her. She reflected on how Tor's glorious physique had been outlined by their sparkling glow moments earlier and could not help but repeat her initial thought – he looked like a god.

Tor surfaced now, almost at the opposite edge of the pool. 'It's heaven in here,' he called. 'What are you waiting for?'

He ducked beneath again and she realised he was doing that so she would not feel awkward about undressing in his presence.

Alyssa pulled off her baggy robe and undergarments. Her skin prickled; not from the cool air because it was so curiously balmy here. No, it prickled from anticipation.

Suddenly Tor burst from the water, shaking his head and throwing droplets in all directions which shimmered in the glow of the flames.

Alyssa watched him drink in her nakedness and she cast away her inhibitions. He swam hungrily towards her and stood in the shallows, his arms reaching out. Alyssa stepped into his embrace and the flames dancing around them blazed from their unified gold brilliance into a riot of glorious colours.

Later, they lay entwined on a soft blanket stretched out in a mossy hollow. Alyssa's eyes were closed but she was not sleeping. Tor traced a finger across her face and down the length of her body. She smiled when it tickled her and touched her lips against his mouth once again.

'You are so beautiful to touch, Alyssa,' he said when their lips parted. 'I never want to let you go.'

'Then don't,' she said and meant it.

He stroked her breasts.

She squirmed. 'Aren't you tired?'

'Never.'

'Well, aren't you hungry at least?' she asked, turning to face him.

His eyes, glinting wickedly, gave her his answer but Alyssa was just fast enough to escape his clutch. She rolled away and said, laughing, 'I'm hungry for food.'

Alyssa went to fetch the supper laid out for them. Tor, resting on his arms, closed his eyes and smiled as he recalled each moment of their lovemaking. It had been urgent, clumsy even, the first time. As the intensity calmed, Tor experienced the uncharted layers of pleasure reserved only for true lovers. All of his lusting at Miss Vylet's was put in perspective now. He knew that he would never want another woman. At first light they would marry. He could not wait another day.

He cast to Cloot. The bird was grumpy at being disturbed but Tor was excited and oblivious to the late hour. He told the falcon of his intentions and was surprised when Cloot made no objection.

Will you ask Solyana? Tor persisted.

Yes, now leave me in peace. We have barely two hours before dawn.

'Are you going to join me?' Alyssa called.

'Will you marry me?'

Alyssa put down the juicy berries she was eating and

wiped her mouth. She walked across to where Tor stood and kissed his broad chest.

'It's forbidden. But then I think we've already broken every sacred Caremboche law written for an Untouchable.'

You wished to speak with me, Tor? Solyana's smooth voice woke him. Alyssa was still asleep.

Thank you for coming, Solyana. Did Cloot tell you about our plans?

He did, she said, leading him away from the sleeping Alyssa. *It can be done. There is a holy woman, a hermit. She is respectful of our ways.*

Tor sat beside the wolf.

Her name is Arabella.

Is she far from here?

Solyana laughed in his head. *You of all people should know nothing is far in the Heartwood. But we have transport for you this time. You may leave as soon as you are ready.*

She pointed her snout towards Alyssa. Tor looked over and saw her stretching awake. Solyana made to leave. *I'll see you tonight and we will reunite you with your friends.*

Solyana . . . may I ask about Cyrus?

There was a pause as she considered. *I can tell you that he is in fine health and excellent spirits. He thrives amongst the Heartwood.*

Will I ever see him again?

Perhaps.

Tor knew the subject was closed as he watched the wolf leave.

He heard a snort and turned. 'Kythay?'

Alyssa woke fully and was extremely happy to see her

old friend. She hugged the beast — an action he would tolerate from no other.

'And where's *my* good morning?' Tor said, pulling her into his arms.

'Right here.' She kissed him lightly. 'This is a beautiful place. I could live here for ever.'

'Perhaps we might. Are you happy, Alyssa?'

'Unbearably,' she whispered, holding her cheek close to his.

'Then today we shall make the promise we made at the Floral Dance come true. Get dressed, my love, and we shall away to a priestess.'

'What?'

'Hurry, hurry. Your donkey awaits and your betrothed is eager.'

Alyssa dressed, pleased to have something simple but pretty to wear for her wedding. She never wanted to see a crimson robe or Untouchable robe again. For a moment she regretted not having any flowers to wear in her hair. There were none she could see nearby. As she dismissed the folly of this thought, Cloot arrived, miraculously carrying a small circlet of woodland blooms. It was as though he had heard her thought.

Your guide is here, he said, dropping to the floor in front of her. *Tor, this is for Alyssa.*

As they journeyed, Alyssa told Tor of Solyana's conversation.

Tor had no idea what she was talking about. *Cloot, have you heard of the Trinity?*

The falcon paused quite noticeably before replying, *Yes.*

Well, good. Tell me, Tor said impatiently.

The Trinity will save the land from dying.

And?

There was silence.

Tor repeated Cloot's words to Alyssa in exasperation. 'He does this to me a lot,' he said.

'Saxon too,' she admitted. 'Perhaps they only know so much?'

Tor nodded. It was not Cloot's fault. *Tell me again of the Paladin then*, he said across the link.

Cloot answered immediately this time. *There are ten of them. Two are bonded to each of you and will protect you with their lives.*

You are one, so who is the other? Tor asked.

That is for you to learn, Cloot said.

Tor related this to Alyssa. She thought aloud. 'And Saxon is bonded to me. Solyana is also one of the ten – who is she bonded to? Obviously not us. And why are there ten if there are only two of us to care for? Where is my other protector? Who are we being protected from?'

Tor shrugged. He asked Cloot the same question, expecting the usual vague or evasive reply.

From Orlac, the bird said.

Tor stopped. The answer had taken him by surprise. Alyssa looked back at him.

'He said we're being protected from Orlac.'

Alyssa felt her throat close. 'What else did he say?'

'I think he may have said too much already,' Tor replied, puzzled.

Cloot was back in his head, but briefly. *Arabella awaits.*

They could smell food cooking. When they emerged they saw a tiny hut. Outside stood a tall, handsome woman; her dark hair, flecked with grey, was tied and rolled and the few lines in her angular face sat comfortably on a clear, olive complexion. Dark eyes settled on him and Tor had the sensation that she had known him for ever.

'Torkyn Gynt and Alyssandra Qyn, I have been expecting you. Welcome both.'

The woman lifted a hand towards Cloot who was sitting on the highest branch he could find. 'You are magnificent,' she called to him, completely at ease in new company.

Tor was thrown. Solyana had told him this woman was a hermit. He had expected someone more reclusive.

'You are the holy woman, Arabella?'

'There is no other,' she said. 'Come. Let us break some bread together.'

They shared a light meal. Her food was delicious and the conversation naturally turned to the marriage.

'We have no ring.' Alyssa sounded apologetic.

'We don't need one, child,' Arabella said kindly. 'A ring is symbolic, nothing more. But if it makes you feel better . . .' She slid a hand into a concealed pocket in her robes. 'Perhaps this might suffice.'

She handed Alyssa a tiny ring made from thin, plaited grass. It was exquisite.

'It will do very well,' Alyssa said, her delight obvious.

They hugged like old friends. As Alyssa loosened her grip and turned to Tor, Arabella's hand slipped to the girl's belly.

'Don't be afraid,' the holy woman reassured. Slowly and gently she touched Alyssa's belly, her face all concentration.

Silence gripped the forest. Cloot landed on Tor's shoulder, breaking the tension for just a moment.

Suddenly Arabella fell to her knees. 'It has happened. We are saved,' she shouted into the treetops. 'Alyssa is with child!'

Alyssa had one more surprise to savour that afternoon.

Kythay carried the bride on his back with the groom walking alongside, his falcon friend on his shoulder. The creatures of the Heartwood came to meet them, lining the pathway which seemed to miraculously unfurl ahead of them and close behind them. The sun was setting but the canopy of trees had brought the deepening towards evening much earlier. Already the Flames of the Firmament with their new brilliant cacophony of colours, were glowing luminously against the darkening backdrop. They chimed and danced around the newlyweds.

Tor and Alyssa could see Solyana ahead, waiting for them. As the flames flew to surround her, the couple could make out that the wolf was accompanied by two people. Alyssa's heart leapt. It had to be Saxon and Sorrel; yet could it be? The male figure looked too tall to be Saxon.

You'd better prepare yourself for a scene, Cloot said to Tor.

Tor did not have the time to find out more. He turned just in time to see Alyssa slide off Kythay, pick up her skirt and run.

It seemed impossible, but running towards Alyssa was Saxon. Gleaming golden hair hung proudly in the Kloekish way to his shoulders. He was his full height again, his arms moved freely and his legs had straightened. Tor looked with wonder at Saxon's formerly blinded eyes; now pale and whole, they were filled with glee.

'Alyssa!' Saxon called over and again until she was close enough to hurl herself into his arms. He threw her high into the air, as he used to when she was just a girl and learning the tricks of the circus trade.

Tor felt humbled. He sensed Solyana arrive silently at his side and pushed his hands deep into her fur. He was too choked with joy for Alyssa and her loyal, brave Saxon to speak.

The Heartwood heals its own, Solyana explained.

Saxon, Alyssa and Sorrel sat together. Alyssa excitedly told them of her day's revelations — a wedding, a pregnancy. Saxon related his tale of being summoned by a god, Darmud Coril, and the healing bestowed upon him.

Tor stayed with the wolf, giving Alyssa time with her friends. *Solyana, is Arabella one of the Paladin?*

She is.

He felt a jolt of excitement. He took another chance. *And Cyrus also?*

Yes, Tor. She sounded pleased that he had worked it out.

So, five more to account for. I will not press you for information, Solyana.

I thank you for this, my friend. You will understand when the time is right, I promise. She turned her large, noble head towards him. *Lys will not forsake you*, she added.

He nodded. He trusted them all. *Will all the Paladin gather in the Heartwood?*

Eventually, yes. There is time yet though before we are complete.

Tor desperately wanted to ask her what their role was before they gathered here, but Saxon and a still weepy, excited Alyssa were approaching and the moment was lost. He had never realised just how tall and broad the Kloek was. He looked magnificently strong and healthy.

'Greetings, Tor,' boomed Saxon, loving being able to speak again.

'And to you, my friend.' Tor crossed palms in the Kloek manner. Saxon appreciated the gesture.

Sorrel was with them; Tor could not read her expression but did not dwell on it. She was a secretive old girl and this was probably all news to store and pass on to Merkhud at the next opportunity. He did not mind as much as he had thought he might. For the first time in years, Tor felt in control of his life. He did not fear Merkhud's manipulations.

Saxon clapped him solidly on the back. 'Well, Tor, I thought my news would be the most astounding for today but it seems you and Alyssa have been busy yourselves.'

His smile was full of wicked humour and Tor joined in.

It was time to celebrate.

Sorrel was exhausted. It had been a long night of revelry and she could not begrudge her companions the chance to engage in some high spirits. The Light knew, they had endured such an extraordinary ordeal to arrive here safely. Regrettably she could not share their joy, though outwardly she pretended to.

Alyssa to have a child.

She shuddered at what the Academie Elders would make of this, but then that life suddenly seemed a long time ago.

She knew she must share with Merkhud this remarkable series of events. He knew only of their escape from Goth and arrival in the Great Forest; nothing more.

The others slept. The Heartwood was still. She cast,

knowing the old man would not be sleeping himself. He answered immediately.

What news, my love? I have missed you.

She felt lifted to hear him speak this way.

Stunning events have taken place since we last spoke, Merkhud. Saxon has been magically made whole again.

Tor? he asked quickly.

No. The Kloek disappeared some time through the first night. I slept through it, I'm sorry to say, but he tells me the huge silver wolf guided him to the place where magical healing occurred. I know no more.

Did you see this wolf?

I saw her briefly when we entered the forest so I know he spoke true but I have only met Solyana properly tonight.

Solyana! She heard Merkhud give a rare giggle.

What cheers you, my love?

Your news gladdens me, Sorrel, that's all.

Well, there are more dramatic tales to tell. I will not linger on the details. You should know that Tor and Alyssa have married.

But how is this possible?

What do you mean, possible? They have exchanged vows in secret. She wears a knotted grass ring to prove it.

So priests roam the Great Forest, marrying couples as and when required? he hurled back irritably.

Sorrel suppressed the instant rebuke which sprang to mind. She kept her voice steady. *No. There is a holy woman apparently. A priestess whom Solyana knew of.*

Tell me her name is Arabella, Sorrel. Confirm it! he ordered, suddenly more excited than she had ever heard him in their long life together.

It is true. I heard them speak of her as Arabella.

There was silence but she could tell the link was still open. She held the pause until she heard the old man sigh.

Thank you, my love. You bring great tidings tonight. This news will make Nanak very happy.

She did not bother asking who Nanak was. *There's still more, Merkhud. I hope you are sitting down?* She heard him grunt. *Tor's and Alyssa's tale goes that this Arabella became disturbed when Alyssa hugged her. The holy woman asked them if she could lay hands on Alyssa, which she did. According to Arabella, Alyssa is with child.*

That's it! he yelled and then louder, *That's it!*

What, Merkhud? Tell me.

The Trinity, woman! This is what we've quested for. Tor, Alyssa and a child. They form a trio. The Trinity. Why didn't this occur to me sooner? It's so obvious.

He began to gabble, running over ideas and scenarios. Sorrel was forgotten in his excitement.

She waited patiently until his ramblings petered out. *What do you wish me to do?* she asked finally.

What are they both saying?

They believe that living in the Heartwood agrees with them. Tor says they should remain in its sanctuary for now, at least until the babe is born. After that, who knows.

Well then, you just stay close. Follow along. As I said before, events are out of our control for now. Perhaps with this imminent birth our part is over, my love, and we can finally lay ourselves to rest.

It was a sad notion but her heart felt strangely glad to hear him say it. Sorrel was tired of her quest.

24

The Birthing

They had counted eight moons since the day of their marriage.

Living in the Heartwood was sublime; after so much adversity in their various lives, the forest's generosity and the peace it offered was humbling. All became so used to life there that no one, especially the parents-to-be, wished for it ever to be any different.

Tor and Alyssa lived as man and wife in a lean-to created from fallen branches. Their existence was simple and carefree. Sorrel had reverted to her old ways and they saw little of her as she wandered the forest, gathering her herbs and enjoying a nomadic, untroubled life. Saxon lived in another of the humble erections they had crafted from whatever the Heartwood yielded, but he too spent most of his days rambling and exploring.

Although time felt as though it stood still, with one day much like the next, Alyssa's increasing girth assured Tor that it was passing as swiftly as ever. Their baby grew steadily. Alyssa seemed to glow in her maternal state and all felt confident the birth would be trouble-free.

Arabella visited frequently and her friendship with Saxon and Cloot blossomed. Although all were Paladin, none recalled the other. Vague memories tugged in the darkness of their minds but all had long ago yielded to the frustration of trying to remember. It was Tor who suggested that when their powers were required, they would surface; when their memories of a past became important, they would remember. They agreed and let their restlessness be soothed by this notion.

The Great Forest was so large it was little wonder it took Saxon some time to chance upon the old cart they had triumphantly driven into Sanctuary all those moons ago. At the time of arrival he had grabbed a few necessities, including the old pot they now cooked their food in each day. Anything without immediate value to them, he had left and forgotten about.

He had been gone for an Eighthday stretch when he returned carrying a sack. Alyssa recognised it immediately. She felt her baby kick; it was as though it too felt the anxiety of its mother at being reminded of Orlac.

'Ho, Saxon!' Tor called. He was clearing an area beneath two saplings. He intended hanging a length of cloth between them in which Alyssa could gently rock her newborn. It was thirsty work and he was glad of the interruption. 'Good to see you back. I'll be there in two shakes.'

Saxon nodded towards him and approached Alyssa, swinging the sack. 'Remember this?'

'I wish you hadn't rediscovered it,' she said.

He set the sack down. 'Then don't look at it.'

Alyssa ignored it and rubbed her belly. 'Do I look bigger?'

'You look enormous. I'd say you have a whole circus troupe in there!'

They both smiled, recalling days which felt like a life-time ago.

She groaned. 'I feel so tired all the time.' She poured him a cup of water. 'Here, sit with me a while.'

'I came across Sorrel two days back.'

'Is she well?'

'Oh, grumbling as always. She said she would return soon, just in case the baby arrives a bit earlier than expected.'

'Good. I haven't said anything to Tor but I'm scared, Saxon.'

He held out the cup for a refill. 'Of what?'

'Oh, I don't really know . . . the unknown probably. This baby arriving, us living in a forest.'

'Quieten your fears. Firstly, Sorrel's an experienced midwife. Secondly, you are in the safest of all places – the Heartwood heals its own, remember.' He was glad to see a twitch of a smile appear. 'Thirdly, you have all the help you'll ever need.'

'I know.'

Tor joined them. He looked at the sack. 'What have you got there, Saxon?'

'Alyssa gave them to me for safekeeping before we left the Academie.'

Tor looked at Alyssa. She twisted her face. 'The writings of Nanak.'

'Ah.' Tor too did not want to be reminded and changed the subject. 'The hammock is ready for baby Gynt.' He pointed proudly to his handiwork.

'We may be needing it earlier than we thought.' Alyssa shifted heavily. 'I've had vague pains all day.'

Both men looked startled and this made her smile.

'Not now, just probably sooner rather than later,' she reassured.

By late afternoon, however, none of the trio were smiling any longer.

In just a few hours, Alyssa's pain had escalated dramatically. She paced to ease the discomfort. Tor and Saxon took it in turns to support her. By dusk she was still walking around but she was tiring. The men now took it in shifts; one resting for a period whilst the other worked hard to hold Alyssa upright.

At nightfall they were all relieved to see Sorrel walk into the clearing. Alyssa had linked to her when the pains were still relatively gentle so the old girl was already making tracks when Solyana, alerted by Tor, had found her. She rode to them on Kythay's back, curiously swiftly.

Sorrel told the men to make themselves scarce and promised she would call them back shortly. Her midwifery skills would be much in need tonight, she thought to herself, as she discovered the baby was lying in an awkward position. This would be a difficult birth for the first-time mother. She gave Alyssa a draught of something she pulled from her famous old bag. It seemed to quieten Alyssa for the time being and she drifted into a restless doze.

Sorrel immediately gave the two anxious men, who were lurking on the fringe of the clearing, jobs to do. They were eager to be occupied. Tor began tearing up linen for rags; Saxon set a fire and began to warm a pot of water.

Solyana roamed nearby like a shadow and kept the curious creatures of the forest well away, whilst Cloot kept watch like a sentry on high.

Way up in the tallest trees, his intensely sharp eyes

could still see his friends clearly. He did not want to be too close to Tor, for all day he had experienced a sense of dread and did not want the feeling to become infectious. Tor might lock on to it if Cloot was nearby. His fear was not about Alyssa and her child; this was a new terror to deal with. No, he was fearful about Goth, who had never given up the search, returning again and again to the area where Saxon and Sorrel had entered the Great Forest.

Cloot figured that Goth believed that if he could just find a trace of the cart or its occupants, then he as good as had Alyssa cornered once more. Cloot had watched the Inquisitor's progress very closely over the months since tor and Alyssa had married. Four separate forays had yielded nothing for an infuriated Goth. And now he was back; this time with men from the King's Guard in tow. Lorys was obviously being supportive of this venture, Cloot thought. And was it his imagination or was the Great Forest allowing Goth further in than on previous occasions?

Up to now, Cloot had enjoyed watching the vile man being given the run-around by the forest. Paths suddenly showed themselves beneath undergrowth but led nowhere; others looked promising but led back to the same spot where they had originated. Still others took their travellers to waterfalls, or dense growth through which no one could pass. One inspired path even took the Inquisitors to a bare rock face. Oh yes, Cloot had watched and derived much humour from the clever way the trees outwitted Goth at every turn. But this time it was different. Goth had actually made it to the furthest reaches of the Heartwood itself. That's what was troubling Cloot tonight.

Arabella was not long in arriving. Sorrel was glad of the help of another woman. Together they walked Alyssa around when the pain got too bad.

It was the middle of the night and she had been labouring now for ten hours and there was no sign of the situation changing. Sorrel explained to the others that, of the three stages of a woman's labour, Alyssa was in the early half of her second stage but was not progressing. The birth process was at a standstill when it should be gathering steam.

'We're in for a long night,' Sorrel warned, not allowing anyone else to see the concern she was feeling. It was not going well and she feared for the baby's health. Alyssa, she could tell, was not even close to delivery which meant the baby had perhaps another ten hours to hold its own, maybe longer. Mother and baby would be struggling by then. Sorrel calmed herself, though, trusting the magic which was all around her.

Tor, having long ago exhausted every possible job he could tackle, was now standing nervously in the shadows. He regretted that Cloot had chosen the cover of leaves; he would have preferred the comforting weight of his friend on his shoulder. Both Tor and Cloot were disturbed by Alyssa's groans; even to their unexperienced ears and eyes, it seemed she was weakening.

Tor tried to offset his nervousness by talking to the falcon.

What news beyond the Heartwood?

You don't want to know, Cloot replied, instantly regretting his hasty words.

Tor's attention was momentarily shifted from the struggles of his wife. *What do you mean?*

That slipped out. You've got a lot on your mind, Tor. We can talk about it later. The falcon was anxious to find something else to talk about. *Shall we check with Sorrel?*

No, Cloot. I can see that Alyssa hasn't improved. Tell me what you're trying to avoid discussing.

Cloot was trapped. Tor heard his sigh across the link. *Goth is roaming the Great Forest. He has a special troop of the King's Guard with him.*

How long has he been here? Tor's insides felt suddenly loose. Goth did not scare him but he knew how much the Inquisitor terrified Alyssa.

Five moons, the bird said softly.

This time Tor didn't bother with the link. 'What?' he roared.

Everyone turned to look at him; even Alyssa, in her pain, glanced over. He waved away their enquiries and stepped deeper into the shadows.

What in Light's name are you talking about, Cloot?

Don't make me repeat it, Cloot replied, embarrassed.

When did you plan on telling me?

When the child is born.

If it ever gets born. Goth will probably kill it even if it does.

Enough, Tor! Goth won't find your child. The Heartwood will protect you all. It's already given him the run-around for all this time. But who could have counted on his determination to find you? He is a man possessed.

So what do we do?

Nothing for now. Just concentrate on your wife.

Alyssa shrieked and all conversation stopped. Tor rushed to her side. Saxon came running from his quiet spot in the shadows. He was suffering in silence too.

Blood was gushing from beneath Alyssa's shift. Sorrel

was pale and the face of the normally unflustered Arabella was etched with worry.

'This is a bad sign,' Sorrel growled. She no longer cared about protecting anyone from her anxieties. The blood signalled that death was not far away. There was no way she could lose Alyssa or the precious child like this.

Alyssa opened her eyes as another wave of pain subsided briefly. She gazed at Tor and mustered the barest of smiles through cracked lips. She mouthed the words 'I love you' and then a fresh torrent of pain hit her hard. More blood gushed and soaked the earth where Tor knelt.

He began to weep. This could not be happening. Alyssa was dying in front of him as she slowly lost the battle to bring their child into the world.

'There is nothing more I can do,' Sorrel said helplessly. 'Only a miracle can save the baby. Alyssa may already be too far gone.' She voiced what everyone suspected.

'No!' shouted Saxon, fighting what he knew to be true.

Tor regained his composure. His mind raced as he looked around him. Solyana had padded up and was standing next to Saxon. He looked down at his wife again; she was pale, bleeding, lifeless. This is how her own mother had died – giving birth to her. History must not be allowed to repeat itself. There was no more time to think. Only to act.

Solyana, can we summon Darmud Coril?

'I am present.' The great voice spoke aloud. 'Give her to me,' he commanded.

Tor and Saxon immediately bent to lift Alyssa but the god of the forest had not spoken to them. Tendrils of vines crept swiftly out of the undergrowth and wrapped themselves around Alyssa. Leaves and twigs meshed together beneath her and a large, majestic tree bent to tuck its branches gently under the prone figure and lifted her tenderly into the arms of Darmud Coril.

Huge and imposing, the sparkling colours of the forest twinkling around him, the forest god cradled Alyssa as though she was an infant. Instantly the Flames of the Firmament lit themselves and draped about her, chiming so softly. Vines continued to wrap themselves around those gathered there, until all were linked through the god's power.

Silent awe gripped them as they watched Darmud Coril work the miracle Sorrel required. He began to chant, his deep voice singing a medley of notes which followed no tune. The flames burned brilliantly bright around Alyssa, swaying in time with Darmud Coril's notes and the trees bent in towards her, whispering.

It was only afterwards that they would confess quietly to themselves that they not only watched but felt the god's power. Of all of them, only Sorrel was changed by it, though she did not know at the time the good and the bad of it.

The others had to shield their eyes from the glare but Tor stared through the blaze, absorbing the finest details of the powerful magic being poured into his wife and once again storing its combination and scent.

After what felt like an eternity, the flames resumed their normal intensity, the trees returned to upright and the god of the forest's eyes refocused on those around him.

He lifted Alyssa to his face and kissed her forehead tenderly before returning her to the tree, which laid her gently on the blanket where she had lain earlier.

'She bleeds no more and is in the most powerful of all

sleeps. In that sleep she will heal but she will recall nothing of this event. Deliver her child, midwife. It comes!'

It took Sorrel a moment to realise the god of the forest was addressing her. She scuttled to Alyssa's side and peeped beneath her bloodstained garments.

'He speaks true,' she cried. 'The child is being born.'

Tor fell at the god's feet. 'How do I thank you?' he mumbled, his head bent in awe.

Tor, spoke the great and gentle voice of Darmud Coril into his mind. *You are the One who will save us all. We will one day thank you. But first you have much to overcome and great pain to endure. Instead of you giving me thanks, I must ask your forgiveness for what the Heartwood must do.*

Tor looked up into the sad eyes of Darmud Coril; he saw the colours of the forest there and endless compassion. He could not imagine why the Heartwood should ever need to seek his forgiveness.

He frowned. *I don't understand.*

You will, my son, the god said even more sadly. The flames flickered to black and Darmud Coril disappeared.

'Tor!' called Arabella. 'Your child is almost here.'

Tor turned to see the holy woman and Saxon holding one another, tears coursing down their cheeks. And then the most amazing sound he had ever heard broke through the silence of the Heartwood.

It was the sound of his child crying.

'A boy,' Sorrel said, her voice thick with her own emotions. She was kneeling between Alyssa's bent legs and holding up a baby towards him.

Arabella handed Tor a length of soft cloth. He took the little boy from Sorrel's hands and he wept, unashamedly this time. 'Oh, Gidyon,' he whispered, 'your mother is going to be so proud of you.'

Exploding into the high emotion and celebration of that moment, creatures of the forest broke from the bushes and ran in all directions.

Solyana spoke. *They have been startled*, she warned and trotted quickly in the direction they had broken cover.

Saxon's face was suddenly grim and Tor realised what the Paladin had been keeping from him.

Goth was here.

'Wait here with Alyssa and Sorrel!' Saxon ordered Tor and followed Solyana. Arabella ran behind them.

Cloot! Tor yelled across the link, *what's happening?*

The nightmare has begun. You must get Alyssa and the child to safety.

Tor had no time to think. Sorrel was screaming at him. 'There is another!'

He thought he had misheard her in his panic, thought she had yelled that there was another baby. He walked closer but was shocked to a standstill when she lifted another whimpering infant in her arms. He was lost for words amongst the wonderment.

'A sister. A twin,' Sorrel offered hoarsely. She too was shocked. Alyssa was no longer conscious.

Tor's voice was as cold as his question. 'Is she dead?'

'She lives still,' Sorrel said, no longer looking at him. 'Here, take your daughter. I must attend to your wife.'

Tor tenderly took the tiny child. Her face was red and screwed up and a soft down of strawberry-coloured hair was matted to her head with birth fluids. She was the complete opposite of her brother, whose thatch of dark hair stood up in thick clumps. Where her features were fine and elegant, like her mother, the boy was dark and angular.

'Gidyon . . . we welcome your sister,' Tor said, his voice trembling as he watched Sorrel trying to rouse Alyssa. 'Her name is Lauryn.'

Cloot demanded his attention. *Tor, listen to me, you have to get the children to safety.*

How close are they?

Too close. The others are trying to draw them away. You must take the children and flee.

No! Tor shouted. *All Goth needs is to see me and he will hunt me down. I'm the best diversion we have. He doesn't care about Arabella or Saxon. He wants me; if he finds me he thinks he finds Alyssa.*

Cloot did not disagree. *What do you want to do?*

How much time do we have?

Minutes perhaps. Saxon's got them herded off in the wrong direction now.

Keep the link open. Keep me advised.

Tor wasted very little time telling Sorrel of events. It seemed she too already knew of Goth's presence.

'You must go,' she said.

'What about my family?'

'Listen to me, Tor, and listen well. I will take the children away to a safe place. But you must give me time by keeping Goth away from here. As far away from the Heartwood as possible.'

'Alyssa?' he whispered, shattered at this turn of events.

'I'll get her to somewhere safe in the forest. I can't carry all of us. Remember what Darmud Coril said – she will survive. She will heal and she will remember nothing. Tor, are you paying attention? If Goth finds these children,

he will execute them without mercy and make you and
their mother watch him do it. Then he'll crucify both of
you. He has ancient law on his side and a King who will
sanctify it. Alyssa's status has not changed in the outside
world. These children are a monstrosity to the likes of
Goth.'

'What are you telling me this for, Sorrel? Do you think
I don't know it!' he shouted at the old woman.

She spoke quietly now, not much above a whisper. 'Tell
no one of this. Only you and Cloot and I know of the
girl. We will say the boy died. As far as everyone is
concerned, there are no offspring of Tor and Alyssa Gynt.'
She looked hard into his uncomprehending eyes. 'Not even
their mother will know,' she added.

Tor looked at her aghast. A pain knifed through his
head as he tried to grasp the meaning of her words.

'Betray her?' he whispered.

'Save her!' she snarled. 'Save your wife, save your children and, with luck, save your skin too.'

Tor's head reeled. Somewhere in that horribly cold plan
of Sorrel's lay truth. Her eyes blazed.

'Go!' she screamed again. 'Save your family. Get Goth
away from us!'

Tor stepped back a few paces in shock. The link was
open; Cloot heard the conversation and was stupefied by
it. The infants began to whimper again. Sorrel could
almost read Tor's thoughts as his expression shifted from
shock to despair and finally to acceptance.

'How will I find you?'

'You will find us.' She turned; the two bundles were
beginning to cry. 'You have to leave, Tor, or we will all
die – all of it will have been for nothing. If you do as I

say, there will be no killing. I know you can wield magic; I know you can kill them all if you wish. But you don't wish. You can keep these children a secret and we can preserve you and Alyssa. Please, Tor, let me go with them to safety.'

'Wait,' he cried. He reached into his shirt and pulled out a small leather pouch. He tipped out three blazing orbs. 'Take these. One for each of my children and one for you. Wherever you go, keep them safe and near to you.'

'What are they for?' she asked, taking them. As she did so their colours died and they became dull stones again.

'I don't understand them yet but I believe they will protect you. And . . . I don't know,' he said tiredly, 'perhaps I can use them to reach you.'

Sorrel gave the loveliest of sunny smiles Tor had ever seen on her. He had not known she was capable of such warmth. It seemed almost ugly amidst such despair.

'I'll be waiting for you, Tor. I will keep your children safe.'

She reached up and kissed him. Then she hugged him fiercely. 'Now you must go, my son,' she said gently.

Tor knelt by his unconscious wife and pulled something from a tiny pocket of his clothing. As he kissed her farewell he pressed the archalyt disc onto her forehead. Should Goth find her, it would offer some small protection. He hurriedly kissed his son and daughter then stood. There was nothing more to be said. He spied the sack containing Nanak's books, which he grabbed, and, without a glance behind, disappeared into the black of the Heartwood, relying on his faithful falcon to guide him towards their enemies.

Sorrel, alone with the children and their unconscious mother, wasted no time in casting to Merkhud. This was a dire change of events and it was critical he knew of it.

There was no response.

She frowned, cast again. This time, she realised with deepening fright, it was not that there was no response; she was reaching into nothing. She cast again and once more felt her link shatter and disappear into a void.

Alarm turned to terror when the trees began to close around her and she became aware of the shimmering, almighty presence of Darmud Coril.

'You will do as I command,' he said.

They spent two days playing cat and mouse in the Great Forest. With Cloot's help, Tor allowed himself to be sighted several times and each time Goth hungrily gave chase. Their manoeuvres managed to draw the Inquisitors and the King's Men entirely away from the Heartwood.

Tor did not spy Saxon, Arabella or even Solyana during this time. It was just him and Cloot again. They spoke so little it made them even more depressed, but they kept the link permanently open and an exchange of moods and emotion rolled between them.

On the third day, hungry and cold – for the Great Forest did not provide like the Heartwood and winter existed again – Tor made a bold decision.

He took Cloot by surprise when he spoke. *I'm going back.*

Tor, no.

I am. You can come or you can stay. I care not. I have to find Alyssa. She may be dead. I may never know.

She won't be dead, Tor. Darmud Coril would not let that happen.

Tor looked up to the branch where Cloot sat and pointed angrily at him. *Oh no? He let the butchers in to come after her. Why not help them kill her?*

Stop! the falcon ordered. *This is madness talking now. All right. I'll come with you — if just to prove you wrong.*

He snapped the link shut.

Tor stood wearily and began to backtrack. Strangely, it took them a much shorter time; only a day and a half. But then everything about the Heartwood was strange and neither commented.

It was dusk when they arrived back in the clearing. What Tor saw there astounded him. There was not only no sign of Alyssa; there was no sign that anyone had ever lived there. He swung around to where the lean-to had been: a tree now stood in that spot. The areas they had cleared were densely covered with foliage and undergrowth. And in the place where Alyssa had lain and given birth grew perfect white blooms unlike any ever seen before in the Heartwood.

Tor's resolve crumpled with his tall body which he curled around the white flowers and mourned his family.

The silence was disturbed by an unhurried thrashing through the bushes. Cloot knew who it was before Tor saw Kythay amble into view. Tor was glad to see the beast again; he knew how much Alyssa had loved this old donkey. He stroked Kythay's neck. Normally the grumpy creature would not allow anyone to touch him like this except his beloved Alyssa, but perhaps he too was missing her.

Kythay took a few steps forward. Tor remained still, trying to gather his thoughts. What to do next? Find Arabella perhaps? Maybe Saxon was near?

The donkey brayed at him and moved a few steps forward again then turned to look at him.

'What's going on, old fellow?' he said kindly.

If I'm not mistaken, I think Kythay wants you to follow him, Cloot suggested tentatively.

Where could he be going?

Cloot clicked his tongue in admonishment. *Let's find out, shall we?* He flew down and settled on the donkey's back. *Come on, Kythay.*

As if the donkey could understand this, it proceeded and the trio headed out of the Heartwood again, in a new direction. This time they were making for one of the fingers of the Great Forest.

A day later they emerged from the forest to find themselves on the bank of a narrow, rushing river. On the other side of a rickety bridge stood a cottage, smoke snaking from its chimney. Tor, chilled to the bone, was heartened at the thought of warming his hands and perhaps sharing some food. He wondered what he could pay with and digging inside his pockets found a few coins he had not needed since his afternoon in Ildagarth so long ago.

He was reminded of Alyssa and pushed the thought away lest he become upset again. This was all about survival now. He must plan his next move carefully. Eating was a priority . . . and sleep.

Cloot echoed his next thought. *Why has Kythay brought us here?*

A man stepped out of the cottage to relieve himself

and was startled to see a stranger standing at the river's edge.

'Please,' Tor said, 'I'm alone. A weary traveller in need of a bowl of broth and a moment to warm myself, if I may?' He blew on his hands, suddenly realising how cold they were. He reached into his pockets and dragged out the money. 'I can pay,' he offered.

The man said nothing, just stared. A movement at the cottage door caught Tor's eye. Alyssa stepped out as if in a trance. Tor could not believe it. He ran towards her and then stopped as his relief turned into watery panic.

Right behind her, his hand nonchalantly guiding her elbow, was Chief Inquisitor Goth.

25

Capture

Alyssa looked straight through Tor. It was if she did not see him at all.

Goth's ugly voice snapped his attention away from her. 'Don't do anything foolish, Gynt. There are twenty-five men ready to loose arrows into you, your whore and your fucking donkey for that matter.'

He giggled. It was not a pleasant sound.

'What do you want, Goth?'

'Oh, sorry, don't you know? I'm forgetting my manners. Captain Herek, if you don't mind . . .'

Captain Herek of the King's Guard came out of the cottage. Tor recognised him.

I wonder if the entire army is in the cottage, Cloot remarked.

Where are you? Tor said, not taking his eyes from Alyssa who stood meekly beside Goth. He noticed the Inquisitor whisper something to the captain.

Not far.

Stay covered. You'll have to be my eyes.

He allowed the Colours to surface. They felt safe.

Captain Herek approached. He was a decent man, a

good soldier. Cyrus had always spoken well of him. He stood right in front of Tor and blocked Goth from seeing Tor's face or hearing what he said. He wasted no words.

'I'm here to see that you are brought safely to Tal. This is our sovereign's instruction. Please co-operate so that the rotting flesh behind me has no excuse to hurt you or the woman.'

Tor thought quickly. If the soldiers could keep them safe, it would be worth getting back to Tal whole and having a chance to speak with Lorys. A series of wild ideas flitted through his mind in those few seconds, from pleading clemency to escape. He finally nodded and the soldier stepped aside.

More soldiers showed themselves from hiding positions around the cottage. Tor was furious with himself for not sensing them. Captain Herek was pronouncing his capture in the name of King Lorys and the Kingdom of Tallinor but Tor was not listening. He no longer cared.

Kythay's leaving, Cloot said quietly. *Ambling off back in the direction we came from.*

And they're letting him?

No one's bothering with him.

He has the books? Tor asked anxiously.

Yes.

Tor realised Goth was walking towards him, bringing Alyssa. The soldiers, meanwhile, seemed to be readying to leave. He heard Herek say something about having the horses fetched and then he was staring into the face of evil.

'Did you two want to greet one another?' Goth said, airily. 'It's just that — and I could be wrong — it appears that Alyssa may have recently given birth. Now isn't that just a recipe for death, Gynt? Untouchable, run off with Royal Physic, pregnant. Wonderful stuff. Can't wait to hear what Lorys makes of it.'

Tor bristled. The Colours flared.

Don't, Tor, cautioned the falcon. *Herek's right. You have a chance if you go back.*

Tor's throat dried when Alyssa looked at him. Her eyes were focused but they lacked the brightness he remembered.

'Where's my baby?'

He swallowed. The lie came easily in this moment of threat. 'Our son is dead. It happened within moments of his troubled birth.'

'Oh Alyssa, my dear, that is a shame. I told you we found the dead baby but you wouldn't listen.' Goth patronised her in a sickly sweet voice. 'Such an awful thing, but looks like you're lucky to be alive.'

She had not flinched. 'I wish that I weren't,' she said, looking at Tor.

They were the last words she spoke to him before he died.

It took six days to make the long journey back to the capital. During that time only the soldiers spoke to Tor with civility. Their memories were long and all recalled how Prime Cyrus had boasted that Torkyn Gynt had saved his life. For that alone, Tor was given decent treatment whenever possible.

Alyssa rode stiffly ahead with Goth's men. Once or twice the Chief Inquisitor forced her to ride with him. It tired his horse but, Tor realised with despair, it gave Goth the opportunity to touch her and whisper his wicked words into her ear. For all that, she did not react. Tor did not once see her exchange a word with her captors. She somehow managed to achieve an air of nobility with her stony silence, despite her bloodstained garments and bedraggled look.

One thing alone kept Tor from unleashing his Colours and that was the startling reappearance of Lys in his dreams. She had wrung a promise from him that he would not, under any circumstances, display that he even possessed sentient powers. No one in this company, bar Alyssa, was aware of his ability; to this day Goth believed that Alyssa had somehow been indirectly responsible for the bizarre events on the night of the Czabba Festival.

The Inquisitor had not been able to explain it, of course, but he hated all Untouchables and it did not take much for him to convince himself that someone more powerful in magic had acted for her. That it might be Gynt never entered his mind. And, confusing though it was that his scrying stone had not helped him track down the culprit, he still believed blindly in his own invincibility.

In his dreams Tor saw himself walking in the Heartwood. He was accompanied by Lys but, as usual, could not see her.

What did he mean about the dead baby? he demanded of her.

A trick. I'm sorry to have frightened you.

He was glad to hear of the skullduggery. This might make his case easier to argue at the Palace. A thin plan was threading itself together in his mind.

Tor, do you recall Darmud Coril's warning that there was still much to overcome and pain to be endured?

He sighed in acknowledgement.

This is the beginning of a very long journey for you and you must trust me. I will not let you down. Will you follow me? Will you obey my requests?

Do I have a choice? he questioned angrily.

Of course.

And if I deny you?

Innocents will be killed. The land will perish. The Heartwood will die. And the Paladin, who have endured for centuries, will fail.

All of this because of me, he said, this time with disdain.

Lys's voice did not falter, though he wished he could provoke her. *Everything we do, is because of you, for you. You are the One.*

Is Goth the reason why Darmud Coril asked my forgiveness? He changed tack, hating where their previous conversation was headed.

You know this to be true already, she replied, patiently.

So he let Goth find us?

You could view it that way.

Why, Lys? Why would the Heartwood turn on us?

It did what it had to to protect your children. The correct decision was made. You must trust. She emphasised her words carefully now. *Certain events must occur in order for the Trinity to succeed.*

He made a sound of disgust. *When do I learn what this famed Trinity is?*

You will discover as you journey, Tor.

Lys visited him nightly; again and again they talked, treading the same ground. She was relentless. His power must not be used, no matter what eventuated. By the time he saw the outlying villages of Tal he was exhausted by her demands. He could not sleep by night or feel comforted by day.

On the outskirts of the city itself, they were met by a fresh contingent of soldiers who would escort the prisoners to the Palace. Goth made sure the captives were paraded through Tal as though they were his trophies. Tor saw shock register on the faces of all the folk they passed. He was so well known in the city that word spread like wildfire and soon there was an excited mob escorting the escorts to the Palace.

They entered the Palace gates and Goth rode triumphantly into the bailey. King Lorys and Queen Nyria were standing regaled in full finery on the Palace stairs. As at their farewell, Lorys found it difficult to look Tor straight in the eye. Nyria tried to conceal her feelings, wringing her hands under the cover of her long sleeves but Tor saw her discomfort. He would use that.

It took only a cursory glance at Alyssa for Nyria to demand the girl be taken to a room immediately. Before he was dismissed to a holding cell to await his summons from the King, Tor glanced towards the West Wing. His sharp eyesight picked out Merkhud looking from the window in the highest room. Most would not have been able to see him; Tor could clearly make out the expression of despair on his face.

Tor was surprised when the Queen swept into the small tower where he was being kept. He had been allowed to wash and change into fresh clothes. A small mercy. She demanded privacy and when they were alone, she turned on him.

'You fool!'

'My Queen, I—'

'Any woman you've ever wanted in your life has been yours. And you choose an Untouchable!' she ranted.

He bowed his head and let her rage.

'Lorys tried to forbid it but I have to hear your reason for throwing away a fine life over a slip of a girl, beautiful though she is, I'll admit.'

He opened his mouth to say something but she continued.

'And my ladies are whispering that the blood on her skirts is birth blood. Tell me this isn't true, Tor. My heart couldn't take it.'

'Where is Merkhud, your majesty?' His voice was raspy.

'Answer me, damn you, Tor!' Her eyes filled with tears but she fought them back, staring him down.

He searched her face then gestured to the hard chair. After she was seated, he told her of his beloved Alyssa. How they had been childhood friends, then young sweethearts with dreams of for ever. He told how his appointment to the Palace had taken him away suddenly and he had been unable to get word to her. He watched the Queen's expression soften when he explained how he had lost track of her and spent years and years of torment at the Palace, loving his work and the people, but grieving over his lost love; finding his comfort in the arms of many but never the one.

Nyria marvelled when he told how they had met again and under such strange circumstances; how he had learned that Alyssa had been forced to flee from the Inquisitors and had chosen first the anonymity of a circus and then the Academie's enclosed safety because of Goth. When he told of the rape, her face hardened again. Nyria hated Goth.

Tor stood and began to pace as he described how it felt to be with her again and how, even though he fully understood the consequences of loving an Untouchable, he refused to be separated from her. They had hatched no plan to be together. Their disappearance had been forced by Goth appearing again to trouble her.

'What was I to do, your majesty?'

'Ask for our help perhaps, Tor?' she replied.

'There was no time. She was so terrified. We ran for the forest and found it to be an agreeable place. We were left to ourselves, lived humbly and loved.'

She smiled at his last comment. It was sincere but it was also a trap. He began to relax but her next comment was a dagger.

'I was told of the powerful magic used to spirit you both away, Tor.' She stared intently at him. The Queen had not forgotten his miracle healing of her.

Tor paused to consider his options. He could continue the elaborate lie or he could add some truth and bring the Queen into his camp as an ally. He felt he could trust her. It was an all-or-nothing situation anyway; he took the risk.

'Your highness,' he said, dropping to one knee, 'I will not lie to you. I am sentient.' He saw her eyes light up with this confirmation.

She began to speak but Tor stopped her. He had more to say.

'Whatever the penalty is, it is mine to bear alone. I seduced Alyssa from the very start. She resisted. I'm sure Elder Iris will verify this. We had been apart for years and she had learned to respect and love her life with the Elders. Her only sin, my Queen, is to have loved me since childhood. She did not pursue me. The only reason she agreed to come with me was her fear of persecution from the Inquisitors.'

There. He had played his hand. He was counting on friendship now to save Alyssa.

Laying her hand on his bowed head, Nyria finally spoke. 'I know what it is to love a man with my whole being. Unlike Lorys, I do not fear your powers or those of people like you. How could I? I owe you my life. I have felt the touch of that magic and it was wondrous.'

She stood. 'I will protect your secret, Tor. And I will speak for your woman. Your fate, though, is in the hands of the King.'

Still kneeling, he took her slender hand and kissed it. 'I ask no more. My Queen is merciful.'

'There's a condition.'

'I will do whatever you ask if it saves Alyssa.'

'You must not use your powers against Tal. I will instruct one of my own loyal courtiers to have Alyssa killed swiftly if you move a hand against Lorys or the people of Tal. That does not include the Chief Inquisitor. Feel free to carry out whatever terrible idea comes to mind regarding Goth,' she said darkly.

'You are ruthless, your majesty,' he said, respect in his voice.

'Do not forget, Tor, that I am Queen. My King and our Kingdom is whom I serve. And never forget that I love Lorys as much as you love Alyssa. I would protect him with whatever is in my own humble powers. So, do we have an agreement? I would warn that you will not know to whom I have given my instructions. You would have to kill us all to be sure Alyssa was not harmed.'

'I give you my word,' he said.

That was sufficient for Nyria. Her voice softened. 'And your child?'

'Dead, your highness.' The lie sounded like truth now; he could believe it himself.

Nyria squeezed the healing hand which held hers. 'It is, perhaps, for the best.'

She left quietly.

The hours moved slowly. Life below him in the bailey had not altered its routine in the fourteen or so moons since his departure. He saw soldiers changing watch; pages scurrying about like busy mice; kitchen hands emerging hot from the huge ovens to drink from the castle well; and once he even saw Goth striding across the courtyard – all pomp and arrogance. The Chief Inquisitor glanced towards the tower. They saw one another. Tor's expression steeled. Goth simply sneered.

Finally, the voice he had been expecting since his arrival breezed into his mind. He knew the distinctive signature of the link: Merkhud. There was no cordial greeting or even hesitation.

I am not permitted to meet with you.

We have this at least.

There was a pause. Tor filled it, deciding he would lead this conversation.

Sorrel was left behind in the forest. I have no knowledge of how she fared when the Inquisitors arrived.

He delivered the update in a flat voice but he knew it hurt Merkhud. He intended it to. Tor expected a slippery reply, certainly one with undertones of denial to his accusation that Merkhud and Sorrel knew of each other.

I don't understand. I have not been able to speak with her now for an Eighthday, the old man replied sadly.

Tor counted back in his mind. That would be the day he had left her.

What did Nyria say?

Ah, so Merkhud was tracking events, even if he was not interfering as he normally did, Tor thought.

That she would intercede with the King on behalf of Alyssa. You knew, of course, before I left that she was at Caremboche. It was not a question.

Yes. I hoped you would be together again. Merkhud's voice tone gave nothing away.

I know of Orlac, Merkhud. I am on friendly terms with five of the Paladin. Tell me of the Trinity, Tor said harshly.

The alarm in the old man's silence was palpable. *Who told you?*

Never mind who. Time is our enemy. Tell me.

Merkhud was not ready for this but his plans were falling around him. Sorrel was no longer in contact, had disappeared. Tor was a prisoner. Only Themesius and Figgis remained of the Paladin to keep the god imprisoned. Orlac would soon be free and they were no closer to solving the riddle of the Trinity. He had to tell Tor what he knew.

He began to tell his story which had started centuries earlier. Tor sat in silence, his head cupped in his hands, as Merkhud's voice spoke of a baby being sold to a young man, sentient and grieving over the loss of his newborn son.

26

A Reckoning

Six of the King's Guard escorted Tor. Captain Herek was at his side. 'Don't look at Goth – he will do all in his power to dissemble,' the soldier whispered through gritted teeth. Goth had no friends in the King's Guard.

When the doors to the throne room were opened, Tor, who had walked through this vast hall many times during his life at the Palace, felt suddenly fearful. He had managed to find the courage required to face his sovereign and explain himself. He had strode tall, even showing some bravado with the soldiers, knowing he would speak eloquently and argue his case well. Now, though, as he recognised many familiar faces in the crowded hall, all looking so bleak, he began to feel the first stirrings of fear for his own life. Surely this was not what Lys intended for him? Clinging to that thought, assuring himself that she had a far grander plan for him, Tor cast his eyes over the faces he recognised; most of whom wouldn't meet his glance. But he searched only for Alyssa.

She was sitting straight-backed and composed near a window where the sun lit one side of her very still, very blank, very beautiful face. His heart leapt to see her and his body ached to hold her once again and tell her he loved her; tell her he was sorry. He cast – it was instinctive. Nothing. The archalyt was back in its place and blocking him. She looked at him, though, and he knew she felt something. A nudge perhaps.

Her eyes lost their dreamy look and registered his presence. He could not fool himself that it was a look of love. It was more a look of shared despair. She too felt the lack of hope in this room.

Herek's touch at his elbow recalled his attention. He was asked to stand in front of the throne. Their majesties were not yet present but a gathering hush was beginning to stifle the mutterings of those around him. He saw a slash of purple: Goth. Next to him his henchman, Rhus, just as evil. And there was Merkhud, seated in the shadows, not looking at him though the link opened swiftly.

Are you feeling brave?

I was, Tor answered. *But not since seeing her.*

The old man frowned. *As soon as these theatrics are over, we must talk. No matter what the outcome, don't say anything we have not discussed.*

Are you spinning your threads again, Merkhud? Tor was surprised at the facetiousness of his remark. He was feeling restless, wanted these proceedings to be done.

I had a strange dream last night, Tor, Merkhud said, ignoring the comment. *A woman came to me.*

Her name is Lys.

Is it? The old man shrugged. *I wouldn't know. She whispered in my thoughts. Do you know what Spiriting is, Tor?*

No.

That is why we must talk.

They could say no more for the heralds sounded and everyone stood. The royals entered from the door behind the dais to take their thrones. Nyria's eyes flicked to Tor; they implored him to be strong.

Lorys lowered himself stiffly into the great throne of his forebears. The gathered nobles and high-ranking courtiers returned to their seats. When the medley of coughs, shuffles, throat-clearing and the sounds of people settling themselves fell silent, the King turned and nodded to Goth.

This stage was Goth's dream come true. Normally his audience were peasants; at best merchants, vintners, storekeepers, the odd innkeeper or wealthy brothel-owner. This was different; here was the attention he craved. He must thank Gynt later for giving him this reward.

He had rehearsed well yet he looked to the fancy gilded ceiling of the throne hall and held a long pause as he pretended to search for the right words. Then, as though filled with regret at the tasteless task ahead of him, he proceeded to ensure that his listeners were made absolutely clear about the enormity of the criminal's actions.

'My liege,' he said, bowing to Lorys. 'Your majesty.' He bowed courteously to Nyria but the inflection in his voice as he spoke to her was anything but courteous. 'We are gathered here today for the regrettable duty of bringing to justice one of our own. It is a torrid tale of broken trust, the misuse of power bestowed by the Palace in good faith and the lust of a young man out of control.'

He allowed his opening to seep into the minds of his audience by pausing to sip from a glass of water.

He continued. 'Torkyn Gynt was accepted into our royal community more than six year-cycles ago as apprentice to the revered Royal Physic Merkhud.' He nodded to the old man who ignored him.

'That the lad was talented is not in question, my lord. Torkyn Gynt was, and still is, a most skilled healer and a fast learner. Our beloved Queen herself benefitted firsthand from his ministrations not so long ago in circumstances when most physics would have been calling for my services as priest.' He smiled, though only one side of his face moved into the grotesque expression.

'Gynt has enjoyed privilege, rank and your majesties' benevolence over the years.' Goth saw Lorys nod and liked it. 'When our Queen was ailing and Physic Merkhud was himself too frail to travel, he suggested Under Physic Gynt go in his stead to represent the Royal family at the ten-year Czabba Festival. Gynt was warned of his responsibilities, my liege, and strenuously cautioned by his superior against getting involved with any of the members of the Academie.'

Goth sipped his water again, eyeing Tor.

'Your majesties, I would suggest that Physic Gynt has consciously, actively and without regard for the sanctity of these women ignored a sacred and ancient law. He must pay the penalty.'

He puffed himself up and turned to his King. The hall was silent, save for the sound of a falcon's wings flapping outside one of the windows.

After a deliberate length of time, Lorys spoke. 'And what of the woman known as Alyssandra Qyn, Lord Goth? What penalty must she pay for her part in this?'

'She must be bridled, my liege, like any sentient

woman. I fear she no longer fulfils the status of Untouchable after laying with a man.'

Goth could not wait to see Alyssa on her knees before him wearing the dull bridle studded with archalyt.

'And if laying with him was against her will, Chief Inquisitor?'

'She spent more than ten moons in the forest, King Lorys. I would suggest this is not the action of someone desperately trying to escape.' Goth sniggered and looked around for others to join him. Only Rhus obliged.

Merkhud stood. All eyes turned to him.

'Your majesties.' He bowed as protocol demanded. 'May I approach?'

'By all means, Physic Merkhud. I would wish to hear your thoughts on this matter,' Lorys replied, clearly relieved.

Merkhud nodded and took the floor. Goth reluctantly gave way.

Trust me on this, Tor. Hold your powers. I know what I do, the physic cast before addressing the gathered.

Trust him, Cloot whispered. *Lys is using him,* he added cryptically.

Merkhud pulled thoughtfully at his whiskers and then began.

'It is true that I cautioned the Under Physic about how he must conduct himself while at Caremboche. And he understood this. Confirmed it twice in my hearing.'

Nyria looked rattled. She had expected support from Merkhud for Tor, not attack.

'I would propose that the girl was seduced by an articulate and clever manipulator of women. His success with the fair sex is legendary, and little wonder. I'm sure there is no man in this room who would refute his charm and looks, and no woman present who would not agree that if they were ten years younger . . .' He allowed his voice to trail off and shrugged, and heard the few chortles in the audience he wanted.

Goth's expression darkened. This was not how he had planned proceedings.

'Alyssandra Qyn is young and vulnerable, unused to the wiles of a charming man who was also an honoured guest, a royal visitor and someone whom her Elders expected her to entertain with generosity and grace. I would suggest that if the Under Physic here is asked, he would admit that he seduced the girl; that she is the victim, not a perpetrator.'

Nyria just stopped herself from clapping. The old rogue was crafting his plan beautifully. He had had her worried initially but she felt her spirits lift now as she saw her husband nod.

The King signalled to Herek and Alyssa was brought before him.

It was the first time Lorys had seen her properly; at their first brief glimpse of one another she had been dirty, dishevelled and in a trance-like state. Now she stood proudly in front of him. Her hair gleamed and she wore a simple but fine robe of the palest green which some good soul at the Palace must have lent her. She did it justice. She was an extraordinary beauty and Lorys found his throat dry just looking at those eyes which blazed back at him with defiance.

Tor saw it in his face and Nyria recognised it too. For one of those rare times in his life, King Lorys had been surprised by a woman. All reason was floating away as he was confronted by someone he instantly desired.

Herek cleared his throat quietly and the King realised he had been staring at the girl.

'What do you say in all of this, madam?' he asked gently and cleared his throat from embarrassment.

Alyssa did not hesitate. 'I have nothing to say to a man of such power who would stomp on helpless people – his own loyal subjects, I might add – and encourage their torture and sanction their death simply because they are empowered. Do what you will with us. It seems your Chief Inquisitor wields the sword around here, my liege, rather than you.'

Gasps came from around the hall. This was treacherous talk. Lorys found himself momentarily without words. He was stunned by her accusation but the greater impact came from her courage. He was past being impressed by her glorious looks now – he recognised they were enough to make a man do dangerous things – but he was captivated by her strength. He could not allow this woman to be bridled and secured in some faraway place.

He held his hand up and peace returned instantly.

'You make dangerous accusations.'

'I have nothing to lose, your majesty. If you think I fear for my life, do not. I would welcome death after losing a man I love and my child. And if you think I fear for my freedom, your toad over there in purple took that away a long time ago.'

It was a couched remark. No one but the few who knew about the rape understood it.

'Speak plainly, young woman,' the King requested.

'I have nothing more to say.' Alyssa bowed to the Royals and daringly returned to her place by the window.

This prompted a fresh wave of gasps and mutterings; most of it out of awe that someone would challenge Lorys.

Lorys scratched his beard. This was certainly a difficult situation. If the girl would not bring into the open that which her barbs hinted at, how could he save her from punishment?

While the King pondered, Cloot linked with Tor. *They've got Saxon!*

Imprisoned? Tor had desperately hoped Saxon would escape capture.

No. Herek left some men behind to find him. I think it will work in Alyssa's favour. The captain aims to pull a bluff which might bury Goth's chances of having Alyssa at his mercy.

Goth sensed the King's indecision and moved to restore balance which had weighted itself well against him in recent minutes but he was cut off by Tor who suddenly stood up.

'King Lorys, I have something to say which might make it easier to decide Alyssa's part in this and explain why she was under the protection of the Academie in the first place.'

'Go ahead,' the King offered. He seated himself and shook his head at Goth, whose expression now was thunderous.

'I am totally to blame for where she finds herself, my liege. I admit unequivocally that I seduced Alyssandra Qyn, despite all warnings. That she loves me and I her is irrelevant.'

Someone could have dropped a needle in the throne room at that moment and everyone would have heard it.

'She told me a secret that she will hate me revealing now to these fine people. But, as you have all discovered,

I am not honourable and so I can tell it to you without hesitation.

'Before Alyssa became a member of the Academie, when she was just a young country girl who happened to be mildly sentient, Chief Inquisitor Goth, in the mood to rut, met her in the town of Fragglesham.'

Goth was determined to let this go no further. He interrupted but the King clearly wanted to hear Tor's story and forbade further outbursts. Lorys indicated that Tor should continue.

'At Fragglesham Goth had Alyssa captured. She was taken to a house on the outskirts of the town where he stripped her, tortured her and raped her.'

Chaos erupted in the throne room as people leapt to their feet. Soldiers instantly surrounded the King and Queen, lest violence break out.

'This is preposterous,' Goth spluttered. 'The man is a villain. How can you take his word against mine, my liege? The girl won't speak. There are no witnesses. This is merely a criminal trying to ingratiate himself so that his own punishment may be lenient.'

Tor spoke quietly and looked directly at King Lorys. 'What if there were a witness, my King? An independent witness who would corroborate not my story but that of a terrified young woman?'

'Bring him on!' Goth gestured theatrically. He knew there was no one alive who could bear witness against him. Rhus was loyal and the man called Drell who had captured Alyssa all those years ago was nothing but bones by now. Rhus had seen to his despatch, as he had the people Goth had paid to guide Alyssa in the wrong direction from the burning circus tent.

Tor glanced at Herek. The captain gave him a look reminiscent of Prime Cyrus: a wry smile, a lifted eyebrow. How did Tor know of the Kloek? It had been a master stroke to find him and had taken little persuading to bring him to Tal where the girl was. Herek had no idea what the connection was; he just knew the man was howling for Goth's blood. Bring him on, indeed. Herek nodded.

Tor called out above the noise. 'Your majesties, there is a witness.'

The confusion of voices lowered and people sat down again, enthralled as this tale unravelled. The King gestured that whoever this witness might be, he or she should be presented. Herek signalled to his soldiers near the door.

It opened and a massive, golden-haired man of Kloekish heritage strode in. Alyssa leapt to her feet but Tor's eyes begged her not to show her emotion. It may damage their argument. She caught the look and checked herself.

'Who is this?' Lorys was looking at Goth who was staring open-mouthed at the Kloek. The Chief Inquisitor's twitch had become more pronounced and his unhealthy complexion was pastier still as he blurted out his disbelief.

'But you're crippled. I poked your eyes out. I fed your tongue to the dogs. I had you killed. You are dead!' he shrieked.

Rhus felt the first pins and needles of fear. Merkhud, Tor and Herek suppressed their inclination to smile. This was better than expected – Goth was burying himself with his own words.

Saxon ignored the Inquisitor. He bowed low to the King and then courteously to the Queen.

Nyria's memory stirred and, against protocol, she spoke. 'But wait, you are Saxon Fox of Cirq Zorros.'

Saxon beamed. 'I am, your majesty.' He looked at Lorys. 'Here I stand, my liege, ready to bear witness.'

'Speak!' commanded the King.

'Goth had Alyssa Qyn removed to a place of his choosing where he beat her and raped her mercilessly. I know this because I found them on the night of the circus fire. When I discovered him in the act of raping this young woman, I dealt with him.'

'Shut your filthy mouth, Kloek scum!' Goth screamed.

The King ignored his Chief Inquisitor. 'How did you come to be on the outskirts of town?' he asked the Kloek.

'The fire drove many of us in different directions. I had just "flown" with this lovely woman – then no more than a girl. You would recall that part of our show where we take someone from the audience? We selected her. As we fled the fire afterwards, I noticed her struggling as she was picked up by a man on a horse. I felt I should follow and offer help. But I was on foot and so it took a while.' Saxon stopped abruptly.

'How did you deal with him?' the King asked.

'Pardon me, my liege, for my simple language in noble company. I battered him senseless and used this very blade to ensure he would never rape again.' Saxon shrugged. 'Perhaps you should ask the Chief Inquisitor to prove me false on that matter.'

The King stood. He was angry now and felt he was being made to look a fool. Goth had betrayed his trust. He swung around and pointed at Alyssa.

'Admit this and you will go free.'

She too stood. 'And what of Torkyn Gynt, your majesty?'

'Answer me!' he roared, hating to admit to himself that he wanted this woman. He loved her fire and her complete disdain for authority.

Saxon, Tor, even the Queen turned to Alyssa. They held their breath. Their eyes collectively implored her to save herself.

She felt the weight of their pressure. Thought of her child, rotting somewhere in the forest. Remembered the writings of Nanak and how the mention of Orlac had made the child stir within her. She was required for something and it was not to die or be bridled as a common sentient. She focused on Tor and saw his love pouring out to her. She felt her hatred for Goth and the King who had supported him for so long harden. Her testimony would surely finish Goth's power. She had no choice.

'It is true,' she said clearly, directly to the King.

Herek had already ordered his soldiers to flank the two Inquisitors. Now Goth felt strong arms clamp his own.

'King Lorys,' he called out above the pandemonium of voices. 'She must be spoken for. She is still an accused sentient, discovered by the Inquisitors. The girl must have rank speak for her.'

Goth knew his fate was sealed but he loved that he had once more found a stake to drive into Gynt's heart. No one could speak for Alyssa.

The King knew it too. His heart sank. Goth was clever indeed. Even in this moment of high stress he had dug deep enough to find a catch that may yet see this beautiful woman tormented and imprisoned, perhaps savaged by the brand. He slumped inwardly.

'Chief Inquisitor Goth is right. Ancient law decrees that a sentient must have someone of higher rank than the Inquisitor who accuses them speak for them. Goth is the highest-ranking member of the Palace in this room save myself. I cannot speak for her and so there is no one.'

Goth's twitching face re-arranged itself into a leer of victory.

'Is there not?' said Queen Nyria's clear voice. 'I shall speak for this woman. I am of superior rank to the filth which I see cringing at our feet, my King.'

The throne room erupted. Alyssa had won the hearts of the gathered with her dignity and courage at the beginning of proceedings and her triumph through Nyria was a triumph for them. Some even began to clap.

Queen Nyria had not finished. 'Lorys, I seem to recall that the ancient law states that the accused, if successful in finding a speaker, has the right to decree the punishment. Is that not so?' she asked innocently.

The King nodded. 'Alyssandra Qyn, you are pardoned of all accusations. This man has committed an unforgivable sin against you and it is your right to choose his fate.'

All eyes were fixed on Alyssa. Goth was forced to remain on his knees, his head bent. He wanted to look her in the eye, to frighten her into submission as he had always done before. He was enraged, shaking with fury that he could not stare at her.

'He must burn,' she said quietly and without hesitation. 'Perhaps the flames that moulded him in childhood will cleanse the man's rotten soul.'

'It will be done,' said the King. 'Take him away.'

'Wait!' screeched Goth. He had one more card to play. 'King Lorys, what of Gynt? What is his punishment for having carnal knowledge of the same woman I am accused of lying with?

'I demand the punishment decreed in the ancient law. He is guilty; you have heard him admit it. He must be crucified and stoned.'

Lorys was trapped again. If he could have slashed open Goth's throat himself then and there, he would have done so. For more than two decades he had upheld a barbaric law which his ancestors had decreed. Now he must pass the according barbaric sentence on Torkyn Gynt or his reign would account for nothing. He would be seen by his rivals as weak; worse, he would be seen as a hypocrite.

'Take him away,' he said.

Goth was wrestled to the door. He shrieked over his shoulder to Tor. 'See you on the cross, Gynt.'

'Not if you burn first, Goth,' Tor shouted back. It sounded courageous but he was frightened and he felt his Colours roaring around him. Merkhud must have felt the power surge too for he jumped into Tor's head and begged him to keep control.

Remember the woman in my dream, boy.

But Tor was not thinking of Lys; he was remembering his promise to Nyria. He had given his word to his Queen.

As the doors closed on the struggling Chief Inquisitor and his henchman, the hall filled with an eruption of voices. Everyone, it seemed, had an opinion.

Lorys sat quietly, stunned for the second time that day. Nyria touched his arm gently and looked hard at him.

'You cannot, must not do this, Lorys, I beg of you.'

'I have no choice, Nyria.'

'You pardon the woman, a stranger, yet will execute

the man you have known and liked for so long. He saved my life, Lorys.' Her eyes begged him.

'I must be true to the law I have decreed in Tallinor through all of my reign. Goth is right. I make a mockery of that law and my sovereignty if I flout it now. It is regrettable.'

His eyes flicked helplessly to the beautiful woman at the window. Hers were fixed on him and they were filled with hate.

'Regrettable! Lorys, this is a good man's life.'

Nyria was frightened. She knew the set of his jaw and recognised the look of finality settling on his face. His decision was already made. Nothing she said would change that now.

She turned away. 'May the gods take pity on your soul, Lorys.'

No one except the prisoner himself could look him in the eye as the King passed sentence of death on Torkyn Gynt.

27

Visitors

This will probably be the last time we speak, Merkhud said quietly to Nanak.

That sounds very final, my friend.

It is. That is, if I can achieve the powerful Spiriting magic.

I have heard of this, Nanak said thoughtfully. *I have never heard of anyone achieving it*, he added.

I must try. It is our last hope. Merkhud tried to lift his voice. *How are they?*

Holding for you, Merkhud. Themesius and Figgis are as strong as ever.

And you?

Disturbed since speaking with you, but my spirits were high until then.

Tell me. I need cheering. Merkhud sighed.

I have been visited by the Custodian; an honour I am still shaking from.

Merkhud frowned at Nanak's unmistakable joy. Custodian? Who was that?

Who is the Custodian?

Why, Lys of course.

Merkhud heard footsteps. *Nanak, I must close. I may not get another chance to speak with you.*

Yes, you told me that.

You must know, Merkhud said hurriedly, expecting to hear a knock at his door any moment, *that she visited me also.*

There was a slight pause. *Then you are honoured and must obey her.*

The knock sounded and then a voice. 'I know you're in there, old man. Open up.'

The Queen. Her voice sounded tremulous despite the command.

Farewell, friend Nanak, Merkhud said sadly and closed the link.

He had so much more to say and time was short. He heaved his tired old bones from his seat and walked to the door where her majesty was becoming impatient. He opened it and she crumpled into his arms, sobbing.

'What are we going to do, Merkhud?' she whispered. 'Tomorrow they crucify our Tor.'

For the first time in two decades Merkhud hugged the woman he had adored for all of that time, and thanked any of the gods who were listening for giving him this chance to hold her before he died.

What are we going to do? he echoed silently in his head as he stroked her soft hair. *We shall obey the Custodian.*

When the gaoler opened the cell door to check on the Chief Inquisitor he was cheered to see Goth slumped in the darkest corner . . . just as he had been when the visitors left. He put a plate of weak porridge on the musty floor and pushed it forward with his foot, enjoying the chance to demonstrate the contempt he felt for this monster.

The cell check was not routine but the gaoler was suspicious. One of the visitors had been uncommonly attractive. Of all the people who might bother to see this fiend, she was the least likely, he mused. Even through that veil he could see she was lovely. It struck him as very strange that she had claimed, along with the old crone she had in tow, her right of visitation as a relative.

The gaoler scratched his head as he looked again at the hooded, slowly rocking figure of Goth. His grisly death would occur on the morrow, scheduled before that of the poor physic on the other side of the dungeon. They had been ordered to keep the two men well apart. The gaoler shivered at the thought of the fire which would consume its victim in the most painful way possible.

'Your food's here,' he said gruffly. As he began to pull the door closed he heard the replacement guards arrive for the changeover.

'How is he?' one called.

'The same,' the gaoler said, shrugging.

The new guard peeped in around the half-open cell door. 'Hey, Goth! If you don't eat this now we'll have to warm it up in the flames around you tomorrow.'

Everyone on the watch sniggered. Other than Rhus, all in the castle would be cheering the flames on. The other execution, however, was a different matter.

'I'll tell you what,' he added, 'we'll all bring some bread and break our fast with you.'

Goth finally turned to face his tormentors. Except it

was not Goth. They looked into the rotting smile of the mad woman, Heggie, who roamed the fields outside Tal begging for food.

In his shock, the guard stumbled backwards against the wall. The gaoler pushed him out, fumbling himself with the keys to lock Heggie inside. He did not know why he bothered. She was no prisoner.

Captain Herek arrived to discuss the arrangements for tomorrow's proceedings.

'What goes?' he demanded.

'It's Goth, Captain,' stammered the gaoler.

'And what about him?' Herek snapped.

The guard stood to attention although he felt in a stupor.

'Speak.' The captain was irritated.

'Captain Herek,' the soldier began, 'it's Heggie in there. Goth is gone.'

'Gone? Have you been drinking?' Herek strode over, took the key and opened the door.

He stepped back out almost immediately and addressed another guard. 'Get her out of here.'

Herek fought to keep his own fear under control and the command strong in his voice. 'Gaoler! Explain.'

The gaoler slumped onto a nearby stool.

'He had a visitor today – well, two. Only one spoke. She was veiled and young. Very beautiful. She said she was a cousin and I thought, well, it couldn't hurt – not that I cared if Goth was hurt, mind. The other woman didn't speak, sir. They left minutes after arriving.'

'Who was she, man? Did you get her name?'

'She said her name was . . .' The gaoler had to think

hard, hoping he would not embarrass himself further by
having to consult the ledger. His relief was evident as he
finally recalled it. 'She said her name was Xantia.'

28

The Stoning

Tor came back to the noisy, terrifying present of his execution. There was no point in thinking about the past.

He realised he was squinting into the noon sun again. Blinking, he saw a man not that much older than himself step forward to touch his arm. There was something about his searching look which made Tor glance back. Guards quickly pushed the man back into the crowd but Tor's sharp hearing caught his words clearly. 'I am Sallementro, the musician. I am her protector.'

Tor's heart leapt. He was talking about Alyssa, surely. Another of the Paladin? He nodded at the man who was being swallowed up by broader shoulders and taller heads.

The noise of people shouting at him and crying for his quick delivery was overwhelming. He wondered if he could do this, keep his promises to Merkhud and Lys to trust them. Seeing Sallementro gave him hope, though. Perhaps he could convince himself that this was not the end. Just a new beginning. He felt his spirits lift.

Cloot flew to his shoulder. Tor reached up and touched the falcon.

Cloot's voice was choked. *Tor . . .*

I know. I must trust Lys.

Cloot was as terrified as everyone else that this execution was a reality. He had never questioned the wisdom of Lys over the years but the scene unfolding in front of him now challenged his loyalty. He was not privy to what came next. Cloot wanted to tell Tor to summon the Colours and escape but he held his own fear in fragile check.

A drum began to beat mournfully. Suddenly Tor realised that he was already standing at the hastily erected stage where the executioner was waiting to introduce himself.

The man's name was Jod. Solemn and businesslike, he took Tor's hand in the Tallinese way of welcome. It was strangely reassuring. Herek was at his side in a moment and he felt the captain squeeze his elbow. More reassurance.

Jod spoke quietly and surprisingly eloquently. His voice was rough and deep.

'I do not like my work but I am good at it. Nay, I am the best in the Four Kingdoms, if you'll pardon such arrogance. I am told by Captain Herek that this is not a popular execution, Physic Gynt. I make no judgement upon your sins but since I have heard of your good deeds in the Kingdom, I make you this promise: your death will be swift and as painless as I can make it. I am using dampened hide to bind instead of the traditional twine and first-grade weight stones.'

Tor presumed this meant that the lighter stones were used in order to prolong death and provide entertainment during the execution of a tyrant. He felt lightheaded. He heard Herek speak on his behalf and thank Jod for his compassion.

The executioner grunted and gestured politely towards the cross which was resting on the floor of the stage. 'If you wouldn't mind,' he said.

Tor looked at Herek; suddenly nothing was making sense.

The captain responded gently. 'He needs you to lie on the cross, Tor, so he can tie you to it.'

Tor did not trust his own voice any more. He nodded. All the while, the huge crowd kept up its fierce noise; clearly most were against his death but had gathered to show respect on the day of his execution.

Cloot! Panic gripped him as Herek helped him to lie down on the cross.

I'm here with Alyssa, Tor. Cloot's voice had found its calm and he poured that across the link into the man he had sworn to protect with his own life. *Look at her, Tor. Please.*

Tor had avoided it so far, unsure of whether it might be the one thing which would destroy his fragile composure. But as Jod began to deftly bind his wrists and ankles to the timber frame, Tor tracked Cloot's voice and turned his head to see her. Forcing a trembling smile, Alyssandra Qyn communicated her eternal loyalty to the only man she had ever loved by reaching out her hands towards him.

This simple act of love stirred a variety of reactions. Most of the women in the crowd cried harder. The men looked down awkwardly.

Queen Nyria refused to watch Tor being bound. Instead, the Queen turned to the Royal Physic who had been commanded to stand present with them. She felt a depthless sorrow for Merkhud. She could see he was struggling to keep his composure.

When Lorys saw Alyssa show her love, he felt greater desire for the young woman, if that was possible. Niggling questions surfaced. Shall I stop it now, he wondered? Could my sovereignty withstand the backlash?

Meanwhile, disguised and shrouded amongst the crowd, former Chief Inquisitor Goth and his new companion Xantia lapped up the anxiety swirling about them. Their only disappointment was the knowledge that they could not personally contribute to the death of a young man they both had reason to despise.

Nyria had read Merkhud incorrectly. He was indeed struggling with the sight of his apprentice being prepared for death, but his display of raw emotion was actually connected to his concern about whether an extraordinary piece of magic could be achieved. He sat nervous and shaking, gathering all the power he could muster while he waited for the right moment for the Spiriting.

Silence hit the crowd like a wave. Merkhud imagined Tor was being lifted on the cross.

He was right. Tor was slowly being hefted into an upright position by soldiers of the King's Guard. He knew the three men involved; had sparred and drunk with them regularly in years previous. Herek was directing proceedings, barking sharp orders, trying to hurry things up so they could be done with this ugly event.

Tor felt the cross fall soundly into place. He hung there pitifully, looking out across hundreds of faces he recognised, including Saxon not far away. The crowd pointed and murmured as a majestic peregrine falcon they knew to be Gynt's landed silently on the top of the cross.

Cloot opened his wings aggressively and eyed them balefully. It was instinctive. He had not meant to do this but he was angry. It was not a regular emotion for him.

I'm here, Tor.

Be careful of the stones, Tor answered. His voice sounded shaky.

I do not fear them. Neither do you. We do this together.

Tor couldn't help the tears sliding down his face now. He was past caring about looking brave for anyone.

Don't die with me, Cloot, I beg you.

I promise you I will die only if you do.

Herek began the formalities of proclaiming Tor's sentence. He was not a man of theatrics and Goth hated to see the occasion wasted by a dour man like Herek. The captain was rolling up the parchment almost as soon as he had begun reading it.

Tor realised he was being asked if he wished to say anything. The silence from the crowd was instant. He could hear himself breathing.

'To all those who have loved or called me friend, I am sorry.' He was looking at Alyssa when he said this. Now he turned his bright blue stare on Lorys. 'I forgive you, my King.'

The silence held; filled now with awe for his nobility.

Jod broke the spell, waving back the crowd until there was space for him to stand thirty or so paces from the cross, directly in front of Tor. In his arms was a basket which carried the cruel, heavy stones of death.

Tor felt the link slice open and Merkhud entered his head.

Are you ready? the old man asked.

Can we do this?

*We're going to try. No one has succeeded before. You under-
stand now: our spirits will swap bodies. You will inhabit my
flesh until we are able to return you to your own body. And my
spirit will enter your body.*

Merkhud, Tor whispered as he watched Jod set the
basket on the ground, *why must you die in my body?*

*It is the only way. My time is done. I have found you and
now you must follow your destiny. You must live and I must
die. Use my body to get to the safety of the Heartwood. There
is no more time. Despite all it seems I have done, child, I do
love you. Open up your powers to me now. I shall need them.*

Tor, terrified, dropped all veils and all defences and
allowed the Colours to roar. Merkhud was momentarily
stunned at the enormous power at his command but he
knew he had only moments now; there would be no second
chance.

Jod spoke for the last time. In his hands he carried
two rocks which he had smoothed to form heavy balls
of death.

'Close your eyes, boy. I will aim for your head. It's the
quickest.' Out of habit he weighted the stone in his right
hand. 'And I never miss,' he added, pulling back his arm.

Xantia smiled and Goth felt joy as Tor closed his eyes
to accept death. What they could not know was that he
had closed his eyes to focus his powers towards Merkhud
to enable them both to lose themselves in the mysterious
and most complex of all magic.

Merkhud cast out. Across the extraordinarily powerful
link, almost more than he could handle, he yelled *Now!*

The crowd watched Jod put every ounce of his huge

strength into the launch of the stone. It hit Tor's forehead with such force that his skull split wide open. Blood gushed. Jod followed with two more throws. The first hit expertly at the temple; the second, meant to shock Tor's heart into stopping, landed true.

The shocked, now silent crowd watched as the light in the bluest of eyes winked out and blood cascaded down the front of Torkyn Gynt's white shirt.

The falcon, screeching its despair, lifted into the air and beat powerful wings to escape the scene of death.

Somewhere deep in the Heartwood of the Great Forest a silver wolf howled.

Lorys looked at Alyssa. Her small body shivered with fright and her streaming eyes were riveted on the slumped body of her lover, his face hardly recognisable now.

The King's regret intensified dramatically. Executing Torkyn Gynt was certainly within the framework of the law; it demanded it. But he had the power to deny it. And he could have done so.

If he had wished to.

From that day in the Throne Hall, Lorys had felt uncontrollable jealousy towards the Under Physic. Why should Tor have this woman? Especially as it was not permitted. And with that warped logic, he justified the law and exercised it to the letter.

Now he regretted his decision; his envy, his weakness. He hated himself. Hated his betrayal of Nyria in his thoughts; hated his betrayal of Tor and indeed of this young woman he should have protected, was bound to protect by royal decree.

'My love,' Nyria said through her tears but he stopped

her for the girl was turning her attention from the corpse on the cross to the betrayer on the balcony.

Loathing was etched onto the proud face which stared at King Lorys. Her hand went to her head and Alyssa brushed back a wisp of golden hair. She looked at the Queen, nodded a courtesy and followed her keepers back into the shadows.

'She will never forgive me,' Lorys whispered involuntarily.

'You need never seek her forgiveness, my lord, if you have committed no sin,' Nyria said pointedly before turning away from him. She wanted to leave this room, escape to her chambers. However, the nightmare was far from over. She saw Merkhud struggling to stand from where he had sat throughout the execution. He looked disorientated.

She rushed to him, calling to Lorys.

'Merkhud!'

He leaned against the wall, his legs unsteady and a strange, faraway look in his grey eyes. Lorys grabbed his arm and was looking around to call for help when the old man spoke. 'No, I'll be fine. Just give me a moment.' His voice sounded strange, croaky.

They watched him gulp air until he was able to focus better. The shock of Tor's death has been too much, Nyria thought. A lopsided smile creased briefly across the physic's face. It was gone almost as quickly.

'I have a job to do,' Tor wheezed through Merkhud's mouth.

'Let me call for some help and we'll have you taken to your rooms.'

'No, Lorys!' The old man was determined. 'The body. I have made arrangements for it. Please, I must see to it.'

He pushed their arms away.

'Where are you going?' Nyria was just as determined.

'Away, madam,' Tor said with finality.

Lorys had suspected something like this. 'You are leaving us, old man?'

'I cannot stay, Lorys. I do not agree with what you have done today. I promised that boy's parents I would protect him, nurture him, take care of him.' The old man sighed deeply. 'I have failed them and I have failed him.'

Nyria began to weep.

'So now I must give this boy the burial he deserves.' Tor stared at the King with Merkhud's hard eyes.

The King turned his palms upwards; confusion on his face. 'But Merkhud, we can—'

'And again I say no, Lorys. I am taking Torkyn Gynt to a special resting place. Forgive me for this hasty departure.'

Nyria hugged him and was surprised to see him stagger again. He seemed so weak.

'Please, please, Merkhud, let us at least send some of the Guard with you,' she begged.

'Thank you, Nyria, but I have made arrangements.'

There was nothing else to say. The stunned royals watched the old man, who had attended Kings and Queens for longer than anyone could remember, weave an unsteady path towards the door and out of their lives.

The sound of the door slamming behind him was like a knife into Nyria's already weakened heart.

As Tor stumbled down the stairs, trying to control Merkhud's arms and legs, he spotted Alyssa being escorted back to her room. She was surrounded by King's Men, including Captain Herek who was speaking quietly to her. Seeing only Merkhud, they permitted him to pass.

Tor stopped in front of Alyssa and stared. He could not drag Merkhud's eyes away yet he said nothing. The guards flicked confused looks from one to another as they wondered what this silent confrontation was about.

It was Alyssa who spoke first. 'This is all your fault.' Her voice was hard and cruel.

Tor's mind was misting over. He needed all his strength and wits just to keep Merkhud's body upright and it was hard to stay focused. The old man had warned him not to linger; time was short. He suspected that his words may be slurred but he was determined to say something comforting to her. He just had to be careful not to give too much away. As it was, Herek was eyeing him strangely.

Tor finally spoke in Merkhud's soft voice. 'Look out for Sallementro, Alyssa. He is Paladin.'

The guards moved on with Alyssa in tow. She looked back over their burly shoulders and Tor blew her a kiss.

What an odd thing for the old man to do, Herek mused, standing next to the physic. 'Are you feeling yourself, sir?' he asked.

A sly smile twitched at the edge of the man's mouth. 'No, Herek. I am definitely not feeling myself today. Thank you for your concern, though. Is the cart readied?'

'It is, Physic Merkhud. All as you instructed.'

'I am grateful to you. You are a good man, Herek.'

'There is something I need to tell you, Physic Merkhud. We have withheld it from the King thus far and I am on my way now to give him the bad tidings.'

'Tell me.'

'Goth escaped last night. I have men searching. We will find him.'

Tor felt as though this body too had been hit by one of Jod's stones. Terror for Alyssa struck him. He coughed with frustration and anger, feeling despair course through the old man's body but knowing it was all his.

'Does the girl know?' he asked sharply.

'Not yet, Physic Merkhud; I must tell the King first. I'm only telling you because I know you are involved and that you are leaving us now.'

Herek watched Merkhud lean against the wall. He felt sure that the old man would not make it back from his journey with Tor's body.

'Promise me you will protect her, Herek. And in the meantime, find him!'

Herek nodded. 'On both counts, sir, you have my word.'

Tor continued his unsteady path until he was outside the Palace. It was a ghostly place at the moment. His former home had come to a standstill for a few hours; there was not even a hint in the air of food being cooked. He was grateful for the quiet at this time.

He spied the cart and its cargo. His own body had been wrapped in muslin but the blood was already soaking through. He looked at it for a few moments; he needed to be sure. With great effort, he heaved himself up into the driver's seat and took the reins of the horses who had been waiting patiently. He heard a noise and looked up. As he had expected, Cloot flew overhead as his guide.

Is it you? Cloot asked cautiously.

I am with you, Cloot, Tor answered.

The old man clicked softly to the horses and began the slow journey with Torkyn Gynt's body to the Great Forest and to Merkhud's final resting place.

The Final Betrayal

The Great Forest had wielded its peculiar magics to bring this precious load to its destination in the Heartwood within hours rather than days.

Arabella the priestess watched as the old man called Merkhud almost fell from the cart in front of her.

'I am here as instructed,' Tor croaked in Merkhud's voice. 'His . . . my body is in the cart.'

'You made very good time.'

'Time, I was told, is our enemy.'

'We shall not waste another moment of it,' Arabella replied. 'Help me get your body into the clearing.'

'I fear it will be the last act Merkhud's body does on this earth,' Tor said tiredly.

They struggled with Tor's cooling body and finally laid it out on the forest floor. Together, without speaking, they stripped it of its muslin shroud. Arabella winced at the oozing, gaping head wound which had ended a life. She put her hand on Merkhud's wrist to calm Tor inside. She couldn't imagine how grisly this must be for him. He was breathing very hard now.

'It's time,' she said.

'I know.' He took her hand and kissed it. 'Thank you,' he whispered.

Arabella watched Merkhud struggle to lie down next to the corpse of his apprentice.

'Farewell,' was all he said before closing his eyes. As Tor had done earlier that day, he dropped all veils and opened up his considerable powers.

Tiny flames erupted and chimed gently around them, encircling the trio. Darmud Coril was present. The power was daunting.

Arabella was no longer looking at Merkhud. Instead she stared into the bruised and battered face of Tor's corpse, watching his once-beautiful eyes for the sign. She was patient but nervous. It had been a dangerous plan from the start; fraught with so many problems she dared not think on them. Now was the moment. She pushed her nails hard into the palms of her clenched fists to steady herself and continued to watch the broken face.

She heard a slight noise, like a sigh, next to her. She knew it was Merkhud. The act was done. He had performed the final task required of him by the Host in his quest to secure the Trinity. She glanced towards him and felt a small surge of shock to see only rumpled clothes and a pile of dust where Merkhud's centuries-old body had been. Its dust was already blowing away in the soft breeze.

The great Merkhud was gone but in truth she knew that he had died many hours earlier, when his spirit had entered Tor's body to take his punishment. He had breathed his last within a different person.

Arabella looked back to Tor.

A moment or two later she closed her eyes in prayer to the gods and silent elation after witnessing Torkyn Gynt's beautiful blue eyes flare into life again.

The vines were already snaking their way around Tor, wrapping him gently. The trees bent and their branches lifted the barely alive body into the arms of their god. The Flames of the Firmament burst into glorious rainbow colours.

Cloot, high in the whispering trees, wept. Torkyn Gynt lived and the next part of the journey had begun.

The story continues in
Revenge: Trinity Book Two

And concludes in
Destiny: Trinity Book Three

By Fiona
McIntosh